"Bonjour," l... French than ...

He sat up to see h... ...carrying a tray with brioches, juice and coffee. She wore a navy T-shirt and jeans and was charmingly barefoot.

"Stay where you are. It's Christmas morning and you deserve to be waited on."

She put the tray on the coffee table and handed him a mug of coffee. His attention was drawn to her fragrance and the blond hair she'd left long. It hung over one shoulder.

"Joyeux Noël! Your housekeeper has been helping me with the pronunciation."

Ping went the guilt again, for enjoying this moment with her. He was close to speechless.

"That sounded perfect. But you shouldn't be waiting on me when you're the guest."

"I think we've graduated beyond that point."

Her laughing blue eyes traveled over him, warming him in new places.

AT THE CHATEAU
FOR CHRISTMAS

BY
REBECCA WINTERS

MILLS & BOON

Published in Great Britain 2014
by Mills & Boon, an imprint of Harlequin (UK) Limited,
Eton House, 18-24 Paradise Road, Richmond, Surrey, TW9 1SR

© 2014 Rebecca Winters

ISBN: 978-0-263-91329-3

23-1114

Rebecca Winters, whose family of four children has now swelled to include five beautiful grandchildren, lives in Salt Lake City, Utah, in the land of the Rocky Mountains. With canyons and high alpine meadows full of wildflowers, she never runs out of places to explore. They, plus her favourite vacation spots in Europe, often end up as backgrounds for her romance novels, because writing is her passion, along with her family and church.

Rebecca loves to hear from readers. If you wish to e-mail her, please visit her website: www.cleanromances.com.

Dedicated to my two wonderful grandmothers,
Alice Driggs Brown and Rebecca Ormsby Hyde.

I had these grandmothers in my life
until just a few years ago and consider them
two of life's greatest blessings.

CHAPTER ONE

THE FINANCIAL DISTRICT of San Francisco was known as the Wall Street of the West. Nic got out of the limo into sunny, fifty-eight-degree weather and entered the high-rise that housed the headquarters of Holden Hotels on Montgomery.

There might be no snow in this city by the bay, but Americans were big on Christmas trees. The tall one in the foyer decorated with pink bows, pink angels and pink lights was dazzling. The hotel chain started by Richard Holden had become one of California's finest.

Nic had checked in to one near the airport upon his arrival at 3:00 p.m., a half hour ago. A smaller tree decorated the same way with a giant Santa Claus in the corner had illuminated its foyer. He was impressed by its unmatched American ambience that would enchant children of all ages and nationalities. Once it might have enchanted him, but no longer. These days Christmas was a painful holiday he had to get through.

A security guard at reception in the lounge of the foyer looked up at him. "May I help you, sir?"

"I hope so. I'm here to see Ms. Laura Holden Tate. I understand she's manager of the marketing department."

"Do you have an appointment?"

"No. I'm here on urgent business and must speak to her as soon as possible."

"Your name?"

"Monsieur Valfort. She'll recognize the name."

"One moment, please, and I'll ring her secretary."

Nic had to wait a few minutes for an answer. The man gave him a speculative glance before he said, "If you'll take a seat, she'll be down shortly."

So she was in…that was good. Saved him from having to hunt her down.

The name *Valfort* had probably given Ms. Tate a heart attack. He'd purposely left off his first name to keep her guessing. But Nic wasn't surprised she was willing to drop everything in order to investigate this undesirable intrusion away from the eyes and ears of her staff. He had to admit he'd been curious about a woman who'd shown no interest or love, let alone curiosity, over her grandmother's welfare all these years. It demonstrated a coldness he couldn't comprehend.

"Please help yourself to coffee while you wait."

"Thank you." Except that Nic didn't want coffee and didn't feel like sitting. He'd done enough of both on the flight from Nice, France, which, being on the Côte d'Azur, showed no signs of snow and coincidentally had been fifty-eight degrees and sunny when he'd left.

The errand his grandfather Maurice had sent him on was one he wanted over. He wasn't looking forward to this meeting, let alone the other business his grandfather had asked him to carry out.

There would be fireworks, but with so many people coming in and out of the building, he planned to convince Ms. Tate to talk to him away from everyone. If this woman was as bitter and unforgiving as her mother, then he had his work cut out.

He looked in the direction of the bank of elevators, braced for a confrontation. Every time he heard the ding, he watched another group of well-dressed people step out. Though he didn't have a picture of Ms. Tate, he knew she was a midlevel executive, twenty-seven years old and had been born with blond hair. Not a great deal to go on. At this point all he could do was wait until she approached him.

When he decided something must have detained her, he suddenly noticed an ash-blond woman with silky hair to the shoulders of her chic navy suit walking in his direction from the stairway door on long, shapely legs.

Out of nowhere Nic felt an unbidden rush of physical attraction. Not in years had that kind of powerful reaction to a woman happened to him.

This was the woman he'd flown all these miles to talk to?

Maybe he was wrong and she was meeting someone else, but no one else was standing by him. On closer inspection he noticed that her coloring and five-foot-seven-inch height could have been the way her grandmother Irene Holden would have looked at the same age. Irene had been an exceptionally beautiful woman.

Nic stood there stunned by the strong family resemblance. That had to explain why he'd been so taken with the woman's looks. She had a certain elegance, like her grandmother, and wore white pearls around her neck as he'd seen Irene do many times. Their sheen was reflected in her hair.

The similarity of the two women's classic features was uncanny, though the granddaughter's mouth was a little fuller. *Her mouth...and her eyes...* They were a lighter blue than her grandmother's.

But instead of the hint of wistfulness that was Irene's trademark, he saw guarded hostility as her granddaughter's gaze swept over him with patent disdain.

"I'm Laura Tate. Which of the Valfort men are you?"

Nothing like coming straight to the point with such an acerbic question, but he was prepared.

"Nicholas. My grandfather Maurice married your grandmother Irene."

He heard her take a quick extra breath. Much to his chagrin, it drew his attention to the voluptuous figure no expensive, classy business suit could hide. She was Irene's granddaughter, all right.

"Paul told me your business was urgent. It must be a life-and-death situation for you to make the long flight into the enemy camp."

Nic changed his mind. This woman wasn't anything like her delightful grandmother, which made him more irritated with himself than ever over his unexpected physical reaction to her.

"I'd rather talk to you outside in the limo, where we won't have an audience." He sensed her hesitation. "I'm not here to abduct you," he asserted. "That isn't the Valfort way, *despite* the rumors in your family."

He noticed how her jaw hardened, but ignored the grimace and got down to the business of why he'd come. "I'm here to inform you that your grandmother passed away day before yesterday, at St. Luc's Hospital in Nice."

The second the news left his lips, Laura's facade crumbled for a moment. In that instant her whole demeanor changed, like a flower that had lost its moisture. He knew he'd delivered a message that had rocked her world. For no reason he could understand, he felt a trace of compassion for her. Tears sprang to those crystalline eyes, bringing out his protective instincts despite his initial resentment of her lack of feeling for her own grandmother.

"My grandfather wanted you and your mother to hear the news in person. Since he knew he wouldn't be welcome here, he asked me to come in his place. If you'll walk out to the limo—the most convenient meeting place I could devise—I'll tell you everything."

Irene Holden had been his grandfather's raison d'être. Nic was still trying to deal with the recent loss himself. He'd loved Irene, who'd been a big part of his life. Her death had left a huge void, one this unfeeling granddaughter couldn't possibly comprehend.

Was it true? The grandmother she'd hardly known was *dead?*

If Laura were the type, she would have fainted. This tall, striking Frenchman dressed in an expensive charcoal-colored silk suit and tie had just delivered unexpected news that shook her to the very foundation.

He had to be in his early thirties and wore a wedding ring. She'd noticed something else—Nicholas Valfort spoke excellent English with a seductive French accent, no doubt just like the rogue grandfather who'd beguiled her grandmother. A man like this had no right to be so…appealing.

Is that what had happened to Irene—she'd felt an overwhelming attraction to Maurice the moment she'd met him? Like granddaughter, like grandmother?

The surreal moment made it difficult for Laura to function, let alone breathe, but she had to.

Without further urging on Nicholas's part, she followed him to the front of the building. Once he'd helped her into the back of the limousine, he sat across from her.

She had an impression of vibrant black hair and hard-boned features, but all she could focus on were the moody gray eyes beneath black brows, studying her as if she were an unpleasant riddle he couldn't solve and frankly didn't want to.

"I brought these pictures of her with me. Please feel free to keep them. They were taken in the last year before she became so ill with pneumonia."

Laura groaned. *Pneumonia?*

He opened an envelope on the seat and handed her half a dozen five-by-seven color photos. Five of them showed her grandmother alone in different outdoor settings. The last one had caught her standing in a garden with a man who had to be her second husband, Maurice.

The same Valfort characteristics of height and musculature in the photo had been bequeathed to the arresting male seated across from Laura. But unlike him, the man's hair in the picture had turned silver.

She studied the photos for a long time. Her grandmother had still been beautiful at eighty. Pain caused her throat to constrict.

"I brought her body on the Valfort corporate jet. Maurice called the Sunset Mortuary here in San Francisco to meet the plane. Here's their business card." She took it from him, cognizant of their fingers touching. Something was wrong with her to be this aware of him when she was in so much turmoil.

"They're awaiting your family's instructions. When your mother broke all ties with Irene, she told her that neither she nor my grandfather would ever be welcome at her home in this life."

Searing pain shot through Laura. Her mother had said those exact words to Laura's grandmother? Laura didn't believe it. This man was biased and had colored the situation with his own judgmental version of the scandal. Still, it was so horrifying, the tragedy of it all overwhelmed her.

"My grandfather is still honoring her wishes, thus the reason I'm here in his place."

That was another lie. His grandfather was a coward or he would have come himself!

"Maurice realizes your grandmother should be buried next to her first husband, Richard, and surrounded by her family."

So in death Richard was finally remembered? The heat of anger and pain washed over her. "How thoughtful of him." She hadn't been able to hide the sarcasm.

Calmly he said, "If you have questions and need to talk to me, I'll be staying at the airport Holden Hotel. You can reach me there until tomorrow morning, when I'll be flying back to Nice at seven a.m.

"One more thing. Your grandmother had a will drawn up several years ago and left something specific in it for you. Unfortunately it means you will have to fly to Nice and meet with the attorney within the next seven days. After that, he'll be out of the country for two months. It was her hope that your mother's feelings wouldn't prevent you from claiming it. She never gave up hope of a reconciliation."

At the revelation, Laura couldn't stifle a quiet sob.

"Should you decide to come, phone me and I'll arrange for the Valfort jet to return to San Francisco and fly you to Nice. My grandfather insists on doing this for you to honor Irene's final wishes. I'll meet you at the Nice airport and drive you directly to the attorney's office. This is my business card." He handed it to her. "You can reach me at Valfort Technologies any time."

He didn't work for the fabulously wealthy Valfort family? They'd been hoteliers since the early 1900s. That much she did know about them. Why on earth would he stay in a Holden hotel after what his grandfather had done to their family? Or did he have a sick desire to see how the Holdens were doing business without the founder?

"Do you have any questions, Ms. Tate?"

At this point her emotions were in chaos. "Only two right now." She fought to keep the tremor out of her voice, but to her alarm, she had difficulty keeping her eyes off him. "Did you know her well?"

"Very" came the grating sound of his voice.

Laura sensed a wealth of meaning and possible rebuke behind that one word, stabbing her until she could feel herself bleeding out. But this man knew nothing about the private history of the Holden family and the horrendous gulf caused by his grandfather. She bristled at his unspoken censure of her.

Narrowing her eyes on him she said, "Am I to assume she was happy with your grandfather?"

"With *him,* absolutely."

What exactly was *that* supposed to mean? "That's your interpretation, of course."

She got no response from him. His sangfroid crept under her skin. So did his lack of explanation that spoke volumes about the underlying issues of a marriage that had brought so much grief to her mother and to Laura personally.

Laura averted her eyes, needing to exit the limo and be strictly alone while she absorbed the gut-wrenching news about her grandmother's death.

All these years without contact. Laura hadn't seen Irene since she was six. Year after year she'd secretly yearned to visit her and get to know her. But loyalty to her mother, Jessica, had prevented her from getting in touch with her. Now the lovely older woman in the photos was gone… *Death was irrevocable.*

Another small sob escaped her throat. She traced her grandmother's features with her index finger. These few pictures were all Laura would ever have of the woman who'd brought her mother into the world and raised her. The pain of loss over an opportunity never seized was excruciating. How empty and pointless that loyalty seemed now.

Without lashing out at her, Laura would have to search her soul to find the right words to tell her unforgiving mother that Irene was dead. She lifted her head, looking at Nicholas through dull eyes. Tears trickled down her throat, yet it was hard to swallow.

"It's evident this was a task you would have done anything to avoid. Your loyalty to your grandfather deserves a medal. I suppose the least I can do is thank you for tearing yourself away from business to come all this way with her body."

"You're welcome."

His cool reply had her floundering. Clearly this man found his errand repugnant. But as much as she knew anything, she realized he was a true gentleman, a quality she valued highly in a man. Otherwise he would have flung all this in her face with the greatest of pleasure. His restraint taught her a lot about his character, adding to the potent charisma no man of her acquaintance possessed.

He got out of the back to help her. As her body brushed against his by accident, an unlooked-for awareness of his male presence leaped to life, threatening her in ways she'd never experienced before. The knowledge that he was married only made her reaction to him that much more shocking. She clutched the photos and cards before running toward the building without looking back.

"Telephone, Nic. Line two."

Nic had been making corrections to a drawing on the computer. "*Merci,* Robert."

After three years, his stomach no longer clenched every time a call came through for him, whether it was on his cell or the landline at work. For the first year following his wife's disappearance, he'd imagined every call would be from Lt. Thibault, the investigating detective on the other end, phoning to give him news of Dorine.

"It's five. I'm heading home and will see you after Christmas."

That's right. It was December 23. Nic's assistant, Robert, was going home to a wife and two children. Nic wouldn't be going home to anyone. Except to spend a little time with his family and siblings, he would work through this holiday.

Three years ago he and Dorine had spent Christmas with her family in Grenoble. They'd only been married five months before her disappearance in January. Their marriage had been of too short a duration to put down roots with children.

Robert paused at the door. "Thanks for the gifts. Pierre and Nicole will love them."

He lifted his head. "My pleasure."

"Nic—everyone at the research park is hoping *Père Noël* will bring some news that will give you closure, *mon ami*."

"After three years that hope is all but gone, but I appreciate the thought. *Joyeux Noël*."

Once the door closed, he pressed line two, putting the call on speakerphone while he worked. "This is Nic Valfort."

"Mr. Valfort? This is Laura Tate."

His head flew back, recognizing her California accent. That was another trait she had in common with Irene. Instead of forgetting this woman, to his amazement she'd managed to intrude into his thoughts. Up until he'd flown to San Francisco, his love for Dorine and the reason for her disappearance had been the only things on his mind.

Several times in the limo parked in front of Holden headquarters over a week ago, he'd heard little sobs catch in her throat. He'd had difficulty reconciling Ms. Tate's icy demeanor at one moment and the tears that welled in her eyes in the next. She was an enigma he didn't want to think about. There'd been no word from her since they'd talked.

To his chagrin the two questions she'd asked him had left an indelible impression. Once he'd told her he knew Irene well, her question about her grandmother's happiness with Maurice had haunted him. Had it been a ploy to convince him she cared when she didn't? Had she hoped to give the impression she wasn't the unfeeling person he'd imagined when they both knew the truth?

The seven-day window he'd given her to meet with the attorney had already closed, so he couldn't understand why she was calling.

"Is this a bad time, Mr. Valfort?"

Bad wasn't the right word. More that he'd been in a state of grief-stricken limbo for an endless period of time without knowing the whereabouts of his wife. If she'd run off with another man, he was still having trouble believing it. The woman he'd fallen in love with couldn't have done it, but his sessions with the psychiatrist convinced him it was possible.

Any other reasons why she'd disappeared had tortured him for so long he was desperate for any news, no matter how ghastly, in order to have closure. As for his grandfather, he was in bad emotional shape for another reason. Maurice had lost two women he'd loved and married. In his grief for Irene, he didn't know what to do with himself.

Both womanless men made a pitiful pair. Might as well answer this woman's question with one of his own. "What can I do for you, Ms. Tate?"

"Am I too late to meet with the attorney?"

He grimaced. She couldn't manage to see her grandmother in life, but she wanted to know what her grandmother had left her in death. How predictable. "You've missed the deadline by two days. He's already left on vacation."

A small cry of frustration escaped her throat. "I was afraid of that. Because of some personal matters and the graveside service for her, I couldn't get here any sooner."

His thoughts reeled. "Here? As in—"

"I'm at the airport in Nice."

Nic's adrenaline kicked in for no good reason. He jumped up from his swivel chair in surprise. "How did you get here? On a commercial plane?" She hadn't called to arrange for the Valfort jet.

"The way most people do."

Most people? "Not the Holden corporate jet?"

"I'm not that high up the chain."

"Not yet, you mean."

"In other words you're assuming I'm an ambitious female working my way up to the top of the Holden Corporation. Haven't you learned yet? It's still a man's world in certain venues. Shall we get straight to the point? Your grandfather was decent enough to take care of the arrangements for my grandmother and send you to do his errand. That was more than my family could ever have expected. But I would never have taken him up on his offer to fly me here."

Nic's brows furrowed in resentment. Maurice had bent over backward trying to do the right thing. "It's too bad you've wasted a trip. Call me in two months. By then the attorney will be back and you can make arrangements to collect your inheritance."

"Whatever you insist on believing, I have no interest in one." After a slight pause, she said, "I should have phoned first, but as you say, it's too late now. Before I turn around and fly back, do you think your grandfather would accept a phone call from me? Or is his opinion of me as bad as yours?"

That all depended on how grasping she was. If she

thought she could get Maurice to tell her what her grandmother had left her in the will before the attorney could read it to her, then she was in for a big surprise.

"Hello? Mr. Valfort? Are you still there?"

"Yes." But he wasn't sure he wanted her to talk to his grandfather right off. Maurice had tender feelings for Irene's granddaughter even though he'd never met her. Nic didn't want him hurt because Laura hadn't inherited Irene's sweetness. Death had a way of making all of them vulnerable one way or another. He needed to vet her first.

"My grandfather isn't available right now. Give me fifteen minutes and I'll pick you up at the airport terminal."

"That won't be necessary. I'll go to a hotel to call him and fly home in the morning."

"I'm afraid it's very necessary if you hope to make contact with him."

"You mean I have to get past you first."

He bit down hard. "He's in deep grief, Ms. Tate. I want to protect him. You and I need to talk first, but not over the phone."

That seemed to take her by surprise. "Well, if you're sure you don't mind—"

Mind? She could have no idea how determined he was to find out what she was up to.

"My grandfather would expect me to accommodate you."

"But this will be putting you out."

Now she was going polite on him? He frowned. Was it part of her act? Whatever, she was doing a good job of it. "Au contraire. Since you want to talk to him, something I didn't expect from you, my grandfather would never forgive me if I ignored your request and let you get away."

Nic hated to admit it to himself, but he was curious to see her again. Maybe the second time around she wouldn't impact him in the same way as before. It was something he had to find out.

A pause ensued. "I know this is another one of those tasks you don't want to do."

He let go of the breath he was holding. "You're wrong. This is the one Christmas present my grandfather hadn't counted on." If she was sincere, her arrival might just have saved Maurice from falling into a slump he'd never climb out of. Nic needed time to find out if avarice had brought her here or not. "Watch for me in front of the terminal. I'll be driving a four-door black Mercedes."

"I'll be there."

He heard the click. Making one of his gut decisions, Nic decided to take her to his house. That way no one in his family would know what was going on. Their disapproval of Maurice marrying a foreigner had never truly gone away.

Now the gorgeous granddaughter had arrived. Out of the frying pan…

Laura's physical resemblance to Irene would be a doubly powerful reminder of the woman who'd captured Maurice's heart. Depending on the outcome, more underlying animosity was in store. This had to be handled discreetly for now. Nic and his grandfather had always enjoyed a certain affinity. His loyalty to the older man had never been in question and he wasn't about to desert him now.

Since his grandfather wouldn't be eating dinner for

several hours yet, Nic would make the phone call from his den once she was ensconced. They'd proceed from there.

He drove out of his parking spot and wound around the technology park to the main road leading to the airport. Day before yesterday he'd decided he wouldn't be hearing from Ms. Tate again, but he hadn't had the heart to tell his grandfather yet. Now he wouldn't have to.

Though the sun had set, she wasn't difficult to spot. Like Irene, she had incredible dress sense. When Nic pulled up to the terminal, he saw that Laura drew a lot of attention in a long-sleeved speckled-tweed jacket and slim skirt. The form-fitting dove-gray outfit had white lace appliqués and fringe trim on the jacket. The effect, combined with the silvery-gold glints in her hair, had captured *his* attention.

Her impact on him was even more forceful than the first time. He levered himself from the car and walked around. She carried only one suitcase. Nic helped her inside and stowed it in the backseat. A light, flowery fragrance assailed his senses. "You travel light."

"I didn't plan to be here more than a few days. Thank you for coming to get me, Mr. Valfort." That sounded halfway sincere.

"Nic." He was tired of the senseless formality.

"In that case, call me Laura. I made reservations ahead of time at the Boscolo Excedra. If you wouldn't mind dropping me there." That five-star hotel had recently been restored with a futuristic-themed bar. No surprise she knew about it.

"My grandfather wouldn't hear of it. Maurice asked me to take care of you before I left for California. For the time being, you'll stay at my home. I'll drive you there now and we'll get in touch with him."

Nic felt her glance. "Does your wife know you'll be bringing someone home with you? No woman likes to be unprepared for an unexpected guest."

She'd noticed his wedding ring, of course. He pulled into traffic. "As it happens, my wife is away for the present." She *was* away, maybe somewhere still on earth, but more likely in heaven. He had no proof of either status. "My staff will see to your comfort. If Dorine were here, she'd want to meet you."

His wife hadn't been a Valfort and she'd liked Irene very much. At this point he realized he'd been thinking of Dorine in the past tense for a long time now. No stone had been unturned, no expense had been too great to find out what had happened to her, but there'd been no trace. During the first year, he'd lived for news of her. But for the last two years, he'd had the feeling in his gut she was gone forever. *Like Irene...*

Before long he took a turnoff and entered a wooded area that led to his home overlooking the coast. Dorine had loved the setting on sight and begged him to buy it before their wedding took place. Not too small, not too large. Perfect for several children who hadn't had time to come along. Empty as a tomb with no one home except the efficient husband-and-wife staff who took care of things.

Provence come to life!

This villa with its red-tiled roof looked like one of the fabulous Provençal properties featured in high-end magazines sold throughout the world. Laura's eyelids smarted with salty tears when she realized Irene would have been here many times enjoying the cypress trees and view of the blue Mediterranean.

Laura had traveled to Europe on several occasions and had been to Paris, but she'd avoided the South of France for fear the temptation to drop in on her grandmother would be too great.

What a colossal fool she'd been to honor her mother's wishes to such a great extent! In doing so she'd denied herself the opportunity to know the woman Laura's grandfather Richard had loved and married.

"Does your mother know you've come?" Nic's deep voice broke in on her anguished thoughts.

"Yes." She bit her lip. "She couldn't stop me. We had a fight."

"You mean she tried to?"

"Yes, but I refused to listen. I told Mother she was inhuman to be upset with me now that Irene was dead. I wish I hadn't said it, but I did. Now I have another regret to live with."

There'd been unpleasantness with Adam, too. The man she'd been seeing over the last few months hadn't wanted her to leave without him. He was getting much too serious. This unexpected trip would give her a needed break from him over the holidays.

His aggression had made her uncomfortable. Maybe her mom had been right—she'd hinted that Adam was ambitious and wanted more than her love. After the way he'd reacted before she'd flown here, Laura had begun to fear the same thing, considering a fortune lay behind her name. Because of the painful history that had beset the Holden family, she had major trust issues. Laura wasn't sure she wanted to be with him anymore.

"Family loyalty has its price," Nic murmured, sounding distanced. "You'd be surprised how many times in the past I had to stop myself from phoning to demand you come and visit your grandmother. She loved you a great deal, but my grandfather wouldn't have approved, so I didn't act on my instincts. He always hoped you'd come on your own."

His admission tugged at her heart. "No matter how much I love my mother, I should have followed my instincts, too. Now it's too late." She moaned the words. "Sometimes family loyalty demands too much, in this case more than I can bear—"

At this point she had the impression he didn't know if he could believe anything she said. That was trouble with a tragedy that had torn families apart. She didn't know if she could believe anything he said, either, but she was here now. For the sake of the grandmother she'd always loved in her heart, she wanted some answers.

Laura got out of his car before he could help her. The best thing she could do was avoid getting too close so they couldn't possibly touch. Despite his poor opinion of her, she was afraid her attraction to him wasn't going to go away. It was madness that she felt this awareness of him. He was a married man, for heaven's sake!

Nic reached for her suitcase and walked her to the entrance. The minute he opened the door to the foyer, a large manger scene placed on the credenza greeted her vision. Moving on into the living room, it felt as though she'd stepped into a painting by Matisse, her favorite Impressionist.

The interior reminded her of his work *The Black Table*. Wonderful dark flooring and beams set a backdrop for flowers, blue-and-white-colored prints, priceless ceramics and paintings. Beyond the French doors was a view of the sea dotted with sailboats, even though it was winter.

She wheeled around. "Your home is wonderful!" The compliment flew out of her mouth without conscious thought.

"Thank you." He lowered her suitcase. The man had a brooding sophistication he didn't seem to be aware of. "If you'd like to freshen up, there's a bathroom off the guest bedroom on your left at the end of the hall."

"Thank you."

"Are you hungry? Thirsty?"

"I ate before I got off the plane, but maybe some coffee?"

"I'll ask my housekeeper to prepare it and take your bag to your room."

He was giving her the opportunity to compose herself. Nic had his emotions well under control—unlike Laura—and seemed to sense instinctively what she needed. The consummate host.

On her way back to the living room, she stopped to look at the photographs hanging in the hallway. One of the groupings caught her interest. The French-looking brunette in the photos had to be his wife. She was a cute little thing with stylish short hair. They were laughing together.

Laura couldn't imagine feeling that happy and carefree. It depressed her that she'd never had a relationship like that. The more she thought about it, the more she knew she would have to end it with Adam. They didn't bring out the best in each other. Look at the way Nic and his wife glowed in the photograph. You could feel their happiness.

Upset by her thoughts, she returned to the front room

and found a tray of coffee and variety of cookies waiting for her. Nic was on the phone speaking his native
tongue and stood behind one of the two sofas facing
each other. Separating them was a tiled coffee table
with a large copper tub filled with fresh-cut blue and
red anemones.

While she waited for him, Laura wandered over to
the doors. In the twilight, the terraced garden below the
villa had taken on a surreal beauty.

"When your grandmother came to visit, she used to
stand right there with that same expression on her face.
She had several interests, especially gardening. Do you
also have a green thumb, as you Americans say?"

He was good at making small talk. She needed to
try, too. "I don't know." Laura had been studious in her
growing-up years so she could go into her grandfather's
hotel business. It had been a man's world then. Still was,
in many ways. She had to work hard to make her mark,
and spent a lot of time in the office. That's where she'd
met Adam, who was determined to rise to the top ech-
elons of the company. They had that in common.

This trip to France hadn't been on her agenda, but
she'd seized at the opportunity to learn more about her
grandmother. Laura had put her assistant in charge
while she was gone, satisfied he could handle things
for the few days she'd intended to be away.

She turned in Nic's direction, bursting with questions. He was silent on several subjects, including his
wife, but she needed to remember his personal life was
his own. She felt his distrust, no doubt as great as her
own. They were walking through a minefield, but especially after her rudeness to him in San Francisco,

she had no right to expect information that was none of her business.

"Was that your grandfather on the phone?"

He nodded. "Maurice is coming now."

CHAPTER TWO

LAURA SWALLOWED HARD. The man she'd been taught to hate would be here soon. What was the real truth about him and his affair with her grandmother? No one was all black or white. The muscles in her stomach started to clench with anxiety.

"The château in La Colle is only ten minutes away. Please help yourself to coffee while we wait."

She sat across from Nic and sipped hers. "The word *château* conjures up images. Does it look like one of the Châteaux de La Loire?"

Nic eyed her over the rim of his cup with a bemused expression. "Would you believe me if I told you that when Maurice took her there for the first time, Irene thought he'd brought her to the château where Cinderella was born?"

This was the first time the man had allowed her to see behind that facade of suspicion. Laura couldn't help but smile. "You made that up."

He sat forward to reach for a cookie. One black brow lifted. "Ask my grandfather." In the next breath he got up from the couch and walked into hall. When he returned, he handed her a five-by-seven photo in an antique frame, one she'd seen hanging among the others.

"This is what the estate looks like. Hopefully it will satisfy your curiosity."

With this picture he'd just extended an olive branch of sorts. Even if he wished his grandfather hadn't put him in this position, she would take him up on it in order to uncover the truth. Nic had actually brought her to his home. She couldn't have imagined it when they'd first met in California.

"Maurice said Irene lived for the day when you would come to visit and she would take you through it room by room, because you loved castles and princesses."

"That's true. I can't believe she remembered that."

He studied her for a moment, as if weighing her words. "Apparently you were taken with Cinderella, whose mean-spirited stepsisters had been cruel to her and made her sleep in the attic with the rats."

"She told you all that? I do have a terrible aversion to rats. A married friend of mine has a little boy who loved the movie *Ratatouille*. I start to watch it with them, but I couldn—" She suddenly stopped talking. Good grief. She was babbling.

His mouth broke into the first genuine smile he'd given her. That's when she realized how fabulous *he* was. Probably the most incredible looking and acting man she'd ever seen in her life. Laura had never met anyone remotely like him. Everything he said and did was starting to slide beneath her skin to draw her in. His wife had to be the luckiest of women.

Laura quickly looked down at the picture, only to cry out in wonder. After studying it, she lifted her eyes to him. "It *does* look like some of the pictures in my old fairy-tale book, the one my nana used to read to me. Your family home is beyond fabulous, Nic!"

"My great-grandfather Clement had the seventeenth-century château fully restored. He needed a lot of bedrooms and bathrooms so he could entertain business associates. There's an original baronial-style fireplace, stone spiral staircases and an enviable wine cellar. The conical roof and spring-fed moat add the perfect ambience."

"This is too much," she cried softly. To think her grandmother had lived there for twenty-one years. "Did you love the château, too?"

"*Bien sûr.* My parents lived nearby. The whole Valfort clan congregated there whenever possible."

"You must have had the time of your life!"

His smile slowly faded, letting her know his family had been in hell, too. That solemn pewter gaze of his traveled over her as if he were trying to figure her out. He had no idea that it sent an unwanted rush of guilty heat through her body. Heaven help her, but she was enjoying Nic too much in his wife's absence. This had to stop.

All the talk about her grandmother having had an affair with Nic's grandfather while she was still married to her first husband had horrified Laura for years. She couldn't imagine getting involved with a married man. What would possess a woman to do that no matter how tempted?

Yet here she was feeling an attraction to this man who'd grown up disliking her and her family with the same disdain Laura had felt for his family. Was this how it had started with her grandmother? An attraction that eventually led to an addiction and in the end the two of them had thrown both families aside in order to be together?

One thing Laura did know. She shouldn't be alone in this house with Nic any longer than necessary. Without realizing it, Laura pressed the photo to her chest, reminding herself that the only reason she was here was because of Irene. Not because of Maurice's grandson, who was proving to be a disturbing distraction.

In a mournful tone she murmured, "My grandmother lived here all these years, yet I never once saw her after she married and moved away."

Nic stood there with his powerful legs slightly apart, his hands on his hips in a male stance. "I heard many versions of the Holden-Valfort saga from my own relatives before I was grown up enough for my grandfather to sit me down and tell me the unvarnished truth about their situation."

She lifted tormented eyes to him. "You condoned his version, whatever it was?"

Nic pursed his lips. "I love my grandfather without qualification. But I'd like to hear your version, if you're willing to tell me. We'll see if they match."

She put the photo down on the table and got to her feet. "My grandmother disappeared from my life when I was six. I have a vague memory of her, but I know most of what I know from my aunt Susan, Mother's elder sister, who has never married. She said that my grandmother had an affair with your grandfather even though his wife was still alive."

"That would have been impossible!" Nic bit out.

"I'm just repeating what I was told. All this happened while my grandfather was battling cancer. Grandfather Richard died too young. Soon after his death, Maurice's wife died, so he married my grandmother and they moved to France. Neither Susan nor my mother could ever forgive Irene for having an affair while their father was so ill."

Nic's face had darkened with lines, making her nervous to go on.

"They said your grandfather was an evil man whose ability to seduce her while his wife was still alive created the scandal. They told her to get out of their lives and never come back.

"When I grew old enough to understand what adultery meant, I could see why Mother and Aunt Susan had been so devastated. When I was told the truth, the bitter side of Mother's nature came out. Our home was not a happy one.

"But over the years I've learned that no one is perfect and everyone makes mistakes. To remain so angry at my grandmother was wrong, no matter what she or your grandfather did. I told her I wanted to go see Irene. She forbade it.

"That's when I suggested she get professional help, but she accused me of turning on her. It was awful. Every time I tried to reason with Mother, she'd shut me out and accuse me of not loving her.

"I made things worse when I tried to talk to my aunt Susan. She told me that if I ever attempted to get in touch with my grandmother, my mother wouldn't be able to handle it and it could push her over the edge."

The forbidding expression on Nic's arresting face filled her with alarm. He moved closer. "That story is so wrong and twisted, it'll tear my grandfather apart when he hears it." To her shock he clasped her upper arms, drawing her to his hard muscled body. His intensity was a revelation. "Maurice is euphoric you're here. Promise me you won't tell him what you just told me." A vein stood out in his neck. "Not yet, anyway."

"I—I won't say anything," she stammered. Her silence on the subject appeared of the most supreme importance to him.

His energy drove through to her soul. He was close enough she felt the warmth of his breath on her lips. When she looked up, his dark gray eyes were pinpoints of pain. "Why did you really fly here?" he ground out. "Was the lure of the will so great, you had to find out what amount of money she left for you? Tell me the truth." He gently shook her. "I can take it, but my grandfather can't!"

She was devastated by his reaction. "I guess I'm not surprised by your accusation. Because of the hate on both sides, it appears you really don't know one very important detail."

"What's that?" he demanded.

"My grandfather Richard left millions to our family—to *me*, personally. I've never wanted for money a day in my life and never will. The only thing I could never have was the joy of growing up around my grandmother. And though I'm loath to meet the man who took her away from us, I was determined to see what kind of man he is."

Her eyes flashed with pain. "What kind of power does your grandfather wield to be able to entice her to give up her whole life in California and come live with him in France? She didn't need money. My grandfather gave her everything!" Laura could tell her voice had risen. "Does that answer your question?"

A groaning sound came out of him.

"Mon Dieu," he whispered, sounding utterly desolate. His hands slowly slid down her arms. But when he released her, she wasn't ready. Her legs felt so insubstantial she grabbed for the wing-back chair so she wouldn't fall.

While Laura was trying to recover from being held that close to him, she heard voices coming from the foyer. A woman and a man, both speaking French.

Shaken by the sound, she turned around and saw Nic's housekeeper usher in Irene's silver-haired husband from the photograph. He was dressed in a royal-blue sweater and cream-colored trousers.

In person he seemed young in demeanor for an eighty-one-year-old man whose face showed signs of recent grief. He was remarkably handsome and had passed on those genes to his grandson. Twenty-one years ago Laura's grandmother had no doubt been swept right off her feet.

He crossed the room, staring at Laura with incredulity before he turned to Nic. "You must have seen it the minute you met her." His French accent was more pronounced than Nic's.

"Oui, Gran'père. Laura is most definitely Irene's granddaughter."

Maurice's brown eyes swam with tears as they centered on Laura. "What she would have given to walk in this room and see you standing here! You're *ravissante,* just like she was."

From the first instant, all Laura could feel was love and warmth emanating from him. Though he and Irene had caused indescribable pain to her family, he couldn't possibly be the man her mother and aunt had demonized. She cleared her throat, still shaken by those moments when Nic had reached for her in pain. "We meet at last."

She had the sense he wanted to embrace her. Instead he held back and wept, pulling some tissues from his pocket. "It's a miracle. When she passed away, I thought my allotment had run out, but it isn't so. You've come. Please. Let's sit."

Once again she found a seat on one of the sofas. He sat next to Nic on the other. "How long have you been here?"

"I picked her up at the airport an hour ago," Nic explained. "She made a reservation at a hotel, but I canceled it."

She noticed Nic didn't mention the name. He wanted to shield his grandfather from the fact that she'd chosen *not* to stay at the world-famous Valfort in Old Town. Laura hadn't seen him do that. It must have been while she was looking at the photos in the hallway.

Maurice smiled. "*Naturellement*. You'll come to the château tonight. I'm all alone, rattling around in the place."

He wasn't the kind of man who rattled. Irene's husband seemed in excellent health. He was an exciting man, full of life and appeared athletic. She hadn't known what to expect. Certainly not this.

"That's very gracious of you, but I'd rather not impose when you weren't expecting me." No matter how taken she was by him at first glance, Laura wasn't comfortable about accepting his hospitality. She wasn't comfortable with Nic, either, for several reasons, but she'd had no choice.

Nic must have sensed her distress, because he said, "Laura's staying with me tonight, *Gran'père*. The housekeeper has already made up one of the guest bedrooms for her. Tomorrow will be soon enough for the two of you to get better acquainted. Right now I believe she's exhausted after her flight. It's a long one across a continent and an ocean."

Laura's eyes met Nic's for a second. She felt he was trying to break up this meeting, in the kindest way possible, of course. Was he still afraid she might say something about the will? She was pained over his suspicions, but she understood them. There'd been so much ugliness between the families—this was the result. Could they ever trust each other?

She would have preferred to stay at a hotel. It would have been the wisest thing to do, but clearly Nic had wanted to warn her not to hurt his grandfather before she met him. Maurice nodded. "Of course. Did Nic give you those pictures?"

"Yes. I love them." Laura's mother had refused to look at them.

"Good. I took those during our many walks. We must have logged hundreds of miles throughout our marriage, exploring the countryside. She was a walker."

So was Laura.

The emotions Maurice evoked were choking her. "Nic told me you were very happy."

"We were soul mates. I adored her." His tears ran freely. "Up until the time she came down with pneumonia, we loved getting out every day together. No man could have been blessed with a better, more loving wife. I'm utterly lost without her."

Touched to the core by the sincerity of his love for Irene, Laura stirred restlessly. "How long was she ill?"

"Two months. She caught a cold. It developed into

a secondary infection and before we knew it, she had pneumonia. Two weeks in the hospital on a regimen of strong antibiotics and the doctor was certain she would rally, thus the reason you weren't notified. But overnight she took a sudden, cruel turn for the worse and left this world quickly with one wish…that you and your family would know how terribly you were all loved."

Unable to prevent the tears, Laura got up from the couch and walked over to the French doors, too heartbroken to listen to any more tonight. Nic's words kept running through her mind: *That story is so wrong and twisted, it'll tear my grandfather apart when he hears it.*

After listening to Maurice's outpouring of love, she understood why Nic had asked her not to destroy this man while he was in mourning. This was no act, on Maurice's part or Nic's. She doubted she would ever repeat her version to his grandfather. There'd been enough suffering. Laura had lived an abnormal existence for years because of it. The bitterness in her household had tainted her life. She wanted no more of it.

"We'll get together tomorrow, *Gran'père.*"

At the sound of Nic's voice, Laura turned toward them. "Thank you for everything you've done, Mr. Valfort."

"Call me Maurice."

"All right then. Maurice it is." Moisture blurred her vision. "Thank you for sending Nic with my grandmother's body and arranging with the mortuary. In light of the history plaguing our families, it was a wonderful, noble thing to do. I'm indebted to both of you." Her voice caught.

His features sobered, showing his full years for the moment. "I must confess it was hard letting her body go." He broke down once more, clearly overcome with grief. "But I can always depend on my grandson to help me."

Her throat swelled, making it almost impossible to articulate. "He was very gracious." In light of the way she'd treated him, Nic was a saint. "Two days ago the family held a graveside service for her. She was buried in the family plot."

"Just as it should have been." The tears in his tone tore her apart. "But in return, *you're* here. I thank God you came." His voice shook. "How she prayed for this day."

Laura felt the same way. "I wanted to meet you," she assured him in all honesty, but she just hadn't expected this feeling that he and her grandmother had been wronged in some tragic way. "She had to have loved you beyond anything."

"Not beyond anything," he contradicted her. "A day didn't go by that your name wasn't mentioned. She longed for her little granddaughter."

Laura couldn't take much more. Neither could Maurice, apparently. Nic put a comforting hand on his grandfather's heaving shoulder. "I'll walk you out."

She watched them go, but he didn't leave her long. When Nic returned, his middle-aged housekeeper was with him.

"I did that flight a week ago and it wiped me out. Arlette will bring you a light supper. Sleep as long as you want and we'll talk more in the morning."

"Thank you, but I don't think I could fall asleep yet. I need to relax. If you don't mind, I'll call for a taxi to drive me into Nice." His head swerved in her direction. "I want to go down to the waterfront and soak in the atmosphere for a while. It will help me get a feel for the place where she lived all these years."

His chest rose and fell visibly. "Your grandmother used to walk along the Promenade des Anglais with Maurice at night. They'd stop to listen to music from the mid-'60s at a local brasserie. The place features *chanteurs* who sing the songs Brel and Aznavour made famous." He rubbed the back of his neck absently. "I'm wide-awake myself and will be happy to drive you."

"No, no. You've done enough. I won't stay out long. I'm used to being out at night in San Francisco. A half hour is all I crave."

His eyes narrowed on her features. "Are you refusing me because you can't forgive me for insinuating something about you that is patently untrue?"

No. She was refusing because he was a married man. But if she said that to him, he'd think she was a very unsophisticated, silly woman instead of an executive at Holden who did business with married men all the time.

"If I accept, are you going to accuse me of deciding to leave the villa so you'll feel obliged to take me?"

A half smile escaped Nic. "Maybe I'm using you so I can enjoy a little diversion before I call it a night."

His wife had to have an awfully good reason to be away. If Laura were his wife...but she had to stop her thoughts right there. "Then I won't say no to your chivalry."

"I never expected to hear that particular word fall from your lips."

Her brows lifted. "I never expected you would willingly accompany me anywhere."

His chuckle followed her down the hall as she went

to the bedroom for a sweater. He waited for her in the foyer and they walked out to his car.

Laura couldn't believe it, but they actually rode in companionable silence to the famous beachfront. Laura loved seeing the Promenade des Anglais, with its Italianate buildings, as portrayed in the many paintings of Nice. It ran parallel to the water. There was a magical feel about it.

He found a parking spot on a side street and they walked about a block and a half to the Oiseau Jaune. She could hear the music on their approach.

By some miracle Nic found them an empty bistro table among the crowd on the walkway and signaled a waiter. He ordered them mint tea.

Laura sat back, soaking up the authentic French atmosphere. "When I was in the Tetons of Wyoming last year, I went to a French restaurant in the mountains where they featured a singer who sounded like Charles Aznavour. This singer reminds me of him. I didn't understand the words, but I loved it. I have to admit, there's no place on earth like this. I can't believe I'm here."

"My grandfather can't believe you've come, either. I doubt he'll sleep until he sees you again tomorrow."

She fought tears. "To think I've missed this by staying away the whole time."

He angled a glance at her. "You were a victim of circumstances. That's what we've all been."

Laura took a deep breath. "I appreciate you bringing to this particular brasserie. For as long as I can remember, I've adored the sound and feel of this kind of music. You know, an accordion, a violin. Maybe a clarinet. It's *so* French. There's something about the tunes in your language that bypass conscious thought and find the romantic in you. But I do wish I knew French to get the full effect."

"You're Irene's granddaughter, all right. She had romance in her soul, too, and loved this place."

"That's nice to hear."

"I'll translate for you."

She glanced at him. "Please. I'd love to know what he's saying."

Nic's eyes were veiled. "'Let's dance the old-fashioned way, my love. I want you to stay in my arms, skin against skin. Let me feel your heart, don't let any air in. Come close where you belong. Let's hear our secret song and dance in the old-fashioned way. Won't you stay in my arms? We'll discover higher highs we never knew before, if we just close our eyes and dance around the floor. It makes me love you more.'"

Oh...oh... Trembling, Laura looked away, spellbound by the words, by the way he said them, by his Gallic male beauty. She'd never known such a moment, such a night.

After twenty minutes the singer took a break. Laura smiled at Nic. "This was wonderful." Her voice shook. "I feel I'm really in France now and think I can sleep. How about you?"

"You've given me a new appreciation for one of my country's greatest assets. If your San Francisco legs are ready, I'll take you on a walk up to Castle Hill before going home. We won't go up all the way, but there's a wonderful view of Port Lympia to the east that's quite magical this time of night."

"Tell me about this place," she murmured. Anything

to hear his deep voice speak English with that wonderful French accent.

"Castle Hill juts out a bit, like the Acropolis in Athens, but much greener, of course. It was named for a fortified castle and was redeveloped by King Charles-Felix of Savoy in the 1830s because of its amazing view. He added a landscaped park and an artificial waterfall."

Laura decided she'd been whisked away to a different universe as they climbed a ways above Nice. The music and the words had seeped into her bloodstream, where they would stay. To be out walking in such spectacular surroundings with this man was her idea of heaven.

She looked out at the sea. The romantic night called to her. Maurice had said he and her grandmother had walked hundreds of miles together. Now that she was in the South of France, she longed to see its wonders and clear her head. To see it with Nic left her breathless.

Eventually they returned to his car, but inside she rebelled that any of this had to end.

Wrapped in the beauty of the night, she closed her eyes and rested her head against the window during the drive back to the villa. Laura couldn't relate to the woman who'd flown to Nice earlier.

A change had come over her. Nothing was as she'd thought. Everything was different. The lines weren't clear anymore. She was terrified of what was happening to her.

The next day Nic was sitting at the dining room table reading the newspaper without absorbing any of it. He was troubled that he'd offered to drive Laura down to the waterfront last night. What had possessed him to take her walking afterward?

He couldn't understand himself. His family would *never* understand. If any of them had seen him with another woman while he was still waiting for word about his wife, it would shock them in a cruel way. But to know he'd been with the enemy when they didn't know she'd even come to France...

Ciel. What was wrong with him? Why had he done it?

Nic put down his coffee, crushed by guilt. Apart from Arlette and Jean, who lived in the back, Laura was the only person to have slept in his house since Dorine had gone missing. He'd let her stay here because he knew it was what his grandfather wanted.

And because you were trying to uncover her true agenda. Look how that turned out for you, Valfort!

He heard footsteps and lifted his dark head. Every time he saw Irene's granddaughter, she looked sensational. Yet beneath the surface he sensed her struggle over a situation that had plagued all of them for years. He discovered his own emotions churning. Today she'd dressed in chocolate-colored linen pants and a café au lait–toned blouse with a chic mandarin collar. She'd fastened her hair back with a tortoiseshell comb.

He got to his feet. "*Bonjour,* Laura."

"*Bonjour,*" she mimicked him before putting up her hands. "Don't laugh. I only took Spanish and never could get the hang of the accent to my teacher's satisfaction."

Nic chuckled as he pulled out a chair for her. "Join me for brunch."

"Thank you. This looks delicious. I'm sorry I slept so late. The fabulous walk after the music last night lulled me into a deep sleep."

"No apology needed after that long flight." He saw signs she'd been crying.

She sat down and took a serving of quiche and fresh fruit. "How did my grandmother do in the accent department?"

"Exactly like you in the beginning. But she worked hard at it. Within two years she sounded French."

"So it *is* possible."

"Of course."

"There is no 'of course' about it. I work with people who've been in the States for years and they still sound like they came from somewhere else."

"An accent is something you have to cultivate. But in truth, your grandmother had an excellent ear."

"Being married to Maurice, she was no doubt motivated," Laura quipped. "It's evident he's an exceptional man. He couldn't have been kinder to me last night. I hope I didn't hurt his feelings by not accepting his invitation to stay at the château."

"My grandfather made the gesture in hope, but I interceded to give you time to adjust."

"I know, and I'm very grateful. For what it's worth, I apologize for the way I treated you in San Francisco. Or maybe I should say, the way I didn't treat you. You were sent into a hornet's nest.

"Given the lovely evening out you showed this tourist last night, I should have taken you to some special spots in San Francisco. We could have eaten at my favorite restaurant at Fisherman's Wharf, ridden a trolley, driven up to Twin Peaks for the greatest view. Forgive me for being incredibly rude when you were only carrying out your grandfather's wishes."

"Just as you were holding up your end to the best of your ability," he inserted.

Now that Nic was getting to know Laura, he'd been forced to alter all his old concepts about her. With the gloves off, this woman was showing the perception and human insight she shared with her grandmother. It took that kind of depth to have attracted his grandfather. In truth, it attracted him.

He couldn't believe that in so short a time Laura had stirred up feelings inside of him without any design on her part. How had Nic allowed himself to get in this position when her family had wronged his over several decades? Since he was in love with Dorine and always would be, neither Dorine's nor Nic's family would be able to understand him having a desire to be with another woman. But for it to be *Laura?*

Their shock if they knew she was his houseguest filled him with despair. He would never want to let his family down, or Dorine's, but Laura's presence beneath his roof was important to Maurice. Unfortunately, no matter how pure Nic's intentions, their disapproval would pour down on his head once they found out.

"To be honest, I'm ashamed of my behavior," she confessed.

"No more than I. Yet we've survived our second skirmish intact. Are you ready for the third?"

Her inquisitive gaze darted to his. "Do I take it you've already talked to Maurice this morning?"

Nic nodded. "He and your grandmother were early birds. Naturally he would like to come over. How do you feel about that? No one else will be here to disturb us."

She wiped her mouth with a napkin. "Please tell him to come. Will someone drive him?"

"Not my grandfather. He says driving is his one pleasure at this point and he refuses to give it up."

"It must be so hard to find himself alone. To have lived with someone all those years…I can't imagine it."

"To be sure, he's struggling. He's also apprehensive of your true feelings."

She bit her lip. "Whatever the problem with my family, I wasn't a part of it except to feel the fallout. You have no idea how eager I am to talk to him."

That would thrill Maurice no end. *"Bon."* He pulled out his cell phone and rang his grandfather to give him the go-ahead. The older man sounded elated before they hung up.

"Nic? Does your family know I'm in Nice?"

"Not yet. For the time being this meeting is just between the three of us. My grandfather is aware this is new ground for all of us."

Those lovely blue eyes were filled with anxiety. "Is the animosity as bad on your family's side?"

Time to tell the truth. "To this day none of his siblings or my parents or my aunts and uncles have approved of Maurice's second marriage. They couldn't very well banish Irene from the family, but they kept their distance so that she always felt like an outsider—except with Maurice, of course."

"And you."

He nodded.

"That means all of you have been in pain, like my family. How tragic," she whispered.

"Tragic is the right word. They thought my grandmother Fleurette was perfect. I did, too. At the end she suffered from a severe case of arthritis that deformed her extremities and kept her bedridden.

"My grandfather waited on her with such devotion and grieved for her so terribly, none of us thought he would ever get over his loss. When he announced he was getting married again less than two years after the funeral, it was hard on the family to comprehend."

"Two years?"

"Yes."

"But I thought—"

"I'm afraid you don't have all the information," he muttered gloomily. "There've been huge lapses of the truth on both sides of the Atlantic."

A distressed sound escaped her throat. "Whatever the truth, both sides of our families have suffered a lot of grief that I find appalling."

"You're not alone on that score. My family would have understood his finding a woman—or several women—to be with. But to actually get married again to a woman from another culture and bring her to the family home to live was a particularly bitter pill to swallow. It turned out she was the widow of Richard Holden, another hotelier who'd put Holden Hotels on the map in California."

Nic sat forward. "Did you know your grandparents and mine met at several world conferences with other hoteliers while they were in business?"

"What?" she cried.

"It seems the four of them struck up a friendship and did a little traveling together."

Aghast, Laura shook her head. "I didn't know about the travel."

"I'm not surprised. As they say, the devil is in the details, and you weren't privy to them. Maurice was saddened when he learned Richard was dying of cancer and visited their home several times before he passed away."

"Was your grandmother still alive at that time?"

"*Mais oui.* She went to Richard's home with him."

"So the idea of an adulterous relationship—"

"Is preposterous," Nic concluded for her. "It was two years later before arthritis turned on Fleurette and put her to bed. After her death my grandfather finally rallied and started working all hours. A year later there was an international conference in New York where several hoteliers were being honored. He discovered Irene was there to receive an award posthumously for Richard."

"So *that's* how they met again."

He nodded. "I leave it to your imagination to figure out what happened. Two strong people who'd been friends earlier and had a great capacity to love discovered they wanted more and fell in love."

Laura was fighting her emotions. "What a romantic story."

"Yes. My grandfather flew to California constantly to be with her. He tried to get to know your mother and aunt, but it wasn't meant to be. When he proposed, she said yes and they got married."

"Where?"

"In California. They had a private civil ceremony performed by a justice of the peace. He planned to settle there with her so she wouldn't have to be uprooted from your family. They could travel back and forth to France. Maurice had decided to install his brother, Auguste, to be in charge of the corporation while he consulted from a distance. But it wasn't meant to be, at

which point Maurice brought her to France. He'll fill
you in on the details."

"Their marriage shouldn't have decimated both families," Laura cried softly. "What's wrong with all of
them?"

He shook his head. "I was twelve at the time. After
hearing the family talk, I wasn't prepared to like your
grandmother, who was taking the place of my *minou,*
but that changed when he brought Irene to Nice to live
and I met her. She was one of the most charming women
I ever met, and it was clear to anyone they made each
other happy. She became my unofficial English tutor."

Those blue eyes lit up. "Really?"

"We both enjoyed our informal sessions."

"You helped each other."

"Yes. As I grew older I heard the word *opportunist* in
regard to her come up in hushed conversations at family gatherings. But that was absurd, since Grandfather
told me she had plenty of her own money."

Laura pushed away from the table and stood up. "I
don't understand any of it, particularly not the lie or
the depth of my mother's and aunt's venom. After what
you've told me, it doesn't make sense."

"I agree there's a big piece missing and had hoped
you could enlighten me. Perhaps my grandfather will
be able to shed some more light on the subject. Would
you like to go down to the garden while we wait?"

"I'd love it. I'll get my sweater."

She joined him in another minute wearing a white
cardigan. He opened the French doors onto the patio.
From there he led her down stone steps to the garden.

"You'd never know it was winter here. Look at that
exquisite array of flowers! Everything from pink to

red and purple. No wonder they call Provence God's garden."

Her comment shouldn't have pleased him so much. "I don't pretend to know their names," he murmured. "I leave that to the gardener. Your grandmother could tell you about each variety. I do know she loved the patch of white narcissus over in the corner surrounding the Etruscan urn."

"They look like drops of snow in the greenery."

Nic moved closer, drawn to her in ways he couldn't explain. "Would you believe me if I told you Irene once said the same thing? Besides your looks, you two are uncannily alike."

He saw her shiver, but it wasn't that cold out. "If you want to know, it spooks me a little."

"Surely *spooked* isn't the right word—"

She avoided his eyes. "No one ever commented that my mother and I are alike. I guess my grandmother's genes were passed on to me. It's so strange to hear about how much we have in common when she was absent almost the whole of my life."

Nic found the similarities astonishing. Laura was so—heaven forgive him—alluring, even though he loved Dorine with all his heart. "There are differences, too, of course. Irene claimed to have no interest or head for business. You, on the other hand, hold the impressive title of marketing manager at Holden headquarters. Which means you inherited some of your grandfather Richard Holden's genius. I'm impressed. Maurice held him in great esteem."

His comment caused her to look at him through veiled eyes. "I keep learning things I didn't know. Tell me something else. How come you're not running Val-fort Hotels?"

"That's all in the hands of family—my father, uncles, siblings and cousins. Maurice and his brothers watch over everything."

She cocked her blond head. "You're the dark horse. What do you do for a living?"

He'd wondered when she'd get around to asking him. Pretty soon she would want to know about his absent wife and he would have to explain. But he preferred not to tell her about Dorine while they were dealing with Laura's reason for coming to France. There'd be time enough later for that horrific, ongoing chapter in his life.

"I run my own research-and-development business in the technology park near here. My division deals with specialized information in life and environmental science, including fine chemicals. The park consists of eight competitiveness clusters. In layman's terms, we reinforce synergy between academic research and business through technology partnerships."

"Already you've more or less lost me," Laura said on a gentle laugh, igniting his senses that had been in a deep sleep. He didn't want to be awakened, particularly not by this woman. His family had never been able to accept Irene. Now her granddaughter had come, and the chemistry between the two of them was coming alive, but it just wasn't possible. His guilt was crushing him. "Sounds like the furthest thing from the hotel business one can get."

"I always liked the sciences and went to study in Paris, but my brother and brother-in-law are steeped in the hotel business."

"Yet your grandfather leans on you for everything of the greatest significance in his life."

She had his attention. "Why do you say that?"

"He said himself last night that he can always depend on you. Plus there's a feeling I sense between the two of you. You're strong like he is, or he wouldn't have sent you on a desperate mission that would have struck fear in anyone else."

Her remarks were so on target, they caught him off guard.

"Nicholas?"

CHAPTER THREE

THEY BOTH TURNED at the same time to see Maurice descending the steps, this time wearing his favorite leisure suit and turtleneck. His searching brown eyes darted from one to the other as he approached.

Because Nic bore a strong resemblance to his grandfather, he wondered if Maurice was seeing himself and Irene as they might have looked fifty-odd years ago, long before the two of them had even met. It raised the hairs on the back of his neck to consider the complexity of their incredibly unique situation.

This time Maurice kissed Laura on both cheeks. Their interaction seemed natural. "I'm sure Nic told you that your grandmother left something for you, otherwise you wouldn't have come all this way."

"That's not true!"

He glanced at Nic in query.

"Maurice, if my grandmother left me something, that thrills me, but I didn't come all this way because of a will. I didn't want the silence between our two families to last any longer. I wanted to talk and meet with the man she'd loved all these years. Not even my family could stop me. I've already told Nic this and hope you believe me."

He reached out to clasp her hand. "What you've just said is an answer to my prayer. Now I want to fulfill my wife's wishes. I spoke on the phone with my attorney, *ma chère.* He told me to go ahead and read the will to you. I could do that, but I'd rather show you. Why don't you come to the château around five?"

She nodded. "I'd like that."

"Good. I'll be waiting for you. In the meantime, I have things to do." He clapped a hand on Nic's arm. "I'll see you later."

"*Mais oui, Gran'père.* Let me walk you back to the car."

"No, no. Spend the time with Laura. Make her feel at home."

More guilt swept through him, but this was one time he had to fight it. When Maurice had disappeared inside, Nic turned to her. "What would you like to do in the next few hours?"

She looked all around her. "Nothing could equal the lovely evening last night, but I would like to do a little shopping in the Old Town I've heard so much about."

Nic would never forget last night either. He was haunted by his feelings. "The window kind, or do you have something specific in mind?"

"Specific for sure." She looked all around her. "Since Maurice couldn't bury my grandmother here, I'd like to do something in honor of their love. You say she loved flowers."

Nic nodded. "So did my grandfather."

"Then I'd like to take him some."

"Do you have a certain variety in mind?"

"No. Not yet."

"You'll have a worse time making a decision when I take you to the Marché aux Fleurs Cours Saleya."

Her eyes smiled. "What's that?"

"One of the most famous flower markets in France. Grab what you need and we'll drive there."

Twenty minutes later he parked near the area with the pretty striped awnings. Beneath them she discovered thousands of flowers. "Nic—"

Their gazes met. "I know. Do you get the feeling they're making eyes at you?"

She laughed. "I do!"

They walked around for at least a half hour while she tried to take it all in. "Oh—I have no idea what to choose. It smells so heavenly here. Look at those geraniums!"

There was everything imaginable, from dahlias with their anemone-shaped flowers to vivid impatiens in glorious colors. But in the end he could see her attention was drawn to the mauve fuchsias. She stopped in front of the huge tub. "I think I have to have these."

The vendor spoke to Nic, who translated. "He wants to know how many you want."

"I wish I could have all of them, including everything in this market, but of course that's ridiculous."

"Not if this is your heart's desire."

In the next breath Nic said something to the man and handed him some bills from his wallet. The vendor grinned, then nodded to several of his workers. They picked up the tub and followed Nic to the car. He opened the trunk and they set it inside.

When the workers left, she looked up at Nic. "I don't know what to say," she whispered. Before he could take his next breath, she raised on tiptoe and kissed his hard jaw. "Thank you for another memory I'll always cherish."

The feel of her lips shook him to the core. To throw off the sensation, he said, "Come on. I'm going to take you to Fenoccio's. It's an ice cream parlor that serves exotic varieties."

"Like what?" she asked as they walked along.

"Have you ever tasted ice cream with violets?"

"You're joking!"

But of course he wasn't. In a few minutes they were both sharing a small cup of it. The flavor was different and quite delicious.

"Around this corner is another treat you have to try."

They stopped at Lova's, where he fed her *socca,* a big pancake cut up into little strips and covered in black pepper, then eaten with the fingers. When he fed her a strip, her lips brushed his fingers, sending another curl of delight through his body.

"Um…that's good! We have to stop feeding ourselves if Maurice is expecting us to eat dinner. I need to do one more errand and know the shop. We passed it a minute ago."

Nic checked his watch. "It's getting late. Tell you what, I'll go get the car. When you're ready, call me and I'll pick you up."

"Thank you." As he started to walk away, she called to him. "I've never had so much fun."

Nic had forgotten what fun was like. Yet overnight she'd transformed the black world he'd been living in.

Dorine…forgive me.

Laura knew this afternoon was the only one she would have with Nic. Her guilt weighed too heavily for this to go on.

She was here to get to know Maurice and tried to

imagine what it was her grandmother had left her. Her excitement was tangible. But intermingled with those thoughts was a growing awareness of the married man who'd just left her. She found him so appealing, she was afraid.

Laura had been rubbing shoulders with married businessmen for years, some of them very attractive. But nothing like this had ever happened to her before.

Was this how her grandmother had felt when she'd first met Maurice? Breathless and aware of a male energy that invaded her body, filling it with shocking new sensations? Nic's deep voice penetrated so that even when she wasn't looking at him, her nervous system responded to a force beyond her understanding.

Tomorrow she'd arrange for a flight to San Francisco and put this man behind her. She'd come to France for answers about her grandmother. With nothing else to be resolved, she didn't dare remain under his roof after today. Her guilt had reached its zenith.

Adam had texted her this morning. She'd texted him back that she'd get in touch with him later when she had something concrete to tell him. In truth, she didn't feel like talking to him. Whether her mother was right about his agenda or not, it didn't matter.

Last night Nic Valfort had happened to her...today he'd happened to her again, only with more force.

Maurice's grandson had already made such a breathtaking assault on her life and senses, Laura was reeling. When she could feel this attraction to an unavailable, married man, it meant she couldn't possibly make a commitment elsewhere that was worth anything. Certainly it meant she hadn't met the right man yet.

The old part of Nice was like a lot of the medieval villages she'd seen throughout Europe. She was charmed by its narrow streets curving in irregular fashion between old buildings with their red-tiled roofs. The streets were packed with shops and shoppers still needing to buy gifts. She'd almost forgotten tonight was Christmas Eve, thus the reason for this errand.

She went in one of the wine shops she'd spotted earlier and bought a Riesling and a Pinot Gris for her hosts to thank them for their hospitality. She asked that the bottles be gift wrapped. While she was waiting, she pulled out her cell phone, but it rang before she could call Nic.

Her heart thudded when she saw his name on the caller ID. She clicked on. "Hello?"

"*Bon après-midi,* Laura. Are you ready for a ride home yet?"

She sucked in her breath. "Your timing is perfect."

"Where are you?"

"At Chappuis et Fils. Sorry I pronounced it wrong."

His chuckle wound its way through her body. "I still understood you and will be there in five minutes. I'm already in my car. Don't go anywhere else."

Laura smiled. "I can tell you're a married man." She'd brought it up on purpose, if only to remind herself. "No doubt you've had to chase after your wife many a time, but I'll make this easy on you and promise to stay put."

She didn't know what she expected to hear him say, but it wasn't the long silence that met her ears. "Nic? Are you still there?"

"*Oui.*" Then she heard the click.

Her brows met in a frown. What had she said? Was he separated from his wife? Maybe in the middle of a divorce? Maybe that's why he hadn't spoken of her. She didn't know what to think.

The shopkeeper handed her a bag containing her two parcels. She thanked him and walked outside, but the excitement she'd felt when she'd first heard Nic's voice had evaporated after hearing his dampening one-word response. He'd hung up, leaving her hurt and baffled.

It wasn't long before she saw his car come alongside her. She hurried to get in and shut the door, lowering her shopping bag to the floor of the backseat. He wound his way through a couple of streets to a broader thoroughfare without saying anything. When they reached the main road, he headed in the direction of La Colle-sur-Loup.

His dark countenance unsettled her. Anxious over the tension radiating from him, she stared out the window, wondering what was going on inside him. "Are you okay? Is your grandfather all right?"

"Your presence has infused him with new purpose. You have no idea. He needed me for a while because he wants this visit to be perfect for you."

Nice as that was to hear, it didn't answer her question about Nic himself. They drove another five minutes before he pulled off the road to a gravel drive. A canopy of trees made the interior darker as they continued through the wooded property.

When they rounded a bend, he pulled to the side of the road and stopped the car. By now her heart was thudding in trepidation. He shut off the engine and turned his dark head toward her. "My wife went missing three years ago."

Laura's horrified gasp resonated in the car.

"I'm presuming Dorine is dead, perhaps from the

very first day. I'll never know if it was foul play. Maybe a vendetta against me or my family. If she was attacked and is still alive, the chances of her having amnesia are statistically improbable. If she was kidnapped, there was never a ransom note. If she left me for another man, it's been three years and I've reconciled myself that she's not coming back. If she became ill and died or committed suicide, her body has never been fo—"

"Don't say any more," Laura begged him. Without conscious thought she put a trembling hand on his arm.

Nic glanced down at it. "I was rude to you on the phone. That's because I was angry at myself." He let out a sigh. "When you first asked me if she knew I was bringing you home to the villa, I should have told you about her then. But you were already dealing with the pain of your grandmother's death and I didn't want to add to your discomfort."

"It couldn't have done that—"

"Then you'd be among the rare few who don't believe I had anything to do with Dorine's disappearance."

Her eyes closed tightly for a minute. "The rare few being your number-one defenders, Maurice and Irene. I know what you're about to tell me. The spouse is always suspect. That holds true in every country."

"Yes," he said grimly. "In some circles I still am the prime person of interest. The police turned my house and office inside out and upside down looking for her. The newspapers had a field day exploiting the Valfort name. Jack the Ripper didn't get as much notoriety as I did. My entire family was vetted with criminal relish."

"I—I can't imagine a situation more ghastly." Her voice shook. "You don't need to explain anything to me." She squeezed his wrist before letting him go. "I don't know how you've been holding your world together." He was in such a horrible situation she could hardly bear it.

"In my darkest hours it was Irene who told me not to lose hope. She'd been ostracized from your family and mine, but she wouldn't let me despair. She told me I could rise above the suspicions and that one day justice would prevail and I'd get my life back. Her prediction was something I've held on to. For her to be gone has left me without one of my anchors."

"Oh, Nic—" Tears gushed from Laura's eyes. "I'm mourning the fact that I never got to know her, but I'm so sorry for what her death has done to you and Maurice. It sounds like my grandmother was a saint."

"There's no question about that."

Laura wiped her eyes with her hands. "What was Dorine doing the last time you knew her whereabouts?"

"She worked at one of the other companies in the technology park. On that particular day, she told the secretary she was leaving for lunch. We know she drove her car into Nice and parked on one of the streets near a favorite restaurant of hers. But the proprietor claimed she didn't eat there that day.

"I was at work, but had left for a business lunch in Nice, then returned. It was almost time to go home when I received a call from the secretary. She wanted to know if Dorine was with me, because she'd never come back from lunch. That's when the nightmare began."

Laura kneaded her hands in anguish. "And it's never ended for you."

"It has been torture, I admit. At first I was on tenterhooks, thinking she was still out there somewhere. For the last couple of years, I've felt she's dead, but..."

"But you've had no closure yet and your character has been unfairly impugned. I'm so sorry, I don't know what to say. There are no words to comfort you."

"Thanks for not trying." His voice grated. "That sounded horrible, didn't it?"

"No," she said in a wooden voice. "Just heartbreakingly honest."

"You have an amazing capacity to understand."

"I don't. I'm just trying to put myself in your place. Knowing you, you've done everything humanly possible to find her."

He nodded. "Both her family and mine dedicated their lives to finding out what happened to her. So has Lt. Thibault, the detective who believes in me and wants to solve this case. Yet having unlimited financial resources still hasn't produced one iota of evidence that she's alive or dead."

Vanished without a trace... There had to be an answer someplace, but he didn't want to hear her say it.

"On top of your pain, you've been trying to help your grandfather in his grief." She swallowed hard. "I was terrible to you in San Francisco and wish I could take it all back. If only there were a way I could help you now."

Her sensitivity was yet another quality that made her exceptional. "By flying here you've made a new man of him. That in turn helps me."

"Then I'm glad I came." It was impossible to keep the tremor out of her voice.

"Maurice has planned that we eat first. Normally we dine later, but this is a special occasion. I hope you can pretend to be hungry. If I know him, he's asked the cook to prepare your grandmother's favorite meal."

Don't say any more or I'll break down. "I'll show him I'm starving."

"You're wonderful." He gave her a quick kiss on the cheek.

Her head was bowed. "I can't imagine food tasting good to you when that darling young wife of yours is still unaccounted for. I saw a picture of the two of you in the hall. I could cry buckets for you. How do you stay so strong?"

This time his hand reached out to cover hers. "One day at a time. Three years have passed. I've had to cope."

She nodded. "What kind of work was she in?"

"Chemical research. Our two companies had business dealings from time to time."

"So you met through your work?"

"In a roundabout way, yes."

"Was she brilliant?"

"Very. We both loved science and had that in common."

"Life isn't fair." Laura had trouble breathing normally. "I'll tell the man upstairs when I talk to him again."

"Laura..." He gripped her fingers a little tighter before relinquishing them. "We'd better go before Maurice starts to get worried."

She wiped her eyes. "That's the last thing we want him to do."

Once again they were on their way. After several more bends, the château she'd seen in the photograph appeared. "Oh, Nic—"

Laura had been to the some of the châteaux on the Loire a few hours away from Paris, where the kings of

France had held court. This one peeking through the trees was reminiscent of them, but much smaller in size.

Enchanting was the only way to describe its soft yellow facade. The combination of the Mansard-styled roofing and the coned towers took her breath. Lights shone from the three floors of evenly spaced windows, with their tiny square panes of glass. The sight was more exquisite than any picture in a fairy tale.

Nic pulled up in front of the circular drive and got out to help her. Laura was so mesmerized, she didn't realize how entranced she was until he opened the door. When he touched her now, his warmth seeped right into her bones.

On a shaky breath she said, "Would you mind bringing that shopping bag in the back? There's something in it for your grandfather." For Nic, too, but he'd find out later.

A half smile broke the corner of his compelling mouth. "Didn't Omar Khayyam say something about a bottle of wine and thou? Grandfather's cup will be running over."

She smiled back. Besides being heartbroken for him, she was so smitten by this man she was afraid he could see it in her eyes. Together they approached the entrance. Nic opened the massive door. *"Gran'père?"*

"Come in, *mon fils.* I'm in the *petit salon.*"

Laura felt like a time traveler who'd just stepped into old-world France. Any second now D'Artagnan might appear. No doubt the hundreds of guests lucky enough to have been invited to the Valfort home over the years had entertained the same thought.

Nic walked her through the immense foyer to a small salon. A dining room table with a lace cloth and candles glowing from the candelabra was set for three. Maurice, dressed in a formal suit and tie, came around and reached for her hands.

"Welcome to my home, *ma chère*." That was the second time he'd called her *my dear*.

"I'm very happy to be here."

"She brought you a gift." Nic reached in the bag and brought out two bottles of wine. When he saw the tags, his gray eyes darted to Laura's in surprise. "You got one for me, too?"

Her heart jumped. "Tonight two bottles of wine and thou sounds better than one, don't you think?"

Their eyes held. In that breathless moment, she knew he sensed her attraction to him. Embarrassed and feeling horribly guilty about it, she took the Pinot Gris from him and handed it to Maurice. "Merry Christmas."

The older man's eyes glistened. "We'll open it and drink to Irene, who would have given anything to be here tonight. You can freshen up through those doors at the other end of the room first."

"Thank you."

Talk about a trip down memory lane... But these were Irene's memories. Through the kindness of Maurice and Nic, Laura was privileged to peek in on them for a little while.

A few minutes later she returned to find Nic had brought in the tub of fuchsias and had placed it in the corner. Maurice greeted her with another hug. "You remind me of Irene. She always wanted to buy every flower at the market. Thank you for remembering her this way."

They sat at the table while Maurice opened the bottle and poured them each a glass. "I'd like to make a toast."

Nic caught her eye, letting her know through a silent message that her gifts had made his grandfather incredibly happy.

"To the long-awaited reunion. May there be many more of them to come."

"Amen," Nic whispered.

Laura didn't know how she was going to get through this meal, knowing Nic's hopes for his long and happy marriage had been dashed in the most cruel way she could imagine. If that wasn't enough, he had to go on living with the knowledge that some people still viewed him as the person responsible for his wife's disappearance. It made this moment bittersweet. They touched glasses before she took a sip.

Maurice smiled at her before drinking some of his. "I haven't had a drink of good *Alsacien* wine in a long time. You have excellent taste, just like your grandmother." A maid came in to serve them. "I hope you'll enjoy the coq au vin. Irene would have eaten it every night."

Laura's body broke out in gooseflesh. Too many coincidences. Her favorite meal at the Fleur de Lis in San Francisco was coq au vin. Nic had been watching her reaction and had probably read her thoughts correctly. He had the unusual capacity to see and feel beneath the surface.

"It's delicious, Maurice. Everything is perfect."

"Yet I see a new sadness in your eyes that wasn't there at noon. Why is that?"

While she was trying to find the words, Nic said, "I told her about Dorine."

"Ah. That explains it."

"I'm afraid it's my fault the subject came up." She

explained what she'd said to Nic on the phone at the wine shop.

Maurice nodded. "In that regard you were right. Dorine loved to shop and often lost track of time, to the frustration of my punctual grandson. But that was a long time ago. Tonight let's put all the sadness away." *What else could they do?* "It's Christmas Eve and you're here. I'm going to read you the will right now and hope it will thrill you as much as it did Irene, who worked on your legacy for years."

My legacy? Laura frowned. "For years?"

"Twenty-one of them, in fact. She told me she took you to see the first Superman movie when you were six. When we got married and she came to live with me here, she grieved so terribly for her daughters and you, she decided to do what Jor-El did for the son he sent to Earth to be saved. You'll understand better what I mean in a minute."

Intrigued beyond words, Laura waited while Maurice pulled a paper from his pocket and unfolded it. He cleared his throat. "She made monetary provisions for your mother and aunt. Those provisions have already been sent to Holden headquarters by my attorney. But this provision is solely for you."

He looked down at the paper. "I, Irene Holden Valfort, being of sound mind and body, leave the summerhouse on the Valfort estate and everything in it to my darling granddaughter, Laura Tate. It is hers for the rest of her natural life to do with as she pleases."

Laura felt dizzy and gripped the edge of the table. "My grandmother left me a house?"

"The one she and I lived in after we were married. She refused to stay at the château because it was where my life with Fleurette had been, and those memories were precious. So I restored the old summerhouse no one had used for a hundred years to make it livable for us.

"It was my wedding present to her. When she made out her will a few years ago, she told me she was leaving it to her granddaughter. She asked me that when the time came to go back to live in the château, because it would make my family happy."

"But who has lived in the château all this time?"

"Nic's parents, Andre and Jeanne, and my ailing brother, Auguste. His wife died a few years back. They've graciously allowed me to move in with them. Auguste and I love our card games."

"I couldn't take your home away from you!" Maurice put on a good front, but inside he had to be dying inside after losing her grandmother. Frantic, Laura's gaze swerved to Nic's. "I don't understand."

His gray eyes narrowed on her face. "You'll have to. It's legally yours."

Maurice got up from the table. "Come. Nic will drive us there and you can inspect it for yourself."

When she found the strength to stand, her legs—in fact her whole body—felt like jelly.

Nic drove them on the road leading behind the château and through the woods to a small lake. The summerhouse was half-hidden by a copse of oak trees. It had the same outer structure as the château, but had been built on a tiny scale in comparison. Laura fell instantly in love with it.

"Why is it called the summerhouse?"

"The head gardener lived there and used the rear of it for a greenhouse and nursery. The summer heat provided the perfect temperature for some of the exotic plants he cultivated."

"Nic told me my grandmother loved gardening."

"She became an expert."

Maurice helped her out of the car and walked her to the entrance. The front door opened to a small foyer that yielded a modern-looking, comfortable living room. The fire in the hearth sent up flames that flickered on the walls.

A handmade Christmas stocking with Laura's name hung from the mantel. In the corner was a decorated Christmas tree with twinkling lights. She breathed in the fresh pine scent. Nic must have come earlier in the morning to help get everything ready and put up the lights.

Dozens of wrapped presents had been placed beneath the tree. On one of the couches was a colorful throw made in blues and greens. A beam running below the vaulted ceiling held all kinds of intriguing-looking ceramics.

"Some of those gifts have been waiting years to be opened," Maurice explained. "Merry Christmas, Laura. This is the Christmas your grandmother has been working on for years. All of it for you."

Overcome by too much emotion, she broke down sobbing and buried her face in her hands.

The outpouring of grief, love and remorse coming from Laura was gut-wrenching. Three pairs of eyes were wet as Nic and his grandfather stared at each other. Nic was so moved he couldn't speak.

Maurice walked over and pulled Laura into his arms. The way she rested her head on his shoulder—

like a young granddaughter might do—was a sight
that would live with Nic all his life. It wasn't fair that
they'd been denied this experience for so many years,
but this Christmas had brought an end to the cycle of
pain for Maurice. Nic was positive there could be a certain amount of healing for Laura now, too.

She finally lifted her head and kissed his cheek.
"There are no words that could thank you for all this,
Maurice."

"I don't need words. What I want you to do is sit
down and watch a special DVD on the television set.
Nic will turn it on for you. When it's over, there's a stack
of them all labeled to watch. I'm going to take the car
back to the château." He looked at Nic. "Call me when
you want me to come for you."

Nic handed his grandfather the keys. After Maurice
left, Nic walked over to the TV set. "I haven't seen any
of these videos. Maurice had them transferred to DVDs.
Go ahead and make yourself comfortable. Your grandmother crocheted that afghan for you several years ago.
Why don't you wrap yourself up in it?"

Wordlessly she pulled it around her and sat down on
one end of the couch. She was so beautiful in profile, it
was hard not to stare. Before he forgot why they were
here, he started the DVD and joined her on the couch.
Suddenly they were both seeing Irene after she'd become ill.

*"I've left a lot of tapes for you, Laura, but this will
be my last one. I feel it in these old bones.*

*"I never got to discuss the afterlife with you, but I
know there is one and that one day you and I will meet
again in person. But I can't leave this world without telling you one more time the joy it gave me when you were*

born. To be a grandmother is a priceless experience for those women blessed enough to enjoy the privilege.

"As soon as you could make sounds, you called me Nana. You were the brightest, smartest, most adorable little girl on the planet. We laughed all the time. You were like a little golden angel from heaven. You loved stories, especially the Three Little Pigs. You were always so worried because they had to go out in the world without their mommy."

A sound between a laugh and a cry came from Laura.

"You had a sensitive heart at an early age and the most incredible imagination. You even made up voluminous stories of your own and drew pictures. I kept everything. You'll find them under the tree.

"Please do me a favor and don't be angry with your mother. She loved her father so much and believed that honoring his memory meant rejecting Maurice. But life's too short not to forgive, so forgive her for keeping us apart.

"You can experience a profound love more than once in this life, as Maurice and I found out. Otherwise, what would be the point of existence?"

Those words jolted Nic to the quick. Possibly what Irene had said was true. But Nic couldn't imagine it. What if that second love came to an abrupt end, too? How did one bear the pain a second time?

"I was so lucky to have met two marvelous men. It hurts me that you never did get to know your grandfather Richard, who fell ill when you were so young. I'm hoping you'll get to know Maurice. To know him is to love him.

"He's a loving grandfather with half a dozen grandchildren. But I have to admit I've had a special spot in

my heart for his Nicholas, who allowed me into his life when the other grandchildren weren't as open. I adored him and loved it when he came around. They are a lot alike. To this day he's been going through a great sorrow no one should have to go through in this life. I'm so thankful he and Maurice have each other.

"*They're both in my prayers continually, as you are.*"

Nic sat there, moved to his very soul.

"*I want you to know I love you and your mom and my Susie more than anything in the world. One day in the next life, we'll throw our arms around each other and all will be forgiven. For now, let me throw my arms around you through this video and the others I've had made over the years. Isn't technology a great thing?*

"*Enjoy this house—use it for a vacation or a place to come when you want to get away from the hotel business. I understand you show great promise in the marketing department and are destined to rise further with time. Good for you, my love. I often teased your grandfather Richard that behind every great man was a greater woman. I have no doubt that's you.*"

Laura smiled sadly.

"*But whatever your future holds, promise me you'll let the grief of the past go. I've urged Nic to do the same. Be happy, my dearest granddaughter. God bless you till we meet again.*"

The machine shut off.

"Oh, Nana—"

All Nic heard were the crackles coming from the fireplace and Laura's sobs. She was bent over, utterly convulsed. Inwardly Nic was, too. He'd learned to love Irene and had never admired another woman more than he admired her. There was wisdom in that woman that defied description. Even in her outpourings to Laura, she hadn't forgotten Nic.

He got up and walked over to the beam to reach for one of the ceramic figures. "Irene bought a kiln and made her own crafts in the back room of the house overlooking the garden. She spent hours painting them. This is one I can remember her working on when I was just a young teenager. I thought it odd she'd chosen to make a pig. Now I understand. She'd obviously hoped to give it to you while you were little enough to appreciate it."

Laura took it from him. Through drenched eyes she examined it. Irene had painted Laura's name on the side. "This is so overwhelming. I can't take it in, Nic."

"Not yet, anyway. It'll require some time to go through everything."

She hugged it to her. "I don't know what to do. Mother and Aunt Susan are spending Christmas together. I told them and Adam I'd be home Christmas night, but I can't leave yet. I—I don't want to." Her voice faltered.

The admission pleased Nic possibly too much, but when she dropped the man's name, his pleasure diminished. "Who's Adam?"

In the next breath she got up and put the pig on one of the side tables. "Adam Roth works in the accounts department at Holden headquarters."

"And?" he probed.

"We've been dating some."

Nic bit down hard. For a reason he didn't have time to examine right now, the news disturbed him. "Under the circumstances, he must be desolate you had to leave."

"He knows my grandmother's death has taken precedence over everything right now."

"Why didn't he come to France with you?"

"Because I didn't ask him," she said without hesitation. "This was something I needed to do alone."

Her response told Nic she couldn't be that deeply in love with Adam, or she would have wanted his support at a time like this. As for Nic, he would have insisted on going with her. Two people deeply in love should have no secrets.

She turned to him. "What I'd like to do is go back to your villa now and make some phone calls. They need to know I could be here for a while. Tomorrow I'll come back here and start going through everything."

"That's a good plan. I'll phone Maurice to bring the car."

CHAPTER FOUR

WHILE NIC CALLED his grandfather, Laura walked over to the tree and hunkered down to look at all the gifts. She reached for a packet the size of a postcard, curious to know what it contained. When she removed the paper, she discovered a dozen letters bundled together. They'd been mailed to her, but on the outside was stamped Return to Sender.

She scanned the dates and let out a horrified cry. These had been sent fifteen years ago. Laura started unwrapping the other presents that looked the same size. Before she was through, hundreds of unopened letters, some addressed to her mother and aunt, littered the Oriental rug.

"Laura?"

"Look at all these letters Nana wrote to us, Nic. Every one was sent back!" She got to her feet, almost hysterical. "How could Mother have done that?"

As she trembled in pain, he put his arms around her. She knew he was only trying to comfort her, but he'd chosen the wrong moment. In her vulnerability she fell apart against him. For a little while he simply cocooned her in place until she regained control. It felt so good... he smelled so good...

What are you doing, Laura? her conscience nagged at her. "I'm sorry," she said in a dull voice, and finally pulled away from him when it was the last thing she wanted to do. Her emotions were in chaos for too many reasons. "Forgive me for going to pieces like that. I'm so ashamed." She started gathering the letters, but he stopped her.

"Leave everything until tomorrow. Tonight you're emotionally exhausted. We'll come in the morning after breakfast and sort them. Let's be thankful your mother didn't destroy them. This way you'll have your grandmother's letters to read. Little slices of life you'll be able to savor."

Nic was wonderful beyond belief. She nodded and looked at him. "You're right. I don't know how I'll be able to make this up to you and your grandfather, but I'm going to try."

Whatever he would have said was interrupted by his cell phone ringing. "He's here. Let's go."

She put one of the letters in her purse and took the afghan with her. Nic grabbed one of the DVDs and turned out all the lights. They left the house for the car, where they found Maurice sitting in the back.

On the short drive to the château, he said, "I'm aware this has been an emotional night for you, Laura. Go home and get a good sleep. We'll talk more tomorrow."

"Definitely. Thank you, more than you'll ever know, Maurice."

"I've only carried out your grandmother's wishes. Don't forget the bottle of wine for you, Nic. It's here in the back. *Bonne nuit.*" He patted both their shoulders before getting out. She watched him go inside the château before they drove away.

"I don't see a sign of anyone else around the château, Nic."

"No. When my parents learned you'd come, they went to my sister's for a few days to be with the other members of the family."

Laura was filled with fresh pain. "So the pariah from San Francisco descended, forcing them to leave."

"Never say that again!" he exploded.

"Do they know about Irene's will?"

"Not yet. Maurice will tell them soon enough."

"Nic—"

"I know what you're going to say, but let's not discuss it tonight."

"I have to. I can't live there and come and go from time to time with your parents close by." *I couldn't live in the same country where you are, Nic.*

"Maurice will be there."

"Of course! This estate and everything on it belongs to him and your family, including the summerhouse. He restored it to accommodate Irene's wishes, and, yes, it was their home together for a period of his life. But she's gone now and he should be able to embrace his whole family again."

"He does that."

"It wouldn't be the same with me around and you know it! Maurice ought to be able to spend time at the summerhouse and the château where everyone can congregate with no more outsiders. You know deep down I'm right."

She saw his hands tighten on the steering wheel. "Do me a favor and humor Maurice right now. He's made it possible for you to discover your grandmother. Let her message to you sink in. The rest will work itself out in time."

"No. It won't work itself out at all unless I take the proper steps to make things right."

He accelerated onto the main road, headed back to his house. "What steps?"

Her pulse picked up speed. "I realize my nana wanted to show me how much she loved me, but she didn't really expect me to keep the house."

"Say that again? You heard Maurice read her will."

"I also know that she refused to live at the château when Maurice took her there. There's no way I'm going to live on the estate. That would be the same thing." She turned to him. "It was the gesture that counted, don't you see? But that's all it could be."

"Laura—"

"The day after Christmas I plan to hire an attorney here in Nice. I'll have him draw up the papers and will the house back to Maurice."

"You can't do that."

"Oh, yes, I can. That way your family will never know about my grandmother's will. I don't want them hurt. As for Maurice, it will be my gift to my step-grandfather for uniting me and Nana. But I'll make him the promise that we'll talk on the phone all the time and I'll come to visit him often."

She heard Nic's sharp intake of breath. "If you do that, he won't be able to handle it."

"That's your love for him talking. But remember that he's in the throes of grief, trying to hang on to Irene. She knew he'd suffer. That's why she willed the house to me. By doing so, he'd have something of hers to hang on to, through me. Admit I'm right."

He kept silent, but she knew he'd heard her. The man was too intelligent not to know she was speaking the truth.

"Those two loved each other to distraction. It's so rare to see a love like that, with both of them trying to help the other. I'm so touched by it I could cry all over again. But it doesn't have to work that way now. I'm alive and I love him already. I swear I'll come to see him a lot. Our visits will keep her alive for both of us without the house to drive another wedge."

As for tomorrow, Laura planned to spend Christmas Day opening her presents and getting them packed to ship back to San Francisco. But by now Nic was silent in that scary way that broke her heart, because he was dealing with unresolved grief of his own. She decided not to tell him any more of her plans tonight.

By the time they reached the villa, the tension between them was palpable. After they went inside, he put the DVD on the table and unwrapped the bottle of wine she'd given him. He uncorked it and poured some into a couple of wineglasses.

"I think we could use a drink." So did she.

He handed her one before tasting it. "Thank you for this. I haven't enjoyed Riesling in years."

She took a sip. "Hmm. It *is* good."

They stood facing each other. "Need I remind you how guilt ridden Maurice has been all these years, keeping Irene away from her own family? He desperately wants to make it up to you. If you will the house back to him, it will be like a slap in the face."

"That's why I intend to have a long talk with him about guilt." Nic had said his grandfather might be able to shed some light on why Laura's mother and aunt had lied to her, but it was a talk she wanted to have with him in private.

"I don't think it will do any good."

"Maybe not, but after hearing my grandmother on the video, he has nothing to feel guilty about. You saw all those returned letters she wrote. Those two committed no sin just because they loved each other. My mom and aunt are the culprits here, no one else. They should be writhing in guilt for keeping everyone apart."

Nic's black brows furrowed. "He won't see it that way."

"He will after I point out the facts. Clearly Nana loved Maurice so much she went to France to live with him. He didn't haul her off at gunpoint."

At that remark, his lips twitched, letting her know he was listening. Nic was handsome in the way that hurt.

"She went willingly because she was compelled by her deepest feelings. A lesser love wouldn't have held her. A lesser love on his part wouldn't have stirred him to marry her."

He drank what was left in his glass, communicating his agreement without words.

"You said they were strong people, Nic. They were and are. It's my opinion that everyone on both sides of the ocean was intimidated by such a profound love in the beginning. But all of that could have been overcome if something evil hadn't happened."

"Evil?" His expression reflected surprise.

"Yes. I know you were right when you said a big piece of the puzzle is missing. My aunt used the word *evil* in reference to Maurice. How could he possibly be evil when Nana loved him so much? I've always been curious about that. Now that I'm armed with information I didn't have before, I'm going home to get the truth out of Aunt Susan and Mom. I'd like to liberate Maurice from the hell he's been in all these years."

She wanted to liberate Nic from his own wretched hell.

Putting his glass down, Nic reached out to cup the side of her face with his hand. He shouldn't be touching her. She shouldn't be letting him, but she couldn't move. The man would never stop missing his wife... and Laura wanted his touch too much. If anyone was evil, *she* was.

"You're a rare woman," he said in a husky voice.

"Because I want to get to the bottom of this mystery? I think not. As it is, I let it go too long." Struggling with all the willpower she possessed, she eased away, forcing his hand to drop. "What is it they say? Those who don't know their own history are doomed to repeat it? I never want to cause a repeat of what happened to our two families because of ignorance."

"Nor I."

She wandered over to the couch and sat down. "Nic? Before I go to bed, I want to ask you a question about something else not related to our grandparents."

He found himself a chair opposite her. "Go ahead."

"I haven't been able to get your wife's disappearance off my mind. Is there any new avenue I could help you pursue while I'm here? Do you want to brainstorm?"

Nic sat forward with his hands joined between his legs and shook his dark head. "That's a kind offer. Don't think I don't appreciate it, but I've been stuck for three years now."

"You said she drove her car to a street near her favorite restaurant."

"In the same block."

"Did she normally eat with friends?"

"Not often. Once in a while someone from out of town working on the same project would fly into Nice. They'd always eat at the Bonne Femme."

"Was her work classified?"

"Some of it."

"Where do those people live who were working with her at the time she disappeared?"

"She had several projects going. One team in India, the other in China."

"Did she travel to those countries?"

"Sometimes."

"Has the detective on her case learned of any deaths or disappearances of people in those countries associated with her company before or after she went missing?"

"Not that I've been told."

"Maybe she was the victim of a corporate espionage scheme and those countries have withheld information. It's possible she was lured away from her office by someone on the team she would never have suspected could do her harm. Did she have her laptop with her?"

His head reared. He stared hard at her. "Yes. She took it back and forth from the office." Nic got to his feet. "Where are all these questions coming from?"

She took a deep breath. "I work for a big corporation. When I go out for lunch, it's usually with a regional manager who flies in to talk business. It would never dawn on me that one of the hotel managers I routinely visit throughout the state would come looking for me to injure me. But if so, I would have no reason to be nervous when first approached."

He looked tired as he rubbed the back of his neck. She wished she hadn't said anything. "I'm sorry I brought up something so painful."

"No. I'm glad you did. It prompts me to call Lieutenant Thibault and run your thoughts by him. The French Sûreté has resources at Interpol that could find out if evidence from those countries to do with her firm has been suppressed over the last few years."

She got excited. "It wouldn't hurt." To be excited sounded so awful, but if Nic could finally find out what happened to his wife, he could learn to live again. To get through each day *wasn't* living, not when certain fingers were still pointed at him. Her heart ached for him.

"You're right." His eyes played over her with a thoroughness that sent a tingling sensation through her body. "What do you say we do something happy and watch another DVD? I brought the one sitting on top of the stack."

"You just read my mind." They needed to get off painful subjects.

"We'll go in the den and watch on the big screen. I need a large one for my work. Bring your wineglass."

She reached for the afghan and did his bidding, following him into the next room on the other side of the house. One lamp was burning. No clutter in here. Just state-of-the-art equipment, bookcases with scientific tomes and some wonderful framed black-and-white photos of an eclipse of the moon in many stages. Riveting!

He poured more wine for them, then put the disk in the machine. The rounded couch filled one wall and part of the other. It was roomy and comfortable. A long, narrow coffee table was placed next to it.

Laura took off her shoes and sat on the end of the couch with her feet curled up under her, throwing the afghan over her.

Nic watched her. "Maurice used to hold the skeins of yarn while Irene wound it into balls while she was working on that afghan for you."

"A labor of love," she mused aloud. "I would have given anything to see them together."

"Perhaps you will through the videos." Nic removed his suit jacket and tie. After unbuttoning his collar, he rolled up his sleeves to the elbow.

When he sat down, he extended his hard-muscled legs and crossed them at the ankles. She was far too conscious of his arms spread across the top of the cushions. His nearness filled her with unassuaged longings.

He glanced at her and sipped a little more wine. "This is nice. Maurice isn't the only one who's been rattling around in an empty house."

Nic.

Their eyes clung for a minute. "After all you've done and been through, I'm glad you're able to relax with me. Who would have thought it after our inauspicious beginning in San Francisco?"

His quick smile melted her bones. "That's what your coming has done for me."

She looked around. You have such a beautiful home."

"Dorine found it and decorated it."

Laura was surprised. "Where did you live before your marriage?"

"At an apartment in Nice she found uninspiring." Laura smiled. "I was so busy building my business, I didn't want to be a home owner, with all the headaches."

"But you took them on with her."

He nodded.

She should stop talking in case it was making his pain worse. "Shall we see what Irene wanted me to see?"

"The DVD case says this was filmed nineteen years ago."

"Nineteen?" she cried. It didn't seem possible.

Once again he smiled that devastating smile that caught at her heart. "You'd be eight, and I, fourteen. I confess I'm totally intrigued to find out what's on here." He pressed the remote.

In an instant there was her grandmother, big as life, but much younger, beautiful, dressed in pants and a blouse and standing against a hilly background. Would that Laura might look half that terrific at her age one day.

"Darling Laura, Maurice has brought me to the fortified city of Carcassonne, famous for the Crusades in 1209. One day you'll learn about them in school. My husband is taking the movie right now. You always loved palaces and castles. I thought you'd like to see this place. I wish you could be here. Maurice's grandson Nic has come with us. I call him Nic even though his name is Nicholas. The longer name is too formal.

"He's as fascinated by this place as I am. Come over here, Nic, so Laura can see what you look like."

A lean fourteen-year-old Nic, with longer hair, already getting tall, made a face for the camera. He appeared in a turtleneck and jeans, showing the promise of the breathtaking man he'd become one day. Laura jumped to her feet.

"Nic—that's you! Pause it for a minute! This is unreal. Do you remember that day?"

He chuckled and leaned forward. "Vaguely. Was I really that pathetic?"

"This movie is priceless. Press the remote again."

Pretty soon Irene took a picture of Maurice looking sporty in a windbreaker. His hair was still black and quite full, with only a few streaks of silver. Then Nic placed the video camera on a nearby ledge while he took a picture of the two of them. Maurice kissed Irene, hamming it up for the camera. They acted like teenagers. Laura heard Nic say, *"Oh, là là, Gran'père—"*

At this point both Laura and Nic collapsed with laughter. Laura had never enjoyed anything so much in her life. The teenage Nic larked around as they toured the battlements and fortifications. When the video came to an end, Laura made him play it again. She couldn't get enough. After the second run-through, he turned it off.

She darted him a glance. "Our grandparents left us both something precious, Nic. Now I know how Superman felt when he saw his father for the first time."

Nic's half smile made her legs shake.

"If Maurice didn't make another set of these for himself, then I'll have them made for you. The first time I saw you with Maurice, I could tell there was an affinity between you. Now I know why. Did your parents make movies with you and your siblings?" She wanted to know anything and everything about him.

"A few. My father doesn't like to bother with a camera. Maurice calls him what would be the equivalent of 'sobersided' in English."

"My mom was more like that, too."

Much as Laura wanted to stay up all night with him and talk, she didn't dare. He had a wife who could be alive somewhere. *What do you think you're doing, Laura?* Her guilt was killing her. The more time she spent alone with Nic, the worse it was getting. She didn't even want to think about saying goodbye when the time came.

After thanking him for letting her see the video, she put the afghan over her arm and walked through the den into the living room. Nic was close behind her, making her go weak in the knees.

Laura picked up her purse from one of the chairs. When she reached the hallway, she turned to him. "Good night, Nic. Thank you for the most wonderful day of my life. I have to believe a day is going to come in your life when you feel the same way."

Nic watched her disappear. For a while tonight he'd known a happiness he hadn't thought he'd feel again. He'd found himself concentrating on Irene. Being able to see Laura in her, the way they both laughed and got excited over everything, tripled his enjoyment.

It had been so marvelous sharing the video with her, he hadn't wanted it to end. Laura's arrival in Nice had brought Christmas back into his life.

But following those feelings came this excruciating attack of guilt. Nic buried his face in his hands. "Dorine, darling." He broke down sobbing. "I haven't given up on finding you. I haven't. Forgive me. Where are you? Please, God. Help me."

When he'd recovered, he texted the detective on his wife's case. Once he'd made the request prompted by Laura, he went back to his den to watch TV.

When he was next aware of his surroundings, it was morning. For the first time in ages he'd fallen asleep before going to his bedroom. To his surprise Laura's afghan had been thrown over him. That's why he'd felt warm—she had to have come in here again.

"Bonjour," Laura said in better French than before. He sat up to see her walk in the den carrying a tray with brioches, juice and coffee. She wore a navy T-shirt and jeans and was charmingly barefoot. "Stay where you are. It's Christmas morning and you deserve to be waited on."

She put the tray on the coffee table and handed him a mug of coffee. His attention was drawn to her fragrance and the blond hair she'd left long. It hung over one shoulder. "Arlette told me this is the way you like it—lots of sugar and cream. *Joyeux Noël!* Your housekeeper has been helping me with the pronunciation."

Ping went the guilt again for enjoying this moment with her. He was close to speechless.

"That sounded perfect. But you shouldn't be waiting on me when you're the guest."

"I think we've graduated beyond that point. I told Arlette we're family. After watching that film, I'd say you and I are the long lost grandcousins of Atlantis or some mysterious forbidden continent like that, united at last."

She grabbed herself a mug. "Here I thought I'd sneak another look at the movie for my Christmas-morning treat. But lo and behold, I discovered Santa had arrived ahead of me, totally exhausted after his trip around the world spreading joy." Her laughing blue eyes traveled over him, warming him in new places.

He burst into laughter that resounded in the room. "If I snore, I don't want to know."

Her chuckle filtered to his insides. "I would never tell. But I must say you don't look a thing like *Père Noël.*"

Nic rubbed his jaw, feeling the growth of his beard. "I don't remember the last time I slept in my clothes."

"That's good for you. I knew Santa had to be wearing something else beneath his red suit. It means you were rid of tension for a change. You've managed to make me and your grandfather so happy, it's time someone did something for you. No one deserves happiness more than you," she murmured with an ache in her voice she couldn't disguise.

Everything Laura said and did was getting to him. What in the hell was he going to do about it? She handed him one of Arlette's Christmas rolls on a napkin. Then she took one for herself and sat down on the other end of the couch.

"When we left the summerhouse last night, I grabbed one of the letters from the floor that had been addressed to me specifically." She pulled it out of her pocket, and his eyes were drawn to the feminine curve of her hips. "Do you realize all these were handwritten? She had the kind of penmanship you don't see anymore. After I got in bed last night, I read it. You need to hear what it says."

Nic felt Laura's magic distill over him like a fine mist. He turned toward her, munching on his roll. He'd never felt so conflicted in his life. All he could do right now was be happy for her. "I'm all ears."

"'My darling Laura, today Maurice and I will have been married ten years. We're in Venice. He's gone out to get a newspaper, but I know he left because he was upset and didn't want me to be aware of it.

"'The only shadow on our marriage has been the inability to share it with our loved ones. Today he got all broken up when he asked me if I'd been happy. A question like that is impossible to answer. He *knows* I've been blissfully happy with him, but deep inside he's not convinced.

"'Tonight he asked me if I wanted to leave him and go back to all of you. He believes that if we end the marriage, you will forgive me.'"

On a groan Nic sat forward, hurt for what the two of them had been forced to endure over the years. But he also groaned for the loss of Dorine, for the situation that had developed since Laura's arrival in Nice.

"'I've never seen him this upset before. Maurice blames himself for taking me away from you. I don't understand it. I feel he's keeping something from me, but I don't know what it is.

"'No matter what I say, I can't talk reason with him. The truth is, your mother and Susie will never forgive me for loving a man other than their father. Without Maurice's knowledge, I've been seeing a therapist in Nice about our situation.'"

Nic grimaced. "Her pain had to have been exquisite."

Laura nodded with glistening eyes, then went on reading. "'He's a doctor of psychology. He said that my children's anger has its roots in something much deeper than their not wanting to accept my marriage. His advice is to confront my daughters openly.

"'I've tried that. They won't see me or accept my phone calls. Tonight I tried to get Maurice to open up and tell me why he feels so guilty. If he's holding something back, what is it? To my devastation, he left to do an errand. It breaks my heart.'"

Until now Nic hadn't realized that Maurice had felt such crippling guilt.

"'Forgive me for baring my soul to you, but you're a part of me. When I write to you, I can imagine us being together face-to-face. I need that. All my love, Nana.'"

Heartsick over their grandparents' pain, Nic got up from the couch. The joy of Christmas had been but a fleeting moment after all. The letter Laura just read had managed to darken the sky once more. Both men had lost the loves of their lives. Nic never wanted to open himself up to this kind of pain again. Maurice had lived through it twice. Nic couldn't.

He glanced down at her. That lovely face had taken on a sober cast. Her eyes searched his. "Do you believe Maurice knows something he was never able to tell Irene?"

"I don't know," he murmured, "but I'm going to find out, because this has gone on long enough."

She jumped up. "I'm so glad you said that. Let's confront him together with this letter. He needs to know Irene went to a therapist to try to help them. The two of them loved each other too much, always trying to shield the other from pain."

Nic rubbed his chest absently. "That's exactly what they did. Whatever secret still lurks, it robbed them of a lot of happiness."

Her features hardened. "It robbed everyone on both sides. Yet their love was so strong, they managed to survive it. That's what real love is all about. Nic...you and I have the power to turn things around."

He admired her courage more than he could say. "We'll do it." He finished off his orange juice. "After I've showered and changed, I'll drive us to the summer-house. We'll open all the presents under the tree. Maurice will join us after he's spent time with the family. Then we'll talk to him about this letter."

"While you do that, I need to make those phone calls I forgot to do last night."

Being Christmas, naturally she'd ring her mother and Adam, the man who desired her. What man with a pulse wouldn't want her? But Nic couldn't be that man. He didn't want to be. He needed to find his wife.

"Laura?"

"Yes?" He heard the throb in her voice.

"Santa thanks you for Christmas breakfast. He hasn't had such a pleasant surprise in ages."

"It *was* fun before I spoiled it and read you the letter."

"I'm glad you did."

Her eyes clouded over. "I hope you mean that."

He meant it all right. With Laura on their grandparents' side, it added the kind of leverage needed to get the truth out of Maurice. Irene had suspected he hadn't told her everything. That woman's instincts couldn't be wrong. For twenty-one years they'd all been in a straitjacket. It was time to remove it.

Nic watched Laura reach for the afghan and leave the den ahead of him. Filled with a new sense of purpose, he found Arlette and asked her to prepare a basket of food for the three of them to enjoy at the summerhouse. With that accomplished, he showered and shaved, then put on trousers and a crewneck sweater.

Laura was ready and waiting for him in the living room, still dressed in the same outfit, but wearing sandals and her cardigan. He couldn't tell by her expression how her phone calls had gone, but if Nic were Adam, he would have taken the first plane to Nice and demanded to find out why she hadn't wanted him there. Didn't the man know not to take love for granted? It could be snatched from you in a minute, and Laura was a prize.

When they reached the car, he put the basket in the back and turned to her. "Isn't there a song in your country about over the river and through the woods?"

Her mouth broke into an enticing smile. "To grandmother's *petit* château we go," she sang, improvising as she went. "Clever Santa knows the way, in his dishy Mercedes sleigh, to avoid the ice and snow."

Nic grinned in spite of himself. He kept trying to control his feelings about her, but then she'd say something like that and his delight in her just kept growing. She had an amazing sense of humor that came out at the oddest times. A spontaneity so different from Dorine, who was a more controlled, structured kind of person.

In that moment he realized that the woman he'd once thought was the enemy had sung her way past his defenses and was close to— *Don't say it, Valfort.* He didn't want to, but his mind finished for him anyway. He feared she was reaching his stronghold.

They stepped inside the house, noticing that Maurice had sent some staff over to light another fire and turn on all the Christmas lights. But they hadn't touched anything else. The letters still lay scattered on the floor.

Nic put the basket on the table. "I'm going to hunt for some boxes. We'll sort the letters by date."

"I can't wait to read all of them."

"You have months of reading pleasure ahead of you, but I would wager you're anxious to open all the other packages first."

He heard her breath catch. "I admit it. I'm as bad as a child."

They worked together and soon the letters were

neatly packed. Nic set them out of the way. "Now I'll play Santa and give the presents to you one at a time."

She knelt down next to him, her blue eyes shining in anticipation. In the video, Irene had painted an image of Laura at six years of age. Nic could almost see her as she'd been then. It clutched at his heart to think she'd been deprived of her grandmother all these years.

Each present had a tag with an explanation. Maurice and Irene had traveled a lot. Before long a series of gifts from around the world surrounded them, hand-picked to bring Laura pleasure. Nic enjoyed witnessing her reactions.

She particularly loved the porcelain mask from Florence. But then the miniature Hans Brinker ice skates from Amsterdam thrilled her. Before long she was enraptured by the hand-carved music box from Vienna that played "Waltz of the Flowers." The last, from Egypt, was a hand-carved wooden Mary. She was holding the baby Jesus while Joseph led her on the donkey.

When the gifts came to an end, Laura shook her head. "This is too much."

"Twenty-one Christmases in one is a lot to take in," Nic murmured. "There's still more."

He handed her another gift, which turned out to be a box. "What on earth?" She reached inside and pulled out dozens of sheets of artwork made by a child. "Nic," she virtually squealed. "She saved the drawings I made for her!"

Nic moved closer. Together they looked at each one, some large, some small, each paper filled with scenes of stick figures done in crayons and markers. There were several pictures of castles.

"Like Nana said, I was preoccupied with fairy tales.

Oh, look—I've done pictures of the Three Little Pigs. My pigs are pathetic! I made the brick house go up to the very top of the page."

"You've drawn the wolf climbing up the wall. You didn't want him to get the pig," he teased.

"This is incredible. Look—I made my *L* backward in my name. The *A* looks like a snail."

More laughter ensued from both of them.

"But you turned it around in the pictures at the bottom of the stack," Nic pointed out. "These latest ones are very revealing. Do you see what I see?"

She nodded. "I've drawn me and my mother and father. But I also included my nana and grandfather. It has to be Nana because I put blond hair on her and brown on Mom."

"You printed her name above her head."

"The *N*s are sideways and look like *Z*s."

"I see you drew glasses on your grandfather and made his hair brown. He's shorter than your father here. You put black hair on him."

"My grandfather was only five foot nine. Dad was six feet. Daddy—" she whispered as a pang of remembrance hit her. "I loved him so much. I can't believe Nana kept all this. If I could see her and tell her what this means to me..."

"Don't forget her promise. In the next life you'll throw your arms around each other," Nic reminded her.

Laura sniffed. "She made up for every Christmas with this one."

Nic slipped an arm around her shoulders. "She was a unique woman to do all this for you." He pulled her closer and kissed her hair. Laura almost had a heart attack. "What a treasure she has left you. This artwork is very revealing of your talents. Even as young as you were, you drew with spatial accuracy. I'm impressed."

Nic was sitting too close to her. He had no idea what that kiss had done to her. His virility played havoc with her senses. It was impossible to concentrate. "Where's your aunt Susan?"

They looked through the rest of the pictures. He acted as though he hadn't been affected by that impulsive moment, but she could hardly breathe. "I didn't draw any of her. That seems so strange."

"Not really. She wasn't your immediate family. Did she live with you?"

"Oh, no."

"Then that explains it." His arm brushed hers as he helped her put everything back in the box. "For Irene to keep these drawings shows what a loving grandmother she was."

Laura got up from the floor, needing to separate herself from Nic before she did something impulsive and unforgivable. So far her guilt held her back, barely, but she was getting in deeper and deeper.

She'd just lost her grandmother. The thought of loving Nic and then losing him, too, made her positively ill. *He's not yours to love, Laura.* Her family would never understand. This was a nightmare.

Nic stood to his full height. "It must have torn Irene apart to be separated from you."

CHAPTER FIVE

"YOU'RE RIGHT, *MON FILS*."

They looked around. Maurice had come into the room.

"She never got over it." His mournful voice pained Laura.

She ran across the expanse to hug him. "Merry Christmas, Maurice. I've never known such a Christmas in my whole life. Thank you with all my heart." She kissed him on both cheeks. "Do you mind if I call you *Gran'père,* too?"

He made a strange sound in his throat and started to weep.

"Come and sit down by the fireplace," she urged him. "Your grandson brought food we can enjoy."

Nic walked over to help. "You'll enjoy the Riesling she bought me. We drank part of it last night, but there's still plenty." He took out the bottle and poured wine into goblets before passing them out. "To you, *Gran'père.*"

"*Joyeux Noël.*" Laura followed, but she knew Maurice was overcome with emotion. He took a few sips, but he looked older than his eighty-one years right now. Nervous, she asked, "Would you like to lie down for a while?"

"I think that's a good idea," Nic said. He must have noticed how drained Maurice was, too. "Come on. Let's set you up on the couch and prop your head."

He didn't fight them as they walked him over so he could stretch his legs. "I'm all right," he said with a sigh. "I guess I'm missing Irene too much."

"Of course you are." Laura kissed him again.

"Your parents are hoping to see you before the day is out, *mon fils*."

Nic nodded. "I'll run over to Marie's a little later."

"Dorine's parents have also arrived there. They know you have a guest, but they'd like to see you at some point."

"I'll do it soon."

Feeling excruciating guilt because she was here and had taken up all Nic's time, Laura looked at him. "Why don't you take care of everything you have to do while Maurice and I enjoy this time together? We have all we need right here."

She could sense his reluctance to leave. He was worried about Maurice. Though she never wanted to be apart from Nic, she had to face reality. "I'm going to stay right here with our *gran'père*. Enjoy the rest of the day with your family, Nic. I'm sure they all miss you terribly. I can only imagine how much Dorine's family is grieving, especially today. You go and don't worry about us."

His dark gray eyes thanked her. "I'll hurry."

After he left, she and Maurice talked for a little while until he fell asleep. The dear thing had done too much, and had worn himself out. She took the time to clean up the mess. Then she read another couple of letters that caught at her heart while she ate the delicious food Arlette had prepared.

"Laura?"

He'd awakened. She walked over with a chair and sat by him. "Feeling better after a catnap?"

"Much, but I was afraid you'd gone."

She smiled. "You can't get rid of me. I'm glad we're alone, because I want to read one of Irene's letters to you. I showed it to Nic earlier. She wrote it from Venice on your tenth wedding anniversary."

A shadow crossed over Maurice's face before he nodded in remembrance.

"Maybe you can answer a question for me." Laura pulled it from her pocket and started in. When she'd finished, she stared at him. "Something terrible happened at the time of your marriage, Maurice. It tore both families apart. I know in my heart you have the answer. Whatever it is, I can take hearing about it."

He blinked. "If I told you, it would do damage that couldn't be repaired. That's why I couldn't tell Irene. It would have destroyed her."

"I knew it was something like that," she whispered. "But you don't have much faith in the Holden women. The truth is, my mother's attitude about you and my grandmother destroyed my happiness years ago. Irene knew you held a secret. If you could tell me what it is, it would help me to put this behind me. And I believe it would help you, too. You've carried the burden far too long. We haven't known each other very long, but I already love you to pieces."

Maurice grasped her hands. "I love you, too. Are you absolutely sure you want to hear this? I've never told this to a living soul. If it had been anyone, I would have told Nic. But when he heard it, he would have done something I couldn't allow to happen."

She knew what Maurice meant. Nic had been so fierce when she'd told him the story that had circulated in her family, it didn't bear thinking about. "You've got me to confide in. Don't forget I'm your granddaughter now and I'm begging you."

He sat up a little. His color had improved since his nap, which was a relief. "All right. It started when Fleurette and I visited your grandfather while he was sick. That's when we met your mother and your aunt."

When Nic pulled up to the summerhouse four hours later, he noticed Maurice's Renault still there. The sun had already set. His in-laws were coping all right and doing as well as could be expected. But there was a grim atmosphere they'd never be able to shake off until there was news of Dorine, whatever it was.

When Dorine's mother got Nic alone, she'd wanted to hear about Irene's granddaughter and had thought it was wonderful that Laura had come to try to make things right now that Irene had passed away. Nic could tell Dorine's disappearance had changed her mother, who was normally more rigid in her thinking. She'd applauded Laura's desire to mend wounds and said she was proud of Nic for aiding in the process.

"You have to hold close the ones you love while you have the chance. We know all about that, don't we, Nicholas?"

Shattered by more guilt after their conversation, he left for the summerhouse.

He found grandfather and granddaughter watching another DVD. He heard chuckling from both of them.

Maurice was sitting in a chair and waved to him. As far as he could tell, the older man felt physically better. Nic was relieved to find him recovered. That was Laura's doing. Despite the storms, she spread sunshine like the six-year-old child Irene had described.

"Come on in, *mon fils*. You've missed all the fun."

"Surely it's not over," Nic teased, his gaze flicking to Laura. She hadn't looked at him yet. That told him something of significance had gone on in his absence.

"I'm afraid it is for me," Maurice stated. "Some of our friends will be coming to the château for the *souper*. I promised to be there." He got up from the chair and kissed Laura before heading for the entrance. "We'll see each other tomorrow."

Nic walked him out to his car. "Why don't I drive you?"

"I'm not too far gone to drive back to the château on my own." Nic frowned. "You two go on enjoying yourselves."

Something had changed. He'd felt it when he'd first laid eyes on Laura. Now Maurice seemed anxious to leave.

Once back inside the house, he walked over to Laura, who was still sitting in the chair. "What happened here?" The distress on her face was evident. "Did you tell him you were willing the summerhouse back to him?"

She looked up at him. "No. I read him the letter sent from Venice. The moment seemed right. I'm sorry I didn't wait for you."

Nic found a chair. "Did he take it hard?"

"No. I think he was relieved to be able to talk about

it. Nic—he's broken the long silence. I now have the missing piece."

He leaned forward, his eyes imploring her. "What did he tell you?"

She moistened her lips nervously. "That my aunt Susan made a play for him when he went to see Irene after they both were free."

"A play, as in—"

"Yes," she answered, reading his mind. "It was something so shocking, I can understand why Maurice never spoke of it."

"What exactly did she do?"

"Let me give you the background first. Susan is eight years older than Mother and was an only child for a long time. I guess when Mother came along, she grew very jealous of her, especially when she married my father. Growing up I saw that jealousy in a lot of ways. Maybe that's why I never drew her in my pictures."

"Jealousy between siblings happens in a lot of families," Nic murmured.

"I know. It's sad that Susan never married, because she's attractive in her own way. But the tragedy here is that after Maurice saw Irene in New York and flew to California to be with her, Susan thought he'd come to see *her.*"

"What?" Nic jumped to his feet. "Where on earth would she get an idea like that?"

Laura lowered her head. "Susan had met him those few times when he and your grandmother Fleurette went to visit Richard during his illness. I guess when he came to California again a few years later, Susan was under the impression he'd come to seek her out."

His gray eyes glittered. "She was delusional."

"I agree. But even being older, you know how charming your grandfather is. In his effort to win my mom and aunt around to the idea of him marrying their mother, he swept Susan off her feet without realizing it. Maurice had no idea and was clueless about her feelings until he returned to the hotel one night and found her waiting for him."

"Laura..."

Unable to sit still, she got to her feet. "By then Susan was thirty-nine and desperate to be married, especially to a handsome, wealthy widower like Maurice Valfort. Possibly she wanted to believe the myth that every Frenchman had a mistress. It's evident the twenty-year age difference didn't matter to her. He's very attractive and looks younger than he is—probably the way you'll look when you get older."

Despite the compliment, Nic shook his head.

"Needless to say, he told her he loved Irene. Susan swung at him in a jealous rage and scratched the side of his jaw. I saw the scar earlier while he was resting."

"That was how he got it?"

"Horrible, isn't it. Susan ran to my mom with lies that Maurice had not only tried to seduce her, but that he'd seduced their mother while their father was dying."

"Impossible. Fleurette was with him."

"Apparently there was one afternoon when Fleurette didn't go with Maurice because her arthritis had acted up. Susan painted him and Irene as evil people. Because Mother was the younger sister and intimidated by Susan, Mom believed her. Together they told my grandmother that they hated her and Maurice. They said they never wanted to see either of them again in this life. It was exactly as you told me."

"Maurice's only sin was in not telling Irene immediately," Nic broke in. "But he knew how much she adored her daughters and was afraid it would damage Irene forever."

Laura nodded. "You want to know something? I'm glad Irene never knew the truth. It was too ugly."

"Agreed," he emoted.

"To her they were her darling daughters, whatever their faults. Think what your grandfather has been living with all these years...but there's more, Nic."

"What do you mean, more? How could there be?" His eyes were haunted.

"When the two of them married, Susan sent a letter to your great-uncle Auguste, telling him about Maurice's affair with Irene while he and Fleurette went to visit Richard during his illness. Her poison did its damage. *That's* why your family never accepted Irene. In Auguste's words, Maurice had defiled the memory of Fleurette and they didn't consider Irene a God-fearing woman."

Sickness filled Nic's gut.

"Maurice demanded to see the letter. He still has it in his possession."

Nic raked his hands through his hair. "That tale is so horrendous, you couldn't make it up."

"It explains everything. I assured Maurice he'd done the right thing to keep quiet. He broke down and we both cried for a long time. It was cathartic."

"I can imagine." Nic drew closer and put his hands on her shoulders. "You've removed a huge weight from him, but now you're the one I'm worried about."

She managed to put space between them, denying him that moment of closeness. "You don't need to be.

I'm so thankful to know the truth. I'm now free to act. Maurice's hands were tied, but mine aren't! I have a phone call to make and I don't care if it's the middle of the night in San Francisco."

"You're sure about this?"

Her jaw hardened the way it had when he'd first met her at Holden headquarters. "I've never been more sure of anything in my life." Laura looked for her purse and pulled out her cell phone.

"Do you want me to leave?"

"No." Her blue eyes beseeched him. "I'm putting this on speakerphone and want you to stay right here. I—I need your support." Her voice faltered. "No more secrets. No more lies."

He agreed. "I'm not going anywhere."

"Thank you." She pressed the digits and soon she heard her mother's voice.

"Laura?" Her mother sounded alarmed. "What's wrong, darling?"

"I'm all right, Mom. I know it's not the best time to be calling, but this couldn't wait."

"Are you still angry with me? Is that what this is about?"

She gripped the phone tighter. "No."

"I'm sorry we quarreled."

"So am I. Please listen to me. I'm calling because you need to come to Nice on the company jet as soon as you can get here. Throw a few things in a suitcase. Your passport is still good."

"Surely you don't mean it."

"But I do, Mom. It's desperately important. I'll tell you everything when you get here. You have to come alone. No Aunt Susan. Do you understand? I need my mother and no one else! Are you at her house?"

"No. I came home earlier this evening. Laura—"

"That's good," she cut her off. "On the way to the airport you can text her that you had to go out of town unexpectedly. No plans you have could be as important as this. I'm begging you to come, Mom. When I meet the plane, I'll answer all your questions."

Laura clicked off so her mother wouldn't keep talking, then she raised her eyes to Nic. "I'm going to force her to face Maurice so she hears the whole truth from him. We'll do it here. He has the letter Susan wrote Auguste and can show it to her. When she knows everything, *you* are going to call the entire Valfort family together and we'll all meet here. Maurice and Irene have been vilified long enough. It's time everyone knew the truth."

"What about your aunt Susan?"

"I'll worry about her later." She smoothed the hair off her forehead. "Do you mind if we go home now and take the box of letters with us? I plan to read all of the ones Irene wrote to Mom and Susan before Mother arrives. I want everything out in the open."

"We'll read them together even if it takes us all night."

Laura lifted moist eyes to him. "I don't know what I'd do without you."

Nic had been thinking the same thing about her as they loaded up his car and drove back to the villa. Arlette served them a meal in his den while they got comfortable on the couch and started in.

But at two in the morning, he could see and hear

her fatigue. "Laura, you need to go to bed. We'll finish these tomorrow after breakfast."

She flashed him a tired smile. "So far there's nothing in these letters but Irene's love. My grandmother
truly had no idea about Susan. If she were still alive and
could be told the truth, she would probably remember
troubling things about her firstborn daughter. But it's
clear Irene wasn't a suspicious person."

He got up from the couch. "She was wholesome and
wonderful. That's why your grandfather and Maurice
couldn't help but be in love with her. You've heard of
people everyone loves. Irene was one of them. You may
not have been allowed to enjoy her all these years, but I
daresay you know her better through these letters and
videos than you might have otherwise."

She wiped her eyes. "I think you're right. I just wish
I'd seen her at the end and had been able to wrap my
arms around her."

Nic's heart ached for her, but he didn't dare comfort
her the way he wanted to. He'd come close to kissing the
daylights out of her at the summerhouse. That couldn't
happen again. Instead he extended his hand and pulled
her to her feet. "Come on. It's time for sleep."

Her eyes had gone a smoky blue. "You're one of the
wonderful ones, too. I'm convinced Maurice couldn't
have made it all these years without you. You've been
his rock even though your world has been torn apart. I
admire you immensely, Nic. Thank you for being here
for me." She kissed his cheek before leaving the den
ahead of him.

When they reached the living room, she turned to
him. "Your wife couldn't possibly have gone off with
another man, not when she had you for her husband.

No matter the truth about her disappearance, be comforted by that thought at least."

Those words gave Nic comfort, but the touch of her lips sent a tremor through him that kept him awake for most of the night. He eventually did sleep, haunted by dreams of her. Dorine wasn't in them. This woman had come out of nowhere to change his world. It would never be the same again.

Nic rose early the next day despite his lack of sleep. Grabbing a cup of coffee from the kitchen, he learned from Arlette that Laura was already up. He walked through the house and discovered she'd gone outside to the garden. This morning she'd dressed in a dusky-blue top and beige pants. He called to her from the terrace. When she turned around, her long blond hair swung onto one shoulder. "Hi!"

He smiled. "How long have you been out here?"

"Just a few minutes."

"Have you heard from your mother yet?"

She sheltered her eyes from a strong sun. "Yes. She'll be in at five this evening."

Pleased with that news for his grandfather's sake, he said, "That means we have plenty of time to do whatever we want. Would you like to go out in the cabin cruiser? It'll be somewhat cool, but it will give you a chance to see Nice from the water. If you get uncomfortable, there's always the afghan."

Her soft laughter warmed him. "I live in San Francisco, remember? I'm used to cooler temperatures than you."

"Then come on up and grab a bite of breakfast with me before we leave."

She left the garden and walked up the stairs toward him. With every step she took, his heart pounded harder.

"Have you had a chance to get in touch with Adam?"

"I let him know I won't be home for a while, but I don't want to talk about him."

Nic had no right to feel the relief that swept through him.

"What about your grandfather?"

"I've told him we plan to meet him at the summerhouse this evening and will be bringing Jessica with us, so he's prepared. Now that you've given me a time, I'll let him know so he can tell the château staff to have dinner ready for us at six."

"That's perfect. Once we've eaten, I'll ask Maurice to tell Mother everything he told me and we'll go from there. I'm going to take the last video she made back to the house so Mom can watch it."

"It might be too much for her," Nic mused aloud. Irene's final words to her family were gut-wrenching.

"Maybe, but she needs to hear and see how much Irene loved her."

"Laura, plan for her to stay in the other bedroom next to yours while she's here." It was the room he'd hoped that one day would be turned into a nursery. Having her mother there would be the buffer he needed to stay away from Laura.

"Thank you. It seems that's all I ever say to you. The debt just keeps growing."

"You're the instrument to bring your mother to France. Maurice owes his future happiness to you. Needless to say, I couldn't be more relieved that this chapter in our lives is going to put an end to the pain for all of us."

"It *has* to." Her voice throbbed. "I'll give her the letters when she goes to bed so she can start reading them. By the time she and I are back home, we'll decide on the best way to handle Susan."

Home to her meant San Francisco. He couldn't think about that right now.

Before long they'd eaten and driven down to the port where he kept his cruiser. He pulled into the private parking area. In a minute he helped her step in the boat and handed her a life jacket. He would have liked to help her on with it, but she thanked him and did it herself, denying him the pleasure of touching her. His desire for her was growing. It terrified him.

"Do you come out in this often?" The breeze blew her hair into enticing disarray.

"When I have the time I bring Maurice fishing with me, or my friends Yves or Luc." He started the motor and headed out at a wakeless speed.

Laura looked all around. "It's the perfect size. What do you catch?"

"Bass and swordfish. Even an occasional tuna."

"I've sailed quite a bit, but I've never been deep-sea fishing."

"You'd love it, unless you have a problem with the *mal de mer.*"

"Knowing me, I probably would get seasick in rough seas, but I'd love to try it one day. Did Dorine go out fishing with you?"

"No. Her pursuits were more academic."

"To each his or her own poison, right?"

He grinned. She had a great attitude about life. "All you have to do is ask if you want to go fishing while you're here, but since we can't be out all day, let's forgo that pleasure today and I'll give you a tour of the sights closer to shore."

"Perfect!"

They took off and cruised for a time without saying anything.

Those heavenly blue eyes scanned the coastline. "It may be winter, but Nice has a subtropical appearance, with all the palm and citrus fruit trees."

"That's why people from around the world come here to vacation in winter. For your information, we're in one of the large bays, called Villefrance-sur-mer, which is enclosed. In a minute we'll pass the main expanse of Nice, between the old port city and the airport, by crossing another bay."

She studied the terrain. "What mountains are those?"

"The western edge of the Ligurian Alps."

"Irene and Maurice must have explored a lot of this." Her gaze suddenly swung to his. "They *were* happy, weren't they? Despite their pain?"

Her anguished cry had surfaced. All the time they'd been making small talk, he'd been waiting for it to emerge. She was seated across from him. He cut the motor. "Come here, Laura."

She almost stumbled into his arms getting there. Nic pulled her onto his lap. Despite her life jacket, he crushed her against him. For a little while he held her tight while the breeze rocked the cruiser.

When she finally raised her head, her cheeks were wet. "I'm sorry to break down like this."

"Hush," he whispered, kissing each feature the way he'd done in his dreams. Once he found her lips, his mouth closed over hers, needing her the way he needed air to breathe. Her mouth trembled, driving him to seek deeper until she opened up to him. He heard her small groan of pleasure as fire leaped between them.

Nic couldn't fight his desire for her another second. He would never stop loving Dorine, but Laura was right here with him, giving him one kiss, then another. The giving and taking went on and on. Each one grew longer and more passionate. He felt himself drowning in ecstasy. To be loving again like this after so long—he couldn't believe it.

She filled his arms, his heart. Who would have thought Irene's death would have resulted in this wonderful woman coming into his life? If she could respond to him like this, then whatever she felt for Adam was too pale in comparison to matter.

"Do you have any idea how much I want you?" he whispered against her throat. "I've never felt like this in my life. I feel so guilty. Believe me when I tell you I've been trying to honor Dorine's memory."

"So have I," she murmured in an aching voice. "You must think me so terrible. I need to go home."

"Laura, there's no way I'm going to let you leave me. I need you, and I *know* you need me."

He embraced her with refined savagery. Besides her beauty he loved her sweetness, her strength and intelligence. Her fun-loving ways. She was so natural and real. "Talk to me, *mon amour.* Tell me what I want to hear," he cried. But when he started to devour her again, she wrenched her lips from his.

"I—I can't say the words you want to hear, Nic. We can't do this!"

"We already have" came the fierce response before he sought her mouth again with a consuming hunger neither of them could deny or satisfy. Once he'd met and married Dorine, he'd never wanted another woman. After she'd gone missing, he hadn't been able to imagine wanting any woman, not ever again. But he hadn't met Irene's granddaughter...

"This isn't right." She half moaned the words when he let her up for air.

He closed his eyes tightly. "Because you're committed to Adam?" Nic didn't want to think about her return to the States. "You couldn't be madly in love with him or you could never kiss me like this." His eyes blazed into hers. "Have you ever kissed him with the kind of urgency and passion you've just shown me?"

She buried her face in his shoulder.

That had to be his answer, but he needed to hear the words. "Answer me, Laura." Was her bond with Adam stronger than Nic wanted to believe?

"Adam's not the reason this has to end. You're a married man, Nic. While there's still a wedding ring on your finger, no matter how much I might desire you, this is wrong—"

"Laura—"

"Don't say any more." She sounded frantic. "You're still looking for your wife." She grabbed the lapels of his Windbreaker. "I want you to find her. Even after three years, she could still be alive somewhere, waiting for help, waiting to get back to the man she loves."

He caressed the side of her neck with his hand, kissing her with growing hunger. "For the first year I believed she was alive. But two years have passed since then." His voice grated. "I sense she's gone."

"Even so, there has to be a part of your heart that hasn't given up yet. I know it hasn't and I won't give up on her either."

Laura moved off his lap and returned to the seat opposite him. "You and I have been caught up in two family tragedies we're still sorting out. My emotions are ragged and so are yours. Naturally I'm not going to forget what happened between us just now. We're both human and turned to each other for comfort. But let's put it behind us, where it has to stay."

He raked a hand through his hair. Though he felt Dorine was dead, he didn't have absolute proof. In that sense Laura was right—this was still a betrayal of his wife if there was the slightest chance she was alive. Nic had never been so conflicted in his life. Because of the precariousness of their situation right now, he was willing to go along with Laura, but only to a point.

"Let's get back to the car." Once he'd started kissing her, he'd lost track of time. He started the motor and they once again shot through the water toward the port. "With all the traffic, we'll be lucky to pick up your mother on time."

Even though they weren't touching, he could feel how shaken she was. After they reached the car, she opened her purse and started to brush her hair. Then came the lipstick. By the time they reached the airport a half hour later, she'd restored herself. But Nic still discerned the heightened color that revealed what they'd been doing out on the water.

A few minutes later Jessica Tate emerged from the Holden corporate jet. The moment Nic saw her, he understood Laura's earlier comment about no one thinking she and her mother looked alike. She had brown hair and was shorter, yet attractive in her own way, especially for a woman in her mid-fifties.

She wore a good-looking two-piece suit in a melon

color and a single strand of pearls. All three Holden women had exceptional dress sense. Though he picked out certain similar familial characteristics, it was a different experience than his first glimpse of Laura, whose resemblance to Irene had left him staggered.

Laura hugged her mother and spoke privately with her for a few minutes. Then she put an arm around her waist and walked her over to Nic.

"Mom? This is Nicholas Valfort, Maurice's grandson. Nic, please meet my mother, Jessica Tate, Irene and Richard's second daughter."

CHAPTER SIX

"JESSICA. I'VE BEEN anxious to meet you."

The blue eyes were like Laura's in color, but they stared at him without warmth. "How do you do, Mr. Valfort." She turned to her daughter. "Will you please tell me what's going on? I'm very uncomfortable. You made it sound like this was a life-and-death situation."

"It is, Mom. My life and Maurice's."

Nic eyed Laura. A nerve was hammering at the base of her throat, revealing her tension. "Excuse me while I put her suitcase in the car."

"Where are we going?" Jessica demanded after Laura climbed in the backseat with her. Nic was already at the wheel and watched them in the rearview mirror. Only a little while ago she'd been in his arms and they'd kissed each other with an abandon he hadn't thought possible. He'd never be able to put it from his mind.

"If you recall, Irene left me something in her will. It's a house on the Valfort estate, the one Maurice lived in with her. We're going there now to have dinner."

Her mother's face filled with alarm. "I can't."

"Yes, you can. You *have* to!"

As he drove them to the château, Nic marveled at Laura's courage to deal with this tragedy head-on.

"Did you receive the money Nana left you and Susan? Maurice had the attorney send it to Holden headquarters."

Jessica looked at a complete loss. "I haven't seen any money."

"Then check with Aunt Susan," said Laura. "I'm sure she has taken charge of it."

"Why do you say that?"

Her bewilderment convinced Nic that Laura's mother wasn't the architect of the horror story that had torn families apart.

"Because she has run your life ever since I can remember. In the process, she ruined all our lives. Your sister is a sick, manipulative woman. Because of her lies, she not only deprived us of your mother and my grandmother, she poisoned Maurice's family against him and Irene."

"How can you say that?" her mother cried.

"Because it's true. In a few minutes we're meeting with Maurice."

Jessica shook her head. "No. Don't try to force me."

"Mom, you owe this to him and to us. Our three lives are on the line. Susan ruined the Valforts' happiness and ours. I need you here so together we can make amends to Maurice and his loved ones before we fly back to San Francisco. He'll tell you just how disturbed Susan was and still is. You're not going to like it, but when you've heard everything, you'll understand that she needs psychiatric help. However, we'll talk about that later. Right now it's not too late to rectify the situation with his family."

Nic grimaced. Touched as he was by Laura's desire to make certain the Valfort family knew the whole

truth, the thought of her leaving Nice was unaccept-
able to him.

When he drove up in front of the summerhouse,
Maurice opened the doors and walked out to greet Jessica. "It's been a long time since I last saw you. Your
mother and I waited many years to see you cross over
this threshold. Thank you for coming."

Laura turned to her mother, who looked frightened,
before she said something that surprised Nic. "Mom?
You and Maurice need to spend this evening alone.
Here's a DVD Nana made for you and me. At the right
time, Maurice will show it to you." Laura's eyes darted
to Nic, imploring him to go along with this, before she
eyed her mother again. "When you're ready, we'll come
back for you. Tonight you'll be staying with me at Nic's
villa."

Maurice gave Laura a kiss on the cheek.

"I hope I did the right thing." Laura's voice shook
after Nic helped her back in the car. The other two had
gone inside the house.

"Was there any doubt? I know my grandfather inside
and out. That kiss was his way of letting you know he
was grateful for the time alone with your mother." He
started the engine and drove away.

"This has to work, Nic."

He reached out to squeeze her arm before releasing
it. "It will, but it'll be a long night for them. I suggest
we drive into Nice and have our own dinner at a café
bar I think you'll enjoy. The seafood menu is traditional
Nicoise—snails, clams, blue oysters, shrimp. Take your
pick. But if you're a pasta lover, we can—"

"I prefer fish whenever possible. You've sold me.
Can we do takeout?"

"Bien sûr."

"Then why don't we get some and drive to the technology park? I'd like to see where you work."

Laura didn't dare to go a place to eat where there might be dancing. She couldn't handle being in his arms one more time. They'd crossed a line. He'd loved Dorine enough to marry her and was still a married man.

She was tortured by it and vowed never to get that close to him again. But she could satisfy her longing to get to know him better by learning more about where he worked, what made him tick.

He drove to the Place Garibaldi, where she waited for him to get their food. Once back in the car with a bag, he headed for the main route leading away from the city center. "My work is about ten minutes from here."

"How nice for you."

"It's definitely convenient."

Pretty soon they came to a turnoff. "What does that sign say?"

"We're entering Sophia Antipolis. It's regarded as one of the world's most prestigiouscenters for voluntary integrated economic development."

"There you go again, speaking over my head."

He chuckled. "It's called a technopole. There are twelve hundred companies with seventy countries represented here."

"How incredible!" They drove deeper into the park with its heavy foliage. "Oh look, Rue Albert Einstein. When you think of the French Riviera, somehow you don't associate a humongous brain trust with brilliant minds like yours all working together here."

"Some more brilliant than others," he quipped. "It has pine-covered hills, hiking trails, jogging paths, a riding stable, golf courses and reflecting pools." They wound around until he pulled in a parking space near one of the buildings: Valfort Technologies.

"You don't need to take me inside, Nic. I just wanted to see it. You work in a world all its own."

"That was the original idea." He turned off the engine and handed her a carton with a fork. They began eating.

"Um." She tested the clams first. "This seafood is excellent."

"I'm glad you like it."

"Did your wife work close by?" Where Nic was concerned, her curiosity was insatiable.

"About five minutes from here by car."

"Did you meet jogging or horseback riding?"

"Neither. She wasn't that great a driver and failed to stop at one of the intersections. She hit the rear end of my car."

"Uh-oh. But when you got out to inspect the damage, you immediately forgave her when you saw how adorable she was."

One side of his mouth lifted in a smile. "You're right."

"Was she your first love?"

"No. I had several relationships over the years before our accident."

"What happened that you didn't end up with one of them?"

"Though my parents are happy enough, I wanted a marriage like Maurice and Irene's. Somehow the reality never lived up to the spiritual essence I was hoping for."

"Until you met Dorine."

"Ours was more a meeting of the minds."

This trip to Nice had taught Laura one invaluable truth. She knew that when she went back to San Francisco, she was going to end it with Adam. Theirs was not that one heart, one soul mating, the kind Nic had just referred to when he'd talked about their grandparents.

"I'm surprised you aren't married yet," Nic murmured. "That means you've turned down a lot of men already."

Her brows lifted. "You think?"

"I know." His husky tone sent shivers down her spine.

"By high school I had my sights set on the corporate office. Mother told me that if I wanted to make it in business, I shouldn't let romance distract me. She told me I had years before I needed to worry about marriage. When I started working there and saw the number of fouled-up office relationships, I made up my mind to put business first."

His eyes gleamed in the semidarkness. "How long have you known Adam?"

She sighed. "He was moved into the accounting office from San Jose about a year ago. We were introduced and—"

"That was it for him," Nic broke in. "Is that when you amended your decision not to get involved?"

"No. I didn't start dating him until October. On Thanksgiving he took me to meet his parents. Adam comes from a fine family. His parents are so stable."

"But what about your feelings for him?"

She averted her eyes.

"I shouldn't have asked that question, but you remind me of myself when I was trying to decide whether to marry Dorine or not. I enjoyed her family very much.

And family—or the lack of it—is of vital importance, as we both know."

"You're right."

"So tell me, what are the qualities that attract you to Adam?"

The questions were painful because Nic was getting closer and closer to the truth about her feelings for Adam. "He's attractive and clever. I can tell he's ambitious, but that isn't necessarily a bad thing for business."

"Maurice would agree with you. To make a company succeed, you have to have fire in the belly, but sometimes that quality is hard on personal relationships."

Laura nodded. "My mother feels he's a little too eager beaver."

"You're a Holden," he blurted. "She's entitled to want to protect her only chick from the fortune hunters out there."

She stopped eating. "You saw right through that, didn't you."

"Don't forget I'm a Valfort. Fortune hunters come male and female."

"Yet you knew that wasn't the case with Dorine."

"My wife was raised with the good things in life and had more than money on her mind."

Laura smiled at him. "You're talking about her brain, the kind that understands what *you're* talking about. You two had your own private club. How wonderful." She closed the carton she'd emptied, envious for that kind of loving relationship. "I'm so sorry for what happened to you I can hardly fathom it."

"Though I didn't think it possible at the beginning, I'm doing better these days. Your coming to Nice has helped in remarkable ways. No one in my family will talk about Dorine. They're afraid of hurting me, and that's understandable. But it's felt good to open up to you."

"I'm glad. One of my friends married a soldier who returned from Iraq with PTSD. They're the ones who have the little boy I spoke about. Through counseling she learned that he needed to talk about his experiences. It helped him a lot once he could share the pain with her, no matter how hideous or traumatizing. Not talking about it is the worst thing you can do.

"The counselor explained that PTSD doesn't just happen to soldiers. You've gone through a life-altering experience, Nic, and need to talk about it and your life with her. How are her parents holding up?"

"They're strong, and they have each other. It's the waiting for news of any kind that's been hard on them."

"Of course. Do you talk to them every day?"

"Not as much during this last year. Their lives are busy."

"I'm sure you're a great comfort to them. I know you have close family, but I assume you and Maurice have relied on each other the most for emotional support."

He put his empty carton back in the sack. "Always. Let's hope he and your mother are going to find relief before the night is over."

She rested her head against the window. "I wonder how it's really going with them."

"So far no phone call."

"I know. It has to be a good sign, doesn't it?"

His gaze wandered over her. When he looked at her like that, she found it hard to breathe. "You're anxious. Do you want to go back home?"

No. But much as she wished they could stay right

here and keep on talking, she knew it was for the best that they leave. What had happened on his cruiser could easily happen again if she gave in to her longing for him. "Maybe we ought to, just in case."

She had the impression he didn't want to go anywhere, either, but after hesitating he started the engine. Nic was riddled with guilt. She could feel it, and she loved him for his devotion to his wife. Their situation was impossible. "By the time we get there, your mother might call you. Fortunately the villa's not that far from the estate."

The villa was his home. *And Dorine's.* But there was a problem, because Laura had started thinking of it as home, too. When she imagined returning to her condo in San Francisco, the realization that Nic wouldn't be there filled her with an emptiness that refused to go away.

While they drove back, she couldn't help staring at his compelling profile. "I meant what I said the other day. I'm going to give the summerhouse back to Maurice. He needs his own place. I believe it will be a great comfort for him to continue living where he knew such happiness with Irene. As long as he has his health, he needs his independence. You know very well he doesn't want to live with your father and mother. Not yet, anyway."

He glanced at her. "I would ask you how you got so smart, but then I remember you're Irene's granddaughter."

"In the morning, will you go with me to get the legal work done?"

"Since I can see your mind is made up, I guess I don't have a choice."

She smiled. "Good. With that fait accompli, Maurice will be able to get on with his life. He can continue overseeing the Valfort empire from the summerhouse. Set him up with a computer that's linked to the mainframe. Depending on the longevity of the Valfort genes, he could conceivably be running the company for years yet."

"Better watch out," he murmured. "He might decide to steal you from Holden headquarters and give you a prominent position as his executive assistant."

Don't hold out that idea to me, Nic. We can't think that way. We can't have a future.

"He'd never do that to your family. It would start another war."

Lines marred his handsome features at the thought. Little did he know her body quickened at the very suggestion she work for his grandfather. To live here in Nice and be so close to him… But it was impossible.

"I'll be perfectly happy to remain his American granddaughter."

"Neither of you will feel that way if you're on the other side of the Atlantic, out of reach."

She wished he hadn't said that. Didn't he realize there was no hope?

While she was waiting for her mother's call, Nic's cell phone rang. After he answered, the conversation went on for a few minutes. She'd been nervous enough, but now she feared the meeting between her mother and Maurice hadn't gone well. Her body tensed in apprehension.

"What's wrong?" she asked the moment he hung up.

"Are you prepared to learn that a miracle has happened? Maurice showed her the DVD before they began talking. Your mother was so overcome by it, she asked him to tell her the truth of everything the moment it ended. It was quite a conversation. After he showed her the letter Susan had sent to Auguste, she broke down and begged his forgiveness. Their meeting couldn't have gone better."

"Thank heaven." It was Laura's turn to fall apart with relief.

"Your mother asked if she could talk to his family. He made a call and then drove her to the château, where she met with my parents and Auguste."

Hot tears trickled down her cheeks. "I—I can't believe it."

"They've all been talking, and now she wants us to come and get her."

She sniffed. "I'm surprised Mom can even function."

"I don't think I am," he said on a solemn note. "You have Irene's strength. It seems that having heard the truth, your mother does, too. This has made a new man of my grandfather. I could hear it in his voice."

The next hour turned out to be a revelation. After they arrived at the château, Maurice introduced Laura to the assembled group. At last she met Nic's family, who seemed genuinely sorrowful for the part they'd played in judging Irene.

His parents were very gracious to Laura. They commented on her strong likeness to Irene. Interestingly enough, Nic only faintly resembled his mother and father. He was Maurice's grandson in every way.

As the night wore on, one glance at her mother and she could tell Jessica was almost ready to faint from all the strain. Nic saw it too and suggested it was time to leave.

Maurice walked them out to the car. He gave Laura a tender hug while Nic helped her mother into the backseat. Finally Laura climbed in next to her. "Talk to you tomorrow, *Gran'père*," she called out.

All was quiet after they started down the drive, but Laura's heart thudded with anxiety.

"Mom?"

"I'm all right, darling." She grasped Laura's hand. "The question is, how do you feel, and can you ever forgive me?"

"Now that we know the truth, there's nothing to forgive. We owe Maurice everything because he never told Nana about Susan. I'm glad I didn't know about it until now, and I love him for sparing all of us that horror."

"Mother was right. He's a wonderful man. She said that when we all meet in heaven one day, we'll throw our arms around each other and all will be forgiven."

"Oh, Mom." Laura hugged her for a long time.

"I've already forgiven Susan and know you have, too. She's not in her right mind. Susan was always different, but I never suspected her problems went so deep. I don't think the videos or the letters would be helpful to her in her condition."

Laura kissed her mom's cheek. "I agree."

"Tomorrow I'm flying back to San Francisco and will talk to a psychiatrist about the best way to handle her. Are you coming with me?"

She couldn't leave Nic yet. Not yet… "I can't. Tomorrow I'm going to see an attorney and have papers drawn up to give the summerhouse back to Maurice."

Jessica didn't fight her on it. "Your nana knew what she was doing when she left it to you."

"I'm sure she hoped this would be the outcome. When I've packed the things she gave me, I'll fly home."

"How soon do you have to be back at work?"

"Not until after New Year's."

Her mother squeezed her hand harder. "Because of Susan, I judged Maurice and Mother, and will always be sorry for keeping you from her. But it's not too late for me to ask your forgiveness for judging Adam. He's in love with you. Forget what I said about him. If you love him, then so do I. That's all that matters."

On a burst of deep emotion, Laura held on to her mother until they reached the house without saying anything. It was over with Adam.

The only man she loved was Nic. She couldn't imagine a future without him, but she would have to deal with that reality, because he was still married. If by some miracle his wife were returned to him unharmed, it still wouldn't change her feelings for him. Unless another man came along who could make her forget Nic Valfort, she was doomed to go through life alone.

Jessica's sentiments to Laura drifted forward to torment Nic. The only thing that saved him was the knowledge that Laura wasn't going home tomorrow. Hopefully the legal matter would take several days to resolve, delaying her departure for as long as possible.

He drove them back to the villa. While Laura got her mother settled in the other guest bedroom, he went to the den to check his voice mail. No call from the detective yet. His assistant, Robert, had called to ask for a few more days off because extended family was still visiting. Nic phoned and told him to take all the time he wanted. Right now he intended to spend every second possible with Laura.

There was a second call from Yves, his good friend from childhood who'd gone through a nasty divorce two years ago and was still trying to recover. He suggested they get together over drinks before the holidays were over. Yves had helped in the search for Dorine. Nic owed him and still had a Christmas gift for him.

Why not set things up for tomorrow night? He'd invite Laura to go with him. It would be a legitimate way to take her out for an evening. Yves would probably bring a girlfriend. His friend wouldn't think anything about Laura being with Nic when he learned she was Irene's granddaughter. In fact he'd see the resemblance, since he'd been at the summerhouse with Nic many times over the years, before and after Nic's marriage.

Once he'd made the phone call, he walked back to the living room, where he found Laura waiting for him.

"I wanted to touch base with you before I go to bed. Mother has made arrangements with the pilot to fly out tomorrow morning at nine. She'll phone for a taxi. I just wanted you to know I'll go with her to see her off."

He frowned. "Would she rather I didn't drive her?"

Color rushed into her cheeks. "No—" She put her hands out. "It's nothing like that. She doesn't want to intrude on your hospitality any more than necessary."

"It's no intrusion. She's Irene's daughter and your mother."

"I know, but don't forget how terrible she feels deep down. She needs time."

Nic nodded. "In that case, take my car. I have another one in the garage if I need it. To make it easier,

I'll make myself scarce in the morning." He pulled out his keys and took the Mercedes key off the ring.

Her blue gaze looked darker than usual before she reached for it. Their fingers brushed. If her emotions were in as much turmoil as his, then she was barely holding on. "You belong to a family with a forgiving nature. They couldn't have been kinder to Mother or me. Now I know why you're a prince."

"Laura—" His voice came out sounding husky to his own ears.

"It's true." Her eyes clung to his. "A miracle happened to the Valfort and Holden families tonight, but I'm greedy because I'm praying for another one. The one that brings your lovely wife safely home to you. I mean that with all my heart. Good night."

He stood there long after she'd gone to bed, trying to get a grip on his feelings. Nic had no doubt she meant what she said. It might have only been a few days, but he'd learned enough about Laura's character to know she would never entertain an affair with him. Whatever physical and emotional bond they'd forged out on the boat, she wouldn't act on it, because she wasn't that kind of woman.

He wasn't that kind of man.

If Dorine were never found, it would be four more years before she would be declared legally dead. Four more years before he could even *think* about getting married again to any woman, *if* that's what he desired.

But after four years Laura wouldn't be available, let alone still wanting to be with him.

No matter how he looked at it, a relationship with her was out of the question. Deep down in his gut, he realized she'd just sent him a coded message. Without saying the exact words, she'd told him that she intended to go home soon. And whether or not she married Adam, she'd keep her distance from Nic.

He turned out the lights and headed for his bedroom, knowing sleep might not come to him tonight.

After taking her mother to the airport the next morning, Laura returned to the villa. She found Nic at his desk in the den on the phone. Realizing he was busy, she started to walk out, but he motioned for her to stay where she was. His all-encompassing glance sent her pulse off the charts.

"How was your mother this morning?" he asked after hanging up the phone.

"Anxious to get back and meet with a doctor who knows how to treat a situation like this. Mom has needed therapy for years. Now she'll get it."

"What about you? How are you holding up?"

"Now that there are no secrets, I'm doing better than I would have thought. You're the one I'm worried about."

He shook his dark head. "You don't need to be. From here on out things are going to be different in my family. Vastly improved." One black brow lifted. "That's a relief only *you* could understand."

"A weight has been taken from both our shoulders, but you sustain a pain that doesn't leave you alone."

"I've been living with it for three years. And don't forget I have my work, which is flourishing."

"I don't doubt it." She sighed. "Speaking of work, I'm facing mounds of it when I get back. I've implemented some new marketing incentives at a few hotels around the state and need to follow the results closely. It means I'll be traveling for a while."

His features sobered. "Sounds like you're anxious to get back. To expedite things, I've retained an attorney for you," he announced, "but he won't be available until tomorrow. Unless you have other plans, I've arranged for a moving company to meet us at the summerhouse at noon with some boxes. We'll get everything packed up and they'll store them. When you're ready to fly home, they'll load them on the company jet."

"A man who can move mountains. That's you."

He got to his feet and moved closer to her. A tightness around his eyes and mouth revealed his suffering. "Would that I could divine where to look for Dorine."

Laura would give anything to help him. He needed an ending. "Nic—after all this time, what do your instincts tell you?"

She waited a good minute for his answer. "Unless I was married to a woman who was unbalanced or kept secrets and was operating with an unknown agenda—destructive or otherwise—my feeling is that she was kidnapped. That's the detective's hunch, too."

"I think you're probably right."

"What happened to her after that I've tried not to think about."

Laura shuddered. "Was her purse missing?"

"Yes, along with her cell phone. It has never been used, or a credit card. No emails, no bank account accessed. Nothing. Our combined families have offered an enormous reward for her safe return, but it never happened."

"Maybe she was at the wrong place at the wrong time. If she went out during her lunch hour, maybe food wasn't on her mind and she decided to do a little shopping or run an errand."

"All the secretary said was that Dorine was leaving for her lunch break."

Laura sighed. "Yes, it's not much to go on."

"No, but I remember her saying Dorine was working on a project that needed to get finished. I assumed that meant she'd intended to hurry."

"What kind of project was it? Would she have needed to buy something in order to complete it?"

"They have technicians for that."

"Maybe she went out to get some information she needed."

He gave her a resigned smile. "Now you're playing the maybe game. In the beginning I played it until I drove myself mad."

"I can understand that." She'd been pacing the floor but came to a standstill. "The police would have combed that neighborhood where her car was found."

"Thoroughly. So did I on my own time. My hunch was that she must have gone in a store or building where she was abducted away from the street through a rear entrance. It could have been a business where she was a regular and knew them. Or they knew her and watched for her. The car showed no evidence of foul play or a struggle. No fingerprints were picked up except hers."

Laura hunched her shoulders. "Or there's the possibility she was abducted in the technology park with all that heavy foliage. Someone who knew her and her habits could have stopped her on some pretext after she left the office."

He cocked his head. "You're thinking she knew him?"

"Yes. Maybe someone from the team who had an

accomplice. While one dealt with her, the other could have driven her car into town and left it there to throw the police off the trail. Nic, did the authorities question the companies within the park?"

"Yes. Every one of them," he said in a grating tone.

"What about the woods? Did they search them?"

His black-fringed eyes darkened until she couldn't see the gray. "Only near her office building."

"Why not the whole park?"

"You're talking six thousand acres."

"I had no idea it was so huge. But if the crime happened in the park, then the whole place should be scoured. If the police used dogs, they might turn up some evidence."

He studied her for a long time. The stretch of silence told her to stop talking because she'd taken this painful inquisition too far.

"I'm sorry, Nic. Forgive me for getting into this with you when you've tried to put it behind you."

His hands reached out to grip her shoulders. He shook her gently. "There's nothing to forgive. You've only put voice to my own thoughts. The park could be hiding many secrets. I marvel that you've given it this much consideration. It means more to me than you know."

You mean more to me than you know, Nic. "I want to help you the way you've helped me."

A groan escaped his throat before he put her away from him with a reluctance she sensed. It was a good thing he let go of her when he did—another second and she wouldn't have been able to stop herself from kissing him, with or without his permission.

"I told you last night, being able to talk to you about

Dorine has been cathartic for me. I'm going to talk to the detective about doing a massive ground search of the entire park and vehicles."

Her spirits lifted. "I know it will take hundreds of men and man-hours and the cost will be prohibitive, but if they can turn up even one clue…"

"Cost be damned! I'll spend any amount to find out what happened to her," he muttered fiercely.

Yes, she mused to herself, because he was a man who loved deeply and was the most exceptional human being she'd ever known. Before she broke down and told him how she felt, she looked at her watch. "I think we'd better leave for the summerhouse or the movers will get there first."

"You're right." But he sounded far away.

They gathered their things and went out to his car. On the drive, he darted her a speculative glance. "If it sounds good to you, we're going to have dinner tonight at the Gros Marin. You can't go back to the States without eating there. Nice's finest restaurant hovers right over the sand and serves delicious Mediterranean seafood. You'll enjoy the sight of the yachts all lit up."

The thought of returning to California was killing her. "It sounds lovely."

"Yves LeVaux, my best friend from childhood, will be joining us."

Though she'd give anything to spend the evening alone with him, the addition of another person would provide the necessary buffer. "Is your friend married?"

"Divorced. He may bring someone with him. We haven't seen each other in a while. Yves helped me during the initial search for Dorine."

"What a wonderful friend," she murmured.

"The best. I'm indebted to him."

Laura's sorrow dragged her down. If Nic's wife were never found, he'd suffer from this tragedy his whole life.

Soon after they reached the summerhouse, the movers arrived and they spent the rest of the day packing. Once the cartons were put on the truck and the men left, Laura helped Nic take down the Christmas tree and decorations and put everything away. He carried the tree outside seemingly effortlessly while she cleaned and vacuumed.

"Now Maurice can move back in," she said when he walked into the room. "After I've been to see the attorney tomorrow, let's bring your grandfather here and tell him what I've done. If he doesn't want to live here again, maybe someone else in the Valfort family will want to take up residence. Possibly one of your cousins? Is anyone in the family planning to get married?"

"Not yet, but it could happen before long. Since our work here is finished, I'll drive us back to the villa to get changed for dinner."

On the way home Laura thought about what to wear. She hadn't planned to be here long and had only brought one dress for evening. It was a black crepe kimono-sleeve wrap dress with a high neck. The hem fell to the knee. She'd been to several marketing dinners in it.

When they reached the house, she disappeared into the bathroom to wash her hair and blow-dry it. Deciding to leave it long, she brushed it before applying lipstick and some blusher. Once she'd put on her dress and had slipped into her sling-back black heels, she walked into the living room and discovered Nic had a guest. He stood by the French doors facing the garden below. It drew everyone's attention.

The good-looking dark blond man in the tan suit was probably six feet. When he heard her come in, he wheeled around and fastened warm hazel eyes on her. "So you're the missing granddaughter, Laura Tate," he said with a strong French accent, and walked over to her.

"Guilty as charged." *And filled with guilt.*

His eyes filled with male appreciation. "Your resemblance to Irene is amazing. I'm Yves LeVaux." They shook hands.

"Nic told me what a great friend you are to him. It's a pleasure to meet you."

"I'll return the compliment. He said to come in and make myself at home while he got ready. I'm glad I did. Since his wife disappeared, you have the distinction of being the only woman to capture his attention, let alone step inside this house. I for one am delighted to see it happen."

She'd known Nic was an honorable man. He couldn't be anything else. Now his friend had just confirmed it. Unfortunately Yves had the wrong idea about them. "As I told his housekeeper, Nic and I are almost family."

He flashed her a curious smile. "But the point is, you're not."

Laura took a quick breath. "The more important point is, he's married."

Yves's smile faded. "So was the man my wife had an affair with. No doubt Nic told you I'm divorced."

She felt his pain. "I'm so sorry, Yves. They were both fools."

His brows lifted. "I think so, too. Anyway, where have you been all day, let alone my life?"

Despite his grief, he could still be charming. It was a trait shared by the three Frenchmen she knew. "We just came back from the summerhouse. My grandmother left me a lot of gifts. I was getting them packed to take home."

"But let's hope that won't be for a while. I'd like to get to know you better. How soon do you plan to leave?"

"That's a good question," Nic answered in his deep voice before she could say anything.

With thudding heart, she turned in time to see him approach with a small Christmas present in his hand. The light gray suit with the charcoal shirt fit Nic's well-honed body to perfection. Laura's mouth went dry just looking at him.

After his slow appraisal that brought heat to her face, his gaze slid from her to his friend. "I see you two have already met." Nic handed Yves the present. "No date tonight?"

Yves shook his head. With a half smile he said, "I decided I wanted to have a good time for a change."

Laura couldn't help but chuckle. "That was honest."

He trained his eyes on her again. "I see honesty is something we have in common. Did Nic tell you I haven't had much luck meeting the right woman?"

She decided she liked him very much. "Finding the right man is a tall order for a woman, too. You're still young and there's plenty of time."

"Your grandmother told me the same thing the last time I saw her."

A lump lodged in her throat. "I'm jealous of you and Nic. Both of you spent time with her. It's my fault I didn't get to know her, so anything you can tell me about her, I'll relish."

"Have you got a month or two?" Yves teased with a twinkle in his eyes.

"I wish." *If I could have a lifetime here*... "But I have to get back to my job." She needed to get away from Nic before she changed her mind and took up residence in the summerhouse.

"Nic tells me you're the marketing manager for Holden Hotels. That speaks highly of your business acumen. Your grandfather was never one for nepotism." Before she could say anything, he exchanged glances with Nic. "Mind if I open my present before we go?"

"Be my guest, *mon ami.*"

Yves undid the wrapping and opened the box. *"épatant!"* He held up a three-inch gold lure.

"It's the latest Shimano waxwing," Nic explained. "In the fall I caught some amazing fish with one just like it. Next time we go out together, you should try it."

"I plan to. *Merci, mon vieux.*"

"De rien. Do you want to drive with us to the Gros Marin?"

"No. I'll follow you in my car. My folks are expecting me to drop by their house later."

"Then let's go."

CHAPTER SEVEN

TWO HOURS LATER the three of them left the restaurant and walked over to Yves's car. He hadn't taken his eyes off Laura throughout their dinner. "This was the best time I've had in ages," he said, smiling at Nic.

"My sentiments exactly. We'll get together soon and do some fishing."

Yves nodded before his hazel gaze swerved to Nic's houseguest once more. "You'll really be gone after New Year's?"

"Afraid so. Business calls. Until then I hope to spend as much time as possible with Maurice."

"Lucky man." He winked at her before getting in his car. "*À bientôt*, Nic." His parting comment was an afterthought. Nic could tell Yves had been blown away by Laura.

After his friend drove off, Nic escorted her to his car. "If you stayed in Nice any longer, Adam would be in for serious competition."

She smoothed some hair behind her ear. "Yves is hurting. I hope he can find someone who appreciates what a terrific man he really is."

He helped her in the car, then went around to get

behind the wheel. "That's been my hope for quite some time."

"I'm sure it will happen. When it does, *she'll* be the lucky one."

Nic put his key in the ignition, but he didn't turn the car on. He flashed her a glance, eager to spend the rest of the evening with her doing something that had nothing to do with other people. It was impossible not to feel possessive of her tonight. "The evening's still young. How would you like to see a sight you'll never forget?"

Her smile captivated him. "That's a trick question. After arousing my curiosity, even if I told you I'm too tired, I couldn't possibly say no."

Laura...

"I promise you won't be sorry. It's only twelve kilometers away." He joined one of the arterials headed east. "It's been my experience that America has some of the great road movies, but it's my country that has the great roads. Do you remember that scene in *To Catch a Thief* with Cary Grant and Grace Kelly, when she was driving the sports car?"

"I must have watched that cliff-hanger scene half a dozen times."

"It was filmed on the Grande Corniche, the stunning coastal highway we're traveling on right now. The engineering feat was built to facilitate Napoleon's Italian campaign. We'll drive to the little medieval village at the top called Eze. At fourteen hundred feet above sea level, it perches like an eagle's nest. You can see everything from that vantage point."

They rode in silence, but the tension between them was building by degrees. Once they reached the summit, Laura let out an exclamation. The ancient little town set on a narrow rocky peak overlooked the Mediterranean.

He pointed to a ruin in the distance. "Those are the remains of a twelfth-century castle. Inside the grounds is the well-known Jardin Exotique. In my opinion this is the best view of the coast on the Côte d'Azur." Nic parked the car. "We walk from here."

She climbed out of the car and they started making their way around the stone village in the night air. It formed a circular pattern at the base of the castle. The old buildings had high stone walls while the narrow roadways were made of redbrick-centered stone. "Everything is so well restored, Nic!"

"It keeps the tourists coming."

"Well, this tourist is grateful."

"I love it here," he murmured. "No cars here. Only donkeys have the right of passage. This is the best time to be here, when there aren't so many tourists."

"I'm crazy about it, Nic. All of it!" She peeked in every nook and cranny, where small art galleries and tiny gift shops were hidden, infecting him with her unique brand of enthusiasm for everything. Climbing a set of steps, they came upon a shop displaying jewelry and women's scarves. The soft gray chiffon with circles of white caught his eye. He could see it on Laura and bought it.

"Here." He looped it around her neck. "This looks like you."

She felt the material with her hands before lifting her eyes to him. The urge to kiss her was killing him.

"You shouldn't have done this."

He shrugged his shoulders. "Why not? You bought

me a bottle of wine. This is my Christmas gift to you, a small thing I hoped would bring you pleasure."

Her features looked pained before she averted her eyes. "You've given me more pleasure than you can imagine, Nic. Thank you," she whispered before moving ahead of him.

Laura was wrong about that. He could imagine pleasure with her beyond belief, but he had to tamp down his desire for her. The wife he'd loved could still be alive. Even if she wasn't, she needed to be found and laid to rest before he could think about anything else.

They followed the village trail that eventually led to a vista point with the whole Mediterranean coast sprawled at their feet. He waited to hear what she'd say.

Laura was quiet for a long while. Finally she spoke. "You were right. It's a sight I'll never forget. I can't think of another spot on earth more beautiful than this."

Nic could not think of a woman more breathtaking than the one standing in front of him.

"Nana would have come here with Maurice. Maybe their trip is on one of the DVDs I haven't looked at yet."

"It's possible." But he didn't want to talk about their grandparents. This night was for him and Laura, no one else.

"If you want to know the truth," she said in a tremulous voice, "this whole trip has changed my life. When I go home, I'll be leaving a part of my heart here."

The ache in her voice matched his longing for her. "Let's not talk about your going back to the States yet. I have an idea. Tonight why don't we stay in the little hotel we passed a minute ago?"

She spun around, visibly shocked.

"We'll each get a room with a seafront view. You have to be here when the sun starts to come up in the morning. I'll set my watch alarm and we'll enjoy it together from one of our terraces. There's a faint lavender that emerges from the darkness and starts to turn to pink, bathing the coast in fantastic colors every great artist has tried to capture on canvas."

Laura stared at him. He could hear her mind turning it over. "We didn't bring anything with us."

"Besides ourselves?" His heart thumped in his chest. She hadn't said no. He held his breath. "No, we didn't, but does it matter? One night out of our lives?" Laura had to know what he was asking. They were running out of time. Meanwhile, Nic's' sorrow over her imminent departure was killing him. If they had to say goodbye, he wanted to do it here.

"No," she answered softly. "I'd love to stay here."

Adrenaline surged through his veins. "After we eat breakfast on the terrace, we'll go back to the villa. There'll be plenty of time to get ready and be at the attorney's office by ten."

She nodded.

Together they retraced their steps to the charming little hotel carved out of the rock. He arranged for two rooms side by side on the second floor, overlooking the water. He flicked her a glance. "There's coffee or tea in the rooms. Would you rather have something in addition sent up?"

"After that marvelous dinner I couldn't manage anything else, but thank you."

He took the keys and handed one to her before they ascended the circular staircase. "I'll come by in five minutes to say good-night."

* * *

Laura let herself inside and locked the door. She should have told Nic she wanted to go back to the villa, but when she thought of never seeing him again, she couldn't stand it. A sadness washed over her, so intense she felt sick.

At first her mind waged the inner argument that staying here in separate rooms wasn't any different than staying in the guest bedroom at his villa. Except that it *was* different.

Though the whole world might not know what was going on, *she* knew. She'd fallen desperately in love with Nic. She wanted to be with him all the time, in every way. But he was Dorine's husband. Being here with him under these circumstances was wrong.

She couldn't do this!

In the next breath she bolted out the door and ran straight into his tall, hard body.

"Nic—" She recoiled from the contact.

His features looked drawn. "Let's go home. I saw guilt written in your eyes before you shut the door."

He knew her too well. "I—I'm sorry."

"No. I'm the one who's sorry for putting you in a compromising position."

"Don't forget I came with you."

"Nevertheless it won't happen again." She heard it in his voice. He meant it. "Do you need anything from the room?"

"Just my purse."

"Then get it and I'll meet you downstairs in the lobby."

Though she was relieved that they were leaving, another part of her cried out that she'd just ruined the night they could have had together away from everyone else. Before she changed her mind again, she grabbed her purse and hurried below to join him. Neither of them spoke as they walked along the trail to the car.

"Nic," she began once they were headed back to Nice, "I—"

"Don't say anything."

"I have to! We talked about this on the cruiser. I should have had the strength to tell you I wanted to go home after we said good-night to Yves." She lowered her head. "I won't deny I find you very attractive. I wanted tonight to go on and on. This has taken me by complete surprise. I thought Adam meant more to me than he does."

"Laura—" His voice rasped.

"No. Let me finish while I can. You're a red-blooded man. After three years without any news of your wife, you have every reason to want to be with another woman. But Yves confided in me that in all that time, you haven't been disloyal to Dorine's memory. That says more about the kind of honorable man you are than anything else I can think of. So I've made a decision.

"After we visit the attorney in the morning, I'm going to tell Maurice I need to get back to San Francisco. I know he wants to send me on the Valfort jet, so let's arrange for the boxes to be put on board and I'll fly out later tomorrow. He'll understand when I tell him that I need to get back to Mom, who needs my support. I must get home and deal with that situation before any more time passes."

She saw his hands tighten on the steering wheel. "Maurice will have a hard time letting you go."

"I'll stay in close touch with him. We'll video chat

and talk on the phone. I love him and want him in my life. If he's up to it in a few months, I'll invite him to come and stay with me for a week at my condo."

A grimace marred Nic's features. He didn't comment. They rode the rest of the way in silence.

When they reached the villa, she turned to him. "I'll get my bag packed tonight so I'll be ready to go to the airport after we go to the attorney's office tomorrow."

He didn't say anything, but she was relieved they were home. She hurried inside and ran straight to her room. After undressing, she took a shower, then packed everything except what she'd wear for the flight home.

Before she climbed under the covers, she picked up the scarf. This was all she would have of Nic to take home with her. Once the lights were out, she clutched it to her, remembering how it had felt when he'd put it around her neck. Their lips had only been a centimeter apart.

The memory was too much for her. Her need for him was too great. She turned over and buried her face in the pillow until it was sopping wet.

When morning came, she saw herself in the bathroom mirror and moaned at her blotchy face. Her eyes were actually red from crying. It took a good hour to restore herself to some semblance of order.

After arranging her hair in a twist with one of her clips, she dressed in the tweed suit she'd worn when she'd first arrived in Nice. Somehow she managed to pull herself together. From a distance, the person standing in front of the mirror looked like the professional businesswoman. But she'd never fool Nic.

As Laura walked through the house with her suitcase, she found him by the French doors talking on the phone. Their eyes met for a heart-pounding moment before she searched out Arlette to thank her for everything. Then she returned to the dining room and sat down to help herself to breakfast.

This would be her last meal with Nic. Everything she did with him today would be for the final time. She couldn't bear it, but somehow she had to find the strength.

This morning he'd put on a claret-red turtleneck sweater and dark trousers. Combined with his black hair and hard-muscled physique, he couldn't have looked more dashing. To never see him again was something she couldn't comprehend.

He clicked off and joined her. His features had taken on a chiseled cast. "That was the detective. He's learned nothing from Interpol and doesn't feel the answer lies with overseas team members. I told him about the conversation you and I had about the park. I've convinced him a search is worth doing—I told him money is no object. He has agreed to arrange for a massive ground search of Sophia Antipolis. He's hoping to get it underway within the next seven days."

She looked down at her roll. "The expense will be enormous, Nic."

"It'll be worth it. Even if nothing turns up, I will have done everything possible to find Dorine. I have you to thank for that."

Laura couldn't swallow for a minute. "I didn't do anything."

"Oh, but you did. I'd put aside the idea of searching the whole area a long time ago, feeling it would be futile. Then you talked to me about it. Even if it's been three years, you convinced me some kind of a clue could turn up. It's worth any amount of money and man-hours to find out."

Her eyes smarted with tears. "I'm going to pray they find something, Nic."

"Me, too," he whispered. "I plan to join them. Yves will help. So will my cousins."

For a number of reasons Laura couldn't stay to help in the search, but it didn't mean she didn't want to. For him to find closure would help him to really live again. "I'm so glad the detective is planning to organize it soon."

Nic glanced at his watch. "It's time we headed for the attorney's office in Nice."

She nodded. "I'll just get my purse."

Laura had put it on the dresser. As she reached for it, she noticed the scarf lying on the floor at the side of the bed. After a slight hesitation, she picked it up and draped it around her neck. She wanted him to know she loved it.

With the sun shining, she needed to put on her sunglasses to shield her red-rimmed eyes. Nic sent her a piercing glance as they drove out to the main road. It was as if he were telling her it was too late to hide anything from him. "I had that suit in mind when I saw the scarf."

"You have a discerning eye. It goes perfectly with it. I'll always treasure it." Her voice caught.

He reached out a hand to squeeze hers before releasing it. "I phoned the pilot, who will have the jet fueled and ready to go any time after two. The storage company will deliver your boxes before takeoff."

"You always take care of everything." She crossed

her legs restlessly. "Have you talked to Maurice this morning?"

"No. I thought we'd drop in on him at the château when we've finished our business with Monsieur Broussard. He's in the same firm with our family attorney and has spoken with him about your decision to will the property back to Maurice. There won't be any problem. Since you didn't take possession or sign anything yet, you won't have to pay taxes."

Laura groaned. "I forgot about those. A fine businesswoman I am."

"These were unusual circumstances."

The man seated next to her was a breed apart from other men. How was she going to get through the rest of her life without him?

"Nic—" She glanced over at him. "Do you think Maurice will be terribly hurt?"

"To be honest, I know he's so happy you came to Nice in the first place, he'll be fine with your decision. After all, it was your grandmother who willed the summerhouse to you. He was only carrying out her wishes. In exchange he got himself the granddaughter he'd always wanted to know."

She bit the underside of her lip so hard it drew blood. "What do you think he'll do with it?"

"Before he makes any decision, I'm thinking of buying it."

Laura sat straight up. *"You?"*

He eyed her curiously. "Though I loved the château, the summerhouse was my fort when I was young."

"You're kidding!" she cried softly.

"Being that it was abandoned, it provided the perfect *endroit* for playing war with no one else around.

Yves and I spent years there with our friends. It was my favorite place to be. I thought that when I grew up, I'd make enough money to buy it."

"That's so touching, Nic."

"Unfortunately because I thought of it as my own, it took me time to adjust to the idea that Maurice decided to restore it so he could live there with Irene."

At this point Laura was totally fascinated. "Did Maurice know how you felt?"

"I doubt he knew that in refurbishing it, he'd robbed me of part of my boyhood delights. But after they moved in, they welcomed me to come any time. Irene always encouraged me to stay over whenever I felt like it, so it took away the sting."

"Until you found out he'd given it to my grandmother. That would have hurt."

He shook his head. "By then I was all grown-up and liked her too much to be upset."

"Even though she willed it to the enemy?"

He flicked her a glance. "We know how that turned out, don't we," he said in a husky voice.

Her heart jumped. She'd fallen in love with the enemy.

Laura had no idea all this had been going on inside him. "If you bought it from Maurice, what would you do with it?"

"Live there."

She blinked. "But what about your villa?"

"I need to separate myself from the past. The villa was Dorine's idea from start to finish. Since her disappearance I've thought of moving, but haven't been able to settle on anything I've seen."

"Except for the summerhouse," she whispered.

"Yes."

"You don't think he'll move back in?"

"Frankly, I don't. It has too many memories for him.
But if *I* lived there, he could come and go at will. I'd be
near enough to help watch out for him. He's not getting
any younger. Neither is Auguste. My parents already
need additional help in the caretaking department."

"He loves you so much."

"It's mutual. I have a few ideas to convert the greenhouse in the back into a laboratory for my work. The
light is exceptional. Since he had it remodeled, my siblings and cousins would all love the chance to buy it.
If I tell Maurice I want it, he'll be fair and announce it
to the family. Everyone will make a bid for it. Hopefully mine will come in higher than the other offers."

During their conversation they'd driven into the heart
of Nice. Nic turned a corner and parked in front of an
office building. "Let's get this over so you can spend the
rest of the time with Grandfather before you fly away."

Fly away. That's what Laura would be doing in a
few hours. She wondered if you could die from the
pain of heartache.

Once they were inside the building, a secretary escorted them to a suite where Monsieur Broussard was
waiting. Nic made the introductions before the brown-
haired attorney asked them to be seated.

"I've been alerted to the particulars, Ms. Tate, and
have all the papers here. It's your wish to will the property willed to you by your deceased grandmother to
Maurice Valfort?"

"That's correct. I live and work in San Francisco,
California. I couldn't be here enough or maintain it in
order to warrant keeping it."

"I understand. What we'll do is issue a quitclaim deed. It will take about ten minutes. When you're ready to sign, I'll ask two of my colleagues to step inside and witness it."

"Wonderful."

"What is the full name of Maurice?"

"Maurice Sancerre Valfort," Nic supplied.

"Excellent."

Laura heard Nic's cell phone ring. He checked the caller ID before looking at her. "I need to take this call. It's Lieutenant Thibault."

She couldn't have been happier about it. "Go ahead."

"I'll be right back." He stepped out of the office.

If he hadn't gotten that call, she would have been forced to ask him to leave on some errand for her. This had worked out perfectly. The second he closed the door, she leaned forward. "Monsieur Broussard, while we're alone, I need to change something on the deed."

He lifted his head. "What do you mean?"

"I'm not willing the house to Maurice. It's going to go to someone else, but I don't want Maurice or Nic to know about it until it's signed, sealed and delivered."

His brows furrowed. "I don't understand."

"It's very simple. Since I own the house and my grandmother told me I could do whatever I wanted with it, I've decided I'm going to give it to the one person who should have it."

"Who would that be?"

"Maurice's grandson, Nicholas Valfort. Nic watched out for his grandfather and my grandmother for years. As you know, the château is close to the summerhouse. Maurice lives in the château now. With Nic living in the summerhouse, they'd both be closer so Nic can help look after him. But we need to do this quickly before he comes back inside."

The older man had to digest it for a minute. "If you're certain."

"I've never been so certain of anything in my life." He needed to live in a place he'd always loved that wouldn't have the same reminders of Dorine.

"I'd like you to send all the paperwork to Maurice. While you're finishing up, I need to write a note." She reached in her purse for small notebook and tore out a sheet. "When I've finished, will you ask your secretary to type up what I've written and put it with the documents? Maurice can be the one to let Nic know what I've done." The attorney nodded. "Do you swear you'll keep this a secret until after it's been delivered to Maurice?"

He eyed her for a long time. "I swear."

"Thank you. You have no idea what this means to me. Nic is the most wonderful man alive. This gift is going to make him so happy you can't imagine."

A faint smile broke out on Broussard's face. "Do you have any concept of the value of that property? Some would be willing to pay a king's ransom for it."

"I don't care about that."

"Then you're a very generous woman."

"A thankful woman," she corrected him. "Because of Nic, I was united with the grandfather I never knew. He, in turn, helped me to know the grandmother who'd been lost to me. I owe Nic a debt of gratitude I can never repay. He flew my grandmother's body back to California and let me know she'd left me a gift. It's beyond price."

If she wasn't mistaken, the lawyer's eyes looked suspiciously bright. "I'll just grab a new sheet and start over again."

"Thank you."

It wasn't any too soon. Suddenly Nic swept back in the room. Before long the transaction had been completed. The notaries signed the documents. Laura's signatures came last and Nic was none the wiser about the transfer or her personal note, thank heaven.

When they reached the car, Nic helped her inside and they left for the château.

"What did the detective want?"

He looked over at her. "To let me know the whole department is behind the search. He's worked tirelessly on this case and is anxious to solve it. While I was out in the hall, I heard from Maurice. He's asked us to meet at the summerhouse, where he has one more surprise waiting. It's your bon voyage gift."

"Do you know what it is?"

"No."

She laughed gently. "There's never a dull moment with him. No wonder my grandmother was so crazy about him." After that comment he drove faster than usual and whizzed through the estate to the summerhouse.

Pain of a new kind had a stranglehold on her. It wouldn't be long before she was gone. She didn't know if she could take it. There was no way they could make small talk right now. When they reached the house, she got out of the car the minute he stopped and hurried inside without waiting for him.

"Et voilà, mes enfants." Maurice hugged both of them. "I'm so glad you're here. Come and sit down. I have something to show you that I couldn't find until

the other day. I had it put on a DVD immediately. It was in my old valise, the one I was using at the time Irene and I got married."

His excitement was so contagious, they did his bidding and waited until he started the machine. "When Irene and I decided to get married, I asked the concierge at the hotel where I was staying to find someone who would film our wedding."

Laura was thunderstruck as he started the DVD and Maurice and her grandmother suddenly appeared on the screen. "You look like movie stars!" she cried.

Maurice nodded with tears in his eyes. "She was a vision in that white suit."

"You look just like her in that suit you're wearing," Nic murmured.

Nic...

Unable to sit still, she got up to move closer. "In that dark suit you're so handsome, my grandmother couldn't have helped but be in love with you, *Gran'père*. I never saw two people who looked so happy."

"For that day, we were divinely happy."

Even amid all the fighting that surrounded their union.

She had to blink away the tears.

The rest of the film showed them coming out of the building and getting in a limo. More video followed of the two of them eating at a restaurant she didn't recognize. They kissed several times for the camera. It was so sweet, so loving.

When it came to an end, Laura walked over and put her arms around him. "You've discovered a treasure."

"I want you to have it." He sounded choked up.

"No. You've given me everything else. This is for

you. Now you can watch it whenever you like and remember that joyous time. The next time I come to Nice, I'll watch it with you and then we'll take walks together."

He got to his feet. "I know you have to go, but it's hard."

"For me, too," she admitted and kissed his cheek. "Is there anything I can do for you before I leave?"

His moist brown eyes studied her. "You can decide to stay here. This is your home now."

No, it isn't, but don't tempt me.

"There's nothing I'd love more, but I can't and you know why. Remember, I'll come for visits. In the meantime, tell you what—I'll call you every day to get your advice on my marketing schemes. What better tutor than the man who put Valfort Hotels on the map!"

"You flatter me, but that was *my* grandfather."

"According to the letters Nana wrote me, you were known as the Valfort who brought the hotel business into the twenty-first century. With your help, I might make it to CEO one day."

"Is that what you want?"

She swallowed hard. "I need a goal." How else was she going to survive her life unless she had a goal that drove her day and night? "Why not rise to the top? It might be interesting to be the first woman on the board."

"If you're that ambitious, why not move to France and work for me? You're practically a Valfort, after all."

Laura cocked her head. "Is that a serious job offer?"

"What if it were?" Maurice fired back. "Would you seriously consider it? Don't answer that question yet.

See what happens after you get back to San Francisco, then call me and we'll discuss it."

The authority in his voice gave her a glimpse of the steel behind the charm. It was that same steel she'd heard in Nic's voice. She'd never forget the moment when he'd first grasped her arms and made her promise not to tell his grandfather what she'd just told him about her family's lies.

"I promise to call you." She kissed his cheek. "Now I'm afraid we have to be going."

He looked at Nic. "I'll drive to the airport with you to see you off."

Laura reached for her purse, then looped her arm through Maurice's. They walked out of the house together. Nic went ahead of them and opened the back door of his car for his grandfather. Laura took advantage of the moment to get in the front seat without his help. The less touching, the less torment.

"Nic? En route could you stop by a store that sells picture frames? I'll only be a minute."

"Bien sûr."

They drove through the estate to the main road. After Nic parked in front of a shop so Laura could run her errand, they headed for the airport. She looked around one last time. Talk about pain.

She didn't think Nic would ever get answers about Dorine, so it might be four more years before he was free again. Laura had reconciled herself to the fact that it might be that long before she could have a relationship with him, *if* he still wanted one with her. That would put her at thirty-one and him at thirty-seven. But it didn't matter, because she'd wait twenty years for him if she had to.

The truck from the storage company had already arrived on the tarmac and was loading boxes in the rear of the jet with the steward's help. Nic pulled up next to it. While he went around for her suitcase in the trunk, she got out and opened Maurice's door.

"I forgot to give this to you at the house." She pulled a small photograph of herself from her wallet and fit it into the little frame she'd purchased. "This was taken a month ago at a marketing conference."

Maurice studied it for a moment before putting it in his pocket. *"Merci, ma chère fille."*

"God bless you, *Gran'père*. Don't get on the plane with me. This is hard enough." She gave him a huge hug.

"Promise you'll phone me the second you've arrived in San Francisco. I have to know you got there safely."

"Of course I will." Tears blurred her eyes as she moved toward the jet and hurried up the stairs.

Nic followed her on board with her suitcase and put it up in the rack. He noted with satisfaction she was still wearing the scarf.

"That little photo meant the world to Maurice."

Those iridescent-blue eyes stared up at him. "I came to Nice totally unprepared for what I'd find here. I'll send him more."

He sucked in his breath and moved closer to her. "How soon do you think you'll be back to visit Maurice?"

A tiny nerve was throbbing in the base of her creamy throat. "With my travel schedule, not for a long time." Moistening her lips nervously she asked, "Did the detective tell you how soon he's starting the ground search?"

"January 2."

"The day after New Year's. That's not very far away."

"It can't come soon enough for me."

"For me, either." Her voice throbbed. He realized that was a big admission on her part. "I want your pain to end."

They stared at each other. "Hopefully because of the resources I've put behind it, there will be a big turnout of volunteers."

"If you ran ads over the television, the word would spread like wildfire."

"I'm not sure if the police will do that, but they have their methods when it comes to a search like this."

"Of course."

His lungs had locked tight. "I'm going to miss you, Laura."

She averted her eyes. "The three of us have been through a life-changing experience together. Nothing will ever be the same again, not for any of us."

He was fast losing control. "Do you have any comprehension of how hard it is to let you go?"

Her body had started trembling. He could see it. "Don't you know it's killing me to leave? Please go, Nic. I can't take any more."

The steward made an appearance. "The captain is ready to take off."

She paled visibly.

This was torture of a different kind than Nic had ever known before. "Have a safe flight, Laura."

Nic had to get out of there now or he'd never leave. He wheeled around and exited the jet. Maurice had gotten in the front seat of the car and was waiting for him. Forcing himself to slide behind the wheel, he started the engine and took off. By the time they reached the main road, the Valfort jet had risen in the sky and would be out of sight any minute now.

A groan escaped him he couldn't prevent.

"I feel the same way, *mon fils*. What do you say we go back to the summerhouse and finish the Pinot she gave me for Christmas? I believe there's enough to help us get through the night."

Nic shook his head. "If your doctor could hear you talk…"

"If my doctor knew how we felt right now, he'd give us his blessing and join us."

CHAPTER EIGHT

AFTER LANDING IN San Francisco, Laura texted Maurice to let him know she was home safe and sound. A phone call would have wakened him. As for Nic, she didn't dare contact him and start anything. Tomorrow she'd ring Maurice, who would communicate any news to his grandson.

Once she was back in her condo and settled, she phoned her mom to let her know she was back. Then she called Adam and had the conversation with him that ended their relationship. He wanted to come over, but she told him no. After explaining she wasn't the same woman who'd left, he quieted down.

"When I went to Nice, certain things happened that have changed my life."

"This has to do with your grandmother."

"Yes. I got answers, but that isn't all. My grandmother's husband has a grandson, Nic Valfort. I stayed at his villa while I was in Nice. He was the one who came on the Valfort jet with my grandmother's body."

"Are you telling me you got involved with him?"

"I didn't mean to. It just happened."

"Are you saying you slept with him?"

"No. Not even close."

"But you wanted to."

Her heart was in her throat. "He's a married man." In the next few minutes she told Adam about Dorine and the ground search that would be happening after New Year's.

"You're in love with him."

"Whatever it is I feel, it's strong enough that I can't go on seeing you."

"You mean you're going to wait for him?"

"Yes."

"Has he asked you to wait?"

"No."

"If he never finds her, how do you know he'll want you in four more years?"

"I don't, but while I feel like this about him, I can't be with another man."

"You know all this in a week's time?"

"Yes. Forgive me."

"My hell, I can't believe this is happening."

"This thing that happened was out of my control." From the first moment she'd met Nic in the Holden headquarters foyer, she'd been drawn to him. "I'm so sorry. You have no idea how terrible I feel. I would never deliberately hurt you. You must know that."

"I'm not sure I know anything anymore! You've just smashed all my dreams!" He clicked off first. It was better this way.

With that hurdle taken care of, Laura showered and changed into her robe. Later she went through her business emails and checked for any emergencies, but it seemed her assistant had taken care of everything.

She paced the floor. It was Nic she wanted. When

she thought of him, she couldn't breathe. The next best thing to being with him was watching a video of him.

Along with the first video she'd seen of him at fourteen, she'd grabbed half a dozen of the DVDs and packed them in her suitcase. She hadn't looked at any of those yet. He'd probably be in one or two of them. The boxes containing all her treasures had been picked up by the movers who'd met the jet. They'd be delivered tomorrow. Tonight she couldn't wait to watch the ones that were handy. She put the disk from the top of the pile in the machine. Finally she could get comfortable on the couch and immerse herself in her grandmother's gifts that kept on giving.

The screen showed an old church on a busy street lined with trees.

"My darling Laura—Maurice and I are in Grenoble. Today is Nic's wedding to Dorine Soulis."

Laura gasped.

"We attended the Mass, but came outside so we could take a picture as they walk out the doors. You can see the families assembled on the steps. It was a beautiful wedding. She's petite and so chic. I think she makes the most adorable bride."

Adorable was the word Laura had used in describing Nic's wife. Suddenly the doors opened and there stood an impossibly handsome, smiling Nic in a black tux with his arm around Dorine's waist. Dressed in white with a flowing veil, she looked like a dark-haired angel.

"They're leaving for a honeymoon in Spain. They plan to be gone two weeks. Maurice and I will miss them, so we've decided we're going to take a trip to Australia. I'll make another video when we get there. By the time we get back, they will have returned to their

new home in Nice. It's not that far from us. She found them the perfect villa. Dorine is quite the decorator."

The camera moved closer and showed Nic helping Dorine into the limo. While she was smiling at everyone, Nic lowered his head and kissed her fully, to the joy of the crowd. Laura could hear the clapping and cheers from family and friends.

But she couldn't stand another second and shut the video off with the remote. Pain stabbed her repeatedly until she felt faint. Nic's darling bride was no more. All that happiness wiped out one afternoon on her lunch hour, and Nic still didn't have answers.

Beside herself with grief for him—for Dorine and what horrors she must have suffered, for the horrors Nic would have conjured up wondering what had happened to her—Laura fell sideways on the couch and sobbed until oblivion took over.

Jet lag must have caught up with her, because she didn't wake until she heard her doorbell ring the next morning. By prearrangement the movers were here and she'd slept in her robe all night!

She buzzed them through, then stumbled to the door and opened it to let them in, knowing she looked a wreck. They put everything in the living room. Once she'd signed the receipt, they left.

Laura sank back down on the couch, burying her face in her hands. So many emotions were bombarding her she could barely function. After seeing the radiant look on Nic's face in that video, a look that would never come again, she was thankful she'd flown home before she'd done something she'd regret through eternity.

Laura had provided a few days of distraction for Nic's grief. Because she was Irene's granddaughter and he was Maurice's grandson, they'd both been caught off guard by the unwitting attraction. But that's all it was on his part. An attraction. It couldn't be anything else and never would be. That man had loved his wife and still did.

There was a love song with the lyrics, "If it takes the rest of our lives, I will wait for you." It was one of Laura's favorites. She'd told Adam she'd wait four years for Nic, but that was before she'd seen the video.

Nic wasn't hers to wait for...

The video had made her mind up for her.

If there was to be any visiting from here on out, Maurice would have to come to her while he was still healthy enough to travel. She'd already dismissed the idea of working for him. That would be madness.

As she'd told him, with a lot of hard work she was aiming for CEO of Holden Hotels, like her grandfather Richard. That would be a goal to help her forget there was such a thing as a personal life.

But while she sat there feeling utterly helpless and wishing there were something she could do to help Nic, an idea came to her that wouldn't let go of her. She jumped off the couch and hurried to her bedroom. He would never have to know about it.

In the next hour she put through a call to police headquarters in Nice, asking to speak to someone who spoke English and could tell her about the Valfort search.

In a minute someone came on the line. "Yes? This is Jean-Jacques, one of the coordinators."

"Oh, good. I'm a friend of the Valfort family. I understand you're putting a massive search group together to look for the missing wife of Nicholas Valfort starting on the second. I've never been trained for this sort of thing, but I'd like to help in any way I can, both physically and monetarily."

"*Très bien!* We can use volunteers who will help feed the rescuers coming and going off shift."

"I can do that. Just give me an address and a time and I'll be there."

"*Excellent.* We are working in grids. The address I'm giving you will be in the north end of the park. There will be signs to help you find the exact spot." The man gave her the specific information. "Bring warm clothing, boots and gloves. The forecast calls for eighty percent rain over those days. We could be working through three or four nights."

There hadn't been a cloud in the sky during Laura's stay there. She couldn't believe the weather would turn like that. "Understood. Thank you."

After she'd hung up, she called the airlines and scheduled a flight to Nice on New Year's Day, two days from now. Once that was done, she got on the internet and found information for several hotels near the entrance to Sophia Antipolis. She booked a room at one of them and arranged for a rental car.

After thinking it over, she decided that when she reached Nice and was given an orientation with the other volunteers, she would make arrangements with a local restaurant to supply food and coffee.

There wasn't enough she could do for Nic. Sitting here in San Francisco feeling helpless was untenable. If the search didn't produce anything, at least she would have the satisfaction of knowing she'd shown her love for him in the only way she knew how.

Relieved to be doing something constructive at last, Laura showered and got ready to drive over to her

mom's. The issue with her aunt Susan was all that occupied Jessica's thoughts right now. Finding the right
psychiatrist was crucial.

Later in the day she'd run to headquarters and tell
Dean about the emergency that meant she'd be leaving the country again. Her assistant would have to re-
schedule her travel plans to the various hotels around
the state. The marketing ideas were important, but they
took a backseat to the search for Dorine.

Nic had been in prison too long. If his wife's case
could be solved, it would add ten years to Maurice's
life, too. Maybe Laura was being fanciful, but she'd like
to think her nana would be helping out from the other
side. Irene had loved Nic, too.

Nic was still working alone in his office at seven on
New Year's Eve when his cell rang. He checked the
caller ID and clicked on. "Gran'père? I thought you
were at the family party at the château."

"I am, but something has come up. Where are you?"

"I'm finishing some work at the office. I'll join you
eventually."

"Quit whatever you're doing and meet me at the summerhouse."

Nic's black brows knit together. "You mean now?"

"Yes. Hurry."

"Are you all right?"

"Of course, but we need to talk!"

"I'm leaving now."

He turned off lights and walked out to the parking
lot. Something told Nic the attorney had couriered the
documents about the quitclaim deed to his grandfather
and he was upset about it. Laura had filled the days for

his grandfather while she'd been here, but now that she was gone, Maurice hadn't been able to throw off his depression. By willing the house back to him, she'd made his outlook worse.

Ever since Nic had watched Laura fly out of his life, he'd lost sleep and his emotions had been too raw to be around other people. It was a good thing his office had been closed over the holidays. Even between working on company business in solitude and putting together a search team with the detective, he'd barely managed not to go off the rails.

The lights of the summerhouse beckoned. He pulled up next to the Renault, but almost dreaded stepping inside because Laura wasn't there. Nothing was the same now that she'd gone. *"Enfin,"* his grandfather called out when Nic entered the living room. The older man held a sheaf of papers in his hand, just as Nic had suspected. "Take a look at this!" He handed him the top sheet.

"I already know what Laura did."

Maurice squinted at him. "You do?"

"Yes. Don't be upset with her, *Gran'père.* You've found out she's a wonderful, unselfish woman just like her grandmother. She could no more take your house with its memories away from you than she could stop breathing."

"But she *did* take it away from me."

Nic thought he hadn't heard his grandfather correctly. "Say that again."

"You'd better look at this sheet."

Puzzled at this point, Nic reached for it. The quit-claim deed had been filled out with another name. *Nicholas Honfleur Valfort.*

"She willed the house to *you*."

As memories of a certain conversation with Laura flashed through his mind, the evidence before his eyes rendered him speechless.

"She also left this note. In the state you're in, I'd better read it to you. 'My dear Maurice—Nana told me I could do what I wanted with the summerhouse. So many happy memories reside there because of the love between the two of you. But I know of other happy memories of a Frenchman whose early youth was enriched because of the years he played in the old greenhouse and ruled his own fort.

"'Nothing would please me more than to know he can call it his own again. No one deserves a little piece of happiness more than your magnificent grandson, who once upon a time was a carefree boy Irene loved like her own.'"

Maurice handed him the note. After clearing his throat he said, "When you've pulled yourself together, come to the château and join the party, *mon fils.* Your parents have assembled family and friends from afar to be of help to you in your search after New Year's Day. The first thing we're going to do is say a special prayer that your agony will end soon."

Long after his grandfather had left the house, Nic stood there, incredulous over what Laura had done. His mind went back to something Irene had said in the video. Her words had never spoken to him the way they did at this moment.

You can experience a profound love more than once in this life, as Maurice and I found out. Otherwise what would be the point of existence?

January 4

Portable tables with a protective canopy had been set up all around the technology park to serve as a rest stop for hot food and first aid. Laura and a college guy named Patrick, who was on crutches, had been manning the station from the get-go. They gave out sandwiches and coffee from several bistros and restaurants. She'd funded everything from her bank account, which included paying the drivers in the trucks who made continuous deliveries.

The light rain had pretty well kept up the whole time, forcing her to pull the hood of her water-resistant Windbreaker over her head. But on the third night of the search, it finally stopped long enough to give the volunteers working the grid in her sector some relief.

Every so often a patrol officer would come by for coffee. She'd listen as they spoke with other officers on their radios, then she'd ask for a translation. They were counting on the dogs from the canine corps units to turn up something, but nothing had been found yet. It was a laborious, exhausting process for those walking in lines following a set pattern so that every inch of ground was covered. Their sacrifice was carried out in less than favorable conditions, but everyone there was committed.

Her heart swelled to see the dedication. She could only imagine how Nic felt to know so many had turned out to search for Dorine. From what she could see, it looked as though a small portion of the city had come to lend their assistance. Cars, trucks and buses were parked everywhere. The tragedy that had befallen Nic and his wife was everyone's tragedy.

All the while she gave out food and drink, she was aware that Nic was somewhere in the park, walking the lines with his family and friends. Knowing Maurice, he would be waiting at the château with his brother for any word.

By noon of the fourth day, word circulated that the search would be called off within the hour. The light rain had started up again. In the unnatural silence that followed the announcement, Laura's spirits sank to think this entire effort might not have produced results, but they'd had to try and no one wanted to give up. Though it was time for her to go back to the hotel, she couldn't leave yet.

"I'll stay until it's over, Patrick. You've done your part. Go home and get some sleep."

"I couldn't do that. I'll wait it out to the end. If my fiancée had gone missing, I'd move heaven and earth to find her, too."

She handed him a cup of coffee. "You took the words out of my mouth. You're a good person."

"So are you. Not every tourist would interrupt her vacation to help."

Laura moaned for Nic's pain while they prepared to feed the last shift coming in. As she was putting fresh sandwiches out on plates, she heard voices coming from far off. Lots of shouting. The sound grew in strength to a roar. Her heart jumped to her throat. She looked at Patrick. "They've found something!"

For the next few minutes Laura couldn't breathe while they waited for word. Pretty soon a patrol car came by.

"I'll find out." Patrick hurried over on his crutches to the officer. When he turned and moved toward Laura, she could tell he was excited. "The dogs found a grave with two bodies. Through certain physical evidence, one of them was positively identified as Dorine Valfort. They've called off the search."

A cry of thanksgiving poured out of Laura.

Nic...Nic...it's over, my love.

He had to be overcome with so many emotions. Exquisite relief that she'd been found, of course, but now he would have to deal with the reality of what his wife's trauma had been and all she must have gone through, plus the dawning realization that all hope that she could return to him was lost. This was a time for mourning and Laura feared for Nic. He could go into a depression of a different kind and might not come out of it for who knew how long.

Laura started putting the food and cups back in the cartons for the trucks to haul away, but her hands were shaking. Filled with questions about the unidentified other body, she did her part to clean up, then hurried to her car. This news would be all over the media. She raced back to her hotel to check out and drive to the airport.

Nic's new grieving process was just beginning along with the families'. They would have a funeral, followed by more rivers of sorrow, to endure now that they could give in to their emotions.

The thing to do was fly home and immerse herself in work. Laura had never known Dorine, but she mourned her death, too. One day Laura might see Nic again, but probably not, because he was sensitive to the feelings of Dorine's family and his own. There'd be talk otherwise. His life needed to go in an entirely different direction now.

CHAPTER NINE

March 3

"Nic?"

"*Oui*, Robert?"

"Lieutenant Thibault is here. He says it's important."

"Tell him to come in." Nic jumped up from his office chair. He'd almost lost his mind waiting for news.

The detective entered his office. "The case is now officially closed, Nic. The Sûreté tracked down the man responsible. He's now in custody in Rouen. They got a confession. It'll be all over the evening news."

"Thank God." This was the information that had sprung his prison door at last.

"The lowlife and his wife worked at the Valfort Hotel in the Old Town. After resigning their jobs, they kidnapped your wife to collect a ransom. When they followed her from her office, they created a diversion so she would stop.

"While his wife held a gun on your wife, he drove Dorine's car into town and left it. Then he came back. But upon his return he found your wife dead in their car. His wife claimed there'd been a struggle and the gun had gone off by accident. In an angry rage because everything had gone wrong, he shot his wife and dug a grave for them that night before disappearing."

The news that Dorine hadn't suffered long before she was killed went a long way to bring Nic peace, but he needed to be alone. "Thank you, Lieutenant."

Once the detective left, Nic told Robert he was going home. When he reached the villa, he told Jean and Arlette he needed his privacy.

After they retired for the night, he went into the bedroom he'd shared with Dorine and collapsed on the bed. Great sobs shook his body. If he ate or drank, he didn't remember it. Three days later his grandfather walked in on him.

"I don't pretend to know the deep suffering you've gone through, *mon fils,* but I do know Dorine is in heaven and happy. She's been there over three years and wants you to be happy, too."

Nic turned over on his back, looking at Maurice through red-rimmed eyes. "How terrified she must have been."

"Yes. But how moved she must have been to hear all the wonderful things said about her at the funeral, especially the outpouring of love from her honorable husband."

"Don't ever call me honorable."

"Why? Because you lost your heart to Irene's granddaughter during your Gethsemane? Want to know a secret? I lost my heart to her too. That dear girl helped both of us keep it together at the darkest moment of our lives. Now it's time to get on with living and put all the pain, all the guilt and all the suffering away. It's time to move into the summerhouse and dream new dreams."

* * *

Nic phoned Robert. "You're going to have to run the office for a while, because I'm leaving for California within the hour. I'll let you know when I'll be back."

On his way to the villa he phoned the pilot to get the jet ready. After he'd packed some clothes and was on his way to the airport, he phoned Maurice and gave him the news. "I'm flying to San Francisco."

"It's about time, *mon fils.*"

Long past time, was more like it Nic mused as he entered Holden headquarters the next day. It was two in the afternoon. When he saw the security guard in the foyer, it was like déjà vu.

"I'm here to see the marketing manager, Laura Tate."

"I'm sorry, but this is her first day of vacation, sir."

Nic felt as if he'd been punched in the gut. "For how long?"

"A week."

"Thank you." He turned on his heel and went back out to the limo. Maybe she hadn't left yet town yet. He'd try her condo. When he entered the foyer, he had to buzz her suite. If she didn't answer, then he'd phone her mother and find out her destination.

He was about to walk away when he heard her voice. "Yes?"

Beyond elated she was home he said, "I thought you were on vacation."

There was such a long silence, he wondered if she'd even heard him. Then, *"Nic?"* The joy in that one word would live with him all his life. "Is it really you?"

His eyes closed tightly for a moment. "Why don't you let me in and find out?"

"I'm on the second floor," she said in a tremulous

voice. "Just take the stairs and I'm around the corner, number six."

He heard the click of the inner door, then hurried through and took the stairs three at a time. She met him when he'd reached the top step.

"Nic—" Her crystal-blue gaze played over him, blazing with a hunger to match his own. Deep in his soul he sensed nothing had changed between them. If anything, their love had deepened. "I've imagined this a thousand times in my dreams. I was afraid I might never see you again. I—I can't believe you're here." Her voice faltered.

"Invite me in and I'll convince you."

She backed into the condo, never taking her eyes off him. He shut the door behind him.

"I've done my grieving, Laura. Dorine is at peace now, and so am I. We can catch up on everything later, but right now I don't want to talk. I just want to hold you."

In the next instant she ran into his arms, enveloping him with her intoxicating fragrance. He crushed her beautiful body against his. The reality of her hadn't begun to sink in yet. He needed more of her, wanted all of her. He wanted too much all at once. He was still trying to get it through his mind and heart she was here with him at last. No barriers to keep them apart.

Impatient for everything denied them, he picked her up and carried her over to the couch. She clung to him with a hungry moan as he followed her down. He was desperate for this closeness while he kissed the mouth he craved over and over again.

They lost track of time trying to merge, but no kiss, no matter how long and deep, could satisfy his need. He would never be able to get enough of her. Their

REBECCA WINTERS   179

legs tangled while his hands became enmeshed in her silvery-gold hair.

"I love you, *mon amour*. I've wanted to say that since Christmas Eve, when we watched the video in my den. You changed my world."

Laura covered his face with kisses, thrilling him as he hadn't thought possible. "I knew I'd fallen in love with you before I climbed out of the limousine that first day. I love you so much I hurt to the palms of my hands." She sought his mouth again with the kind of passion that was burning him alive.

"We need to get married. Since you willed it to me, I'm thinking the summerhouse. A small, intimate ceremony. We'll make our home there after we come home from our honeymoon."

"I think I'm dying of happiness."

"Tomorrow we'll fly back to Nice. You'll have to handle your corporate job long-distance. I don't ever want to be separated from you again. These past months..." His voice cracked. He couldn't finish.

"Hush, darling. It's over. All of it." She pressed his head to her chest. For a little while they both let go of their emotions and wept. While she rocked him, she kissed his hair and told him how she'd flown to Nice to help in the search.

"You were there?"

"Yes. I heard the noise and the barks of the dogs."

"I can't believe it. You never told me or Maurice."

"No. That was your private time. I knew how much you loved Dorine. I saw the video of your wedding after I got back to San Francisco. That's why I didn't come near you at the time, or phone you. I knew I had to wait and hope that like our grandparents, who were given a second chance at happiness, one day you might grow to love me enough to come for me."

Laura's love astounded and humbled him.

A week later the family priest officiated at the late-afternoon wedding ceremony in the living room of the summerhouse. The first person to embrace Laura after she and Nic became man and wife was Maurice.

In a croaking voice he said, "Little did I know when I had to say goodbye to my beloved wife for the last time, I'd be welcoming a new Madame Valfort into the family. My own beautiful granddaughter."

She let out a gentle laugh. "Don't get me started on the tears, *Gran'père,* or I'll never stop and my brand-new husband won't know what to do with me."

Nic's strong arms went around her waist from behind. He was never far from her. "If you believe that, then you don't know me at all," he whispered into her neck, thrilling her. Her cream-colored lace suit, which she'd chosen rather than a wedding dress, made it easy for him to pull her against him. She'd wanted simplicity.

It was a day of intense happiness. Her gaze took in her mom and Yves, who both broke off talking to hug them. Yves had videotaped the wedding and had also volunteered to drive her mother back to the villa. She would stay the night before he drove her to the airport to return to San Francisco.

All of Nic's family had assembled and welcomed her as one of their own. What Maurice and Irene hadn't been able to enjoy had come back to bless Laura and Nic in profound ways. Two families were healing. Her aunt Susan was in therapy in San Francisco. Laura had a feeling her grandmother was looking down and smiling.

Nic tugged on a strand of her blond hair, which she'd left long the way he loved it. "I don't know about you, but I'm ready to leave."

She turned in his arms. "We can't go yet. You *know* we can't."

"Then kiss me so I can stand it."

In this mood Nic was irresistible. She raised up to press a kiss to his lips, but he took advantage and gave her a husband's kiss, hot with desire. Heat swarmed her cheeks because everyone would have noticed. She burrowed against him for a moment to gain her composure. "Be good, darling."

"I'm being as good as I can for a new bridegroom."

"No, you're not."

"But you love me."

"You *have* to know that by now. I've been living to become your wife."

"I want more proof."

Her pulse raced. "I promise you'll have it later tonight."

"Don't you know I have a voracious appetite for you and want it for the rest of our lives?"

They heard someone tapping on a Champagne glass. Flushed with love and desire, she turned in his arms. Maurice's brother, Auguste got to his feet with difficulty.

"I'd like to propose a toast to Nicholas and his bride. Everything good started to happen the day she flew in to Nice. I wish we had gathered like this for my brother and Irene. Our family should have celebrated their marriage and I'm sorry about that. But we can celebrate new beginnings with the new generation of Valforts. May Nic and Laura be happy and fruitful."

"To new beginnings," everyone joined in.

Nic's arms held her tighter. "Did you hear that, *mon amour?* It's time to go and fulfill every wish. Our bags are packed and waiting for us in the car."

She blushed again. "Where are you taking me?"

"It's not far, believe me." He reached for her hand and pulled her toward the foyer with him. Everyone rushed forward as they slipped out the front door to the car. Yves kept filming them as Nic helped her inside.

"Let's have a kiss," he called out, but Nic didn't respond.

Surprised, maybe even a little hurt, she lowered the window. "*À bientôt, Gran'père.* I love you. See you soon."

"Take your time," he called back. "There's only one honeymoon."

In another minute Nic had started the car and they pulled away. He grabbed hold of her hand. "Before you leap to the wrong conclusion, I had two reasons for not kissing you just then. Dorine and I saw Maurice's video of our wedding after we got home from our honeymoon. When I realized you'd seen it, too, I didn't want you having to make comparisons that could hurt y—"

"Don't say any more." She cut him off and squeezed his hand. "I love you for being so sensitive to my feelings. I'm afraid I love you too much."

"If you want to know my second reason, it's because I almost devoured you in front of our guests after the ceremony. To be honest, I didn't trust myself not to do the same thing again given the chance."

"If we're talking truths, I never trusted myself with you from the moment you picked me up at the airport in Nice."

"Ours was a trial of fire from the beginning."

She nodded. "Thank heaven that part is over. Do you swear we don't have much farther to go? I don't think I can stand to be this far apart from you any longer."

"Do you recognize this highway?"

She looked around and let out a half squeal. "You're taking me back to Eze—"

"This time I only booked one room. Just remember that after we get there, I won't let you out of my bed, let alone my sight."

"You think I feel any different?"

Once they reached the parking area, he grabbed their bags and they walked the trail to the little hotel.

"The night is so glorious, Nic."

"Balmy, just the way I like it."

The concierge greeted them and handed Laura the card key. Her body trembled with anticipation as they ascended the stairs to the next floor. She opened the door for them. This was so different from last time. For a moment she wondered if this was really happening.

"It's really happening," Nic murmured and put down the bags. He knew her so well he'd read her mind. After he opened the glass door to let in the night air, he turned to her. "Come here to me, my love."

The second she walked into his arms, she knew pleasure beyond anything in this life. They took their time getting to know each other in ways she hadn't even dreamed about. Nic was such a beautiful man. To think he was her husband. His possession of her was to die for.

But she didn't die. She was vibrantly alive and sought the rapture of fulfillment he gave her again and again. Toward morning he fell asleep. She lay at his side and watched him as the lavender tint he'd told her about illuminated the sky. Minute by minute the color changed to the indescribable pink he'd talked about.

The magical hues filled the room, bringing out the Gallic features that made him such a gorgeous man. She gasped quietly in awe, but he heard her. His eyelids opened. The gray of his irises between his black lashes had turned crystalline in the early-morning light.

"What is it, *ma belle?*"

Laura loved it when he called her that. She leaned over to kiss his mouth. "Nothing's wrong. I simply felt like looking at you. No woman could be as lucky as I am. I'm hoping that one day soon we'll have a baby. It won't matter if it's a boy or a girl, because either way, they'll have the Valfort traits and qualities."

He kissed the palm of her hand. "Don't forget the Holden genes."

She smiled. "While I was getting ready for the wedding, Mother said you're the most sinfully handsome man she ever saw. I thought the same thing the first time I laid eyes on you, but I've never heard her express herself like that before."

"Sometime you'll have to ask Yves what I said about you." Her heart thudded in reaction. He raised up on one elbow. His eyes radiated excitement. "You honestly want a baby soon?"

Suddenly she felt anxious. "Don't *you?*"

"Now that I've got you, I want it all."

"If I was pregnant right now, would you mind?"

"Mind?" He pulled her on top of him. "How can you even ask me that?"

"Because we didn't ever really talk about it, but last night we didn't take precautions."

"So you're not on the Pill?"

"No. I've never slept with any man, so I didn't need to be."

A cry of joy escaped his throat. "So I could have made you pregnant during the night?"

"Yes. You have no idea how much I want your baby. I want us to be a real family. You're going to make the most wonderful father."

Suddenly he rolled her over so he was looking down at her. "I don't want you to move. We're going to stay in this room for the next couple of days. I'll order breakfast, lunch and dinner for us. In between meals we're going to be busy doing what I love doing best with you. Have I told you yet what a wonderful lover you are? You're the light of my life. I love you, *mon amour. Je t'aime,*" he cried, burying his face in her hair.

Laura's joy was full. She held the world in her arms and sang a certain song to him she'd memorized because of that night.

"Let's dance the old-fashioned way, my love. I want you to stay in my arms, skin against skin. Let me feel your heart, don't let any air in. Come close where you belong. Let's hear our secret song and dance in the old-fashioned way. Won't you stay in my arms? We'll discover higher highs we never knew before, if we just close our eyes and dance around the floor. It makes me love you more."

"Laura—"

* * * * *

"Could you take me on a tour of the inside of the house?" she asked brightly.

"I could," the cowboy answered, but made no effort to follow through on her request.

"But?" she asked.

She made him think of a stick of dynamite about to go off. He was about ten inches taller than she was, but a stick of dynamite didn't have to be very big to make a sizable impression.

Just who was this woman and what was she doing here? "I don't even know who you are."

"I'm not dangerous, if that's what you're thinking," she told him.

As if he believed that.

Finn's mouth curved ever so slightly, the left side more than the right. He wondered just how many men this woman had brought to their knees with that killer smile of hers.

"There's dangerous, and then there's *dangerous,*" he replied, his eyes never leaving hers.

She raised her chin just a little, doing her best to generate an air of innocence as she assured him, "I'm neither."

"I don't know about that," he said.

COWBOY FOR HIRE

BY

MARIE FERRARELLA

MILLS & BOON®

Published in Great Britain 2014
by Mills & Boon, an imprint of Harlequin (UK) Limited,
Eton House, 18-24 Paradise Road, Richmond, Surrey, TW9 1SR

© 2014 Marie Rydzynski-Ferrarella

ISBN: 978-0-263-91329-3

23-1114

USA TODAY bestselling and RITA® Award-winning author **Marie Ferrarella** has written more than two hundred books for Mills & Boon, some under the name Marie Nicole. Her romances are beloved by fans worldwide. Visit her website, www.marieferrarella.com.

To
Dianne Moggy,
for being nice enough
to call and reassure me.
Thank You.

Prologue

There had to be more.

There just had to be more to life than this.

The haunting thought echoed over and over again in Constance Carmichael's brain as she sat in her father's dining room, moving bits and pieces of chicken marsala around on her plate.

Her father was talking. But not to her—or even *at* her, as was his custom. This time his words were directed to someone on the other end of his state-of-the-art smartphone. From what she had pieced together, someone from one of his endless construction projects. Carmichael Construction Corporation, domiciled in Houston, Texas, had projects in different stages of completion throughout the country, and Calvin Carmichael thrived on the challenge of riding roughshod on *all* of his foremen.

The table in the dining room easily sat twenty. More if necessary. Tonight it only sat two, her father and her. She was here by mandate. Not that she didn't love her father, she did, but she had never been able to find a way to bond with him—not that she hadn't spent her whole life trying. But she had never been able to approach him and have him see her as something other than the ongoing disappointment he always made her feel that she was.

Calvin Carmichael didn't believe in pulling any punches.

Rather than sharing a warm family dinner, Connie had rarely felt more alone. She felt utterly isolated—and distance was only part of the reason. Before the call came in, her father had insisted that she sit at one end of the table while he sat at the other.

"Like civilized people," he'd told her.

He was at the head of the table and consequently, she was at the foot—with what felt like miles of distance between them.

If merely sharing a meal had been her father's main objective, it could have been more easily attained than this elaborate command performance. Connie was aware of restaurants that were smaller than her father's dining room. She'd grown up in this enormous house, but it had never felt like home to her.

She watched Fleming, her father's butler, retreat out of the corner of her eye. It was no secret that Calvin Carmichael enjoyed with relish all the perks that his acquired wealth could buy, including not just a cook and a housekeeper but a genuine English butler, as well. The latter's duties included serving dinner, even if the only one at the table was her father.

Connie sighed inwardly, wondering when she could safely take her leave. She knew that if her sigh was audible, her father would make note of it. Moreover, he'd grill her about it once his phone call was over, finding a way to make her feel guilty even if he was the one at fault.

Sitting here, toying with her food and watching her father, Connie felt a numbing malaise, a deadness spreading like insidious mold inside her. Surrounded by wealth, able to purchase and own any object her heart desired, no matter how extravagant, she found she desired nothing.

Because nothing made her happy.

She knew what she needed.

She needed to feel alive, to feel productive. She needed to accomplish something so that she could feel as if she finally, finally had a little of her father's respect instead of always being on the receiving end of his thinly veiled contempt.

"You're not eating. I invited you for dinner, you're not eating. Something wrong with your dinner?"

Connie looked up, startled. Her father had been on the phone for the past twenty minutes, but the slight shift in his tone made her realize that he had ended his conversation and had decided to find some reason to criticize her.

Connie lifted her shoulders in a careless, vague shrug. "I'm just not hungry, I guess," she replied, not wanting to get into an argument with the man.

But it seemed unavoidable.

"That's because you've never *been* hungry. Had you grown up hungry," Calvin stressed, "you would never waste even a *morsel* of food." Crystal-blue eyes narrowed beneath imposing, startlingly black eyebrows.

"What's wrong with you, little girl?" If the question was motivated by concern, there was no indication in either his inflection or his tone.

Little girl.

She was twenty-seven years old, and she *hated* when her father called her that, but she knew it was futile to say as much. Calvin Carmichael did what he pleased *when* he pleased to whomever he pleased and took no advice, no criticism from anyone. To render any would just get her further embroiled in a heated exchange. Silence usually won out by default.

"Haven't I given you everything?" Calvin pressed, still scowling at his only daughter. His only child according to him. He had long since disowned the older brother she had adored because Conrad had deigned to turn his back on the family business and had struck out on his own years ago.

Connie looked at her father for a long moment. This feeling wasn't about to go away, and if she didn't say anything, she knew it would only get worse, not to mention that her father wouldn't stop questioning her, wouldn't stop verbally poking at her until she told him what he claimed he wanted to know.

As if he cared.

"I don't want to be *given* anything," she told her father. "I want to *earn* it myself."

His laugh was belittling. "Earn it, right. Where's this going, little girl?"

She pressed her lips together for a moment to keep from saying something one of them—possibly both of them—would regret. Her father didn't respond well to displays of emotion.

"I want to helm a project." It wasn't really what was bothering her, but maybe, just maybe, it might help squash these all but paralyzing doldrums that had infiltrated her very soul.

"You? Helm a project?" Piercing blue eyes stared at her in disbelief. "You mean by yourself?"

She tried not to react to the sarcasm in her father's voice. "Yes. My own project."

He waved a dismissive hand at her. "You don't know the first thing about being in charge of a project."

Anger rose within her, and she clutched to it. At least she was finally *feeling* something. "Dad, I've worked for you in one capacity or another for the last ten years. I think I know the first thing about being in charge of a project—and the second thing, too," she added, struggling to rein in her temper. An outburst would only tilt the scales further against her.

Her father was a formidable man, a man who could stare down his opponents and have them backing off, but she was determined not to allow him to intimidate her. She was fighting for her life—figuratively and, just possibly, literally.

Calvin laughed shortly. But just before he began to say something scathing in reply, his ever-present cell phone rang again.

To Connie's utter annoyance, her father answered it. It was time to leave, she decided. This "discussion," like all the others she'd had with him over the years, wasn't going anywhere.

But as she pushed her chair back and rose to her feet, Connie saw her father raise a finger, the gesture meant to keep her where she stood.

"Just a minute."

She wasn't sure if he was speaking to her or the person on the other end of the call. His next words, however, were definitely directed at her.

"Forever." For a moment, the word just hung there, like a single leaf drifting down from a tree. "Let's see what you can do about getting a project up, going and completed in Forever."

Something in her gut warned her she was walking into a trap—but she had no other choice. She had to do it—whatever "it" turned out to be.

"What kind of a project?" she asked warily.

Her father's attention already appeared to be elsewhere. "I'll have Emerson give you the particulars," he said in an offhanded manner, referring to his business manager. "Just remember, little girl, I started with nothing—I don't intend to wind up that way," he warned her, as if he was already predicting the cost of her failure.

Adrenaline was beginning to surface, whether in anticipation of this mysterious project or as a reaction to her father's condescending manner, it was hard for her to tell—but at least it was there, and she was grateful for that.

"Thank you," she said.

But her father was back talking to the person on the other end of the cell phone, giving that man his undivided attention.

She had a project, Connie thought, savoring the idea as it began to sink in. The world suddenly got a whole lot brighter.

Chapter One

"I can't believe what you've done to the place," Brett
Murphy said to Finn, the older of his two younger
brothers, as he looked around at what had been, until
recently, a crumbling, weather-beaten and termite-
riddled ranch house.

This morning, before opening up Murphy's, Forever's one and only saloon, he'd decided to look in on
Finn's progress renovating the ranch house he had inherited from one of the town's diehard bachelors. And
though he hadn't been prepared to, he was impressed
by what he saw.

"More than that," Brett added as he turned to face
his brother, "I can't believe that you're the one who's
doing it."

Finn never missed a beat. He still had a lot to do before he packed it in for the day. "And what's that supposed to mean?" he asked. He'd been at this from first
light, wrestling with a particularly uncooperative floorboard trim, which was just warped enough to give him
trouble. That did *not* put the normally mild-tempered
middle brother in the best frame of mind. "I built you

a bathroom out of practically nothing, didn't I?" he reminded Brett. The bathroom had been added to make
the single room above the saloon more livable. Until
then, anyone staying in the room had had to go downstairs to answer nature's call or take a shower.

Brett's memory needed no prodding. It had always
been a notch above excellent, which was fortunate for
his brothers. It was Brett who took over running Murphy's and being financially responsible for them at the
age of eighteen.

"Yes, you did," Brett replied. "But don't forget, you
were the kid who always wound up smashing his thumb
with a hammer practically every time you so much as
held one in your hand."

His back to Brett as he continued working, Finn
shrugged. "You're exaggerating, and anyway, I was
six."

"I'm not—and you were twelve," Brett countered.
He inclined his head ever so slightly as if that would
underscore his point. "I'm the one with a head for details and numbers."

Finn snorted. It wasn't that he took offense, just that
their relationship was such that they took jabs at one
another—and Liam—as a matter of course. It was just
the way things were. But at bottom, he was fiercely
loyal to his brothers—as they were to him.

"Just because you can add two and two doesn't make
you the last authority on things, Brett," Liam informed
his brother.

"No, running Murphy's into the black pretty much
did that."

When, at eighteen, he had suddenly found himself in charge of the establishment, after their Uncle Patrick had died, he'd discovered that the saloon was actually *losing* money rather than earning it. He swiftly got to work making things right and within eight months, he'd managed to turn things around. It wasn't just his pride that was at stake, he had brothers to support and send to school.

"Look, I didn't swing by to squabble with you," Brett went on. "I just wanted to see how the place was coming along—and it looks like you're finally in the home stretch. Liam been helping you?" he asked, curious.

This time Finn did stop what he was doing. He looked at Brett incredulously and then laughed. "Liam? In case you haven't noticed, that's a box of tools by your foot, not a box of guitar picks."

Finn's meaning was clear. Of late, their younger brother only cared for all things musical. Brett still managed to get Liam to work the bar certain nights, but it was clear that Liam preferred performing at Murphy's rather than tending to the customers and their thirst.

"I thought Liam said he was coming by the other day," Brett recalled.

"He did." Finn's mouth curved. "Said watching me work inspired his songwriting."

"Did it?" Brett asked, amused.

Finn shrugged again. "All I know was that he scribbled some things down, said 'thanks' and took off again. I figure that *he* figures he's got a good thing going. Tells you he's coming out here to help me then when he comes here, he writes his songs—and calls it working." There was no resentment in Finn's voice as he summarized his younger brother's revised work ethic. For the most part, Finn preferred working alone. It gave him the freedom to try different things without someone else second-guessing him or giving so-called advice. "Hey, Brett?"

Brett had wandered over to the fireplace. Finn had almost completely rebuilt it, replacing the old red bricks with white ones. It made the room look larger. "What?"

"You think our baby brother has any talent?" he asked in between hammering a section of the floorboard into place.

"For avoiding work?" Brett guessed. "Absolutely."

Finn knew that Brett knew what he was referring to, but he clarified his question, anyway. "No, I mean for those songs he writes."

Brett could see the merit in Liam's efforts, especially since he wouldn't have been able to come up with the songs himself, but he was curious to hear what Finn's opinion was. Since he was asking, Brett figured his brother had to have formed his own take on the subject.

"You've heard him just like I have," Brett pointed out, waiting.

Finn glanced at him over his shoulder. "Yeah, but I want to know what you think."

Brett played the line out a little further. "Suddenly I'm an authority?" he questioned.

Down on his knees, Finn rocked back on his heels,

the frustrating length of floorboard temporarily forgotten. Despite the fancy verbal footwork, he really did value Brett's take on things. Brett had been the one he'd looked up to when he was growing up.

"No, not an authority," Finn replied, "but you know what you like."

"I think he's good. But I think he's better at singing songs than he is at writing them," he said honestly, then in the next moment, he added, "But what I *do* know is that you've got a real talent for taking sow's ears and making silk purses out of them."

Never one to reach for fancy words when plain ones would do, Finn eyed him with more than a trace of confusion.

"How's that again?" he asked.

Brett rephrased his comment. Easygoing though he was, it wasn't often that he complimented either of his brothers. He'd wanted them to grow up struggling to always reach higher rather than expecting things to be handed to them—automatic approval readily fell into that category.

"You're damn good at this remodeling thing that you do."

Finn smiled to himself. Only a hint of it was evident on his lips. "Glad you like it."

"But you don't have to work on it 24/7," Brett pointed out. Finn had immersed himself in this huge project he'd taken on almost single-handedly. There was no reason to push himself this hard. "Nobody's waving a deadline at you."

"There's a deadline," Finn contradicted. He saw

Brett raise an eyebrow in a silent query, so he stated the obvious. "You and Lady Doc are still getting married, aren't you?"

Just the mere mention of his pending nuptials brought a wide smile to Brett's lips. Just the way that thoughts of Alisha always did.

Until the young general surgeon had come to town, answering Dr. Daniel Davenport's letter requesting help, Brett had been relatively certain that while he loved all the ladies, regardless of "type," there was no so-called soul mate out there for him.

Now he knew better, because he had met her. Not only was she out there, but he would be marrying her before the year was out, as well.

"Yes," Brett replied. "But what…?"

Finn anticipated Brett's question and cut him short. "This is my wedding present to you and Lady Doc—to say thanks for all the times you were there for Liam and me when we needed you—and even the times when we thought we didn't," he added with a touch of whimsy. "And this is, in a small way, to pay you back for staying instead of taking off with Laura right after high school graduation, the way she wanted you to.

"In other words, this is to say thanks for staying, for giving up your dream and taking care of your two bratty younger brothers instead."

While Finn and Liam were aware of Laura, he had never told them about the ultimatum she'd given him. Had never mentioned how tempted he'd been, just for a moment, to follow her to Los Angeles. All his brothers knew was one day, Laura stopped coming around.

He looked at Finn in surprise. "You know about that?"

Finn smiled. "I'm not quite the oblivious person you thought I was."

"I didn't think you were *oblivious*," Brett corrected him. "It was just that you saw and paid attention to things the rest of us just glossed over." His smile widened as he looked around the living room. Finn had outdone himself. "But seriously, this is all more than terrific, but this is *our* ranch house," he emphasized, "not just mine."

Finn looked at him and shook his head in wonder before getting back to work. "You bring that pretty Lady Doc here after you've married her and she finds out that she's sharing the place with not just you but also your two brothers, I guarantee that she'll walk out of here so fast, your head'll spin clean off."

He might not be as experienced as Brett was when it came to the fairer sex, Finn thought, but some things were just a given.

"Now, I don't know nearly as much as you do when it comes to the ladies, but I do know that newlyweds like their own space—that doesn't mean sharing that space with two other people. Liam and I'll go on living at the house. This'll be your place," he concluded, waving his hand around the room they were currently in as well as indicating the rest of the house.

"But the ranch itself is still *ours,* not just mine," Brett insisted.

"Earl Robertson left it to you," Finn stated simply. The man, he knew, had done it to show his gratitude because Brett had gone out of his way to look in on him when he had taken sick. That was Brett, Finn thought, putting himself out with no thought of any sort of compensation coming his way for his actions.

"And I've always shared whatever I had with you and Liam," Brett stated flatly.

Finn allowed a sly smile to feather over his lips, even though being sly was out of keeping with his normally genial nature.

"I see. Does that go for Lady Doc, too?"

Brett knew that his brother was kidding and that he didn't have to say it, but he played along, anyway. "Alisha is off-limits."

Finn pretended to sigh. "It figures. First nice *thing* you have in aeons, and you're keeping it all to yourself."

"Damn right I am."

Finn changed the subject, directing the conversation toward something serious. "Hey, made a decision about who your best man is going to be?"

Brett was silent for a moment. He'd made Finn think he was debating his choices, but the truth of it was, he'd made up his mind from the beginning. It had been Finn all along.

"Well, Liam made it clear that he and that band of his are providing the music, so I guess you get to be best man."

His back to Brett, Finn smiled to himself. "I won't let it go to my head."

"Might get lonely up there if it did," Brett commented with affection. He glanced at his watch. "Guess

I'd better be getting back or Nathan McHale is going to think I've abandoned him," he said, referring to one of Murphy's' two most steadfast patrons.

Finn laughed. "Wonder how long he'd stand in front of the closed door, waiting for you to open up before he'd finally give up."

Brett began to answer without hesitation. "Two, maybe three—"

"Hours?" Finn asked, amused.

"Days," Brett corrected with a laugh. The older man had been coming to Murphy's for as many years as anyone could remember, motivated partially by his fondness for beer and most assuredly by his desire to get away from his eternally nagging wife, Henrietta. "I'll see you later tonight."

Finn nodded. "I'll be by when I get done for the day," he said. He was back to communing with another ornery section of floorboard before his brother walked out the front door.

CONNIE HAD DECIDED to just drive around both through Forever and its surrounding area to get a general feel for the little town. For the most part, it appeared she'd stumbled across a town that time had more or less left alone. Nothing looked ancient, exactly, and there were parking places in front of the handful of businesses rather than hitching posts, but all in all, the entire town had a very rural air about it, right down to the single restaurant—if a diner could actually lay claim to that title.

She'd been amused to see that the town's one bar—

how did these cowboys survive with only one bar?—
had a sign in the window that said Hungry? Go visit
Miss Joan's diner. Thirsty? You've come to the right
place. That had told her that there was obviously a division of labor here with territories being defined in
the simplest of terms.

Given its size and what she took to be the residents'
mind-set, Connie doubted very much if a place like
this actually *needed* a hotel—which, she had a feeling, had probably been her father's whole point when
he had given her this *project,* saying if she wanted to
prove herself to him, he wanted to see her complete
the hotel, bringing it in on time and under budget. The
budget left very little wiggle room.

"Newsflash, Dad. I don't give up that easily," she
murmured to the man who was currently five hundred
miles away.

Challenges, especially seemingly impossible ones,
were what made her come alive. At first glance, the
sleepy little town of Forever needed a hotel about as
much as it needed an expert on wombats.

It took closer examination to see that the idea of
building a hotel had merit.

Connie could see the potential of the place forming itself in her mind's eye. She just needed the right
approach, the right thing to play up and the hotel-to-
be would not only become a reality, it would also be a
success and eventually get its patrons.

But it wouldn't get anything if it wasn't first built,
and she had already decided that while she could have
materials shipped in from anywhere in the country that

could give her the best deal, to get the structure actually built, she was going to use local *talent,* so to speak.

She naturally assumed that living out here in what she viewed as *the sticks* made people handy out of necessity. Unlike in the larger cities, there wasn't a range of construction companies, all in competition with one another, all vying for the customer's money. Driving down here from Houston, she had already ascertained that the nearest town, Pine Ridge, was a minimum of fifty miles away. That alone limited the amount of choices available. If anything, out here it was the unhandy customer who wound up searching to find someone to do the work for them.

Just like faith, the right amount of money, she had learned, could move mountains.

She had no mountains to move. But she did have a building to erect, and in order not to be the outsider, the person who was viewed as invading their territory, she would need allies. In this particular case, she needed to have some of the men from Forever taking part in making the hotel a reality.

Granted that, once completed, the hotel would belong to the Carmichael Construction Corporation until such time as they sold it, but she had to make the locals feel that building the hotel would benefit the whole town as well as provide them with good-paying jobs during construction.

Connie knew the importance of friends; she just didn't exactly know how to go about making them.

But she had done her homework before ever getting behind the wheel of her vehicle and driving down here.

As she drove around now, Connie thought about the fact that on the other side of the town, located about ten miles due northwest, was a Native American reservation. She couldn't remember which of the tribes lived there, but perhaps they would welcome the work, along with Forever townspeople. Given the local state of affairs, who wouldn't want a job?

So, armed with her GPS, Connie was on her way there. She was driving slower than she was accustomed to for two reasons: one, she didn't have a natural sense of direction, and she didn't know the lay of the land and two, she wanted and *needed* to get to know this land she was temporarily camping out on.

The reservation was her destination, but something—instincts perhaps—made her closely scan the immediate area she was traversing.

Which was when she saw him.

At first she thought she was having a hallucination, a better-than-average morning fantasy that could easily trigger her latent libido if she let it. The trick to being a driven woman with not just goals, but also the taste of success tucked firmly under her belt, was the way she responded to things that needed life-long commitments. It required—demanded, really—tunnel vision. Eye on the prize and all that sort of thing.

Even so, Connie slowed her pristine, gleaming white BMW sports car down to an arthritic crawl as she stared at the lone figure in the distance.

No harm in just looking, she told herself.

Even at this distance, she could easily make out that the man was around her own age. She was keenly aware that he was bare-chested, that his muscles were rippling with every move he made and that, pound for pound, he had to be the best-looking specimen of manhood she had seen in a very long time.

Moving closer, she could see that perspiration covered his body, causing practically a sheen over his chest and arms.

At first she wasn't aware of it, but then she realized that her mouth had gone bone-dry. She went on watching.

He didn't seem to be aware of the fact that he was under scrutiny. The worker turned his back to her and went on doing whatever it was that he was doing. She couldn't quite make it out, but it had something to do with construction because there were tools on the ground, surrounding an empty tool chest.

As she continued observing him, Connie saw that the man appeared as if he not only knew his way around tools, but he also definitely seemed comfortable working with his hands.

It came to her then.

He was just the man she was looking for to be her foreman, to act as her go-between with whatever men she wound up hiring to do the actual work. Watching him, she couldn't help wondering how well someone who looked like that would take instructions from a woman.

Or was he the type who didn't care who issued the orders as long as there was a guaranteed paycheck at the end of the week?

Enough thinking, start doing, she silently ordered herself.

The next moment, she turned her vehicle toward the cowboy and drove straight toward him.

Chapter Two

He'd been aware of the slow-moving, blindingly white sports car for some time now. It was a beauty—much like the woman who was driving it.

But unlike the woman behind the wheel, the vehicle, *because* of its make and model, stuck out like a sore thumb. Regardless of the season, Forever and its outlining area didn't see much through traffic. Every so often, there was the occasional lost traveler, but on the whole, that was a rare occurrence. Forever was *not* on the beaten path to anywhere of interest, except perhaps for the reservation and a couple of other tiny towns that had sprung up in the area. On its way to being a ghost town more than once, the town stubbornly survived despite all odds. Like a prickly-pear cactus, Forever, a few of the much older residents maintained, was just too ornery to die.

The owner of the sports car, Finn decided, had to be lost. Nobody driving that sort of a vehicle could possibly have any business being in or around Forever. Even Dan, the doctor who had initially come to town out of a sense of obligation mixed with a heavy dose of guilt, hadn't been driving a car nearly that flashy and unsuitable for this terrain when he'd arrived.

As the vehicle came closer, Finn tossed down his hammer and approached the car. The woman, he couldn't help noticing, was even better-looking close up than she was at a distance.

"You lost?" he asked her, fully expecting her to sigh with relief and answer "Yes."

She didn't.

Instead, she shook her head and said, "No, I don't think so."

Finn regarded her thoughtfully. "In my experience, a person's either lost or they're not. There is no gray area."

The woman smiled at him. "Didn't think I'd find a philosopher all the way out here."

"It's not philosophy, it's just plain common sense," Finn told her.

To him, so-called *philosophers* referred to the gaggle of retired old men who got together every morning and sat on the sun-bleached bench in front of the general store, watching the rest of the town go through its paces and commenting on life when the spirit moved them. He was far too busy to indulge in that sort of thing.

"Well, if you don't need directions, then I'll get back to my work," he told her. The woman was clearly out of her element, but if she didn't want to talk about what she was doing out here, he wasn't about to prod her. Lost or not, it was strictly her business.

"I don't need directions, but I do have a question."

She raised her voice as if to get his attention before he began hammering again.

Finn turned back to face her. She looked rather fair. He could see a sunburn in her near future if she didn't at least put the top up on her car. Skin that fair was ripe for burning.

"Which is?" he asked casually.

"Did you build this yourself?" The woman got out of her car and crossed to the freshly rebuilt front steps of the house.

Thanks to Brett, honesty had always been at the core of his behavior. His older brother expected and accepted nothing less than that. Anyone can lie, Brett maintained, but it took a real man to tell the truth each and every time, even when it wasn't easy.

"No," Finn replied. "The ranch house was already here. I just changed things around a little, replaced what needed replacing, added a little here, a little there—that kind of thing," he told her simply.

He made it sound as if he'd hammered down a few loose boards, but one look at the exterior told her that the man with the impossibly appealing physique had done a great deal more than just that. The structure looked brand-new. She knew for a fact that this part of the state was hard on its buildings and its terrain. Summers could be brutal, and they left their mark on practically everything, especially structures. The ranch house she was looking at had been resurfaced, replaced and renovated—and recently.

Connie couldn't help wondering if that craftsmanship extended to the inside of the building, as well.

There was only one way to find out.

"Could you take me on a tour of the inside of the house?" she asked brightly.

"I could," the cowboy answered but made no effort to follow through on her request.

"But?" she asked.

She made him think of a stick of dynamite about to go off. He was about ten inches taller than she was, but a stick of dynamite didn't have to be very big to make a sizable impression.

Just who was this woman, and what was she doing here? "But I don't even know who you are."

"I'm not dangerous, if that's what you're thinking," she told him.

Like he believed that.

Finn's mouth curved ever so slightly, the left side more than the right. He wondered just how many men this woman had brought to their knees with that killer smile of hers.

"There's dangerous, and then there's *dangerous*," he replied, his eyes never leaving hers.

She raised her chin just a little, doing her best to generate an air of innocence as she assured him, "I'm neither."

The cowboy continued looking at her. The image of a human lie detector flashed through her mind for an instant. She discovered that breathing took a bit of concentration on her part.

"I don't know about that," he said. But the next moment, he seemed to shrug away his assessment of her and said, "Okay, why not? Don't lean against anything," he warned before going up the porch steps. "The paint's still fresh in places."

She had no intentions of taking away any part of this house on her person. "I'll keep that in mind," she told him.

Connie waited for her tour guide to open the front door. If the inside looked nearly as good as the outside, she was ready to be blown away.

"After you," the cowboy told her once he'd opened the front door.

Connie crossed the threshold, taking it all in at once.

She hadn't missed her guess. The inside of the house was simplistic and all the more captivating for that. It was a house that emphasized all things Western, with just the right touch of modern thrown in to keep the decor from being completely entrenched in the past.

There were only a few pieces of furniture. For the most part, the house was empty, but then, she hadn't asked to come in just to see the furniture. She was looking to take stock of the workmanship firsthand.

She hadn't been wrong.

This cowboy did have a gift for bringing things together—and apparently, a knack for knowing just when to back off.

"How long have you been working on this?" she asked, wanting as much input from the man and *about* the man as she could get.

"Awhile," Finn replied vaguely, as if wondering just what her end game was.

WHILE THIS WOMAN had apparently been taking stock of the house as he went about showing her around the two floors, Finn did the same with her. So far, he hadn't come to any useful conclusion. She hadn't really volunteered anything except a few flattering comments about his work. He still had no idea what had brought her to Forever, or even if she *meant* to come to Forever, or was just passing by on her way to somewhere else.

"Awhile," the woman repeated, going back to what he'd said about his timetable. "Does that mean six months or six years or what?"

"Awhile means awhile," he replied in a calm voice, then added, "I'm not exactly keeping a diary on this."

"Then you're just doing this for fun?"

"Not exactly." Because he could see that she intended to stand there, waiting, until he gave her some sort of a more satisfying answer, he told her. He saw no reason not to. "It's a wedding present."

"For your bride?" she guessed.

Finn nearly choked. He didn't intend to get married for a very long time. Possibly never.

"No," he denied with feeling. "For my brother. It's *his* wedding."

"And this is his house?" she asked, turning slowly around, this time taking in a three-hundred-sixty-degree view. No doubt about it, she thought. The work done on the ranch house was magnificent.

"He says it belongs to all three of us, but Earl Robertson's will left it to him." And as far as he and Liam were concerned, this was Brett's house.

"Honor among brothers. That's refreshing."

He thought that was an odd way to phrase it. "Don't know one way or the other about *refreshing.* Do know what's right, though, and this house is right for Brett and Lady Doc."

"Lady Doc?" she repeated, slightly confused.

"That was the nickname my brother gave Alisha when she first came to Forever. Alisha's a doctor," he told her by way of a footnote. "Look, lady, I'd love to stand around and talk some more—it's not every day that we see a new face around here—but I really do have to get back to work."

The woman raised her hands in mock surrender, showing the cowboy that she was backing off and giving him back his space. "Sorry. I didn't mean to take you away from your work."

Having said that, she turned on her heel and headed back to her vehicle.

As he watched her walk away, Finn found himself captivated by the way the woman's hips swayed with every step she took. It also occurred to him at the same time that he didn't even know her name.

"Hey," he called out.

Ordinarily, that was *not* a term Connie would answer to. But this one time, she made an exception. People acted differently out here. So rather than get into her car, Connie turned around and looked at him, waiting for the cowboy to say something further.

Raising his voice, Finn remained where he was. "You got a name?" he asked.

"Yes, I do," Connie replied.

With that she slid in behind the steering wheel of her car, shut her door and started up her engine.

Always leave them wanting more was an old adage she had picked up along the way, thanks to her grandfather. Her grandfather had taught her a great many things. He had told her, just before he passed away, that he had great faith in her. The only thing her father had ever conveyed to her was that she was a huge and ongoing source of disappointment to him.

Her grandfather, she knew, would have walked away from her father a long time ago. At the very least, he would have given up trying to please her father, given up trying to get him to take some sort of positive notice of her.

But she was too stubborn to give up.

Knocked down a number of times for one reason or another, she still got up, still dusted herself off and was still damn determined to someday make her father actually pay her a compliment—or die trying to get it out of him.

CONNIE SPENT THE rest of the afternoon driving around, getting marginally acquainted with the lay of the surrounding land. She took in the reservation, as well—if driving around its perimeter could be considered taking it in. She never got out of her vehicle, never drove through the actual terrain because even circumnavigating it managed to create an almost overwhelming sadness within her.

Her father had been right about one thing. She was a child of affluence. The sight of poverty always upset her. But rather than fleeing and putting it out of her mind, what she had seen seemed to seep into her very soul. She could not imagine how people managed to go on day after day in such oppressive surroundings.

It also made her wonder why the reservation residents didn't just band together, tear some of the worst buildings down and start fresh, putting up something new in their place.

Not your problem, Con. Your father issued you a challenge. One he seemed pretty confident would make you fall flat on your face. It's up to you to show him once and for all that he's wrong about you. That he's underestimated you all along.

THAT THOUGHT WAS still replaying itself in her head when she finally drove back into Forever late that afternoon. She was hungry, and the idea of dinner—even one prepared at what she viewed to be a greasy-spoon establishment—was beginning to tempt her.

But as much as she wanted to eat, she wanted to finish up her homework even more.

In this case, her homework entailed checking out the local—and lone—bar to see the kind of people who hung out there. She wanted to meet them, mingle with them and get to know them, at least in some cursory fashion. She was going to need bodies if she hoped to get her project underway, and Murphy's was where she hoped to find at least some of them.

Right now all she knew was that her father had purchased a tract of land within Forever at a bargain price because no one else was interested in doing anything with it. A little research on her part had shown that the town was deficient in several key departments, not the least of which was that it had nowhere to put up the occasional out-of-town visitor—which she just assumed Forever had to have at least once in a while. That particular discovery was confirmed when she went to book a hotel room and found that the nearest hotel was some fifty miles away from the center of Forever.

The hick town, her father had informed her through Emerson, his right-hand man, needed to have a hotel built in its midst. Giving her the assignment, her father washed his hands of it, leaving all the details up to her.

And just like that, it became her responsibility to get the hotel built for what, on paper, amounted to a song.

Her father had hinted that if she could bring the project in on time and on budget—or better yet, *under* budget, he might just take her potential within the company more seriously.

But she needed to prove herself worthy of his regard, of his trust. And until that actually happened, he had no real use for her. He made no effort to hide the fact that he was on the verge of telling her that he no longer needed her services.

Connie had every intention of showing her father just what a vital asset she could be to his construction conglomerate. She also promised herself that she was going to make him eat his words; it was just a matter of time.

Stopping her vehicle behind Murphy's, Connie parked the car as close to the building as she could. The gleaming white sports car wasn't a rental she was driving, it was her own car. She wasn't superstitious by nature, but every good thing that had ever happened to her had happened when she was somewhere within the vicinity of the white sports car. It was, in effect, her good-luck talisman. And, as the embodiment of her good fortune, she wanted to keep it within her line of vision, ensuring that nothing could happen to it.

She intended on keeping an eye on it from inside the bar.

However, Connie quickly discovered that was an impossibility. For one thing, the bar's windows didn't face the rear lot.

Uneasy, she thought about reparking her car or coming back to Murphy's later, after dinner.

But then she reminded herself that her car had a tracking chip embedded within the steering wheel. If her car was stolen, the police could easily lay hands on it within the hour.

Provided they knew about tracking chips and how to use them, she qualified silently. She took measure of the occupants within the bar as she walked in. The first thought that crossed her mind was that the people around her could never be mistaken for the participants in a think tank.

Still looking around, she made her way to the bar, intending on ordering a single-malt beer.

A deep male voice asked her, "What'll it be?" when she reached the bar and slid onto a stool.

The voice sounded vaguely familiar, but she shrugged the thought away. She didn't know anyone here. "What kind of beer do you have on tap?" she asked, continuing to take inventory of the room.

"Good beer."

The answer had her looking at the bartender instead of the bar's patrons. When she did, her mouth dropped open.

"You," she said in stunned surprise.

"You," Finn echoed, careful to hide his initial surprise at seeing her.

Unlike the woman seated at that bar, he'd had a couple of minutes to work through his surprise. It had spiked when he first saw her walk across the threshold. Disbelief had turned into mild surprise as he watched her make her way across the floor, weaving in and out between his regular patrons.

When she'd left the ranch this morning, he'd had a vague premonition that he would be seeing her again— but he hadn't thought that it would be this soon. He should have known better. The woman had asked too many questions for someone who was just passing through on her way to somewhere else.

"So what are you?" The woman posed the question to him. "A rancher or a bartender?"

"Both," he said without the slightest bit of hesitation. Around here, a man had to wear a lot of hats if he planned on surviving. "At least, that's what my brother says."

"The one who's getting married," she recalled.

So, she had been listening. That made her a rare woman, Finn concluded. The women in his sphere of acquaintance talked, but rarely listened. "That's the one."

"You have any more brothers?"

"Yeah, he's a spare in case I wear the other one out."

The woman looked around, taking in the people on either side of her. The bar had its share of patrons, but it was far from standing-room only. Still, there were enough customers currently present—mostly male— for her to make a judgment.

"Something tells me that the men around here don't wear out easily."

"You up for testing that theory of yours out, little lady?" Kyle Masterson proposed, giving her a very thorough once-over as he sidled up to her, deliberately blocking her access to the front door.

Chapter Three

Although he remained behind the bar, Finn's presence seemed to separate the talkative cowboy from the young woman who had wandered onto Brett's ranch earlier. Finn was 85 percent certain that Kyle, a rugged, rather worn ranch hand, was harmless. But he was taking no chances in case Kyle was inspired by this woman and was tossing caution to the wind.

"Back to your corner, Masterson," Finn told him without cracking a smile. "The lady's not going to be testing out anything with you tonight."

Kyle, apparently, had other ideas. "Why don't you let her speak for herself, Murphy?" the other man proposed. "How about it, little lady?" he asked, completely ignoring Finn and moving in closer to the woman who had caught his fancy. "We could take us a stroll around the lake, maybe look up at the stars. See what happens."

His leer told her exactly what the hulking man thought was going to happen. Amused, Connie played out the line a little further. "And if nothing happens?" she posed.

"Then I will be one deeply disappointed man," Kyle

told her, dramatically placing a paw of a hand over his chest. "C'mon, little lady. You don't want to be breaking my heart now, do you?" He eyed her hopefully, rather confident in the outcome of this scenario he was playing out.

"Better that than me breaking your arm, Masterson," Finn informed him, pushing his arm and hand between them as he deliberately wiped down the bar directly in the middle.

Kyle glanced from Finn to the very appealing woman with hair the color of a setting sun. It was obvious he was weighing his options. Women came and went, but there was only one saloon in the area. Being barred from Murphy's was too high a price to pay for a fleeting flirtation.

"Oh, is it like that, now?" the cowboy guessed.

"Like what?" Connie looked at the man, not sure she understood his meaning.

Amazingly deep-set eyes darted from her to the bartender and then back again, like black marbles in a bowl.

Kyle grinned at the bartender. "Don't think I really have to explain that," he concluded. Raising his glass, he toasted Finn. "Nice work, laddie." And with that, the bear of a man retreated into the crowd.

Brett approached from the far side of the bar. "Problem?" he asked, looking from his brother to the very attractive young woman at the bar. He'd taken note of the way some of his patrons were watching her, as if she were a tasty morsel, and they were coming off a

seven-day fast in the desert. That spelled trouble—
unless it was averted quickly.

"No, no problem," Finn replied tersely. As grateful as he was to Brett and as much as he loved and
respected him, he hated feeling that his older brother
was looking over his shoulder. He wasn't twelve anymore, and hadn't been for quite some time. "Everything's fine."

"That all depends," Connie said, contradicting
Finn's response. She had a different take on things,
one that had nothing to do with the hulking cowboy
and his unsuccessful advances.

Brett looked at her with interest. "On?"

"On how many men I can get to sign on with me,"
Connie replied.

The sudden, almost syncopated shift of bodies, all
in her direction, plainly testified that the exchange between the young woman and two of the saloon's own-
ers was far from private. Leers instantly materialized,
and interweaving voices were volunteering to sign on
with her no matter what the cause.

In Finn's estimation, it was obvious what the men's
leers indicated that they *believed* they were signing up
for—and tool belts had nothing to do with it.

To keep the crowd from getting rowdy and out of
control, Finn quickly asked the question, "Sign on to
what end?" before Brett could.

Crystal-blue eyes swept over the sea of faces, taking preliminary measure of the men in the saloon. "I
need a crew of able-bodied men to help me build a
hotel," she answered.

"Build a hotel?" an older man in the back echoed incredulously. By the way he repeated the proposed endeavor, it was obvious that a hotel was the last structure he would have thought the town needed. He wasn't alone. "Where you putting a hotel?"

Connie answered as if she was fielding legitimate questions at a business meeting. "The deed says it's to be constructed on the east end of town, just beyond the general store."

"Deed? What deed?" someone else within the swelling throng crowing around her asked.

Connie addressed that question, too, as if it had everything riding on it. She had learned how *not* to treat men by observing her father. He treated the men around him as if they were morons—until they proved otherwise. She did the exact opposite.

Employees—and potential employees—had her respect until they did something to lose it.

"The deed that my company purchased a little less than three weeks ago," she replied, then waited for the next question.

"Deeds are for ranches," Nathan McHale, Murphy's' most steadfast and longest-attending patron said into his beer, "not hunks of this town."

Connie shifted her stool to get a better look at the man. "I'm afraid you're wrong there, Mr—?" She left the name open, waiting for the man to fill it in for her.

Nathan paused to take a long sip from his glass, as if that would enable him to remember the answer to the newcomer's question. Swallowing, he looked up, a somewhat silly smile on his wide, round face.

"McHale."

"Don't worry about him, missy. Ol' Nathan's used to being wrong. The second he steps into his house, his wife starts telling him he's wrong," Alan Dunn, one of the older men at the far end of the bar chuckled.

Nathan seemed to take no offense. Instead, what he did take was another longer, more fortifying drink from his glass, this time managing to drain it. Putting the glass down on the bar, he pushed it over toward the bartender—the younger of the two behind the bar.

Connie noticed that the latter eyed his customer for a moment, as if deciding whether or not to cut the man off yet. She knew that she definitely would—and was rather surprised when the bartender decided not to.

For all his girth and folds, McHale looked like a child at Christmas, his eyes lighting up and a wreath of smiles taking over his rounded face. He gave the bartender who had refilled his glass a little salute as well as widening his appreciative smile.

Using both hands, he drew the glass to him, careful not to spill a single drop. Then, just before he took his first sip of his new drink, McHale raised it ever so slightly in a symbolic toast to the newcomer. "You were saying?"

"I was saying—" Connie picked up the thread of her conversation where it had temporarily stopped "—that my construction company has purchased the deed for a section of the town's land."

"You here to see if the town wants to buy it back?" Brett asked, curious.

There'd been complaints from time to time that there

was nowhere to stay if anyone was stranded in Forever overnight. But things always got sorted out for the best. The sheriff enjoyed telling people that was how he and his wife, Olivia, had first gotten together. On her way to track down her runaway sister, Olivia'd had no intentions of staying in Forever. Her car had had other ideas. She'd wound up relying on the hospitality of the town's resident wise woman and diner owner, Miss Joan.

"No," Connie replied patiently, "I'm here to build a hotel."

"A hotel?" It was someone else's turn to question the wisdom of that. Obviously, more than one person found this to be an odd undertaking. "What for?" the person asked.

"For people to stay in, you nitwit," the man sitting on the next stool informed him, coupling the sentence with a jab in the ribs.

"What people?" a third man asked. "Everyone around here's got a home."

Connie was ready for that, as well. She'd read up on Forever before ever setting out to see it. She knew her father wouldn't have given her an easy project. That had never been his way.

"Well, if there's a hotel here," she said, addressing her answer to the entire bar, "it might encourage people to come to Forever."

"Why would we want people to come here?" the man who'd asked her the question queried again. "We got all the people we know what to do with now."

Several other voices melded together, agreeing with him.

Connie was far from put off, but before she could say anything, the good-looking man she'd seen this afternoon beat her to it.

"She's talking about the town growing, Clyde," Finn pointed out. "You know, *progress.*"

Connie fairly beamed at the bartender, relieved that at least *someone* understood what she was trying to convey. "Exactly," she cried.

"Hell, progress is highly overrated," Clyde declared sourly. He downed his shot of whiskey, waited for it to settle in, then said, "I like this town just fine the way it is. Peaceful," he pronounced with a nod of his bald head.

This was not the time or the place to become embroiled in a hard sell. The land officially now belonged to her father's company, thanks to some negotiations she had not been privy to. That meant that the decision as to what to do or not do with it was not up to the people lining the bar.

Be that as it may, she was still going to need them, or at least some of them, to help with the hotel's construction. That meant she couldn't afford to alienate *any* of them. Besides the fact that local labor was always less expensive than bringing construction workers in, hiring locals always built goodwill. There wasn't a town or city in the country that hadn't felt the bite of cutbacks and didn't welcome an opportunity to obtain gainful employment, even on a temporary basis.

This was not the first project she was associated

with, although it was the first that she was allowed to helm on her own. She already knew she was going to need a few skilled workers, like someone who could handle the backhoe, and those people would be flown in. But as for the rest of it, the brawn and grunt part, those positions she hoped she would be able to fill with people from in and around the town. The one thing she knew she could count on was that extra money was always welcomed.

Connie raised her voice, addressing Clyde. "I promise not to disturb the peace." For good measure, she elaborately crossed her heart. "I came here to offer you jobs. I need manpower to help me make this hotel a reality."

This time it was Kyle Masterson who spoke up. He hired out to some of the local ranchers, but he had never been afraid of hard work. "What kind of money we talking about?"

She made eye contact with the big man. "Good money," she responded in all seriousness.

"How much?" Brett asked, trying to pin her down not for himself, but for the men who frequented Murphy's, men he knew were struggling with hard times and bills that were stamped *past due*.

"Depends on the level of skills you bring to the job," she replied honestly. "That'll be decided on an individual basis."

"Who's gonna do the deciding?" another man at the bar asked.

The question came from behind her. Connie turned to face whoever had spoken up. They were going to find out sooner or later, might as well be sooner, she thought. "I am."

"Big decisions," the man responded with a laugh. He eyed her in clear amusement. She obviously looked like a slip of a thing in comparison to the men she was addressing. "You sure you're up to it, honey?"

Connie had never had any slack cut for her. Her father had made sure that she was treated like a crew member no matter what job she was doing. The fact that she was willing to—and did—work hard had not failed to impress the men, even if it seemed to have no effect whatsoever on her father.

Connie looked the man asking the question directly in the eye and said with no hesitation, "I am. Are you?"

Her answer generated laughter from the other men around the bar.

"She's got you there, Roy. Looks like you better make nice if you want to earn a little extra for your pocket," the man next to him advised.

"It'll be more than just a *little extra*," Connie was quick to correct. "And if you work hard and get this project in on time and on budget, everyone on the project will get a bonus."

The promise of a bonus, even an unspecified one, never failed to stir up positive goodwill, and this time was no exception. Snippets of responses and more questions furiously flew through the air.

"Sounds good!"

"Count me in."

"Hey, is the bonus gonna be as big as the salary?"

"You calculating that by the hour or by the day?"

Finn had stood by, holding his tongue for the most part. The woman doing the talking had intrigued him right from the start when she'd first approached him this morning. Since his bent was toward building, anyway, he figured that he might have to do a little negotiation with Brett to get some free time in order to get involved on this construction project.

But he didn't see that as being a problem. Brett was fairly reasonable when it came to things like this. He'd given Liam a lot of slack so he could practice and rehearse with his band. As far as older brothers went, a man would have to go to great lengths to find someone who was anywhere near as good as Brett.

"Looks like you've got them all fired up and excited," Finn commented to the young woman as he checked her glass to see if she needed a refill yet.

"How about you? Do I have you all fired up and excited?" she asked, going with his wording. Connie shifted the stool to face him. The man was still her first choice to head up the work crew. The other men might be good—or even more capable—but so far this so-called bartender's handiwork had been the only one she'd seen firsthand.

But the moment she phrased the question, she saw her mistake.

Finn had every intention of giving her a flippant answer, but there was something in her eyes, something that had him skidding to a grinding halt and reassessing not just his answer, but a hell of a lot of other things, as well. Things that had nothing to do with tools and construction.

The woman on the stool before him probably had no idea that she had the kind of eyes that seemed to peer into a man's soul while making him reevaluate everything that had happened in his life up to this singular moment in time.

A beat went by before he realized that she was still waiting for him to respond.

"Yes," he answered quietly, his eyes on hers. He found he couldn't look away even if he wanted to—which he didn't. "You do," he added in the same quiet tone.

Despite the surrounding din, his voice managed to undulate along her skin and lodge itself directly beneath it.

It took Connie more than a full second to come to, then another full second to find her voice and another one after that to realize that her mouth and throat had gone bone-dry. If she said more than a couple of words, they could come out in a comical croak, thereby negating whatever serious, or semiserious thing she was about to say.

Taking the drink that was on the bar before her, she emptied the glass in an effort to restore her voice to its initial working order. Tears suddenly gathered in her eyes as flames coasted through her veins. She'd forgotten her glass contained whiskey, not something less potent.

"Good," she managed to say without the word sticking to the roof of her mouth. Taking a breath, she willed herself to be steady and then completed her sentence.

Nothing could interfere with work. She wouldn't allow it to. "Because I have just the position for you."

Most likely not the same position I have in mind for you.

The thought, materializing out of nowhere, took Finn completely by surprise. He was extremely grateful that the words hadn't come out of his mouth. It wasn't his intention to embarrass either himself or the young woman.

But he found that he was having trouble banishing the thought out of his head. The image seemed to be all but burned into his brain. An image that was suddenly making him feel exceedingly warm.

Finn focused on the hotel she had been talking about. This represented the first move toward progress that had been made in Forever in quite some time.

"What kind of a position?" he asked her out loud, rubbing perhaps a bit too hard at a spot on the bar's counter.

"Is there someplace we can talk?" she asked him.

Finn thought of the room that was just above the saloon. Initially, their uncle Patrick had lived there when he'd owned and operated Murphy's. On his passing, it had been just an extra room that all three of them had sporadically availed themselves of if the occasion warranted it. Currently, however, Brett's fiancée was staying there, but only when she wasn't working—or staying with Brett at the ranch. The clinic was still open, which meant that the room would be empty.

But Finn didn't feel comfortable just commandeering it—besides, Brett would undoubtedly have his head if he found out.

The next moment, Finn felt he had come up with a viable alternative. "Have you had dinner yet?" he asked the woman.

"No." She had been so worked up about this project, so eager to get it going, that she had completely forgotten about eating.

"Then I know just the place we can talk. Brett," Finn called, turning toward his brother. "I'm taking my break now."

Motivated by his interest in anything that had an effect on the town, Brett had discreetly listened in on the conversation between Finn and this woman. He appeared mildly amused at his brother's choice of words. "You planning on being back in fifteen minutes?"

"A couple of breaks, then—plus my dinner break," Finn added for good measure.

"You already took that, don't you remember?" Brett deadpanned.

"Then my breakfast break," Finn shot back, exasperated.

Brett inclined his head. "That should work," he told Finn. "Just don't forget to come back," he called after his brother as Finn made his way around the bar.

Escorting the woman through the throng of patrons, most of whom were now keenly interested in what this newcomer to their town had to offer, Finn waved a hand over his head. This signified to Brett that he had heard him and was going to comply—eventually.

"Where are we going?" Connie asked once they made it through the front door.

"To dinner," Finn repeated.

"And that would be—?"

Finn grinned. "At Miss Joan's," he answered.

"Miss Joan's?" she repeated. The name meant nothing to her.

"The diner," Finn prompted. "It's the only restaurant in town."

For now, Connie corrected silently. Plans for the hotel included a restaurant on the premises.

But for the time being, she thought it best to keep that to herself.

Chapter Four

Since she had already ascertained that it was the only so-called restaurant in town, Connie had initially intended on checking the diner out after she left Murphy's. But seeing the cowboy who had, she admitted—although strictly to herself—taken her breath away—both because of his craftsmanship *and* his physique—she'd temporarily lost sight of the plan she'd laid out for herself to round out her first day in Forever.

The bartending cowboy opened the door for her and she stepped into the diner. Connie scanned the area, only to discover that everyone in the diner was looking right back at her.

Before taking another step, she unconsciously squared her shoulders.

Inside the brash, confident young woman who faced down all sorts of obstacles, beat the heart of a shy, young girl, the one whose father had always made her feel, through his words and through his actions, that she wasn't good enough. That she couldn't seem to measure up to the standards he had set down before her.

Even though he had told her, time and again, that she was a source of constant disappointment to him, Calvin Carmichael had insisted that, from the relatively young age of fourteen, his only daughter replace her late mother and act as a hostess at the parties that he threw for his business associates.

It was while acting as hostess at those very same parties that she developed her polish and her poise—at least on the surface. Only her father knew how to chip away at that veneer to get to the frightened little girl who existed just beneath that carefully crafted surface.

To be fair, her father had been just as demanding of her brother, Conrad. But Conrad had been far more rebellious than she ever was. He absolutely refused to be bullied and left home for parts unknown the moment that he turned eighteen.

She would have given *anything* to go with him, but she was only fourteen at the time, and Conrad had enough to do, looking after himself. He couldn't take on the burden of being responsible for a child, as well.

At least that was what she had told herself when he'd left without her.

So Connie resigned herself to remaining in her father's world, desperately treading water, determined to survive as best she could. Not only surviving, but vowing to one day make her father realize how wrong he'd been about her all along. It was the one thing that had kept her going all this time.

The *only* thing.

Was it her imagination, or were the occupants of

the diner looking at her as if she were some sort of an unknown entity?

She inclined her head in her companion's direction, lowering her voice to a whisper. "You weren't kidding about not many tourists passing through this town. These people really aren't used to seeing strangers walking their streets, are they?"

Finn's mouth curved ever so slightly. "Forever's not exactly on the beaten path to anywhere," he pointed out. Although, even if Forever was a regular bustling hotbed of activity, he could see this woman still turning heads wherever she went.

"That's becoming pretty clear," Connie whispered to him.

"Been wondering when you'd finally step in here," the thin, older woman with the somewhat overly vibrant red hair said as she sidled up to the couple to greet them. "What'll it be for you and your friend here, Finn?" she asked, nodding her head toward the other woman. "Table or counter?"

Connie was about to answer "Counter," but the man the hostess had referred to as "Finn" answered the question first.

"Table."

The woman nodded. "Table it is. You're in luck. We've got one table left right over here." So saying, the redhead led them over to a table near the kitchen. There was only one problem, as Connie saw it. There was a man still sitting at it.

Connie regarded the other woman. "But it's occupied," she protested. Did the woman think they were going to join the man?

The woman appeared unfazed. "Hal here finished his dinner," she explained, indicating the table's lone occupant. "He's just a might slow in getting to his feet, aren't you, Hal?" she said, giving her customer exactly ten seconds of her attention. Then she looked around for the closest waitress and summoned her. "Dora." She beckoned the young blonde over. "Clear the table for Finn and his friend, please." She offered the couple just a hint of a smile. "I'll be back to get your orders in a few minutes. Sit, take a load off," she encouraged, patting Connie on the shoulder. And then she added, "Relax," and turned the single word into a strict command.

Dora was quick to pick up and clear away the empty dinner plate from the table. Within two minutes, Dora retreated, and Connie realized that she and the cowboy were left alone with their menus.

Connie was only mildly interested in glancing over the menu and that was purely out of a curiosity about the locals' eating preferences. As always, eating, for Connie, took a backseat to orientation.

She decided to begin with the very basics. Names. Specially, his name. "That woman, the one with the red hair, she called you Finn."

"That's because she knows my name," he replied simply. Finn had a question of his own to ask her. "But I don't know yours."

"I didn't tell you?" The omission on her part surprised her. She'd gotten so caught up in getting her op-

eration set up and hopefully rolling soon in this tiny
postage-stamp-size town that common, everyday details had slipped her mind.

"You didn't tell me," Finn confirmed, then added
with yet another, even more appealing hint of a smile,
"I'm not old enough to be forgetful yet."

Not by a long shot, Connie caught herself thinking.
Just for a moment, she got lost in the man's warm, incredibly inviting smile.

*Get back on track, Con. Drooling over the employ-
ees isn't going to get this project done—and it just
might mess everything all up.*

One way or another, she'd been lobbying her father
for a chance to show her stuff for a while. Now that she
finally had it, she was *not* about to allow something as
unpredictable as hormones betray her.

"My name is Constance Carmichael," she told him,
putting out her hand.

"Nice to meet you, Ms. Carmichael." Her hand felt
soft, delicate in his, he couldn't help thinking.
His hand all but swallowed hers up. "I'm Finn Murphy."

"Like the bar?" she asked, trying to fit two more
pieces together.

"Like the bar," he confirmed.

"My father's Calvin Carmichael," Connie added.

She was accustomed to seeing instant recognition
whenever she mentioned her father's name. The second
she did, a light would come into people's eyes.

There was no such light in the bartending cowboy's

eyes. It prompted her to say, "He founded Carmichael Construction Corporation."

Still nothing.

Finn lifted his broad shoulders in a self-deprecating shrug and apologized. "Sorry, 'fraid it doesn't ring a bell for me."

That was when it hit her. "I guess it wouldn't," Connie said. "The corporation only erects buildings in the larger cities." The moment she said it, she knew she had made a tactical mistake. The man sitting across the table from her might take her words to be insulting. "I mean—"

Finn raised his hand to stop whatever she might be about to say. "Forever *is* small," he assured her. "And that leads me to my question for you."

Her eyes never left his. "Go ahead."

Having given him the green light, Connie braced herself for whatever was going to be coming her way. Something told her that Finn was one of the key players she would need to solidly win over and keep on her side if she hoped to not only get this project underway, but completed, as well.

"If your dad's company just builds things in big cities, then what are you doing scouting around someplace like Forever?" It didn't make any sense to him. He loved the place, but there wasn't anything exceptional about Forever to make outsiders suddenly sit up and take notice.

It's personal, Connie thought, silently answering him.

Granted, the man was pretty close to what one of

her friends would have termed *drop-dead gorgeous,* but she didn't know a single thing about him other than he was good with his hands and could tend bar, so trusting him with any part of her actual life story would have been beyond foolish, beyond reckless and definitely stupid.

Connie searched around for something neutral to say that would satisfy Finn's curiosity. And then she came up with the perfect response.

"He's branching out," she told him, then fell back on what had always been a sure-fire tactic: flattery. "Besides, there's a lot of potential in little towns like yours."

Though he wasn't quite sold, Finn quietly listened to what this stunningly attractive woman had to say. For now, he'd allow her to think he'd accepted her flimsy explanation. Since she was obviously sticking around, he figured that eventually, he'd find out just what part of what she had said was the truth.

Miss Joan picked that moment to all but material- ize out of nowhere, a well-worn pad held poised in her hand. "So, you two ready to order yet?" she asked them.

Finn had barely glanced at the menu, but then, he didn't really have to. His favorite meal was a perma- nent fixture on the second page.

"I am," he told Miss Joan, "but I don't think that Ms. Carmichael's had a chance to look at the menu just yet."

Rather than go with the excuse that Finn had just provided her with, Connie placed her menu on top of his and told the woman, "I'll just have whatever he's having."

"How do you know it's any good?" Finn challenged, mildly surprised by her choice. "Or that you'll like it?"

"I'm a quick judge of character, and you wouldn't order anything that was too filling, or bad for you. You told your brother that you were coming back to work the rest of your shift. That means that you can't be too full or you'll get drowsy," she concluded. "Besides, I'm not very fussy."

Miss Joan smiled in approval, then nodded toward her as she said to Finn, "This one's smart. Might want to keep her hanging around for a bit. Okay, boy," Miss Joan said, shifting gears when she saw the slight change of color in Finn's complexion, "what'll it be?"

Finn placed his order, asking for a no-frills burger and a small order of home fries, along with some iced coffee. Miss Joan duly noted his order, then murmured, "Times two," before she glanced over toward Finn's companion. She waited for the young woman to change her mind.

She didn't.

About to leave, Miss Joan turned abruptly and looked at Finn's tablemate. "Ms. Carmichael," she repeated thoughtfully.

"Yes?" Connie considered the older woman, not quite knowing what to expect.

The light of recognition came into Miss Joan's sharp, amber eyes. "Your daddy wouldn't be Calvin C. Carmichael now, would he?"

"You know my father?"

She would have expected the bartender and the people around his age to know who her father was. Since he apparently didn't, she felt it was a given that someone around this woman's age—someone she assumed had been born here and most likely would die here—would have never even *heard* of her father.

"Mostly by reputation," Miss Joan admitted. She thought back for a moment. "Although I did meet the man once a long time ago. He was just starting out then," she recalled. And then her smile broadened. "He was a pistol, all right. Confident as all get-out, wasn't about to let anything or anyone stop him." Miss Joan nodded to herself as more facts came back to her. "He was bound and determined to build himself an empire. From what I hear now and again, he did pretty much that."

Rather than wait for any sort of a comment or a confirmation from Finn's companion, Miss Joan asked another question, a fond smile curving her mouth. "How's your mother doing?"

"She died a little over twelve years ago," Connie answered without missing a single beat, without indicating that the unexpected reference to her mother felt as if she had just been shot point-blank in her chest. Twelve years, and the wound was still fresh.

Usually, she had some sort of an inkling, a forewarning that the conversation was going to turn toward a question about or a reference to her mother. In that case, Connie was able to properly brace herself for the sharp slash of pain that always accompanied any mention of her mother. But this had been like a shot in the dark, catching her completely off guard and totally unprepared and unprotected.

Sympathy flowed through Miss Joan and instantly transformed and softened the woman's features.

"Oh, I'm so sorry to hear that, dear." She placed a comforting hand on the younger woman's shoulder. "As I recall, she was a lovely, lovely woman. A real lady," she added with genuine feeling. Dropping her hand, Miss Joan began to withdraw. "I'll get that order for you now," she promised as she took her leave.

The woman sitting opposite him appeared to be trying very hard to shut down, Finn thought. He was more than familiar with that sort of reflexive action, building up high walls so that any pain attached to the loss was minimized—or as diminished as it could be, given the circumstances.

"I'm sorry about that," Finn said to her the moment they were alone again. "Miss Joan doesn't mean to come on as if she's prying. Most of the time, she just has a knack for getting to the heart of things," he told her gently.

"Nothing to apologize for," Connie answered, shaking off both his words and the feeling the older woman's question had generated. "The woman—Miss Joan, is it?" she asked. When Finn nodded, Connie went on. "Miss Joan was just making idle conversation."

Her mouth curved just a little as she allowed herself a bittersweet moment to remember. But remembering details, at times, was becoming harder and harder to do.

"She actually said something very sweet about my

mother. At this point, it's been so long since she's been gone that there are times I feel as if I just imagined her, that I never had a mother at all." She shrugged somewhat self-consciously. She'd said too much. "It's rather nice to hear someone talk about her, remember her in the same light that I do."

Because his heart was going out to her, Finn had this sudden desire to make her realize that she wasn't the only one who had suffered this sort of numbing loss so early in her life.

"I lost my mother when I was a kid, too. Both my parents, actually," Finn amended.

Despite his laid-back attitude about life and his easygoing manner, to this day it still hurt to talk about his parents' deaths. One moment they had been in his life, the next, they weren't. It was enough to shake a person clear down to their very core.

"Car accident," he said, annotating the story. "My uncle Patrick took my brothers and me in." A look Connie couldn't fathom crossed his face. The next moment, she understood why. "A few years later, Uncle Patrick died, too."

Completely captivated by his narrative, she waited for Finn to continue. When he didn't, she asked, "Who took care of you and your brothers after that? Or were you old enough to be on your own?"

"I was fourteen," he said, answering her question in his own way. "Brett had just graduated from high school. He was turning eighteen the following week, so he petitioned to be officially declared our guardian."

What he had only recently discovered was that his

brother had done that at great personal sacrifice—the girl Brett loved was setting out for the west coast. She'd asked Brett to come with her. Given a choice between following his heart and living up to his responsibility, his older brother had chosen responsibility—and never said a word about it.

"I guess you might say that Brett actually raised Liam and me—it just became official that year," Finn concluded fondly.

He and Brett had their occasional differences, but there was no way he could ever repay his brother for what Brett had done for him as well as Liam.

Connie laughed shortly. "When I was fourteen, my brother took off." She said the words dismissively, giving no indication how hurt she'd been when Conrad left her behind.

"College?" Finn guessed.

She actually had no idea where her brother went or what he did once he left her life. She hadn't heard from him in all these years.

"Maybe." She thought that over for a second. It didn't feel right to her. Conrad had been neither studious nor patient. "Although I doubt it. My father wanted my brother to go to college, and Conrad wanted to do whatever my father didn't want him to do."

"Is that why you're working for Carmichael Construction?" he asked. "Because your father wants you to?"

Remembering the look on her father's face when they had struck this deal, Connie laughed at the suggestion. Having her as anything but a lowly underling in the company was *not* on her father's agenda. The man was not pushing her in an attempt to groom her for bigger, better things. He was pushing her because he wanted to get her to finally give up and settle into the role of family hostess permanently.

"Actually," she replied crisply, "my father doesn't think I have anything to offer the company. I'm working at the corporation because *I* want to," Connie emphasized.

Reevaluating the situation, Finn read between the lines. And then smiled. "Out to prove that he's wrong, is that it?"

It startled her that he'd hit the nail right on the head so quickly, but she was not about to admit anything of the kind to someone who was, after all, still a stranger.

She tossed her hair over her shoulder. "Out to build the very best damn hotel that I can," she corrected.

Her voice sounded a little too formal and removed to her own ear. After all, the man had just been nice to her. She shouldn't be treating him as if she thought he had leprosy.

So after a beat, she added, "And if that, along the way, happens to prove to my father that he'd been wrong about me all these years, well, then, that's just icing on the cake."

Icing. That was what she made him think of, Finn realized. Light, frothy icing—with a definite, tangy kick to it.

Finn leaned back in his chair, scrutinizing the woman he'd brought to the diner. The next few months were shaping up to be very interesting, he decided.

Chapter Five

"How would you like to come and work for me?"

The question caught Finn completely off guard, but he was able to keep any indication of his surprise from registering on his face.

Rather than laughing or turning the sexy-looking woman down outright, he decided to play along for a little while and see where this was going.

"Doing what?" he asked her, sounding neither interested nor disinterested, just mildly curious as to what was behind her offer.

He'd lowered his voice and just for a split second, Connie felt as if they were having a far more intimate conversation than one involving the construction of the town's first hotel.

His question caused scenarios to flash through her brain, scenarios that had absolutely *nothing* to do with the direction of the conversation or what she was attempting to accomplish.

Scenarios that included just the two of them—and no hotel in sight.

She'd never had anything that could be labeled as

an actual *relationship,* but it had been a while between even casual liaisons. The truth of it was, she'd gotten so involved in trying to play a larger part in the construction company, not to mention in getting her father to come around, she'd wound up sacrificing everything else to that one narrow goal.

And that included having anything that even remotely resembled a social life.

Just now, she had felt the acute lack.

The next second, she'd banished the entire episode from her mind.

Without realizing it, she wet her lips before answering his question. "I want you to head up my construction crew for the new hotel."

She might not have been aware of the small, reflexive action, but Finn definitely was. It drew his attention to the shape of her lips—and the fleeting impulse to discover what those lips would have felt like against his own.

Reining in his thoughts, Finn focused on what she had just said. The only conclusion he could reach was that she had to be putting him on.

"The fact that I've never headed up a construction crew before doesn't bother you?" he asked, doing nothing to hide his skepticism.

Connie shrugged carelessly.

"There always has to be a first time," she told him.

That wasn't his point. "Granted, but—"

She wanted him for the job, but there had to be others in this blot of a town who were qualified for the position. What she'd seen at Murphy's convinced her of his leadership qualities. She was not about to beg.

"Look, if you don't want the job, just say so. I'll understand."

He raised his hand to stop her before she could go off on a tangent—or for that matter, leave. When he came right down to it, he'd be more than happy to accept her offer. But there were extenuating circumstances—even if he was to believe that she was really serious.

"Trust me," he told her, "it's not that I don't want to."

If this had been a legitimate offer, he would have snapped it up in an instant. He'd had a chance to compare how he felt when he was working on making something become a tangible reality—first the bathroom for the room above the saloon, and then restoring and renovating Brett's ranch house. He had to admit that was when he felt as if he'd come into his own, when he felt as if he'd finally found something he enjoyed doing that he was really good at.

Those were all reasons for him to pursue this line of business—God knew there was more than enough work for a builder in the area.

But that notwithstanding, Constance Carmichael had no way of knowing any of that. The woman had only been in Forever a few hours, not nearly enough time to orient herself about anyone or anything. Besides, there wasn't anyone to talk to about the quality of work he did because Brett—and Alisha—were the only ones who would have that sort of input for this woman. As far as he knew, Connie hadn't talked to either one of them about him—or about anything else for that matter.

Since she'd seen for herself that strangers really *were* rare in Forever, her fishing around for workers would have instantly become the topic of conversation.

He had no doubt that now that they had left Murphy's, the rest of the patrons were busy talking about the hotel that she had come to build. The skeptics would maintain that the project would never get off the ground because Forever didn't need a hotel, while the hopefuls would declare that it was high time progress finally paid Forever a visit.

Every one of those patrons would secretly be hoping that the promise of extra employment would actually find its way to Forever, at least for the duration of this project.

And he was definitely in that group.

"It's just that," he continued honestly, "I don't quite understand why you would want me in that sort of capacity."

The simple truth was that Connie had good gut instincts, and she'd come to rely on them.

"When I drove by the ranch house this morning, I liked what I saw."

The second the words were out of her mouth, Connie realized what they had to have sounded like to Finn. It was a struggle to keep the heat from rising up her cheeks and discoloring them. She did her best to retrace her steps.

"I mean, you looked like someone who knew what

he was doing." That still didn't say what she wanted to say, Connie thought in frustration.

She tried again, deliberately refraining from apologizing or commenting on her seemingly inability to say what she meant. She did *not* want this cowboy bartender getting the wrong idea.

Trying it one more time, Connie cleared her throat and made one last attempt at saving face as well as stating her case.

"What I'm trying to say is that I was impressed with what you had apparently done with the ranch house you said that your brother inherited."

"How do you know what I did and what was already there?" Finn asked.

"When you've been in the construction business for as long as I have, you develop an eye for it," she told him.

Finn didn't bother challenging that outright, instinctively knowing that she would take it as a personal attack on her abilities. But what he did challenge was her timeline, her claim to having years of experience.

"And just how long have you been *in the business?*" he asked. "Ten weeks?" he hazarded a guess, given her fresh appearance and her less than orthodox approach to the work.

Connie's eyes narrowed. Maybe she was wrong about this cowboy. "Try more like ten years."

Finn stared at her. The woman before him was far too young to have had that many years invested in almost *anything* except for just plain growing up. "You're kidding."

"Why would I joke about something like that?" she asked, not understanding why he would ever *think* something like that. "I got a job in the company right out of high school, working part-time. What that amounted to was any time I wasn't in college, working toward my degree, I was on one site or another, learning the trade firsthand."

Since she'd brought the subject up, he was curious. "What was your major in college?"

"It was a split one, actually," she answered. "Architecture and engineering. And I minored in business," she added.

New admiration rose in his eyes as he regarded her. "A triple threat, eh?"

She didn't see herself as a triple threat, just as prepared—and said so. "I wanted to be prepared for any possibility."

Finn nodded. His opinion of her was taking on a different form. The woman sitting opposite him, seemingly enjoying a rather cheap dinner, was multidimensional. To begin with, she had the face of an angel and the body, from what he could tell, of a model.

If she wasn't exaggerating about her background, the woman wasn't just a triple threat, she was a barely harnessed dynamo.

"Well, I think you've covered that," he told her with no small appreciation.

Because of her father, Connie was accustomed to being on the receiving end of a great deal of empty flattery uttered by men who wanted to use her as a way to get ahead with her father. She would have been inclined to say that was what was going on now, but something told her that Finn Murphy wasn't given to offering up empty flattery—or making empty gestures, either. That put his words under the heading of a genuine compliment.

"Thank you," she said quietly.

Finn leaned across the table. "Let's say, for the sake of argument, that I'm interested in working for you," he began. "Exactly what is it that you see me doing?"

"What I already said," she told him. "Heading up the work crew."

"You mean like telling people what to do?"

She nodded. "And seeing that they do it," she added with a hint of a smile. "That's a very important point," she underscored.

This didn't seem quite real to him. Who did business this way, just come waltzing into town, making snap decisions just by *looking* at people?

"And you really think I'm the one for the job by spending fifteen minutes looking at my handiwork on the ranch house?" he asked her incredulously.

"That and the way you handled yourself at the bar," she told him.

"You intend to have me serve drinks on the job?" he asked wryly. In actuality, he had no idea what his job at Murphy's would have to do with the job she was supposedly hiring him for.

"The way you handled *the men* at the bar," Connie corrected herself, emphasizing what she viewed was the crucial part. "You have an air of authority about you—it's evident in everything you do. And just so you know, that air of authority doesn't have to be loud," she told him, second-guessing that he would point out that he had hardly said a word and when he had, none of the words had been voiced particularly loudly.

"The upshot of all this is that men listen to you," she concluded.

She was thinking specifically of the man who had tried to hit on her at the bar. Finn had made the man back off without causing a scene of any sort, and she appreciated that—and saw the merit in that sort of behavior—on many levels.

"When's this job supposed to start?" he asked. "Brett's getting married in a couple of months. I can't just leave him high and dry. He needs someone to run Murphy's while he and Alisha are on their honeymoon."

She assumed that *Alisha* and the woman he had referred to earlier as *Lady Doc* were one and the same, although she wasn't really interested in names.

"We can make arrangements regarding that when the time comes," she promised. "Besides, I gather that most of Murphy's' business is conducted after six." She raised a quizzical eyebrow, waiting for his confirmation.

"Most of it," Finn agreed. "But not all of it. Brett opens the doors officially at noon, just in case someone really needs to start drowning their sorrows earlier than six."

"There's a third brother, right?"

"Liam's more into providing the music for Murphy's than he is into actually serving the drinks."

"But he can, right?"

Finn inclined his head. "Right."

That meant the solution to Finn's problem was a very simple one.

"Then you or Brett tell Liam that his services as a bartender are more important than his playing whatever it is that he plays."

"Guitar," Finn prompted. And family pride had him adding, "And he's pretty damn good. A better musician than a bartender," he told her.

That might be so, but in her estimation, this third brother's talent was not the source of the problem. Apparently, Finn needed a little more convincing.

"I guess it all boils down to what do *you* want more? To continue working at the bar, or to stretch your wings and try doing something new, try challenging yourself," she urged. "Maybe," she concluded, "it's time to put yourself first for a change."

What she had just suggested he saw as being selfish and self-centered. "That's not how family works," he told her.

"That's *exactly* how family works," she corrected with feeling. "*If* the members of that family want to get ahead in the world," she qualified, her eyes meeting his, challenging him to say otherwise.

For a moment, Finn actually thought about terminating the informal meeting then and there. He debated getting up and walking out, but then he decided that the young woman with the blue-diamond eyes apparently was here on her little mission and that if someone didn't come to her aid and pitch in, this whirling dervish in a dress would spin herself right into a huge pratfall—and a very painful one at that.

But first, she needed to be straightened out.

"I think there's something you have to realize," he told her in a slow, easy drawl that belied what he felt was the seriousness of his message.

"And that is…?" she asked.

"The people in Forever aren't really all that interested in 'getting ahead in the world' as you put it," he told her. "If they were, they would have left the area when they graduated high school, if not sooner. We're well aware that there's a big world out there, with bigger opportunities than Forever could *ever* possibly offer.

"But that's not what's important to us," he stressed, looking at her to see if he was getting through to her at all. It wasn't about the money or getting ahead; it was the pride in getting something done and done well. "You might find that bit of information useful when you're working with us."

This is a whole different world, Connie couldn't help thinking. It was totally foreign from anything she was accustomed to. But there was a bit of charm to this philosophy, to this way of viewing things—she just didn't want that *charm* getting in the way of her end goal: completing the hotel and ultimately getting it on its feet.

"I appreciate you sharing that with me," she told Finn.

He grinned. He could still read between the lines. "No, you don't. You think what I'm saying is hopelessly lazy at its worst. Horribly unproductive at its very best."

"Fortunately, I don't have to think about it at all," she told him, then smiled broadly. "Because I have you for that—" And then she realized that he still hadn't accepted the job in so many words. "Unless you've decided to turn down my offer."

"It's not an offer yet," he pointed out to her. "It's only a proposition. To be an offer," he explained when she looked at him in confusion, "you would have had to have mentioned a salary—and you haven't."

"You're right," Connie realized, then nodded her head. That, at least, could be fixed immediately. "My mistake." She rectified it in the next breath by quoting Finn a rather handsome salary.

"A month?" Finn asked, trying to put the amount in perspective. She had just quoted a sum that was a more than decent amount.

Connie shook her head. "No, that's payable each week," she corrected.

Finn stared at her. It was all he could do to keep his jaw from dropping open. The amount she'd quoted was enough to cause him to stop breathing for a moment, sincerely trying to figure out if he was dreaming or not.

"A week," he repeated, stunned at the amount of money that was being bandied about. "For someone with no work experience in the field?" he asked incredulously.

She had to be testing him, he concluded. To what end he had no idea, but nobody really earned that sort of money in a week, not unless they were crooked.

"You have life experience," she countered. "That trumps just work experience seven ways from Sunday."

Hearing the phrase made him grin.

"What?" she asked.

"Nothing." He began to wave the matter away, then stopped. What was the harm of sharing this? "It's just that I haven't heard that phrase since my mom died. She liked to say it," he confessed.

That in turn brought a smile to *her* lips.

Small world, Connie couldn't help thinking. The phrase had been a common one for her own mother.

"Wise lady," she said now.

"I like to think so." Finn gave it less than a minute before he nodded his head. "She would have liked you," he told Connie. And as far as he was concerned, that cinched it for him. Besides, it wasn't like he was signing away the next twenty years of his life.

Putting out his hand, Finn said to her, "Well, Ms. Carmichael, looks like you've got yourself a crew foreman."

Connie was fairly beaming when she said to him with relish, "Welcome to Carmichael Construction," and then shook his hand.

Chapter Six

"Well, you two seemed to have come to some sort of an amicable agreement," Miss Joan noted.

Having covertly observed the two occupants of the table from a discreet distance for the duration of their conversation, Miss Joan decided that now was the proper time to approach them.

Not that she was all that interested in restraint, but this was someone new to her, and she wanted to start out slowly with the young woman. Picking up a coffeepot as she rounded the counter, she used that as her excuse to make her way over to their table.

It was time to see if either of their coffee cups was in need of refilling. High time.

Pouring a little more coffee into both their cups, Miss Joan looked from the young woman to Finn. They had dropped their hands when she had come to their table and had now fallen into silence.

Silence had never been a deterrent for Miss Joan. On the contrary, it merely allowed her to speak without having to raise her voice.

"Anything I might be interested in knowing about?" the older woman asked them cheerfully.

Connie could only stare at the other woman, momentarily struck speechless. Granted, she was accustomed to her father's extremely blunt approach when he wanted to know something. The man never beat around the bush. His demand for information was nothing if not direct.

However, everyone else she'd ever dealt with was far more subtle about their desire to extract any useful information from her.

Miss Joan, apparently, was in a class by herself. Polite, but definitely not subtle.

Since she was in Forever for the singular purpose of getting this hotel not just off the ground but also completed, and to that end she was looking to hire local people, Connie told herself that she shouldn't feel as if her privacy had been invaded—even though she had a feeling that Miss Joan would have been just as straightforward and just as blunt with her query.

You're not here to make lasting friendships—just to get the hotel erected, Connie told herself sternly. *Act accordingly.*

So Connie smiled at Miss Joan, a woman her gut instincts told her made a far better ally than an enemy, and said to her, "Mr. Murphy here has just become my first hire."

Miss Joan's shrewd eyes darted from Finn back to the young woman. "You're looking to hire men?" she asked with a completely unreadable expression.

Finn could see that Connie's simple statement could

easily get misinterpreted and even once it was cleared up, there would undoubtedly be lingering rumors and repercussions. He came to Connie's rescue before she could say anything further.

"Ms. Carmichael is going to be building a hotel in town, and she's looking to hire construction workers," Finn told Miss Joan succinctly.

Miss Joan leaned her hip against the side of the table, turning his words over in her head.

"A hotel, eh? Something tells me you'll get the show on the road a hell of a lot quicker if you two stop referring to each other as *Ms.* and *Mr.* and just use each other's given names." And then she considered the project Finn had mentioned a moment longer. Her approval wasn't long in coming. "Might not be a bad idea at that, putting up a hotel around here. Give people a place to stay if they find themselves temporarily in Forever for one reason or another."

She straightened up then and looked directly at the young woman. "Speaking of which, where is it that you're going to be staying for the duration of this mighty undertaking, honey?" she asked.

Connie wasn't used to being accountable to anyone but her father, so it took a second to talk herself into answering. The woman was just being nosy.

"I've got a room reserved at the hotel in Pine Ridge," Connie replied, thinking how ironic that had to sound to anyone who was listening.

"Pine Ridge?" Miss Joan repeated incredulously. The expression on her face went from disbelief to dismissive. "That's at least fifty miles away from here.

You can't be driving fifty miles at the end of the day," Miss Joan informed her authoritatively. "You'll be too damn tired, might hit something you didn't intend to."

As opposed to something she *had* intended to hit? Connie wondered. She shrugged in response. "I'm afraid it can't be helped."

"Sure it can," Miss Joan insisted. "You can come and stay with me and my husband. I've got an extra bedroom you can have. No trouble at all," she added as if the discussion was over and the course of action already decided.

But it wasn't decided at all. Again, Connie could only stare at the other woman, completely stunned. How could this Miss Joan just come out and offer her a bed under her roof? Things like that just weren't done where she came from.

Wasn't the woman afraid she might be taking in a thief—or worse? Apparently, people around here were far less cautious.

"But you don't know me," Connie pointed out.

Miss Joan snorted as if that made no difference at all.

"Finn here seems to trust you, and that's good enough for me," the older woman told her. "Besides, you just said you were building a hotel here. That'll put some of our boys to work, earning more money than they have in a long while, and that's *really* good enough for me. Especially if you include some of those boys on the reservation. They're a proud bunch, but they need work just like the others." Miss Joan leveled a gaze at the younger woman. "Whatever you need," she told Connie, "you come check with me first. I'll see that you get it."

With that, Miss Joan took her leave and sauntered away.

Finn could almost see what his table companion was thinking by the stunned expression on her face. Survivors of a hurricane had the exact same expression.

"Well, that's Miss Joan all right," he commented. "She's pretty much a force of nature. But she means well. She comes through, too. And just so you know, you wouldn't be the first person who's stayed with her when they first came to town."

Connie didn't care if the woman had a guest registry a mile long, she wasn't about to accept anyone's charity. "Thanks, but I do have that hotel room reserved, and I don't mind the drive."

The latter statement wasn't really true. Connie very much *did* mind the drive, especially since she was going to be doing it at night. She was, perforce, independent, but that didn't mean that she wouldn't have preferred not having to drive a long, lonely, relatively unknown stretch of road in the dark. But she had no choice—unless she got a pup tent and camped out.

What she *did* plan on getting sent down, once the work got underway, was an on-site trailer. She'd definitely be able to sleep in it. That way, all she'd have to do was step outside her door, and she would be at work. And once her day was over, her bed wouldn't be far away.

"Suit yourself," Finn was saying. "But if I know Miss Joan, her offer stands and will continue to stand until either the hotel is finished or you actually move into someone's place here in Forever."

Connie paused for a moment, captivated by what he was saying despite the fact that her mind was racing around a mile a minute, pulling together myriad details and things she had to take care of before this work got fully underway.

She was having a hard time accepting what he was telling her. "Are you people really this open and generous?"

The corner of Finn's mouth rose in an amused semismile, just like the one, he was told, that on occasion graced his older brother's face.

"I wouldn't know about open and generous," he confessed. "We see it as business as usual," Finn told her matter-of-factly. "Everyone just looks out for everyone else here in Forever."

Any moment now, the people here were going to join hands and sing, Connie thought sarcastically.

"Yes, but I'm not an insider," she pointed out—needlessly, in her opinion. "I'm an outsider."

He laughed at her statement. "An outsider is just an insider who hasn't come in yet," Finn informed her very simply.

He was kidding, right? "That's very quaint," she told him.

He took no offense at the dismissive note in her voice. Finn had learned that some people needed a little more time to come around. He had no doubts that once her hotel was framed, she would see things differently. He could wait.

"And also true," he added.

"If you say so." Connie looked down at her plate. Dinner had somehow gotten eaten without her taking much note of it or of the process of consuming it.

Okay, it was time to call it a day for now, Connie decided. She discreetly pushed back her plate, away from her.

"Thank you for dinner," she told him, rising to her feet. "I'm going to start heading back to Pine Ridge now, but I'll be back here in the morning. We can start signing up workers then."

Finn was on his feet, as well. Knowing the prices on the menu by heart, he took out several bills and left them on the table.

"Sounds good." Getting up from the table, he walked her to the front door, acutely aware that Miss Joan was watching their every move, no matter where she was in the diner. "Where do you plan to set up?"

She stepped across the threshold. "Set up?"

He nodded. "I figure I can spread the word, round up a bunch of people for you to interview, but you're going to need to set up somewhere so you can conduct these interviews."

He was right; she needed a central place, somewhere everyone was familiar with and felt comfortable in. It took Connie less than a minute to think of the perfect place.

"How about at Murphy's? Could you open early for me?" she asked, turning directly toward him. "I could conduct interviews there, although if you vouch for the people you bring to me, I don't foresee the interview process taking very long."

She supposed that her father would have accused her of being crazy. She'd had just met this man, and she was behaving as if he was a lifelong trusted friend. But there was just something about Finn Murphy that told her he was the kind of man who always came through, who wouldn't let a person down, not even for his own personal gain. If he told her that someone was worth hiring, she saw no reason to doubt his assessment.

"Murphy's is doable," he told her.

Brett might take some convincing, Finn thought, but he had no reason to think that his brother wouldn't come around. After all, this was ultimately for the good of the town, something that always interested Brett.

"How soon are you looking to get started?" he asked.

"Yesterday," Connie answered.

He believed her.

"Then *we* have some catching up to do," he told her, walking her to her car.

It was a long drive, Connie thought as she *finally* saw the lights of Pine Ridge come into view in the distance.

It wasn't a drive she relished. Maybe she'd see about having that trailer brought in as soon as possible. Granted, the road between Forever and Pine Ridge was pretty empty, but that didn't mean she couldn't find herself accidentally driving into some sort of a ditch, especially if she fell asleep. The road was exceedingly deserted and boring. Monotony put her to sleep, hence her problem.

Mornings wouldn't be a problem. She'd be fresh in the morning, far less likely to have an accident. But even so, it was still time wasted, time she was taking away from getting the actual hotel completed.

For the good of the job, Connie began to seriously entertain taking Miss Joan up on her offer. God knew she valued her privacy, and she liked keeping to herself, separating the public Connie from the private one, but this was business and, as such, she was willing to sacrifice a lot of her own personal beliefs.

Anything to show her father she could live up to her word and be the asset to the company he was always saying he wanted.

The first thing she did when she got into her room at the hotel—besides immediately kick off her shoes and allow her toes to sink into the rug—was place a call to her father's business manager on her cell phone.

Stewart Emerson answered on the second ring. "Hello?"

The familiar, deep voice vibrated against her ear, magically creating a comfort zone for her. "Stewart, it's Connie."

Instant warmth flooded his voice. "By the tone of your voice, I take it that all systems are a go."

She laughed. Good old Stewart. The man seemed to be able to read her thoughts before she ever said anything. She'd discovered long ago that a simple hello could tell the man volumes.

Ever since she could remember, Emerson was like

the father that Calvin Carmichael wasn't, the man who made her feel that she had a safety net beneath her if she ever really needed one.

She knew without being told that he had her back in every project she had ever gotten involved in. He'd always made sure that her father only received the positive reports.

Granted, the senior Carmichael paid his salary, but Calvin Carmichael's lifelong associate reasoned that his boss's daughter had a great deal to contend with as it was; he just wanted to make it a little easier for her. He knew the sort of demands that Carmichael placed on his daughter—and he also knew that each time she came close to meeting those demands, Carmichael would raise the bar that much higher.

He had watched her grow from a little girl to the woman she had become. Watched, too, as she heartbreakingly attempted to cull and gain her father's favor, only to fail, time and again. Carmichael was the type to drive himself—and everyone in his world—hard. It made for a very successful businessman—and at the same time, a rather unsuccessful human being.

Emerson strived to somehow prevent the same sort of fate from ultimately finding Carmichael's daughter.

"So tell me how everything's going," Emerson encouraged.

"I found someone in town who's willing to help hire the right people for the crew," she told him.

"Does he have any kind of experience with construction?" Emerson asked her.

"I came across him rebuilding a ranch house. I was really impressed with what I saw," she told him.

"Are you talking about the man, or the job he did?" He put the question to her good-naturedly.

"The job he did. I don't have time for that other stuff," she told him.

"Maybe you should make time," Emerson tactfully suggested.

"Someday, Stewart," she promised strictly to placate the man. "But not today. Anyway, from the looks of it, the man seems pretty skilled."

"And you can work with him?" Emerson questioned.

"I think so," she answered honestly. There was only one problem in the foreseeable future. "But I'm still worried that it might be hard meeting the deadline Dad set down."

"You'll do it," Emerson told her with no hesitation whatsoever.

"Thanks, Stewart." And then, radiant even though there was no one to see her, or to appreciate the sight, she added, "Hearing you say that means a lot to me."

"I'm not just saying it, Connie. I know you. You're just as determined and stubborn to succeed as your old man. The only difference is that you're still human," he qualified. And then he warned her, "Don't drive yourself too hard."

She smiled to herself. "I won't."

There was a slight pause, and then he asked her, "Are you remembering to eat?"

Connie caught herself laughing at that. "Now you're beginning to sound like my mother."

"There are worse people to sound like," Emerson responded. There was a fond note in his voice, the way there always was when the conversation turned toward her mother.

Connie had long suspected that there had been a connection between Emerson and her mother. He'd never actually said as much, and she hadn't asked him. But one day, Connie promised herself, she intended to ask him. Not to pry, but to feel closer to not just her mother, but to the man she was speaking with, as well.

Her father had been no kinder to her mother than he had been to her brother, or to her. It would make her feel better to know that while she was alive, her mother'd had an ally in Stewart, someone she could turn to for emotional support, even if not a single word had been exchanged between them at the time.

That was Stewart Emerson's power, she thought now. He could make a person feel safe and protected without saying a single word to that effect. He conveyed it by his very presence.

"How about the supplies?" she asked, suddenly stifling a yawn. "Are they still coming?"

"They're already on their way," Emerson confirmed. "Now if you've had dinner, I suggest you get to bed and get some rest. If I know you, you're going to drive yourself relentlessly tomorrow—and all the tomorrows after that," he added.

Because no one ever fussed over her, she allowed herself a moment just to enjoy Stewart behaving like an overprotective mother hen.

"Been looking into your crystal ball again, Stewart?"

"Don't need one where you're concerned, Connie," he told her. "I know you like a book."

She didn't bother stifling her yawn this time. Instead, still holding her cell phone to her ear, Connie stretched out on her bed for just a moment. With little encouragement, she could allow her eyes to drift shut.

"You need new reading material, Stewart," she told him with affection.

"No, I don't. You are by far my very favorite book. You don't get rid of a favorite book, Connie, you treasure it and make sure nothing happens to it. Now say good-night and close your phone," he instructed.

"Good night," Connie murmured obediently.

She was asleep ten seconds after she hit End on her cell phone.

Chapter Seven

Connie was not unaccustomed to sleeping in hotels. In the past few years, she'd had to stay in more than her share of hotel rooms, most of which were indistinguishable from the hotel room she now had in Pine Ridge. Despite all this, it was not a restful night for her.

Exhausted though she was, Connie found she couldn't sleep straight through the night. Instead, she kept waking up almost every hour on the hour. The cause behind her inability to sleep in something more than fitful snatches was not a mystery to her. She was both excited and worried about what the next day held.

There was a great deal riding on this for her and although, despite her father's mind games Connie *did* have faith in herself, she was not narcissistic enough to feel that everything would turn out all right in the end—*just because*. That was her father's way of operating, not hers.

As a rule, Connie tried to proceed confidently, but keeping what to do in a worst-case scenario somewhere in the back of her mind. She knew better than to believe that the occasion would never come up. She was also well aware that while she seemed to have the beginnings of a decent relationship going with the man in charge of the crew, she wasn't exactly home free in that department yet.

Added to that, she wanted the people who would be working for her to like her. It just stood to reason that employees worked a lot better for people they liked and admired than for people whom they feared and who rode roughshod over them. This would not be an ongoing job for the people she hired but rather a one-time thing. She had to get the very best out of them in the time that she had.

And, if that wasn't enough to prey on her unguarded mind, there was that added *thing* that kept buzzing around in her brain. She had no succinct description for this feeling, other than to call it unsettling. She could, however, easily trace it back to its source: one Finn Murphy. There was something about him, something above and beyond his capability, his craftsmanship and his obvious connection to the men of the town.

Though she would have rather not put a label on it, Connie had always been honest and straightforward with people—and that included herself.

With that in mind, she forced herself to admit that there was no other way to describe it. The man was sexy—not overtly, not in a showy, brash manner, but more in an inherent way. It was part of the fabric of his makeup. Sexiness seemed to be just ingrained in him. There seemed to be no way to separate the trait from the man. They were, apparently, one and the same.

But no matter how she described it, how she qualified it, the bottom line was that she was attracted to him.

This was going to be a problem, she thought uncomfortably.

Only if you let it be, her inner voice, the one that always kept her on an even keel, told her firmly.

The internal argument continued back and forth for the duration of her morning drive from Pine Ridge to Forever, blocking out whatever songs were being played on the radio station.

The argument was so intense, she wasn't even aware of the time as it went by. One moment she was half asleep, slipping behind the steering wheel of her car, aware that she wanted to arrive in town early, the next, miraculously, she found herself there, parking in front of Murphy's, wondering if Finn had remembered their conversation about conducting the interviews in his establishment.

She shouldn't have worried, Connie realized as she got out of the vehicle. There was a line of men that went out the saloon's front doors and wound its way down the street.

Some of the men were standing in clusters, talking, others were on the ground, sitting cross-legged and giving the impression that they had been sitting there for a while. A handful looked as if they had just stepped out of a movie about cattle ranchers from the last century, complete with cowboy hats, worn jeans and dusty boots, and still others appeared downright hungry for work.

The last group was the one she paid attention to

most of all. Born into the lap of luxury, she nonetheless had an endless capacity for empathy and could just
imagine how it had to feel, facing financial uncertainty
each and every morning.

The moment the men saw her approaching, everyone got to their feet, their posture straightening as if
they were elementary school students, lining up for the
teacher and hoping to pass inspection.

Connie glanced at her wristwatch, half expecting
to discover that she had somehow managed to lose an
hour getting here.

But she hadn't.

She was early, just as she'd initially intended. The
men were even earlier.

Butterflies suddenly swooped in, clustering around
her stomach, pinching her. Connie did her best to ignore them.

Approaching the entrance to Murphy's, she greeted
the hopeful applicants. "Hi, I'm Constance Carmichael.
I'll be conducting the interviews today." She quickly
scanned the line, amazed at how many people had
turned up. Finn was to be commended—either him,
or Miss Joan, she amended. She had no doubt that the
older woman had been quick to pass the word along
that there would be jobs available. Still, she thought it
judicious to ask, "Are you all here about the construction crew jobs?"

To a man they all answered in the affirmative, the
chorus of *yeses* all but deafening.

Connie nodded, letting the moment sink in. She felt
a little overwhelmed but she did her best not to show it.

"Okay, then I guess we'd better get started. Give me five minutes to get things together and then we can begin."

Hurrying past the long single line, Connie made her way into the saloon.

In contrast to the way it had looked when she'd first seen it, the place was lit up as brightly as any establishment that didn't require an ambiance for its clientele.

Finn was there along with his older brother, Brett, and another, younger man with blond hair. She took a closer look at the latter and realized that this had to be Liam, the youngest of the Murphy brothers. The family resemblance was hard to miss.

But Finn wasn't talking to either one of his brothers when she walked in. Instead, he seemed to be deep in conversation with a tall athletic man with straight, thick, blue-black hair, and skin that looked as if it would be right at home beneath the hot rays of the Texas sun.

The other man's bone structure intrigued her for a moment. It was all angles and planes, and there was almost a regal appearance to it. The man's most outstanding feature, at least for the moment, was that he was wearing what she took to be a deputy sheriff's uniform.

Did they expect things to get a little rowdy? she wondered uneasily.

Only one way to find out, Connie decided, braced for anything.

Walking up to Finn and the man he was talking to, she greeted one and introduced herself to the other. "Hi, Finn, I didn't think you'd be ready so early. I would have been here sooner if I knew," she told him honestly. Her eyes darted over to the other man. "I'm Constance Carmichael. Is there something wrong, Officer?"

"Deputy," the man corrected her. "I'm Deputy Sheriff Lone Wolf, but you can call me Joe, and no, there's nothing wrong."

Finn joined in. "Joe brought some of his friends from the rez with him when he heard you were hiring."

"The rez?" she questioned uncertainly.

"That's short for reservation," Finn explained. "Everything gets shortened these days."

Joe had been around long enough to be aware that there were those who still viewed Native Americans differently from others. He'd come to unofficially make sure that there would be no trouble erupting due to any misunderstandings that might flair up.

"You *are* hiring, right?" Joe asked the young woman.

"Absolutely," Connie answered with enthusiasm.

She knew what it was like to have a strike against her for no apparent reason other than a preconceived— and false—notion. Contrary to some opinions, her name did *not* open doors. In some cases, it actually slammed them in her face. Her father was a powerful man, but he was definitely *not* liked.

"I'm looking for able-bodied men with strong backs who don't mind working in the hot sun for an honest day's wage," she told the deputy, summarizing exactly what her criteria was. Once that was met, everything else could be taught.

"How many men are you going to need?" Finn asked her.

"How many men have you got?" she countered, indicating that the number of positions she was looking to fill was far from small.

Finn grinned. This really was going to be good for the town. "Let's get started," he told her.

He gestured to a table he'd set up for her. He and his brothers had temporarily cleared away the others, putting them off to the side for the time being, until the interviews were over for the day.

"Let's," she echoed.

Sitting down, Connie beckoned to the first man in line.

SHE KEPT AT IT, nonstop, until she had seen and talked to every single man in line. She reasoned that if they could stand in line all this time, waiting to talk to her, the least she could do was interview them.

Except for a few who had shown up out of idle curiosity, or had decided after the interview that the work would be too physically taxing, she wound up hiring all the men she interviewed.

Since that number turned out to be higher than she'd initially intended, rather than work a given number of employees full-time, she'd decided to spread the work out, employing all of the men she'd hired on a part-time, as-needed basis. Some, she discovered during the course of the interviews, already had jobs and had approached this position as a way to pick up some extra money, while others were looking to this construction job as a way of feeding their families.

In making her preliminary decisions about the schedule, Connie gave the latter group the most hours while the people in the former group, since they already had some sort of gainful employment, she used accordingly.

In the end, the general schedule Connie ultimately wound up putting together looked a bit complicated, but she was satisfied that she had done the very best job she could and more important to her, had done right by some of the town's residents.

She also found that her initial instincts involved in selecting Finn were right. Finn had remained with her through the entire ordeal. He'd stood off to the side to give her space, but he always remained close enough to be there if she decided she needed backup for some reason, or to resolve some issue.

While acting as her more or less silent second in command, he'd also gotten to observe her more than holding her own. Finn found himself impressed by the way she did business as well as her underlying sincerity. Any doubts he might have still been entertaining about her were laid to rest by the end of the long session. The woman wasn't here just to take advantage of the labor or the town.

Right from the first interview, she made no secret of the fact that this hotel was important to her, but so were the people she was hiring. She made a point of telling them that she wanted them to speak up if at any time they were dissatisfied with the work conditions or the treatment they received from a superior.

All in all, he thought that this newcomer in their midst conducted herself better than some far more experienced people that both he and Brett had dealt with at one time or another.

WHEN THE LAST man had finally filled out a form and given it to Connie, then left the saloon, Finn came up behind her, leaned over and said, "You look like you could use a drink right about now."

Turning her head, her eyes met his, and she allowed herself a weary smile. That had been grueling, she couldn't help thinking. Even so, she felt wired—and very pleased with herself.

"Quite possibly more than one." The one thing that hosting those parties for her father and hanging around with his associates had taught her, other than how to listen and absorb information, was how to hold her liquor.

"That can be arranged," Finn told her. "I happen to know the bartender in this joint. It's a pretty well-established fact that he's a pushover for a pretty woman's smile."

God, but she felt stiff, Connie suddenly realized. She'd been sitting so long in one spot, she felt as if she could have very well melded into the chair.

"Do you know where we can find one?" she murmured, rotating her head from side to side. She could almost hear it making strange, creaking noises.

"I'm looking at one," Finn told her very simply, his eyes on hers.

Connie caught herself raising her chin. It was a purely defensive move on her part. She was waiting for some sort of a disparaging remark to follow because right about now, she felt about as pretty as a dried-up autumn leaf.

"This bartender doesn't set the bar very high, does he?" she quipped dismissively.

"On the contrary, it's pretty much an absolute," he told her.

He realized that she wasn't being cute or angling for some sort of a bigger compliment. She actually meant what she'd said. She didn't think of herself as attractive. How was that even possible? he couldn't help wondering. One glance at her more than established that fact.

"You do have mirrors in your house, don't you?" he asked. How could she possibly not see just how really gorgeous she was? He would have been willing to bet that a number of the men who had lined up today would have been willing to work for her without any monetary compensation, as long as she was on the job with them every day.

"I don't need mirrors," she answered. "I've got my father. He does more than an adequate job of keeping me aware of myself."

He was about to say that, obviously, it was her father who was suffering from some sort of blindness, but Finn never got the chance. Their conversation was abruptly curtailed when one of Miss Joan's waitresses—Dora—walked into the saloon, clutching a large insulated carrier in both hands.

She went directly to the table where Connie had set up her *office*. Seeing that it was covered with stacks of papers, she turned toward the bar instead.

"Miss Joan said you need to keep your strength up," Dora announced, setting the rectangular carrier she'd brought in on the bar.

Unzipping the insulated carrier on three of its sides, Dora extracted what turned out to be a complete three-course meal, along with a container of coffee and a huge slice of coconut cream pie.

The pie was her favorite, Connie thought. Was its inclusion in the meal just a coincidence? Or was this a further example of Miss Joan's talked-about, unusual abilities? At this point, she really didn't know what to believe—or what she ultimately felt comfortable believing.

So instead, she pretended as if all this was just commonplace. "This is for me?" she asked, feigning surprise.

"Miss Joan told me not to let anyone else pick at it but you," Dora told her.

Dora looked at Finn. A rather sharp *no trespassing* look passed between them because the latter looked rather interested in the pie.

Flashing a smile at the waitress, Finn, along with his brother, brought over one of the tables that had been pushed to the side and set it up beside the other one.

Dora brought all the items from the carrier over to that table.

Connie moved her chair over to the new table and regarded the unusual spread. She wasn't accustomed to having anyone concern themselves with her welfare. "I don't know what to say."

"Don't have to say anything," Dora told her, zipping up the carrier and then slinging the straps over her shoulder as if it was nothing more than an oddly shaped shoulder bag. "Miss Joan said for you to consider it her investment in the hotel—and the future."

Connie was unclear as to the message that was being conveyed. She glanced at Finn. "What's that supposed to mean?"

Finn laughed. "You got me. Half the time we're not sure exactly *what* Miss Joan's saying, only that, somehow, in the long run, that very sharp lady always turns out to be right."

"I don't have any great insight in the way people think," Joe began, joining the circle of people, "but offhand, I'd say that Miss Joan just wants to make sure you don't waste away. She doesn't like anyone being as skinny as she is," the deputy added with a dry laugh. He turned toward Brett. "I'll be heading back now." His attention shifted for a moment back to the young woman he had initially come to see this morning. "Thanks for hiring some of my friends."

"No reason to thank me." She thought for a moment, then added just before he walked toward the door, "If there's any thanks to be given, I should be the one to be thanking you for bringing them here today."

"Then you can thank Finn," Joe told her. The man he'd just mentioned had temporarily stepped aside to talk to Brett. "He's the one who told me about this hotel your company's building." He nodded, as if agreeing with something he was thinking before he said out loud, "Finn's a good man."

Connie had no intentions of disputing that. Her gut instincts had already told her the same the morning she had seen him standing before the ranch house, tool belt dipped provocatively at his hips, causing his jeans to dip with them. It had brought a whole new meaning of *fine craftsmanship* flashing through her mind.

Out loud, she murmured to Joe, "I'm beginning to see that."

The problem, however, was that she was also beginning to see a lot more, and that could only have a negative effect on her ultimately getting the job done the way she wanted to.

Chapter Eight

"I'll take that drink now," Connie said, slipping onto the bar stool.

Finn seemed somewhat surprised to see her sitting there. The woman had somehow managed to make it from her table to the bar without a single telltale sound to alert him that she was moving in his direction. Glancing around her, he saw Joe just as the latter went out the front door. He couldn't see the deputy's face from where he was—not that it would have done any good even if he had. As a rule, Joe's face was completely unreadable, giving nothing away that he didn't want to.

"Joe giving you a hard time?" Finn asked her, curious.

It took Connie a second to connect the face with the name. She'd spoken to several "Joes" during the marathon interviewing session today.

"Oh, you mean the deputy?" she finally concluded. "No, he was nice as pie."

Pouring her a shot of Kentucky bourbon, Finn moved the partially filled glass in front of her. "Not that I didn't offer you one just a few minutes ago, but why do you suddenly look as if you actually need this drink?" he asked.

She raised the glass, but rather than throw back the drink or sip it, she just studied the amber liquid in it, moving it slowly from side to side.

"So I can talk myself out of the idea that I'm in over my head," she replied.

He hadn't expected her to say that. From what he had seen, Connie Carmichael struck him as being equal to anything she tackled. But he'd learned long ago that self-image had a lot to do in making decisions that affected more than just yourself.

"Is that how you feel?" he asked.

She laughed shortly, shaking her head. "You're not much of a bartender, are you?"

Although, she silently had to admit, Finn Murphy with his lean, sculpted torso, sexy smile and magnetic green eyes, was every woman's fantasy come to life. She would have to watch her step with him. Really watch her step.

"Come again?" Finn asked.

"Well, isn't this the part where you tell me that, 'no, you're not in over your head. Everything's going to work out just fine and we'll stand to gain from this experience when it's all behind us.'" Her tone of voice was only partially sarcastic.

"Don't see why I should. You seem to have taken care of that part pretty much on your own."

Connie frowned, still regarding the drink in her hand. "Yeah, except that I don't believe myself." And with that, she took a long, savoring sip from her glass. Closing her eyes, she allowed herself to focus on the fiery path the alcohol took through her body. He noted that she didn't toss her drink down, the way people would when they were trying to erase a reaction or memory of a sore point.

"Maybe you should," he told her. "From where I'm standing, you seem like a very capable person. Notice I said *capable,* not *superhuman,*" he pointed out. "If you were shooting for superhuman, I'd say that you had unrealistic expectations. But since you're not, I'd say that everything was A-okay. Now why don't you take that drink—" he nodded at it "—go back to your table and have that dinner Miss Joan sent over before it gets cold?" he suggested. "If I don't miss my guess, Angel made that dinner special, just for you."

"Angel?" Connie tried to recall if she'd met anyone answering to that name in the last two days. She came up empty.

"Gabe Rodriguez's wife," Finn told her. "Miss Joan's got her working at the diner, and that lady's got a way with food that's nothing short of heavenly." He paused to inhale deeply even though it was literally impossible to catch a whiff of the aroma of the meal. The distance was fairly substantial. "I'd recognize Angel's fried chicken *anywhere.*"

He sounded as if he'd enjoy the meal a lot more than she would, Connie thought. Her stomach was badly knotted. As far as she knew, he hadn't had a chance to eat anything, either, so she beckoned him over before she even sat down at the table again.

"Why don't you join me, then? There's more than enough here for both of us," she told him, indicating the food that was on the table.

Finn glanced at the heaping basket of fried chicken that had been placed beside her plate. He knew Miss Joan and the way the woman thought. She had people and their appetites down to a science, and she wouldn't have sent over that much food if she thought that Connie would be eating it by herself. What he was looking at was a deliberate double portion, generous, yes, but definitely a double portion.

Why Miss Joan had sent a double portion, he could only speculate, but he had a feeling that if Connie suspected this was what the older woman had in mind— that they share a meal together for the second time—it just might be the added pressure that would cause Connie's undoing. The woman currently had more than enough on her mind without trying to fathom what was going on in Miss Joan's head.

"Well, if you insist," Finn allowed, crossing over to her table.

"I do."

"Then how can I say no? You're the boss lady," he told her agreeably as he took a seat opposite her at the table.

Boss lady.

That sounded good, Connie couldn't help thinking. She just hoped that this wouldn't turn out to be an isolated incident.

She gazed at the food again and shook her head

amused disbelief. "Miss Joan must think that I have an absolutely *huge* appetite."

"Miss Joan likes to think that when it comes to the food she serves at the diner, *everyone* has a big appetite," Finn told her. "I think that woman feels it's her mission in life to fatten everyone up."

As he spoke, he reached into the basket for another piece of chicken—at the exact same time that Connie went to take one herself. They wound up both reaching for the *same* piece of fried chicken, which was why, just for a second, their fingers brushed against one another. Contact generated a spark that had no business being there, and no tangible explanation for being there, either.

They both pulled their hands back almost simultaneously.

"Sorry," Connie murmured. She was *really* going to have to be careful, she warned herself. Everything, including her entire future, was riding on her success with this project.

"No, my mistake. Go ahead," he urged, gesturing toward the basket. "After all, you're the one Miss Joan sent this to. It's her way of looking out for you," he added.

"Why would she even concern herself with me?" Connie asked. "I mean, not that it's not a nice feeling to k̲ ̲w that someone cares whether I eat or not, but ̲ ̲ly doesn't know me from Adam."

̲ ̲ think she's got that part pretty much figured ̲ ̲ld her with a grin. "There's definitely no ̲ ̲ou for any guy named Adam. As for the rest of it, Miss Joan likes to think of herself as a great judge of character. To give the woman her due, I don't think there was a single time that anyone can recall Miss Joan being wrong about anything."

"Bet that must make her hard to live with," Connie commented.

She knew firsthand what her father would be like under those circumstances. The man already felt he couldn't be opposed, and he had been wrong at least several instances that she knew of. Most likely more that she *didn't* know about, she was willing to bet.

"You'd think so, wouldn't you?" Finn agreed, then went on to say, "But I don't think there's a nicer person in Forever than Miss Joan. Oh, she comes off all prickly and distant at times, you know, crusty on the outside. But she's kind of like French bread in that way. Soft on the inside," he told her with a wink. "Miss Joan's got that famous heart of gold that so many people have benefited from. She thinks you're going to be good for the town, so that's why she's behind you the way she is," Finn told her.

Because her father had made her leery of being on the receiving end of praise, she'd never been one to take a compliment lightly or at face value.

"I don't know about *me* being good for the town," Connie said, "but the hotel's bound to be. If there's a hotel in town, people'll be more inclined to stop here rather than somewhere else. That means they'll eat their meals here, maybe spend a little money here—" And that was when an idea hit her. She looked at Finn hopefully when she asked, "Anything like an annual rodeo take place here?"

Now *that* had come out of left field, he thought. "Nope."

The woman amused him, she really did, Finn thought. It was obvious from the way she conducted herself that she was a city girl—even if she hadn't told him that her father's company was domiciled in Houston, she had the word *city* written all over her. Yet here she was, acting like some kind of an activities director, coming up with ideas about what she thought would be best for a town she'd only set foot in yesterday.

It took a great deal of self-confidence to come across like that—yet when he looked into Connie's eyes, he could see the slight element of fear lurking there. Fear of failure, he assumed. That kind of a thing might ultimately cause her to second-guess herself, which, in his experience, never amounted to anything positive in the long run.

"Maybe you should consider holding a rodeo here," she encouraged. God knew she could picture Finn on a bucking bronco, every muscle tense as he focused on the longest eight seconds of his life.

A warm shiver went up and down her spine. It was an effort to get herself under control and act as if images of Finn hadn't just taken over her brain.

"I'll do that," he told her with a wink, unable to put a lid on his amusement any longer. "I'll consider holding an annual rodeo."

"I'm serious," she told him, leaning in closer over

the table. "That would really bring in more people to Forever."

"People who would have to stay at the hotel," he said with a straight face.

"Yes." And then she took a closer look at him. It wasn't that he thought she was kidding; he thought she had a screw loose, she realized. "You're laughing at me."

He did his best to turn down the wattage of his grin—but she was so damn cute when she tried to be so serious. "Not at you, with you."

Connie frowned. "You might not have noticed this, but I'm not laughing."

"But you will be. Sooner or later, you will be," he assured her. "One thing you should know about the people in Forever is that they kind of move at a slower pace than what you're probably used to."

Connie immediately interpreted the words to mean something that affected her. Instantly on the alert, she asked, "What are you telling me, that we're not going to make the deadline?"

"Oh, no, you'll make the deadline," he told her quickly, wanting to make sure she didn't misunderstand him. "That's a real hardworking bunch of men you just hired today."

Her eyebrows seemed to knit themselves over her narrowed eyes. Finn had lost her. "Then I don't understand...."

"People in Forever are slow when it comes to making changes. They take their time embracing progress, if you will."

"Everything has to embrace progress," Connie doggedly insisted. "If something isn't growing, then it's dying." It was one of the first lessons she'd ever learned—and it had come from Emerson, not her father.

"Or maybe it's just being," he suggested.

"Being?" she asked, not understanding what he was trying to tell her.

"Existing," Finn said, putting it another way. "In general, people work hard to make a living, and they feel that they're entitled to just sit back and enjoy that accomplishment. You know, sit back, take a look around and just be happy that they've managed to come this far and survived. It's not always about reaching the next major goal, or getting the next big-screen TV. In other words, it's not always about getting something bigger, or better, or faster. Sometimes, it's just about enjoying the prize that you have, the thing—however small—you succeeded in doing."

He realized that Connie hadn't said anything in a couple of minutes, hadn't attempted to interrupt him. Not just that, but she was looking at him in a very odd way, like he was speaking another language.

He'd overstepped his bounds, Finn thought, upbraiding himself. The woman wasn't ready to hear this countrified philosophy when all she was interested in was getting a good day's work out of them.

He tried to backtrack as gracefully as he could. "Hey, but that's just me," he concluded, easing himself out of the conversation.

But Connie continued to watch him in what he could

only describe as a thoughtful, strange way. It was obvious that if they were to move on, he had no recourse but to ask her, "What?"

As Finn had talked, she'd stopped embracing the credo that had governed most of her life, and instead listened to what the cowboy was telling her. It didn't take a scholar to realize—rather quickly—that she was hearing the antithesis of her father's number one philosophy.

Her father would probably have this man for lunch— or try to—saying that if everyone was like him, the country would have withered and died a long time ago.

But maybe it wouldn't have, Connie now thought. Maybe the country would continue thriving because people were satisfied and that in turn made them happy. Was that so bad, just being happy?

She couldn't recall the last time her father, with his countless mind-boggling triumphs and successes, had been happy for more than a fleeting moment or two.

For Calvin Carmichael, it was always about the next project, the next conquest. Bigger, better, more streamline, all that was her father's primary focus. That was what had always kept him going even more so since her mother had died.

And, until just now, that was what kept her going, as well. But maybe not, Connie amended. "You sound like the exact opposite of my father," she told him.

"I meant no disrespect," he told her. "I just think that maybe there's room for both those points of view. Think about it," he urged. "Why should someone work so hard for something and not stop to at least enjoy it for a bit?" he asked.

Connie realized that he probably thought she was trying to find a nice way of saying that he was wrong. But the truth of it was, upon reflection, she didn't believe that he was. What Finn had done was succeed in making her think a little—not to mention that he'd managed to generate a feeling of—for lack of a better word—relief within her.

There *was* room for more than just her father's work ethic out there. That was a fact that was good to keep on the back burner, she decided.

"I didn't say I thought you were wrong. I just said you and my father would be on opposite sides of the fence when it came to your idea of what life was all about." She smiled, more to herself than at the man with whom she was sharing this impromptu dinner. "You might have guessed that my father is not the kind of man you could get to stop and smell the roses. He's more inclined to stomp on the roses as he made his way to the next rosebush—just to reach it, not to try to savor it or appreciate it," she confessed.

At this point, Connie decided that a change of subject might do them both some good. This was just the beginning of their working relationship. It wasn't the time to get into philosophical discussions regarding—ultimately—the meaning of life. Or any other serious, possibly life-altering topic. Not if it didn't directly relate to the job at hand.

So instead, Connie turned her attention to the meal they were sharing. "You were right."

"About?" Finn asked.

"This has to be the best fried chicken I've ever had. Does Angel do something different when she makes this?"

"I'd say that would be a safe guess," Finn answered her. "But if you wanted to know exactly what she does, that's a discussion you're going to have to have with Angel."

She understood that chefs had their secret recipes, and she wasn't trying to pry. Her eye was on a much larger prize at the moment.

"You know, Miss Joan might do well if she thought about looking into maybe having a chain of restaurants, or selling a franchise—including this recipe and a few others in the package—" She looked at Finn, her momentum growing. "I'm assuming fried chicken isn't the only thing Angel does well."

She said this as she finished yet another piece of the chicken. Rather than become full, Connie only seemed better able to savor each bite the more chicken she consumed.

"Everything Angel makes is pretty tasty," Finn answered. "She has a whole bunch of regular customers who faithfully turn up at the diner since she came to work there."

"I knew it," she said with feeling. Plans and possibilities began to multiply in her head. "Angel and Miss Joan are missing a golden opportunity," Connie told him.

"I'll let them know you said so," he told her. "But

for right now, I think you're missing a golden opportunity yourself."

"What do you mean?" she asked.

Finn smiled at her. It wasn't a patronizing smile. Instead, it was indulgently patient. The kind of smile a parent had while waiting for their child to catch on to something all by themselves after all the clues had been carefully and discreetly laid out.

But, Finn quickly realized, they came from different worlds, he and this woman, and thus had been raised completely differently, with a different set of rules to guide them. She would need more than just a hint to catch on.

"You're forgetting just to enjoy the moment. Just for a little while, why don't you forget about the project, your father and everything else and just enjoy the meal and what's around you without trying to see if you can maximize it or improve it or market it? Maybe I'm talking out of turn, but you're going to wind up wearing yourself out before you get a chance to make that mark on the world you're so keen on making."

She pressed her lips together. She hated to admit it, but Finn was right.

At least about the last part.

Chapter Nine

The next moment, Connie pulled herself back mentally and rallied. Maybe if she'd lived here, in this tiny speck of a town all of her life, her view of life might match the handsome cowboy's, but she wasn't from Forever. She was from Houston, and things were a lot different there, not to mention that it moved a great deal faster in the city. Oh, she was certain there were people in Houston with the exact same approach to life as Finn had just emphasized, but they were the people who were content never to get anywhere. To be satisfied with their small lot in life and just leave it at that.

But she wasn't. Her father had drummed it into her head over and over again: you were only as good as your next accomplishment.

Finn might not have a father he needed to prove himself to—once and for all—but she did, and until she accomplished that mission, those roses that needed smelling would just have to wait.

Finished with her dinner, Connie pushed herself away from the table and rose to her feet. "As tempting as just kicking back and savoring the moment sounds,

I've got a full day tomorrow. We both do," she reminded him pointedly. "And I've still got a fifty-mile trip ahead of me."

It was that fifty-mile trip that was going to wear her out faster than the rest of it, he couldn't help thinking.

"Why don't you reconsider and just stay in town?" Finn suggested. "That way, you could give yourself a little while to take a well-deserved deep breath, relax and enjoy the rest of today before you go full steam ahead tomorrow."

He made it sound so very simple—but she'd learned the hard way that *nothing* was ever simple.

"And just where do you suggest I spend the night?" Connie asked him. "My car's a little cramped for sleepovers," she added in case Finn was going to suggest that she sack out in her sports car.

"I wouldn't have even thought about you sleeping in your car," he told her. "That's a sure-fire way to guarantee waking up with a stiff neck. Not exactly the way you'd want to start out," he predicted. "Besides, plenty of people in town would be willing to put you up for the night," he assured her.

And just how did he propose that she go about making that a reality? Connie wondered with a touch of cynicism. "I'm not about to go begging door to door—" she began.

Finn cut in. "No begging. A lot of people here have an extra bedroom." Hell, until Brett and Alisha got married and moved into the ranch house he'd inherited, for all intents and purposes, he and his brothers didn't just have an extra room, they had an extra *house*.

"All you'd have to do was say that you needed a place to stay and—"

He didn't get a chance to say that people would line up with offers to accommodate her because Connie cut him off. "Which is just another way of begging," she pointed out, stopping him in his tracks.

But Finn, she quickly learned, was not the type to give up easily. "Miss Joan offered you a room at her place," he reminded her. "That was without you saying anything about even *needing* a place."

She was not about to impose on anyone, or approach them, hat in hand, like a supplicant. "I already told Miss Joan I had a room in the Pine Ridge Hotel. To arbitrarily just ask her if I could stay at her place after that wouldn't seem right." She wanted the workers to trust her, not think of her as some sort of a giant sponge.

"What it would seem," Finn argued amicably, "is practical, and there's nothing Miss Joan admires more than someone being practical."

Judging by the look on Connie's face, he hadn't won that argument, Finn thought. He gave getting her to agree to remain in town overnight another try by offering her another option to consider.

"Or if you really can't bring yourself to do that, my brothers and I have a house right here in town not far from this saloon," he told her. "It's plenty big."

She looked at him incredulously. Was he actually saying what she thought he was saying? "And what, I should stay with you?"

"And my brothers," Finn tacked on for good measure.

"Even better," she murmured to herself, rolling her eyes. If she gave him the benefit of the doubt, best-case scenario, the man thought he was being helpful. She told herself to keep that in mind. "I realize that appearances don't count for very much in this day and age," she began, "but it wouldn't look right, my staying with my crew foreman in his house. Look, I'm not an unreasonable boss to work for, but there are certain lines that just shouldn't be crossed. You've got to know that," she said, searching his face to see if she'd made an impression on the cowboy.

Finn ran the edge of his thumb ever so lightly along the area just beneath each of her eyes. Initially, she began to pull back—then didn't.

There it was again, she realized, that lightning, coursing through her veins. Immobilizing her.

"Only lines I'm worried about seeing are the ones that are going to be forming right here, under your eyes, because you didn't get enough sleep," Finn told her in a low voice that made her scrambled pulse go up several more notches. "And that'll be in large part because of your fifty-mile, round-way trip from Pine Ridge to Forever. Seems like a lot to sacrifice just for appearances' sake."

Finn dropped his hand to his side. "C'mon, Ms. Carmichael, we're both adults," he coaxed gently. "Adults handle situations. Nothing's going to happen if we don't want it to."

If. He'd said if. *Not* because *but* if. *Was that a prophesy?*

Only if she let it become one, Connie silently insisted.

She supposed, in the interest of being here very early—Emerson had promised that the machinery she required to begin the excavation would be here first thing in the morning—finding a place in town to crash for the night was the far more practical way to go. And while staying with Miss Joan seemed to be an acceptable concept, the older woman seemed the type to subject to her a battery of questions. And Connie would feel obligated to answer in repayment for the woman's hospitality.

That was an ordeal she would definitely rather not face.

She slanted a glance toward the man standing beside her.

"What would your brothers say about your impulsive burst of hospitality?" she asked, covering up the fact that she found herself suddenly nervous with rhetoric.

Finn shrugged, as if she'd just asked a question that was hardly worth consideration. "Brett wouldn't say anything because when he knocks off for the night, which is pretty damn late, he usually goes home to the ranch house you saw me working on. Lady Doc stays there, as well, whenever she gets a chance. So Brett's not even in this picture if you're worried about what he thinks," Finn guaranteed. "As for Liam, well, Liam doesn't exactly think," he said with a dismissive laugh.

"What do you mean?" she asked, doing her best to be tactful in her inquiry.

The last thing she wanted to do was insult someone in Finn's family.

"Liam's just plain challenged—challenged by anything that's not a musical note in a song he had a hand in writing. In other words, what I'm trying to say is that if you're not shaped like a guitar, there's little chance that he'd even notice you, even if you stripped down buck naked and pretended you were the dining room tablecloth. On second thought," he amended, taking another look at the woman beside him, "maybe he's not really that far gone yet."

"As intriguing as that sounds," Connie began, but got no further.

Seeing his advantage, Finn pushed to the goal line. "Take me up on the offer. You'll be driving yourself plenty once this thing is in full swing. I can tell just by looking at you," he said, surprising her. "This might very well be your last chance to take in a deep breath and relax. If you don't want to listen to me telling you this as a friend, then maybe you'll listen to the man you're paying to head up your crew and tell you the way he sees things."

Connie stared at him for a moment, confused. "But that's you."

The smile he flashed at her cut right through the cloud of confusion that threatened to swallow her up. "Exactly," Finn agreed. "And the way I see it, your getting a good night's sleep is more important than you worrying about what a couple of people may—or may not—say about you staying at my house," he underscored.

Having laid out his argument, he took a step back. He had a feeling that crowding this woman was *not* the way to go.

"Final decision," he told her, "like with the project, is ultimately yours. But I'd like to think you'd respect my opinion and give it its due consideration. Otherwise, there's really no point in you hiring me. Think of it this way," he added, suddenly coming up with another argument in his favor. "You wouldn't have any objections to staying in the same hotel as I was in, right?"

"Right," she agreed warily, waiting to see where this was going.

"Well, then think of my house as a hotel," he told her, adding with a grin, "a very small, rather limited hotel."

The man really knew how to use his words. To look at him, she wouldn't have thought that he could actually be so persuasive.

"Bed-and-breakfast inns are larger than your house," she told him.

"So, after your hotel is completed, I'll see about adding on some extra rooms to the house," he told her. "You can think of it as a bed-and-breakfast inn in the making," he added with a wink.

She felt something flutter inside her chest and told herself it was just that she was tired. Her reaction had nothing to do with the wink.

"My clothes are all at the hotel," she suddenly remembered, which, in her book, should have brought an end to this debate.

She should have known better.

Finn took a step back and regarded her thoughtfully for a moment. "Lady Doc's about your size, as is Dr. Dan's wife. One of them can lend you something to sleep in. The other can give you a change of clothes for tomorrow. And once we get the assignments straightened out for the day, I can send someone over to Pine Ridge to get the rest of your clothes." He grinned at her. "See? Problem solved."

And just possibly, a brand-new one started, she couldn't help thinking.

"So you've taken care of everything, just like that?" she asked out loud.

There was a note in her voice Finn didn't recognize, but he had a hunch that weather watchers would point out that it might have to do with a coming storm. He quickly got ahead of it—just in case.

"What I've done—just like that—was make suggestions," he told her. "You're the one who makes the final decisions and ultimately takes care of everything," he concluded, looking like the soul of innocence.

It was Connie's turn to look at him for a long moment. And then she nodded, suppressing what sounded like a laugh. She gave him his due. "Nice save."

Finn did not take the bait. "Just telling it the way it is," he countered.

Connie merely nodded, more to herself than to him. She definitely didn't want to spend the rest of the evening arguing—especially unproductively. Instead, she silently congratulated herself on going with her gut instincts. She'd made the right choice putting Finn in charge of all the others. If the man could pull off this side-step shuffle effectively with her, he could do it with anyone. After all, she had seen something in him from the very first moment she laid eyes on him, and it wasn't that he had looks to die for. It was a vibe she got, a silent telegraphing of potential that felt so strong, it had taken her a few minutes to process.

But just for a moment, she had to deal with his suggestion not as his boss, but as a woman. Looking at him intently, silently assuring herself that if he was selling her a bill of goods, she'd be able to tell, she had one more question for him.

"And you're *sure* neither one of your brothers— wherever they might roam—won't mind my crashing at their place—and don't tell me again that they won't be there. It's their place. That counts for something."

"They won't mind," he assured her with feeling.

"Okay, I'll stay in town," she agreed in pretty much the same tone that someone agreed to have a root canal done. She only hoped she wouldn't wind up regretting a decision of so-called convenience.

"In the interest of full disclosure," Finn went on, "I just want to warn you that neither one of my brothers— or I—are exactly good at housekeeping. I mean, it's livable and all that," he was quick to add, "if you don't mind dirt, grime and dust like you wouldn't believe." He looked a little embarrassed as he added, "Lost civilizations have less dust piled on top of them than some of the rooms in this house.

"The place is in sturdy condition," he went on to assure her. "Either that, or the dust is acting like the glue that's holding all this together," Finn told her with a hearty laugh.

Connie couldn't help wondering just how much of what the cowboy was telling her had more than an ounce of truth in it. Instead of repulsed, she found herself intrigued. Now she *wanted* to take a tour of this place where he had lived his entire life, just to see if it was in the less-than-savory condition he was describing.

"Remind me not to put you in charge of the new hotel's travel brochure," Connie told him with a shake of her head.

"I don't think you're going to need someone to re-mind you of that." And then it hit him. They were about to walk out of Murphy's, and Finn caught hold of his boss by the arm. He didn't want to lose sight of her until he had gotten at least this part straight. "Wait, are you saying that I managed to convince you?" he asked her, genuinely surprised. "You've decided that you're staying in Forever tonight?"

"That's what I'm saying," Connie answered—and then she paused. "Unless you've changed your mind about the offer."

"No way," he told her with enthusiasm. "You won't regret this," he promised.

She didn't know about that. Part of her already *was* regretting her decision. As a rule, while she remained friendly and outwardly approachable, she didn't really get too close to the people who essentially worked for her. The reason for that was that she never knew if they were being friendly because they liked her—or because they were using her to get to her father.

Not that that approach ever really worked, since her father could never even come close to being accused of being a *doting* father.

She looked at Finn, hardly believing that she'd actually agreed to allow him to put her up for the night. "So, is this the part where you go asking your friends to donate their clothes to me?"

"No, that comes a little later," he told her. "This is the part where you look up at the sky, say something about being awestruck over how there looks as if there's twice as much sky here as in places like Houston or Los Angeles, and I agree with you—even though I know it's not true. Then I tell you that if you see a falling star, you have to pause and make a wish. Sound too taxing?" he asked her, a hint of a smile on his face.

They had stopped walking again and were standing, in her opinion, much too close, at least for her comfort.

This was a mistake. A big one.

But if she suddenly announced that she had changed her mind about staying the night in his guest room, she'd seem flighty—worse than that, she'd seem as if she was afraid, and she'd lose any chance she had at commanding respect—from him and most likely, from the rest of the men working for her.

Her only recourse was to brazen it out.

Heaven knew it wouldn't be the first time.

"No, I think I can handle making a wish if I see a falling star," she told him.

"Well, then I'd say you've got everything under control."

Finn watched her for a long moment, thinking things that he knew he shouldn't be thinking. Things that would probably get him fired before he ever began to work on the project. But there was something about the woman, a vulnerability despite the barriers she was trying to rigidly retain in place, that reached out and spoke to him. It brought out the protector in him.

He wondered what she would say if she knew. Probably, *You're fired.*

"It's going to be fine," Finn told her.

Startled, she looked at him. "What?"

Connie wished she had as much confidence in her succeeding as Finn apparently had—if she was to believe what he'd just said.

But you don't have everything under control, do you?

She felt another knot tightening in her stomach.

This had to be what opening-night jitters felt like for actors, she theorized. It felt as if everything was riding on this.

"I said it's going to be fine," Finn repeated. "For a second you looked as if you were a million miles away—and you were frowning, so I thought maybe you were worrying about the site. I have to ask—you always this nervous before a project?"

It was on the tip of her tongue to tell him that her emotions were none of his business, that she hadn't hired him to subject her to countless questions, but that would really be starting out on the wrong foot, and he did seem genuinely concerned.

"No, I have to admit that this is a first."

He nodded, giving her the benefit of the doubt. "You've hired on a good bunch of people, and they'll work hard to deliver whatever it is you need done," he assured her, then asked, "Anything I can do to help squelch your uneasiness?"

She smiled at him. "You just did it."

"Good to know," he told her.

They were outside the saloon now. Finn had gently coaxed her over to the side, out of the way of any foot traffic. He directed her attention toward the sky, pointing to a cluster of stars.

"Look." He indicated a constellation. "Isn't that just the most magnificent sight you've ever seen?" he asked.

To oblige him, she looked up when he told her to. Ordinarily, before tonight, the thought of a heaven full of stars did nothing for her. But looking up now, at Finn's request, she found herself at first interested, then deeply moved. The vastness spoke to her—and she could relate. Relate to feeling isolated, desolate and alone.

Shake it off, Con, she ordered herself. *Sentimental and sloppy isn't going to build the future. It's not you, anyway.*

"Beautiful, isn't it?" he asked again.

She couldn't very well pretend to be indifferent. Because she no longer was.

"Yes," she agreed, "it is. It kind of takes my breath away."

She heard him laugh. When she looked at him quizzically, he merely said, "I know the feeling."

Except that when he said it, he wasn't looking at the sky. He was looking at her.

She told herself to ignore it, that she was misreading him. But even so, Connie could feel herself growing suddenly very warm despite the evening breeze.

Growing very warm and yearning for him to kiss her.

That's the alcohol talking, a voice in her head insisted. But she had only had the one drink, a short one at that, and she could hold far more than that and still remain lucid and steady.

It wasn't the drink. It was the man. But that was an admission she intended to take with her to the grave.

"I think we'd better get going," he told her. "The whole idea of you staying in town was for you to get extra rest—and if we stay out here like this any longer, I might wind up doing something that's going to cost me my job before I ever set foot on the construction site."

Her cheeks heated up and for just a second, she felt light-headed and giddy, like a schoolgirl. She hadn't experienced this sensation even when she had been a schoolgirl.

But the next moment, she regained control over herself and willed the moment to pass. "You're right. Let's get going."

Chapter Ten

"If you need anything," Finn told her almost an hour later as they stood on the second floor of his house, "I'm just down the hall." He pointed to the room that was located on the other side of the small bathroom he had already shown her.

Suddenly bone-tired, Connie nodded, murmuring, "Thanks."

They had stopped on the way to his home to borrow the things that she needed in the way of clothing for tonight and tomorrow. Finn couldn't think of a single other thing she needed to know at this point, so he began to withdraw from the room.

"Okay. Then I guess you're all set. See you in the morning," he told Connie.

Again she nodded, softly repeating the last word he'd just said, as if in agreement. "Morning." With that, Connie retreated into the room that he had just brought her to.

Closing the door, Connie took another, longer, closer look around what he'd referred to as the guest room. It looked even smaller now than it had at first glance, barely the size of her closet back home. Perhaps even smaller. There was enough space for a double bed, one nightstand with a lamp and a very small dresser.

The closet itself, which curiosity prompted her to check out, was large enough to accommodate less than half the clothing she'd left at the hotel in Pine Ridge.

Yet from the way Finn had talked about the house as they drove over to it, she got the impression that this small, cramped house had seen a great deal more happiness and love than her father's seven-thousand-square-foot-plus mansion ever had.

There was a kind of worn-down-to-the-nub warmth emanating from the sixty-three-year-old, two-story house that was sorely missing from the place where she had grown up and still vaguely thought of as home.

She found herself envying Finn and his brothers a great deal.

Get it together, Con. You've got a full day ahead of you. Save the pity party for later.

Taking care to lock her door, Connie pushed the room's mismatched chair against it by way of an extra precaution. It wasn't that she didn't trust Finn, because oddly enough, she did, despite knowing the man for less than forty-eight hours. She'd been taught that taking an extra ounce of prevention was always a wise thing to do—just in case.

That hadn't come from her father, but was something that Emerson had taught her. The man at one point had worked as her father's head of security before becoming his general business manager. Emerson had always seemed to be aware of *everything.* She doubted there was a situation in the world that Stewart Emerson was not prepared to handle.

It never occurred to her to dismiss what he said as being useless or inapplicable. She looked to him for guidance the way one should a father. Emerson was the one who always had time for her.

Her father did not.

Connie remembered changing for bed—donning the nightshirt that Brett's fiancée gladly lent her. The verbal exchange between them, with Finn in the middle, had been fleeting. To her chagrin, she could barely recall what the woman had looked like.

But then, she was running perilously close to empty. Connie could vaguely remember lying down.

She didn't remember falling asleep, but she obviously had to have because the next thing she knew, she was looking at the watch she always wore and realizing that it was six in the morning.

Six?

Connie bolted upright. She'd wanted to be up and ready by five. Not because she thought anything actually needed attending to at that time, but because she wanted to be ready—just in case. It was always good to be prepared.

Happily, as far as she knew, everything was proceeding as planned. The necessary machinery was on its way and being delivered by a contractor Emerson had been dealing with for the past fifteen years, Milo Sawyer. Both Emerson and Sawyer knew that failure was not an option for her. Failure would have been worse than death. Emerson had told her that Sawyer took an oath on a stack of figurative bibles that everything would be there when she needed it—if not sooner.

Scrambling, silently lamenting the fact that she needed to sleep as much as she did, Connie was up, dressed and ready in less than twenty minutes.

Her heart kept pace by slamming against her rib cage, reminding her that she was, beneath it all, nervous as hell.

She looked down at what she was wearing. She wasn't keen on starting her first day on a brand-new site in someone else's clothes, but apparently she and Forever's first resident doctor's wife were the exact same size—just as Finn had predicted—and the woman seemed to think nothing of lending her a pair of jeans and a jersey.

Or so Finn had told her when he'd darted into the doctor's house and gotten the items for her. It seemed people just *gave* each other whatever was needed without questioning it. For the umpteenth time it struck her how very different her world was from the world she found herself operating in at the moment.

Moreover, it occurred to Connie, as she glanced in the small oval mirror perched on top of the bureau, that she was wearing something borrowed—the entire outfit—and something blue—the jersey. Not to mention, she also had on something old. Unlike her car, which she laughingly described as her lucky charm, the boots she was wearing were her one *real* concession to superstition: they were her *lucky* boots and they hadn't been considered *new* in the past fourteen years.

Longer, really, because the boots had once belonged

to her mother. Unbeknownst to her father, she'd kept her mother's boots in the back of her closet and as luck would have it, when she reached her present adult height and weight, she discovered that the boots fit her perfectly. She had worn them on every occasion that something good had happened to her.

Connie sincerely hoped that they would continue exerting their *magical* influence and make the hotel's construction come off without a single hitch.

Ready and anxious to begin her day, Connie moved the chair away from the door and pushed it back against the wall where it had been. Unlocking the bedroom door, she ventured down the stairs silently.

Her intention was to slip out of the house and drive over to the site—her car was conveniently parked in front of Finn's house. But when she came to the bottom of the stairs, the deep, rich smell of freshly brewed coffee surrounded her before she knew what had hit her—followed by the aroma of bacon and eggs, a classic one-two punch if ever there was one.

Unable to resist, Connie glanced toward the only source of light on the first floor at this hour. It was coming from the kitchen.

The debate between following her nose or leaving while there was no one watching her was a short one that abruptly ended when her stomach rumbled rather loudly, casting the deciding vote.

She went toward the light.

Finn was standing by the old-fashioned stove. He glanced over his shoulder in her direction the moment she stepped over the threshold. It was almost eerie, as

if he instinctively knew she would come. He supposed
that some people would have said they had some sort
of a "connection." He could think of worse things than
being connected to a woman who could scramble his
insides just with a toss of her flowing, shoulder-length
auburn hair.

"You're up," Finn declared by way of a greeting.

"So, apparently, are you," she countered, nodding
toward the stovetop. He had three frying pans going
at once.

"Everyone gets up early around here. If you don't,
you're either sick—or dead," Finn told her matter-of-
factly.

"That doesn't exactly leave a wide range of choice
available," she commented.

He laughed and shrugged before gesturing toward
the kitchen table.

"Sit down," he told her. "Coffee's hot. I'll pour you
a cup."

"I can serve myself," she told him as she crossed
to the counter.

She looked around for a coffeemaker, but didn't see
one. But she did notice a coffeepot on the last burner
on the stovetop.

Talk about old-fashioned, she thought. Connie duti-
fully poured the extra-black substance into her cup and
retreated back to the table, getting out of Finn's way.

"Where is everyone?" she asked. She glanced out
the kitchen window to see if perhaps one of his brothers was outside, but they weren't. The small area was
desolate.

"Liam's holed up in his room, working on another song for his band—he decided he didn't like his last couple of efforts—and I'm guessing that Brett's over at the other ranch house like I said he'd be." Finn was smiling as he turned away from the stove. "He likes the job I did renovating the ranch house so much, he decided he wanted to stay there, getting it set up for Lady Doc and him once they're married."

Holding the steaming mug of coffee with two hands, Connie made herself comfortable at the table. "Have you thought of taking up that line of work permanently?" she asked.

He frowned ever so slightly, not at her suggestion but over the fact that he had lost the thread of the conversation. "What line of work?"

"Construction, renovations," she elaborated. "That sort of thing. There has to be better money in it than there is in bartending," she insisted. Why was the man wasting his time bartending when he could be earning *real* money?

Finn shrugged indifferently. "I wouldn't know. So far, I've never been paid anything for doing that kind of work."

Connie stared at him. Had she gotten her information mixed up? "I thought you said you installed a bathroom over the bar."

"I did," he confirmed. "But that was for the apartment above the bar—all that belongs to my brothers and me. Seems pretty silly to charge myself," Finn commented.

"And the ranch house?" she asked, referring to the

first time she had seen him. He'd certainly been working hard that day. Free of charge?

"The same," he replied. "Besides, I told you, that's my wedding present to Brett and Lady Doc. I couldn't charge them," he said, shooting the mere notion down as beyond ludicrous.

She had no idea that they *made* men like this anymore. Connie looked at him with renewed admiration. "That's exceptionally generous of you."

He shrugged away her comment. "So, how do you like your eggs?" he asked.

"In the chicken," she quipped.

Finn stared at her. "Wanna run that by me again?" he requested.

She appreciated what he was trying to do, but there was really no need. "I don't eat eggs," she told him. "Never have, never will. I just plain don't like them no matter what you do to them," she added.

He nodded and said, "Fair enough. Got an opinion about bacon?" he asked, testing the waters cautiously.

There was bacon sizzling in the large skillet on the left back burner. "It smells good," she was forced to admit.

Finn's grin hinted of triumph. "Tastes even better," he assured her. Without waiting for her to respond, he proceeded to place four strips of what looked like perfectly fried bacon on her plate. But that obviously wasn't enough as far as he was concerned, so since she had vetoed eggs, he gave her other options: "Pancakes, waffles, French toast or...?"

She regarded him with what could be described as innocent confusion. "What about them?"

"Which do you want for breakfast?" he asked patiently.

He'd already gone out of his way more than was required. He might work for her, but there was nothing in the fine print about serving her hand and foot, and she didn't want him feeling as if this was part of his job description.

"The bacon is more than enough," Connie assured the man. "I usually have just coffee in the morning, nothing else."

Finn frowned, obviously displeased with the answer. "You can't tackle a new day on just coffee," he told her. And then he seemed to study her for a long minute, as if he was making some sort of a major decision.

It took everything she had to wait him out, but she had a feeling that she could lose him if she began to ask him too many questions. So she did her best to appear patient—even if it was the last thing in the world that she was right now.

He was probably trying to browbeat her into eating. Simple enough fix, she decided. "Okay, I'll have toast," Connie finally conceded.

"Just toast?" he asked her.

She stuck to her guns. If she began giving in now, that would carry over to the work site, and she would quickly lose any ground she might have had to begin with. "Just toast," she confirmed. And quite honestly, she didn't even really want that.

Finn frowned for a moment longer then suddenly

brightened—as if an idea had literally hit him—and went to work. A few minutes later, he deposited two large so-called *slices* onto her plate.

Stunned, Connie could only point out the obvious. "I agreed to toast. What is that?" she asked. Whatever it was, it was thick, and it was huge.

"Toast," Finn responded innocently, then a smile slipped through. "Texas style."

Each piece was the size of three regular slices of bread and together with what she had before her comprised more than a full breakfast in her opinion.

She sighed and shook her head, knowing that if she protested, she would wind up with something even bigger. And she had to admit that the aroma was definitely working its magic on her, arousing her taste buds. For the first time in years, she was hungry enough to eat something for breakfast.

"You know, it works better if you pick up a fork and put the food into your mouth instead of staring at it," he advised, sitting down opposite her.

He'd put a plate down for himself. Finn's plate was all but overflowing with bacon, eggs, toast and a sprinkling of hash browns.

Connie could only stare at the heaping plate in complete wonder. "You're really going to eat all that?" she asked him.

"I *need* to," he emphasized. "If I don't, I'll run out of steam in a couple of hours—like clockwork," he assured her.

However, listening to him, Connie sincerely doubted what he'd just said. She'd come to quickly realize that

Finn might appear laid-back, but the man was all go all the time.

"Who taught you how to cook?" she asked as she resigned herself to the meal before her.

She half expected Finn to say that he had picked things up while watching his mother fix meals in the kitchen.

He summed it up in one word: "Brett."

Connie blinked and stared at him. "Your brother?" she asked incredulously.

To her best recollection, her own brother couldn't boil water. She fervently hoped he'd learned how by now, wherever he was.

Finn nodded, seeing nothing out of the ordinary with what he was telling her. "Everything I know how to do, Brett taught me."

"Even construction?" she asked, thinking that perhaps she should have approached the older Murphy brother with a job offer, as well—because what she had seen with the ranch house had impressed her no end, and if Brett had had a hand in that, as well…

"Even construction," Finn echoed. "He taught me the basics. I kind of took off with it on my own after that," Finn admitted without a drop of conceit. "Brett's abilities—and vision—kind of went in a different direction from mine," Finn went on to tell her. "Let me put it this way. Brett can fix a leaky faucet—I can install a new one along with a new sink," he explained in an effort to illustrate his point. "Besides, Brett was always busy. He didn't have time to get caught up in anything fancy. He was keeping our family together, especially after Uncle Patrick died. Brett's the really practical one in the family," he added, as if that explained everything.

She tried to glean what he was actually telling her. "And that makes you what, the dreamer?"

"No, that's Liam. He's the dreamer in the family. Me, I'm just the guy in the middle." He grinned as he illustrated his point for her. "The guy not *too*."

If anything, that made things only more obscure in her opinion. "I'm sorry," she told him. "I don't understand. Not too...?" she repeated, at a loss as to what that meant or was supposed to illustrate for her.

Finn nodded then went on to give her examples. "Not too practical, not too dreamy. You know, not too hot, not too cold, that kind of thing. Always staying on an even keel, never too much of anything, just enough to satisfy requirements."

She held up her hand to get him to stop. Was that how he saw himself? That was awful. "You make it sound so bland," she told him.

Finn laughed softly. "Probably because it is."

Connie looked at the man sitting across from her for a very long, quiet moment, thinking of the way this man she still hardly knew seemed to stir her in ways that she'd never experienced before.

"Not by a long shot," she finally told him, though a little voice in her head warned her that she was giving too much away far too quickly.

"You want seconds?" he asked out of the blue. When she eyed him questioningly, trying to comprehend what he'd just asked, he nodded at her plate—which was somehow miraculously empty. When had she eaten everything? "Do you want seconds?" he repeated.

"No. No, thank you. It was all very good, but in the interest of not waddling onto the construction site, I think I'll just stop here," she told him, pushing back her plate.

That was when he took her plate from her, put it on top of his own and then carried both to the sink. Connie bit her lower lip, curtailing the impulse to offer to wash them for him.

The next moment, as she watched, he quickly rinsed off both plates and stacked them in the dishwasher.

An efficient male, she thought to herself.

She took a deep breath.

It was time.

Chapter Eleven

Looking back at the end of the day, as far as first days went, this had to be the very best one she had ever experienced. The machinery showed up early, as did the men who were to operate it. That meant that excavation and ground preparations could begin right on schedule and even a little bit ahead of it.

Because of the work schedules she had laboriously written up ahead of time, everyone she had hired knew almost from the very beginning exactly what to do and what was expected. Detailed schedules were conspicuously posted in a number of places.

The biggest surprise of the day for her occurred shortly before two o'clock.

Stewart Emerson walked onto the construction site, managing to catch her completely off guard.

Connie had been in the middle of a conversation with Finn, outlining what she hoped would be the project's progress for that week, when she heard a gravelly voice behind her call out her name.

Stopping in midsentence, she turned away from

Finn to see exactly who sounded so much like the man she thought of as her rock.

Her mouth fell open the second she saw him.

"Stewart?" Connie cried in disbelief as the big bear of a man strode in her direction.

As Finn looked on, he watched the rather petite young woman being enfolded and all but swallowed up in the embrace of a man who could have easily doubled as Santa Claus—if the legendary figure had been a towering man given to wearing three-piece suits.

"In the flesh," Emerson confirmed. "I guess I'd better put you down. The men might not react well to seeing their boss whirled around the construction site like a weightless little doll." Emerson's deep laugh filled the immediate area.

With her feet firmly back on the ground, Connie made no effort to put space between herself and the older man. "I wasn't expecting you. What are you doing here?" she asked.

Finn stood by, wondering who this man was to her. He would have had to have been blind not to notice how radiant she suddenly looked. She was all but glowing and her smile resembled rays of sunshine reaching out to infinity. He'd thought she was a beautiful woman before, but what he'd been privy to before didn't hold a candle to what he was seeing now. Whoever this man was, he clearly lit up her world.

The one thing he did know was that this couldn't be the father who was always criticizing her.

"I thought you might need a little moral support," Emerson confessed, then laughed at his own words as he took a long look around the area. The entire grounds were humming with activity. "But you're obviously doing just fine—not that I ever thought you wouldn't. You don't lack for bodies, that's for sure," he ascertained.

"Did he send you to check up on me?" Connie asked out of curiosity.

There was no accusation in her voice. She knew that despite the fact that Emerson had been her mentor and all around best friend all these years, the man did work for her father, which meant that he had to abide by whatever wishes Calvin Carmichael voiced whenever possible. The last thing she wanted was to have Emerson terminated because of her. She knew she wouldn't be able to live with this.

"Oddly enough, no, he didn't," Emerson told her. "I meant what I said. I came down because I thought you might need a little moral support, this being your first real solo project and all. I mistakenly thought you might be in need of a pep talk, but here you are, all grown up and following in your dad's footsteps," he chuckled. "The old man would be proud of you if he saw this." Emerson gestured around the busy construction site.

"No, he wouldn't," Connie contradicted him knowingly. "You know that. If he were here, he'd be pointing out all the things he felt that I neglected to do, or had begun to do wrong..." Her voice trailed off as she eyed the heavyset man.

"All right, he wouldn't," Emerson conceded. "But just because he's always looking to find ways in which you can improve doesn't mean you're not doing a fine job to begin with."

She knew what Emerson was trying to do, and she loved him for it, but she was beginning to resign herself to what she was up against when it came to her father—a bar that was forever being raised no matter how great her achievements.

"It's okay, Stewart, really," she told the man, laying a hand on his arm. "My reward will be in a job well-done, not in any praise I'm hoping to get that'll just never come."

Out of the corner of her eye, she saw that Finn was still standing just on the outskirts of her conversation. "Oh, sorry, I guess your visit threw me. I'd like to introduce you to someone, Stewart. This is my foreman, Finn Murphy," she told the older man, hooking her arm through Finn's and drawing him into the small circle that she and Emerson formed.

"Finn, this is Stewart Emerson, the man who really runs Carmichael Construction Corporation." And by that she meant the man who provided the corporation with a heart.

Emerson pretended to wince. "Ouch, don't let your dad hear you say that or I'll have my walking papers before you can say, 'here's your hat.'" Leaning past the young woman he considered to be the daughter he never had, Emerson grasped the hand that her foreman offered and shook it heartily. "Foreman, eh?" he repeated. He released Finn's hand, but his eyes continued to hold the other man's. "You've done this kind of thing before?" Emerson asked.

Connie immediately placed herself between the two men again. "Don't browbeat my people, Stewart. I wouldn't have hired Finn for the position if I didn't think he could do the job."

Emerson looked at her knowingly. "You'd hire a puppy to do the work if it looked at you with eyes that were sad enough. No offense, Murphy," he quickly told Finn.

"None taken," Finn replied, then added, "as long as you don't think that's why I have this job."

The look in the older man's gray eyes was unreadable. "So this isn't your first time as a foreman? You've been one before?" Emerson asked him.

For the second time, Connie came to the cowboy's defense.

"You're doing it again. You're browbeating. And as to your question, Finn knows how to get men to follow orders." Which, she added silently, he did, just that he did it in his role as a bartender.

"Does he issue those orders himself, or does he let you do all the talking for him?" Emerson asked, a healthy dose of amusement curving his rather small, full mouth.

"Well, I do know enough not to get in her way if she decides she wants to say something," Finn told the other man politely.

Emerson regarded Connie's foreman thoughtfully. For a second, Finn thought that the older man might have felt that he'd overstepped the line. But the next moment, what he said gave no such indication.

"I just want to make sure that Connie's not being

taken advantage of—by anyone," Emerson emphasized pointedly.

"Understood," Finn replied with sincerity. "But Ms. Carmichael isn't someone who *can* be easily taken advantage of. In case you haven't noticed, sir," he pretended to confide, "she's very strong-willed and very much her own person."

"Excuse me, I'm right here," Connie reminded the men, raising her hand as if she were a student in a classroom, wanting to be called on. Dropping her hand, she got in between the two men again, looking from one to the other. "I appreciate what's going on here, but I *can* fight my own battles, you know," she informed them, the statement intended for both of the men on either side of her. "Now, then, Stewart, let me take you into that trailer you remembered to send out for me and show you the plans I drew up. Maybe I can renew your faith in me once you review them."

"My faith in you never faded," Emerson informed her as he followed her to the long trailer that was to serve as both her on-site office and her home away from home, as well.

Finn hung back. He'd already seen the plans, both the ones that she herself had drawn up—strictly from an architectural standpoint—and the ones that the structural engineer she'd consulted with had put together.

In addition, he thought that if he tagged along, his presence might be construed as an intrusion under the circumstances.

Sexy and stirring though he found her, she was,

after all, the one in charge of all this and ultimately, no matter what sort of feelings he might have for her, she was his boss. He had absolutely no business viewing her as anything else.

However, he silently promised himself, walking back to the backhoe, once this project was completed—and before she left Forever for Houston or her next assignment—he intended to carve out a little time alone for the two of them. There was no two ways about it. The lady most definitely intrigued him.

But he could bide his time and wait.

Patience, his older brother had drilled into him more than once, was the name of the game, and anything worth getting was worth the effort and the patience it took to wait it out.

STEWART EMERSON HAD been around the world of construction, in one capacity or another, for a very long time. Ever since fate had stepped in one night, putting him in the right place at the right time to save Calvin Carmichael from being on the receiving end of what could have been a fatal beating.

He had not only pulled the drunken, would-be muggers off Carmichael, but by the time he was done, he had also sent the duo to the hospital—which seemed only fair inasmuch as their plan apparently had been to send Carmichael straight to the morgue.

Shaken for possibly the first—and last—time of his life as well as uncharacteristically grateful, Connie's father had immediately offered the much larger—and unemployed—former navy SEAL a job as his body-guard.

As the business grew, so had Carmichael's dependence on Emerson, causing the latter's responsibilities to increase, as well.

Taking nothing for granted, Emerson made it a point to become familiar with everything that his employer concerned himself with and thus, while he couldn't draw up his own plans from scratch, he developed an eye for what was constructually sound, as well as what made good business sense.

Emerson made it a point to become indispensable to the corporation—and the man—in many ways.

But to Connie, the tall, heavyset, bearded man who could have easily been mistaken for Santa Claus these days would always be her one true confidant, her one true friend.

While for years, she had wanted nothing as much as to finally win her father's approval, nothing meant more to her than Emerson's opinion.

It still did.

"Well, what do you think?" she asked, gesturing toward the two large drawings that were tacked up side by side on the bulletin board that hung opposite the trailer's entrance. Between the two plans, they encompassed both the esthetics and the practical side of the building that was destined to be Forever's very first hotel.

Emerson spent a good five minutes studying first one set of plans, then the other. Finally, he stepped back and nodded his shaggy, gray head.

"I must say that I'm impressed. But then, I'd expect nothing less than the best from you," he told her, hooking his bear-like arm around her waist and pulling her toward him affectionately.

She laughed softly to herself, happily returning his hug. "That makes one of you."

Emerson released his hold from around her shoulders and did what he could to hide his sigh. There were times when he despaired if the man he worked for would ever realize exactly what he had and what he was in danger of losing.

"Your father's a hard man to please, Connie. We both know that. Did I ever tell you about the time that, after standing at the edge of the Grand Canyon, looking down for a good ten minutes, he turned to me and said, 'I could have done it better in probably half the time.' If your dad thinks he can criticize God's handiwork like that, the rest of us can't expect to be treated any better."

Though she gave Emerson no indication, it wasn't the first time she'd heard him tell her the story. Emerson had told it to her at least a couple of times, the first being a long time ago in an effort to make her feel better after her father had mercilessly taken apart a venture she'd been very proud of undertaking.

That was when she'd finally realized that *nothing* was ever going to be good enough to meet her father's standards, no matter how hard she tried.

But she wouldn't be who she was if she didn't keep on doing just that.

Trying.

Over and over again.

"I suppose I shouldn't care about pleasing him," she told Emerson, "but he put so much on this project turning out right, I feel that if I don't meet his expectations, that's it, I'm out of the game. Permanently," she added flatly.

"You'll never be permanently out of the game," Emerson told her, even though he knew that was what he'd heard Carmichael tell her. "Doesn't matter what he says at the time. He needs you, needs your energy, needs you to keep going, to be his eyes and ears in places he can no longer get to. He'll come around," Emerson promised in a tone that made an individual feel that he could make book on the man's words and never risk a thing.

"Meanwhile," Emerson continued, his eyes on hers, "you seem to have put together a pretty good crew. They're moving back and forth like well-trained workers. And that foreman of yours—" He paused for a moment, looking at her significantly. "I'd keep my eye on him if I were you."

"Why?" Connie asked. "Don't you trust him, Stewart?"

Emerson heard the slight defensive tone in her voice and wondered if she was aware of it herself. He had a better-than-vague idea just what it meant in this instance. "Hasn't got anything to do with trust," he told her.

She was trying to follow Emerson's drift, but he did have a habit of going off on a tangent at times. This seemed to be one of those times.

"Then what...?"

For once, Emerson didn't hide his meaning behind incomprehensible rhetoric that left the listener baffled for days—because he wanted to be certain that she was aware of what was going on. It was one thing for him to catch her off guard, and another to have some stranger do it.

"Your foreman looks at you as if you were a tall, cool drink of water, and he had just come crawling in on his chafed hands and knees across the length of the desert."

Connie stared at him in bewildered disbelief. "What does that even mean?" she asked. Finn had been nothing if not polite. If anything, she had been the one who'd stared at him that first day.

Emerson grinned. "That means, don't work any long hours alone with the man or you might find something besides this building being created."

What would Stewart say if he knew that she'd spent the night in Finn's house? Connie couldn't help wondering. She was fairly confident that Stewart would ultimately believe anything she would tell him. However, she was also certain that he'd worry twice as much as before—for no reason.

She shouldn't worry. She trusted Finn implicitly—and more important, even though she was admittedly more than just mildly attracted to Finn, she trusted herself not to jeopardize the project.

That was what was important here. Not the blush of a possibly fleeting romance, but the project.

The hotel.

Winning this invisible wager with her father and being assured that her career with the company was a done deal. Anything else came in a distant second—if that.

"I never knew you had such a rich imagination, Stewart," she said, grateful that her cheeks hadn't suddenly rebelled and given her away. "Finn only thinks of me as his boss. There are plenty of women around for him to choose from if he has other inclinations," she added innocently.

"I think he's already made his choice," he told her pointedly.

"And I think you're being way too protective of me—not that I don't appreciate it," she added, lovingly patting the man's cheek. "So, how long do I have you for?" she asked, effectively changing the subject.

In response, Emerson looked at his watch. "Just another couple of hours, I'm afraid. I'm flying back to Houston at four-thirty," he told her. "Your father's looking into acquiring another company to extend his domain, and I told him I'd be there to sit in on the meeting."

"Extension? Again?" she asked with a shake of her head. Wasn't it ever going to be enough for him? she wondered.

Emerson raised his wide, wide shoulders and then let them fall in a vague shrug. "Your father does have the resources."

Connie sighed and shook her head. "That's not the point. Is it really a smart move to spread himself so thin? What if he suddenly experiences a cash-flow problem? What then?"

Emerson laughed at the objections she raised because those were the exact same ones he'd raised with his employer. "And that's one of the reasons he has his suspicions that you're more mine than his." And then he went on to say what they both knew to be true. "Your father doesn't think that way, and ultimately, he's the boss."

"Still doesn't make him right."

"No," Emerson agreed. "It doesn't. But it also doesn't give us anything to fight with, either. He does what he wants to when he wants to."

Truer words were never spoken, Connie thought. She picked up a clipboard from the table. The next week's schedule was attached to that, as well.

"Well, I've got to get back to work." She paused and then quickly kissed the older man's cheek. "Thanks for coming to check up on me."

"Wouldn't have missed it for the world," he told her in all honesty. "And Connie?"

At the door, about to step out, she paused to look back. "Yes?"

"For what it's worth, I like him. Your foreman," he specified. "I like him."

She hadn't expected that warm feeling to go sweeping through her. It threw her for a second.

"Good. I'll let him know. Maybe the two of you can make an evening of it sometime," she said with a straight face.

The sound of Emerson's booming laugh followed her out of the trailer.

It was, for her, the most heartwarming sound she knew.

Chapter Twelve

Connie looked up from the wide drawing board in her trailer, startled to see Finn walking in. She knew the broad-shouldered man was only six-one but somehow, he just seemed to fill up the entire trailer with hi presence. Given the size of her trailer, that was saying a lot.

"I knocked," he told her. "Twice."

She had no doubt that he had. She'd been lost in thought, oblivious to her surroundings, for the last half hour or so.

Connie merely nodded at his statement. "Is there a problem?" she asked, ready to send him on his way if there wasn't. She was having trouble concentrating, and the schedules were overlapping in areas where they really shouldn't.

He and Connie had been working closely now for the past four weeks, and he'd gotten somewhat accustomed to her being braced for something to go wrong. Thus far, nothing had. If anything, it had been the complete opposite since they'd started work on the hotel.

But that still didn't change her attitude.

"No, no problem," he assured her. "As a matter of fact, it's going pretty damn well, don't you think?"

It did look that way, she had to silently concede. Working in what amounted to two complete shifts, utilizing whatever daylight was available and relying on strobe lighting that she'd had brought in less than six days into the job, Connie had to admit that Finn and the crew had made tremendous headway. The two backhoes were kept humming sixteen hours a day until the excavation was completed.

In addition, the weather had been incredibly cooperative. They had no *rain days* to interfere with the schedules she'd so carefully drawn up. All that had put them ahead of schedule, something she was not about to take for granted.

"We still have a long way to go before we're done," she pointed out.

Despite everything he had said to her at the outset, he noted that the woman just did not know how to relax or even coast along for a minute. He was just going to have to keep at her, Finn decided.

"But not as long as when we first got started," Finn countered.

"No, of course not. The double shifts have gotten us ahead of schedule—but all it'll take is a few rain days and we'll backslide."

It had to be really taxing, he thought, anticipating the worst all the time. She needed to break that habit—or he had to do it for her.

"Weatherman says no rain for the next week," he told her mildly.

Connie stated what she felt was the obvious. "Weathermen have been wrong."

"Look on the positive side," he coaxed.

Easy for him to say, she thought. He didn't have everything riding on this the way she had. Connie glared at him, debating just murmuring some noncommittal thing, then decided that after the way he'd gotten the crew to operate like a well-oiled machine, maybe she owed him the truth.

So, in a rare unguarded moment, she admitted, "I'm afraid to."

"Nothing to be afraid of," he told Connie. "As a matter of fact, I was going to suggest that maybe, for once, we could keep it down to a single shift and even have everyone knock off early."

"Early?" she echoed. "Why?" Her voice instantly filled with concern as she assumed the worst. "*Is* something wrong?" she asked again.

"No, nothing's wrong," he assured her again in a soothing voice.

"Then why would they want to stop early?" she asked. The crew was being paid, and paid well, to work. She didn't understand the problem.

He crossed to her, gaining a little ground. He glanced at the papers she had spread out over the large drawing board. It was a wonder she didn't have a constant headache, he marveled. He got one just glancing at it.

The scent that he was beginning to identify with her—lilacs and vanilla—began to slowly seep into his consciousness. He assumed that it was a cologne, but maybe it was her shampoo. Whatever it was, he found it both pleasing and arousing—a little like the woman herself, he couldn't help thinking.

He'd come here with an ultimate goal in mind, and he forced himself to get back to it.

"Maybe because all work and no play...you know the old saying."

Connie laughed softly to herself. "In my house, we weren't allowed to mention that old saying," she told Finn. "My father did *not* believe in 'playing.' Or smelling the roses, or anything that didn't have goals and work attached to it."

He'd thought he and his brothers had had it rough as orphans. Despite certain financial hardships, their life seemed like a positive picnic in comparison to the one she must have had.

"Your father's not here," he tactfully reminded her, then quickly added, "and Brett and Alisha are having their engagement party at Murphy's tonight, so, if it's okay with you, everything's temporarily on hold until tomorrow morning."

She looked at him for a long moment. He wasn't challenging her, she realized. If he was, then her reaction would have been completely different. Still, she wanted to push the imaginary envelope just a little to see what would happen.

"And if I say that the work has to go on?"

He didn't look away but continued to meet her gaze head-on. "You'll generate a lot of ill will, and you don't want to do that," he said quietly.

Connie suppressed a sigh. No, she didn't. While she

wanted to continue meeting and even surpassing her deadlines, the way her father's crews all did on their construction sites, she really did not want to maintain the kind of tense atmosphere that always existed on one of those work sites.

So, after another moment's debate, Connie nodded and gave her approval. "Fine, tell the men they have the rest of the evening off—but I'll expect them in on time tomorrow," she added, wanting to make sure that Finn didn't lose sight of the fact that she and not he was the one in charge.

"They will be. By the way, you're invited, you know."

She'd already turned her attention back to the schedules, which, in light of the lost shift, now had to be revised.

"To what?" she asked absently.

"To the engagement party."

That had her looking up at him again. "Oh. Well, thank you." She reached for a fresh piece of paper. Instead of using a laptop, she always liked to write her first draft of anything in pencil. "But I think I'll pass." She expected that to be the end of it.

It wasn't.

"Mind if I ask why?"

She indicated the drawing board before her. "If I'm losing an entire eight to ten hours of work, I've got to find somewhere to make it up."

To her surprise, rather than just go along with what she was saying, the way he had been since they had begun working together on the site, Finn took her hands in his and drew her away from the drawing board, saying, "No, you don't."

Stunned at the apparent mutiny, she blinked and stared at him. "Excuse me?"

"You heard me," he told her amicably. "No, you don't," he repeated, then added, "you don't have to do it tonight. Connie." He went on patiently. "It can't always be all about work."

Somewhere in the past few weeks, they had gone from his calling her Ms. Carmichael to using her first name. She wasn't sure exactly when, only that it had evolved rather naturally. She supposed that should have concerned her, but it hadn't.

However, she didn't appreciate being lectured to—especially when she knew in her heart that he was right. "Is this the *look up at the stars* speech again?"

"Think of it as the *let me take you to a party because life is more than just one big work schedule* speech," Finn told her, an amused smile playing along his lips.

She didn't want to be rude, but she couldn't go—for more than one reason. "Finn, I appreciate what you're trying to do—" she began.

"Good, that makes two of us," he replied. "Now, you're coming with me to this thing, and I'm not taking no for an answer."

Connie stared at her foreman in utter wonder. "You're actually going to give me a hard time about this?" she questioned.

"I'm going to *hog-tie* you if I have to," he corrected, "but you are definitely coming to the party."

She didn't understand what difference it made. "Why is it so important to you?"

He never hesitated. "Because you're important to me."

Her mouth dropped open. Did he just say what she thought he said? "What?"

Finn had no doubt that she had heard him the first time. Nonetheless, he went through it again.

"You heard me—and I *am* prepared to hog-tie you if I have to," he said with finality. "Now, are you going to sacrifice your dignity, or will you come along with me quietly?"

She looked into his eyes and had her answer. He wasn't kidding. She definitely didn't want to put him in a position where he had to carry out his threat.

"I guess I don't have a choice in the matter," she said.

"No," he agreed. "You don't. Besides, seeing you join the party will make the men respect you even more."

She was certain that if her work ethic didn't do it, it would take more than just joining in a toast to make her become one of the crew.

"I really doubt that," Connie told him.

She meant that, he realized. Finn shook his head, feeling genuinely sorry for her. "Then you have a few things to learn about the men who you have working for you."

But as he drew her over to the trailer's door, Connie suddenly looked down at what she was wearing.

Jeans and a work shirt. She definitely wasn't dressed for any kind of a party.

"I can't go like this," she protested, digging in her heels.

He gave her a quick once-over. She looked fine to him. Better than fine, actually, though he didn't say so out loud.

"Why?"

"Because I'm not dressed for a party."

"You might not be dressed for one of those fancy parties your father throws in Houston," he told her, "but trust me, you'll fit right in here."

Connie looked at him, surprised at his assurance. "How do you know about my father's parties?" she asked.

Rather than take offense, Finn merely grinned at the woman's question. "Oh, it's amazing what you can find on the internet when you know where to look. We're not nearly as backward here as you seem to think."

Color flashed across her cheeks. She hadn't meant to insult him. It was just that Forever seemed so self-contained and removed from the world she was familiar with.

"I never thought you were backward," Connie protested.

"Sure you did. But that's okay. You can make it up to me by coming to my brother's engagement party," Finn told her. "C'mon, let's go, boss lady. We're wasting time here."

To emphasize his point, he pulled the trailer door closed firmly behind him then immediately turned around and took her arm. Smiling, Finn guided her over to his truck. As he did so, he waved to the men, who appeared as if they were all looking in his direction, and called out, "She says it's okay!"

Instantly, a cheer went up.

Finn grinned in satisfaction. "See? You're responsible for instant happiness. Feels good, doesn't it?"

She had to admit that it did.

THE ENTICING SOUND of laughter coming from Murphy's reached them even before they ever pulled up before the saloon.

There were only a few vehicles, trucks like Finn's for the most part, that were actually parked near the saloon. It appeared that most of the people attending the engagement party that Finn and Liam were throwing for their older brother and his fiancée had walked to the saloon. That way, driving home would not be a problem or hazardous to anyone in the vicinity. The town jail was not built large enough to accommodate more than four offenders at a time.

Connie wasn't sure exactly what she expected to find once she walked into the saloon—maybe seeing the patrons line dancing—but what she did see wasn't all that different from other parties she'd attended. The clothes were definitely not as fancy, but there was live music, thanks to Liam and his band, and appetizing food arranged on side tables, buffet style, courtesy of Angel, Gabe Rodriguez's wife and Miss Joan's resident chef.

It was, all in all, a combined effort with everyone,

first and foremost, wanting the future bride and groom to have a good time.

The warmth within the saloon was unmistakable.

Connie fully expected to feel awkward and more than a little out of place at such a gathering. She was afraid she'd be regarded in much the same light as a parent who was looking over their child's shoulder on the playground during recess.

But to her surprise, she wasn't. She was not only greeted by everyone she walked past, but she was also swiftly made to feel welcomed, as if she *belonged* here with the others, celebrating the fact that two very special people had managed to find one another against all odds.

Connie would have been content to sit on the sidelines, quietly nibbling on the fried chicken that Angel had painstakingly prepared and listening to people talk.

But she quickly realized that Finn apparently had other ideas for her. He waited until she'd had a beer to toast the happy couple—who she confided looked absolutely radiant—and had finished the piece of chicken he'd gotten for her.

Once she had put the denuded bone down on her plate, Finn took the plate from her and put it down on the closest flat surface. She looked at him in confusion. Had she done something wrong without realizing it?

"What are you doing?" she asked him.

"You can't dance with a plate in your hands," he told her simply.

Dance? He couldn't be serious. "I can't dance without one, either," she informed him.

Finn was already drawing her to her feet, away from the table where she'd left her near empty bottle of beer. "Sure you can."

Connie shook her head. "I'm serious, Finn. I don't dance." She had two left feet, and she knew it.

But Finn obviously wasn't accepting excuses. "Don't? Or won't?"

"I won't because I don't," she insisted. With every word, he was drawing her further away from any small comfort zone she'd hoped to stake out and closer to the dance floor.

He laughed at the sentence she'd just uttered. "Practice saying that three times fast," he told her, all the while drawing her closer and closer to the area in the saloon that had been cleared for dancing.

She did *not* want to make a fool of herself in front of him.

"Finn, no, really. I'm going to wind up stepping all over your feet," she warned him.

Her excuse made no impression on him whatsoever. "They can take it. Besides, you're light, how much damage can you do? Don't worry, I'll teach you a few steps. You'll look like a natural," he promised.

Famous last words, she couldn't help thinking. Finn had no idea what he was getting into—but she did, and it was up to her to stop him before it was too late.

"Others have tried and failed miserably," she warned him.

"'Others' weren't me," he told her with a confidence that was neither cocky nor self-indulgent; it merely *was.* He took one of her hands in his and pressed his other hand against the small of her back.

"It's a slow song," he said, bringing her attention to it. "All you have to do is sway with the music and follow my lead."

All. Ha! The man had no idea what he was asking of her.

"I have no rhythm," Connie protested. She wasn't proud of it, but there it was. Connie Carmichael had less rhythm in her body than the average rock.

But Finn was obviously not accepting excuses to-night. "Everyone has rhythm, Connie," he countered easily. "You just have to not be afraid to let it come out. Now, c'mon," he coaxed, "let yourself feel the music. Close your eyes," he urged, "and just *feel* it," he stressed, gently guiding her movements.

This was an experiment that was doomed to fail from the very start, didn't he realize that? "You're going to be sorry," Connie warned him, even as she allowed herself to rest her head against his shoulder.

"I really doubt that," he assured her, his voice low, a whisper only she could hear despite the general din in the room.

A moment later, her eyes flew open.

She could actually feel it. Not just the rhythm, the way Finn had promised her that she would, but she slowly felt the effects of the music as it seemed to seep into her.

Or was that her reaction to the way his body was pressed ever so gently—and incredibly seductively—against hers?

Connie wasn't quite sure, but she could definitely feel herself reacting to the music—as well as to the man.

Her heart got into the act, revving up its pace.

When the music stopped, Connie was almost sorry to hear the notes fade away.

Raising her head from his shoulder, she realized that Finn was still swaying, still moving his feet to a beat that was no longer there.

"Song's over," she told him, whispering the words into his ear.

"Shh," he responded, a mischievous smile playing on his lips. "There'll be another one to take its place in a second."

And then Liam, looking his way, struck up another slow song with his band. Couples around them began dancing again.

"See?" Finn said. "What did I tell you?"

"I should have never doubted you," she told him with a laugh.

"No," Finn agreed, looking far more serious than she would have thought the moment warranted, "you shouldn't have."

SHE WASN'T SURE just how long she and Finn danced like that. Three, four songs came and went, all surprisingly slow in tempo. For her, it felt like just one long, timeless melody that went on.

"I haven't stepped on your foot yet," she marveled when she finally realized that she was *really* dancing and not just keeping time with her hips.

His laughter, soft and warm, ruffled her hair ever so slightly. Ruffled her soul a great deal more.

"The evening's still young," Finn told her. "You'll have more opportunities to live up to that threat if you really want to."

She liked what was happening now. It couldn't continue and she knew it, but just for now, she was content to pretend that it would.

"Actually, I kind of like the fact that I haven't yet," she told him. "How do you do it?" she marveled quietly.

"Do what?" he asked as he whirled her around ever so gently. The movement was so subtle, he had a feeling she didn't even know she executed it.

"How do you get me to move this way?" she asked, mimicking him step for step. "I'm usually completely uncoordinated."

"Magic," he said, whispering the word into her ear. "I do it with magic."

A warm, tantalizing shiver shimmied up and down her spine, instantly spreading out to all parts of her. Claiming her.

Just the same way that the man did.

She knew that Finn was just putting her on with that answer. The funny thing was, though, just for a moment or two there, she could have sworn that it actually *felt* like magic.

Or, at the very least, she was more than willing to pretend that it *was* magic.

Chapter Thirteen

Living under her father's roof, Connie had hosted more than her share of parties and so-called casual get-to-gethers, all to the very best of her ability.

Initially, she'd imagined that she fell woefully below the standard that her late mother had set. Victoria Carmichael had a charming, outgoing personality and the ability to make each person she spoke with feel as if they were the only person in the room. In addition, Victoria had a way of lighting up any room she entered. While Connie knew that her father had never said as much to her mother, after Victoria's death he was always quick to point out how incredibly short of the mark she fell each time he ordered her to take over her mother's role as hostess.

Eventually, through sheer perseverance, Connie grew into the role and became more at ease with the part she had to play. However, she'd never enjoyed herself during any of those gatherings the way she was enjoying herself tonight, here in the small, jam-packed bar, talking with people her father would have been quick to judge, cut off and summarily dismiss as being beneath him.

She began the evening as an outsider and was certain she would remain that way throughout the entire night, but she hadn't counted on Finn taking her in hand, hadn't taken into account the character of the people attending this engagement party.

She'd just assumed that they would regard her as an intruder and laugh about how she didn't fit in behind her back. Instead, to a person, they all went out of their way to make her feel welcome.

She thought perhaps this was because of Finn, that this was somehow his idea, and he had found a way to convey his wishes to the others attending the party. But she never saw him signal anyone, never saw him indicate to the people around them that he wanted them to treat her with kid gloves.

In a way, the opposite of the latter happened because as the evening wore on, she was being teased and kidded, all in such a way that she took no offense and found herself responding lightheartedly.

By evening's end, she came away with the feeling that the people she worked with, the people who essentially worked *for* her, actually *liked* her. Liked the fact that she had come out of her trailer after hours to meet them on their own ground and celebrate that two of their own were getting married.

Each time someone proposed a toast, she was right there with them, lifting her own glass and adding her voice to the well-wishers. And each and every time she did, she was aware of Finn beside her, smiling at her and approving the way she conducted herself.

For the most part, she had lived without approval for a very long time.

As she finished her glass of champagne in what felt like an umpteenth toast, laughter bubbled up within her as she leaned into Finn and whispered, "You were right."

Turning to look at Connie, he nodded. "Of course I was— About what, specifically?" Finn tagged on after a beat.

Her smile was wide and totally uninhibited. She must have looked like that as a child, Finn couldn't help thinking. "I am having fun."

"Yes, you are," he agreed with a laugh.

He noted that she was all but completely effervescent at this point. Connie leaned back a little too far, and he quickly put his arm around her waist to keep her from sliding off her stool. Finn gently took the empty glass from her hand and placed it on the first flat surface he saw on the bar, thinking that was safer than having her accidentally drop it. He knew that once this evening was behind her, she wouldn't appreciate being allowed to look foolish—or tipsy.

"Possibly just a tad too much fun," he speculated.

"There's no such thing as too much fun," Connie murmured. Standing up, she nearly went straight down, feeling as if her legs had mysteriously turned into tapioca pudding right beneath her. "Whoops." She grabbed hold of Finn by his shirt to keep from sinking to the floor. "I swear I only had one drink. Was there something special in it?" she asked, punctuating her question with a laugh that was mingled with a giggle.

"Nothing that wasn't in all the others," he assured her. And then he took a closer look at her. All her features had definitely mellowed. There was only one thing that could accomplish that to such a degree at this point. "How many have you had?" he asked her.

Finn hadn't bothered keeping track of the alcohol she consumed, but then, he hadn't thought he had to. Since she was so straitlaced, he assumed she'd keep track of herself.

Apparently, he was wrong, he realized.

"Just one," Connie said. "That's usually enough...."

She appeared so serious, it was hard for him not to laugh. "You're a cheap date." *Not that this is a date,* Finn added silently.

But he knew she'd be self-conscious later when she realized she'd been slightly tipsy, or even cutting loose. He took better hold of her arm to escort her out of the saloon.

Brett saw them leaving just as the couple reached the massive front door. Excusing himself from the people he was talking to, he quickly made his way over to them.

"Everything okay?" Brett asked, coming up behind the pair.

"Everything's wonderful," Connie answered in a gush before Finn could. "You throw a very mean party," she told the oldest Murphy brother.

"Actually, Finn here and Liam threw it," he gently corrected, "but on their behalf, thank you," Brett responded with a smile as he looked at her. Raising his eyes to Finn, he asked, "Are you taking her out for some air?"

"And then home," Finn added.

Connie whirled around to look at him. "You're taking me to your home?" she asked, visibly beaming. "Good, I've missed it."

Her comment took both men by surprise, especially since her stay at the ranch house had been limited to a single day.

"She's not going to remember saying that in the morning," Finn told his brother.

The latter nodded. Finn had cut her off just in time. "You need any help?" he asked Finn.

Finn smiled as he slanted a glance at the petite woman. "She's a live wire, but I can always tuck her under my arm if I have to."

"Good luck," Brett said before he turned back to the party.

"Why do you need luck?" Connie asked as Finn took her outside. And then she suddenly grinned from ear to ear. "Oh, I get it. You're looking to get lucky. Why didn't you say so?" she asked with a laugh.

"Because I'm not looking to get lucky," he told her patiently, although the idea of getting lucky with her had more than a little to recommend it. He forced himself not to think about it. He'd only be torturing himself. "I'm just looking to get you home."

"Where you'll have your way with me," she concluded with a nod of her head, as if it were already a foregone conclusion.

Finn watched as she got into the passenger side of his vehicle. "I'm not looking for that, either," he told her matter-of-factly, doing his best to bury the fact that this new uninhibited version of her was beginning to stir him.

"Why not?" she asked, confusion highlighting her expression. "Why don't you want to have your way with me? Don't you think I'm pretty?"

They were driving now, and Finn stepped down harder on the gas pedal, going faster than the posted speed limit, but just this once. He figured he could be forgiven for that. There was no one else out on the streets and the entire sheriff's department was back at Murphy's, anyway. He needed to get Connie back to her trailer before his restraint dissolved just like soap bubbles in the spring air.

Because she was staring at him, waiting for an answer, Finn finally said, "Yes, I think you're pretty. Beautiful, actually," he amended.

"But you don't want me," she concluded sadly.

She was making it very, very difficult for him. "You're my boss," he told her, hoping that would be the end of it.

"I know that, but you can still want me," she insisted.

He could almost *feel* his defenses crumbling. "Okay, I want you. But that still doesn't mean I'm going to do anything. It wouldn't be right," he informed her firmly.

He put his truck into Park. They'd arrived at her trailer none too soon, he thought, because he was quickly losing this battle of good intentions allied with restraint. She kept leaning into him, despite the seat belt that should have kept her on her side of the cab. Her hair was seductively brushing against his neck and cheek, making him yearn for her.

Unbuckling his seat belt, Finn quickly got out of the driver's seat and rounded the hood of his truck to get to Connie's side.

She was fumbling with her belt when he opened her door.

She raised her head and he'd never seen her look so vulnerable. "It won't open," she complained.

Finn reached over and uncoupled the seat belt, freeing her. The second he did, she all but slid into him as she got off the seat and out of the truck.

Looking up into his face, she declared, "I give you permission."

"Permission?" he echoed. Very carefully, he made sure she could stand, then removed his hands from her waist. "Permission for what?"

She stepped in closer again, as if there was a magnetic charge between her body and his. "Permission to do something about wanting me."

Oh, God, if only... He caught himself thinking before he shut down his thoughts.

"Connie, you're a little tipsy. Maybe this isn't the right time," he began, desperately trying to do the right thing. But the ground beneath his feet was swiftly eroding.

"I know exactly what I'm saying," she corrected. "What I don't have the courage to say during regular hours."

Finn told himself not to listen, and he tried to get her to go into the trailer. Instead, she whirled around, made a funny little noise about how dizzy that made her feel. Then, before he knew what was happening, she had anchored her arms around his neck, pushed herself up as high as she could and before he could stop her, she'd managed to press her lips against his.

At first, it was just the excitement of making contact that zipped through him like static electricity. But as she pulled herself up a little higher and pressed her lips against his a little more forcefully, all sorts of tantalizing things began happening all through his body.

And not just his body, he realized a second later because the woman on the other side of her all-but-death grip was definitely responding to him. He could feel her body, soft and pliant, against his. Could feel her lips against his, no longer just a target, a passive receiver, but most definitely in the game.

All the way in the game.

Before he knew what was happening, he found himself responding to Connie. *Wanting* Connie with a level of desire that took him completely by surprise and totally threw him off his game.

He enfolded her in his arms, deepening the kiss she had begun even as it took him prisoner.

And then, as a sliver of common sense returned, pricking at his conscience, Finn forced himself to stop kissing her. Forced himself to put some distance, however minuscule, between them.

Taking hold of both her arms—to keep himself at

bay as well as her—he gently pushed Connie back and said, "You don't want to do this."

There was a very strange light in her eyes, mixing in with the definite glimmer of mischief.

"Guess again," she said in a low, husky voice just before she retargeted his mouth again, sealing hers to it.

Finn knew damn well that he was supposed to be the sane one here, the one who was supposed to push her away again for her own good and keep pushing until she finally stopped coming at him. But he had used up his small supply of nobility quickly and she had refused to listen, refused to back away the way he'd told her to.

And damn, he'd been wanting this since the first time he'd turned around and saw her out there on the ranch, standing next to her less-than-useful sports car, looking at him as if she'd never seen a bare-chested man sweating in the hot sun before. She had generated a strong wave of desire within him then, and that wave had never really subsided, never receded so much as an iota.

Instead, it had remained suspended, waiting to be released.

Waiting for an opportunity like this.

Before he knew what he was doing and could discover a way to talk himself out of it, he swept Connie up into his arms. Then, pushing his shoulder against the trailer door to open it, Finn carried her inside.

The second the door was closed—and even before— Connie was all over him—marking his total undoing.

He could hardly keep up with her.

Her hands were everywhere, tugging at his clothing, skimming along his body, coaxing him to let go of his last thread of sanity and come to her.

And then he did.

He remembered the whole scenario taking place in what amounted to a hot haze, a frenzy of activity. A strange wildness had seized him as he found himself wanting her so very badly that it actually physically *hurt*. Wanting her and waiting for even an instant hurt in such a way that it felt as if it almost turned the air in his lungs to a solid substance.

SHE WAS GOING to regret this, a little voice in her head told her over and over, taunting her. Pointing out obvious things.

The actual deed couldn't possibly live up to the expectations she had built up in her head. She was just setting herself up for a fall.

And worst of all, he was going to brag about this to his friends, tell them that she was an easy mark and not really worth the effort in the end.

He'd disappoint her and she him.

All these things raced through her mind at top speed, repeating themselves over and over again. They should have stopped her.

On some level, she knew that.

But even so, her body was begging her not to listen to anything but its own rhythms, its own demands. All along, if she was being honest with herself, she had known that this man was going to be her downfall and yet she'd still hired him, still kept him around. Still allowed his presence to fuel her dreams at night, when her guard was so woefully down.

She couldn't put a stop to it, couldn't rescue herself at the last moment because she discovered that every moment was just too delicious for her to voluntarily end.

She reveled in the way his lips felt against her skin, creating an excruciatingly wondrous moist trail of kisses that covered her breasts, went down to her belly and even farther than that, creating a dizzying warmth at the very core of her.

A warmth that coupled with a fire, which reduced her to a mass of rejoicing whimpers as climaxes blossomed within her over and over again.

Encased in dusky desire, Connie uttered not a single murmur of protest as she heard rather than saw Finn sweep away the schedules she'd labored so hard over, sending them all tumbling to the floor as he cleared the drawing board for her.

For them.

Squeals of ecstasy escaped her as he pushed her down onto the cleared flat surface and proceeded to make love to every inch of her, using his hands, his lips, his very breath to claim each part of her as his very own.

And when restraint tore at the weakened ties that were meant to keep her in place, when she arched and bucked against his body, silently begging for the union it'd promised, he gave in and took her, capturing her mouth at the last second so that they were joined together at all possible points.

The eternal dance began, and it was one that, to her stunned delight, Connie quickly mastered, getting in sync with each of his movements so that only a moment into the dance, they began to move as one, increasing the tempo as one.

And reaching the highest peak of pleasure as one, as well.

She felt the rainbow reach out and claim her, filling her with such exquisite euphoria that she didn't want to ever let it go.

This was where true happiness had been hiding from her all along.

And he had brought it to her.

Chapter Fourteen

Sanity returned far too swiftly.

It wore spurs on its boots and tracked a layer of mud all over Finn's conscience. The weight of his conscience was almost too oppressive to bear.

Pivoting on his elbows, Finn did his best to create space between their bodies, then moved over to one side, separating from her completely. He didn't know whether to apologize to her for what had happened, or just allow the silence to grow until it filled the room and overtook them, leaving no opening for conversation.

Rather than turn from him the way he expected her to, Connie just watched him. If she'd been giddy and tipsy before, she appeared to be totally clear-eyed now.

Was she angry? Did she think he took advantage of the situation and of her?

Did she hate him for it?

The silence continued to grow, becoming unwieldy to the point that he felt he just couldn't tolerate it any longer. Silence had never bothered him before, but it did now.

"Say something," Finn finally urged. But even as he was on the verge of begging her to speak, he braced himself for what he felt was inevitably coming: a barrage of words that would most likely compare him to the very lowest life form on the face of the earth.

What he found he wasn't prepared for was the actual word that did leave her lips.

"Wow."

Finn blinked, utterly positive that he had misheard her. Almost hesitantly, he whispered in confusion, "Say again?"

"Wow," she repeated, this time accompanying the word with a breathy sigh. "You know, I think the earth actually moved." She turned into him to see his face more clearly. "You don't have earthquakes down in this part of Texas, do you?"

"No," he replied uncertainly, studying her. Was she pulling his leg? Getting him to lower his guard before she hit him with a lethal punch?

"Didn't think so," she said, the smile taking on a dreamy quality. "Then I guess *wow* stands."

Her reaction just wasn't sinking in. He was still waiting for an explosion. "You're not angry?" Finn asked, still more than a little uncertain as he studied her demeanor.

"No, why would you think that I was angry?" She sat up for the first time. "Do I look angry?" Connie asked, glancing around to see if there was some sort of a reflecting surface available to her. She wanted to see herself so she could ascertain whether or not *she* thought she looked angry.

"No, you don't," he told her, treading very lightly. "But I thought…well…I thought that you'd feel I took advantage of you, and also you're my boss."

So that was it, Connie thought. At that moment, Finn went up another notch in her estimation. He really *was* a good guy.

"I had one drink," Connie admitted. "Not so much that I can't remember that I was the one who made the first moves—" she pointed out. "I kissed you first, not the other way around."

"So you're not angry," he concluded, wanting to be absolutely sure.

"Right now I'm still too tingly to be angry," Connie freely admitted—another first for her, she thought. She'd made love before, but each time all her feelings, all her reactions, were neatly compartmentalized. This deliriously happy feeling was definitely something new—and it thrilled her. Probably more than it should, she realized. But she just couldn't get herself to put a lid on it. So, just for tonight, she allowed herself to enjoy it.

Connie glanced down on the floor at the flurry of papers scattered there. "I will, however, be upset in the morning when I try to put all those schedules into some kind of order again."

That *had* been his fault. He'd swept her schedules to the floor. "I can help with that," Finn quickly volunteered.

"How?" Connie asked with a laugh. "By sweeping them out of the trailer?" she asked, amusement playing on her lips.

"By organizing them for you on my own time," he told her, sitting up beside her and looking at the mess below their feet. He was acutely aware of her sitting like that beside him. "But right now, if you're sure you're not angry…"

She turned her face to his and softly whispered, "Yes?"

He'd just had her and here he was wanting her again. Wanting her so badly, he felt himself literally *aching* for her. "I'd like to make love to you properly."

She pretended to look at him with wide-eyed confusion. "Oh, then what we just did, that was improper?"

He was fairly certain there were several states where what they'd just done would have been banned. "Highly."

"I see," she murmured thoughtfully. "And now you'd like to show me how it should have actually been done, is that it?"

His smile reached out to all parts of him, shining in his eyes as well as on his lips and in his demeanor. "Yes, I would."

Connie slid off the drawing board, her bare feet touching the scattered papers on the floor. She nodded her head slowly, as if she was thinking it over. "Never let it be said that I refused to leave myself open to a learning experience."

Finn followed suit, standing up beside her. It was all she needed. Connie wound her arms around his neck, vividly aware of the fact that they were both still very nude.

She smiled up into his eyes. "You do realize that I'm still just a little dazed."

His arms went around her, bringing her even closer to him than a sigh. "I'm counting on it." When he saw her raise an eyebrow at his statement, Finn was quick to explain, "You're a lot less inhibited—and a great deal more trusting."

She saw no reason to argue that. He was right. "I'll have to work on that. Tomorrow," she decided. "I'll work on it tomorrow."

Because tonight, she knew she would be otherwise occupied.

And thrilled because of it.

FINN APPROACHED HER carefully a little after eight the next morning, not quite sure what to expect or how to behave. He'd slipped out quietly from her trailer an hour before dawn. He'd wanted to give Connie her privacy, and he wasn't sure just how she would deal with the sight of him in her bed now that they had to go back to work.

If there was shame and discomfort on her part, since he was the cause of it, he wanted to spare her the sight of him for as long as possible.

At the same time, he knew he didn't have the luxury of simply going into hiding. He was her foreman, her second in command and as such, he had to be there, available for her *to* command.

Approaching her trailer, he knocked lightly, gave himself to the count of three, braced his shoulders and then walked in, every part of him prepared for some form of rejection, denouncement or whatever it was that would make Connie feel vindicated.

Finn was far too much of a realist to believe that fairy tales went on forever. He was just hoping that she didn't ultimately hate him for last night because for him, last night would live on in the annals of his mind for a very, very long time.

When she heard the door opening, Connie glanced over her shoulder. "Morning. I was beginning to think you were going to sleep in today."

Connie waved her hand, indicating the tall, covered white container on the side of her drawing board. An opened, partially empty container was standing right next to it.

"Got you some black coffee at Miss Joan's," she went on, turning back to her work. "The woman is selling India ink as coffee, but she swears that it gets your motor running, so drink up. We've got a really full day ahead of us if we've got a prayer of keeping this puppy on schedule."

Though he'd always thought of himself as being able to roll with punches, Finn was having trouble processing what was going on. Not because he was hungover, but because Connie seemed so different, so much—*looser* for lack of a better word—than she had been before. And definitely more upbeat and cheerful. She still looked like the same woman, the same beautiful blue eyes, the same killer figure, but it was as if she was a newer, more improved version of heresf. If she'd been a software program, he would have thought of her as Connie 2.0. He stared at the covered, oversize paper container she'd pointed to on the drawing board. "You got me coffee?" That alone was enough to throw him for a loop.

She nodded again. "Just in case you were having trouble getting in gear this morning."

"You have any of this?" he asked.

"I don't drink India ink," she informed him matter-of-factly. "I did get myself a cup of regular coffee, though. Just enough coffee to give the creamer something to work with and lighten," she told Finn. Now that he looked into her container, he could see that the contents appeared to be exceedingly light, close to the color of milk itself. "Now drink up, Finn," she was saying, "we're wasting daylight."

That was an exaggeration. "It isn't even eight yet," he pointed out.

But Connie absently nodded, as if he'd just agreed with her. "Like I said, we're wasting daylight."

Shaking his head even as humor crept in and curved the corners of his mouth, Finn took the lid off his container and took a very long, savory drag of his very black coffee.

As hoped for, the caffeine hit him with the kick of a disgruntled mule.

FROM THAT DAY FORWARD, work continued at an almost effortless pace. There were a few hitches, and one on-site near accident with a girder, but overall, they kept on track, and the hotel took on its desired shape.

As it transformed from a hole in the ground to an edifice of impressive lines and structure, the citizens of Forever began to redesign their paths so that it took them by the excavation site. They came to note the progress or simply to watch some of their own operate the sophisticated machinery with precision.

They came to watch girders, posts, bolts and nails become something greater than the sum of their initial parts.

And a number of them, mostly the younger females, came to observe bare-chested men sweat and strain as they diligently created something they would all be proud of.

As Connie oversaw each and everyone's progress as they approached the end goal, occasionally issuing orders, or changing directives, her project, the bet she had with her father, turned into something far more meaningful to her. It no longer represented just winning an impulsive bet.

She was no longer the girl who was trying everything she could to get just a drop of her father's praise. There was far more going on here now.

The hotel became not only *her* project, but the crew working on its completion also became *her* men. And, she was delighted to discover, she was proud of them— proud of each and every one of them because of what they contributed to the whole.

And she fervently hoped that they returned the feeling, at least to some degree.

Somewhere along the line, shortly after Brett's engagement party—and her awakening as a woman— Connie began to document the crew's progress with the hotel. She would aim her smartphone at anything she felt should be preserved. This was her very first solo project and as such, like a first-born, each tiny milestone deserved to be forever frozen in time.

What she felt were the best shots she passed on, not to her father, but to Emerson, trusting him to choose which photo her father should see and which he might have found some minor, underlying fault with. It was a given fact that Calvin Carmichael was not known for his tact or restraint, especially where the company logo was involved. Emerson knew her father the way no other living soul did, and she trusted him to make the proper judgment calls on her behalf.

She could also trust him to be on her side. True to his nature, Emerson would send back an encouraging text that praised not just her efforts, but also her progress and the way the hotel was obviously shaping up. He was her own personal cheering section, and Connie loved him for it the way she knew she could never hope to love her father. On the home front, her life was also progressing equally well.

What could have become a very awkward situation between her and Finn—with neither of them knowing how to behave or react to one another—became, in fact, a very comfortable existence that they found themselves falling into without any actual discussion on their parts. Certainly no attempts to lay down any groundwork for themselves.

Connie was a woman who had, from a very young age, lived by her schedules. She always had to have her days mapped out from moment one to way beyond the final time frame. It made her feel as if she had control.

And yet this sort of spontaneous forward movement worked for her. Not knowing worked for her. As did the delicious warmth of anticipation. And holding her breath when Finn walked up behind her, waiting for the first moment that his hand would brush against her shoulder, or touch her face.

Or the first moment that he would make her insane with desire.

They made love every night, the perfect ending to a perfect day. She had never been happier—as long as she didn't allow herself to dwell even fleetingly on the specter looming in the background: the completion of her project.

For now, she just took heart in the fact that the project was progressing well ahead of schedule and she, well, she was progressing in directions she had never dreamed she would.

As the days and weeks went by, Connie began to think of Forever as her special magical place, except that she knew Forever was real, too.

Still, because it had become so very special, she fervently hoped that Forever—and Finn—wouldn't disappear.

"What's that you're humming?" Finn asked her as they stood off to the side one day, observing the day's progress.

"I didn't realize I was humming," she confessed. "Just some nameless tune to keep my spirits up."

She didn't want to admit that what was actually keeping her spirits up was the fact that he was at her side from morning to night—and thereafter.

Work-wise, there had been a problem with the design when it came to the plumbing on the ground floor, but she had managed to resolve it with a few key strokes of her pen on the blueprints, then conveyed what needed to be done by way of integral changes to the men installing the pipes.

All of which had left Finn in complete awe of her—and also drove home the stark realization—again—that she didn't belong here. It was further proof to him that once this hotel, which was so very important to her, was finally finished, Connie would go back to her upscale world and be permanently gone from his life.

Which, had this been any one of a number of other times in his life—involving other women—would have been fine with him.

But it wasn't fine this time.

Because this wasn't like any of those other times. This time, he admitted to himself, was different because *she* was different.

And he was different because of that.

Different because he was in love with her.

It had hit him one night as they were making love in her bed. Hit him with all the subtlety of a rampaging mustang trying to divest itself of a newly cinched saddle. He felt a tenderness toward her, a sensation he hadn't experienced before, a desire to protect her not just for a little while, but for all the years to come.

That part had become clear to him when he discovered his desire to shield Connie from her father's harsh behavior. Something had been bothering her for the past few hours. He was aware of it even as they were making love.

"What's wrong?" he asked her as they lay there together, the sounds of heavy breathing mingling and fading.

"Nothing."

"I know you. That's not *nothing*. Now out with it—or do I have to torture you to get it out of you?" As if to make good on his threat, he wiggled his fingers before her as if he was about to tickle her. The second he brushed his fingers against her, Connie quickly surrendered.

"It's nothing, really. I sent my father a text update, complete with photos and the fact that we were way ahead of schedule."

"Did he respond?"

"Oh, he responded all right. He texted back 'Stop bragging. It's not finished yet. You could still fail.'" Connie shrugged. "I suppose it's just the way he is, and I shouldn't have expected any other response from him. It's just that every once in a while, I keep hoping he'd change. That this one time, he'd tell me he was satisfied."

"And that he was proud of you?" Finn guessed.

"Yeah, there's that, too," Connie admitted with a shrug.

Finn could feel anger building up. Anger aimed at a man who had no idea how lucky he was to have a daughter like Connie. "Leopards don't change their spots," he told her gently.

A smile played on her lips. She knew he was try-

ing his best to cheer her up, to make her focus on what
she had and not feel inadequate because of what she'd
failed to achieve.

"Very profound."

"Also very true," he pointed out.

She sighed and nodded. Finn was doing his best,
and she was grateful to him for it. "My father doesn't
matter."

"Damn straight he doesn't matter," he'd told her,
surprising her with the fierceness in his voice because
up until now, Finn hadn't really commented on her father at all. "He's never going to be satisfied and even
if he thinks you've done better than fantastic, he's not
about to tell you because somehow, he feels that would
be cutting down *his* image." His eyes held hers as he
tried to make her understand what seemed so obvious
to him. "Connie, you could do the best damn job in the
whole world, and that man isn't going to tell you. He's
just going to look for something, *anything,* to point to
and find it lacking." He raised her chin with the crook
of his finger when she tried to look away. "But you and
I know the truth."

"And what's the truth?" she asked with a glimmer
of a smile forming on her lips.

"That no one holds a candle to you. That you've got
a crew that'll follow any order you give them not because it's an order but because you were the one who
gave it. They're not just a crew, Connie, they're *your*

crew. I know these guys. Trust me when I tell you that really has to count for something," he told her.

The smile that rose to her lips told him that, at least for tonight, he'd gotten his point across.

Chapter Fifteen

When her cell phone rang the following morning, Connie was busy finalizing the next week's schedule, which was, happily, far ahead of her original schedule. Things were moving right along, and she was exceedingly pleased with herself and with life in general.

She couldn't remember a time when she was happier—or even just as happy—than she was right now.

Pulling the phone out of her pocket, she pressed Accept without looking at the caller ID. Emerson called her almost daily to find out how things were going, and it was his voice she expected to hear on the other end when she said, "Hello."

But it wasn't Emerson.

It was her father.

Carmichael began without exchanging any pleasantries or even offering a perfunctory greeting. As always, he was all business. "I went over your latest report last night."

When he paused, she knew better than to press him for his opinion. It would come soon enough.

She was right. "I must say, you didn't mess up as badly as I expected you to."

Could she have expected anything more? Connie asked herself wearily. "Heady praise, Dad."

"I'm not in the business of heady praise," he told her curtly. "In case you've forgotten, I'm in the construction business. Which leads me to my next point. I've got a new project for you to supervise—it's a museum. Right up your alley. It's on the east coast so I'm pulling you off the hotel."

She felt as if she'd just walked across a land mine and it had gone off. "But the hotel's not finished," she protested.

"I'm not blind. I can see that," he snapped. "I'll be sending Tyler Anderson to oversee its completion. It's not your concern anymore, Constance. Pack. I want you here by morning."

"But—" She heard a strange noise on the other end of the line and found herself talking to dead air. Her father had terminated the call.

Frustration flared through her. "Damn," Connie muttered to herself as she continued to stare at the now silent phone in her hand.

There was a quick knock on her trailer door and the next moment, Finn stuck his head in. "Hey, we're sending out lunch orders to Miss Joan's, and I just wanted to ask what you wanted to eat today."

That was when he saw the shell-shocked expression on Connie's face. Lunch was forgotten. Finn came all the way into the trailer and crossed to her.

"What's wrong?" he asked.

And then he noticed the cell phone in her hand. His mind scrambled to put the pieces together. Had she just gotten bad news? Was that what was responsible for that completely devastated look on her face?

"What happened?" he prodded again. "Did your father just call?" She raised her eyes to his but still wasn't saying anything. "Talk to me, Connie. I can't help if you don't talk to me."

"You can't help even if I do," she answered quietly, staring unseeingly straight ahead of her. She felt as if everything was crumbling within her.

Taking hold of Connie's shoulders, he gently guided her to a chair and forced her to sit down.

"It was your father, wasn't it?" It was no longer a guess. Only her father could make her look like that. After a moment, Connie nodded. "What did he say? Because no matter what that man said, you know you're doing a damn good job here and—"

Her quiet voice cut through his loud one. "He wants me to come home."

Finn tried to make sense out of what she had just said. "When you finish?"

Connie slowly moved her head from side to side. "No, now."

That didn't make *any* sense. From what she'd told him, her father was obsessive about projects being completed on time, under budget and to reflect everyone's best work to date.

"But the hotel's not finished. You still—"

Connie turned to look at him, focusing on his face

for the first time. She was struggling very hard not to cry.

"He's sending someone else to finish overseeing the job. He says he has another project for me. Seems there's a museum going up on the east coast he wants me to be involved in."

"The east coast?" Finn echoed. That was half a continent away. *She'd* be half a continent away, he thought, something twisting in his gut.

"The east coast," she repeated numbly.

"Are you going?" he asked, doing his best to suppress his anger at this unexpected, sudden blow.

Connie released a huge sigh that felt to her as if it went on forever. "He's my boss. I have to."

Finn wanted to argue that, but he knew he had no right. All he could do was ask questions. "Did he say why he wanted you off this project?"

Connie shook her head. "He's the boss. He doesn't have to explain anything. He never has before."

Finn told himself that his feelings about this unexpected turn of events, his feelings about her, didn't matter. That he'd known all along that this day was coming. It had just arrived a little sooner than he'd anticipated.

The important thing here was Connie. This was what she'd wanted all along, to have her father recognize her ability to helm projects. The man clearly wouldn't be sending her to begin another one if he didn't feel that she was good when it came to setting things up and getting them rolling.

"How soon?" he asked her, the words tasting bitter in his mouth.

Her eyes shifted to his. "Soon" was all she said in reply. She couldn't bring herself to say "immediately" just yet. She knew that she would break down if she did.

"Well," Finn began, doing his best to sound philosophical and supportive instead of angry and exasperated, "this is what you've been hoping for all along, right?"

"Right," she answered without even attempting to sound enthusiastic.

She slanted a glance at Finn. Why wasn't he as upset about this as she was? Did he actually *want* her to go? Didn't he care that she wasn't staying?

Finn was doing his best to find his way through this emotional maze he suddenly found himself in. "In his own way, I guess your father's telling you that he thinks you're capable of representing him, of helming an important project. He's not asking you to accompany him but to go to the location without him. This means that he's admitting that you *can* fly solo," he said with as much enthusiasm as he could summon—all for her sake. But then he looked at her closely. "You're not smiling."

"Sure I am," she responded evasively. "On the inside."

"Oh. Sorry, I left my x-ray-vision glasses in my other jeans," he told her sarcastically. The next moment, he told himself that wasn't going to get him anywhere. He ditched the attitude. "So how much time *do* you have?" he asked, acutely aware of the minutes that were slipping away, out of his grasp. Quite possibly his last minutes with her.

"He wants me to be in Houston in the morning. That means I have to leave by tonight at the latest."

She was saying the words, but they still hadn't sunk in yet. She was leaving. Leaving Forever. Leaving crews who weren't just crews anymore; they had become her friends. Leaving a man who had her heart in his pocket.

"Tonight?" Finn questioned, his voice echoing in his own head. "He really does want you back immediately, doesn't he?"

Don't cry. Don't cry, she kept telling herself over and over again. "Looks that way."

"And he didn't give you a reason for all this hurry?" Finn pressed. He really *hated* things that didn't make any sense.

"I already told you," she said, bone-weary, "he's the boss. He doesn't have to explain himself or give reasons. He just gives orders."

Connie kept looking at him, silently begging Finn to tell her not to go. To come up with some lame excuse why she just couldn't pick up and leave right now. *Any* excuse.

But there was only silence in the trailer.

"The men aren't going to be happy," Finn finally said, speaking up.

"They need the money," she reminded him. That was what he'd told her at the outset of the job, that most of the people being hired were taking this on as an extra job. "They'll adjust."

Finn snorted. "Not readily."

"But eventually," Connie countered sadly.

She knew she was right. Within a few months, nobody would even remember that she had been here, Connie thought sadly. She felt as if someone had dropped an anvil on her chest. The upshot was that she was having trouble catching her breath as well as organizing her thoughts into a coherent whole.

Most of all, she was trying to deal with the realization that Finn seemed to be all right with the thought of her leaving. He hadn't said a word of protest, just asked her a few questions about the situation, that's all.

Well, what did you expect? That he'd fall down on one knee and beg you to stay? That he'd ask you to marry him because he just couldn't live a day without you? Get real, Con. This was a nice little interlude as far as he's concerned, but now it's over and it's time for him to move on. You move on, too. Move on, or become a laughingstock.

Connie raised her head and glanced in his direction. "If you don't mind, I've got a lot of things to do before I can leave, and I can do it faster if I'm by myself."

"Sure," he told her. "I'll get out of your hair" were his parting words as he left.

Connie nodded numbly in response.

But how do I get you out of my soul? she asked him silently, staring at the closed door.

With no need for restraint any longer, she allowed her tears to fall.

"HEY, WHAT THE hell happened to you?" Brett asked when Finn walked into the saloon a few minutes later.

Murphy's didn't officially open for another few hours although the doors weren't locked and even if they were, all three of the brothers had keys to the establishment since it belonged to all of them.

"You look like you just lost your best friend," Brett said, concerned when Finn didn't answer him.

Finn shrugged his shoulders, leaving his brother's question unanswered. Instead, he went behind the bar, took out a shot glass and then grabbed the first bottle of hard liquor within reach.

When he went to pour, Brett pushed the shot glass away. The alcohol wound up spilling onto the bar.

"I can always pour another shot," Finn said.

"And it'll land on the bar, same as the first shot," Brett informed him, "so unless you plan to lick yourself into a drunken stupor, put down the bottle and tell me what's going on with you."

"Always the big brother," Finn said sarcastically.

"Yeah, I am, so deal with it. Now what the hell's going on with you? You're not going anywhere until you tell me," Brett declared with finality.

Finn's throat felt incredibly dry as he said, "She's leaving."

"When the hotel is finished," Brett said, reviewing the facts as he knew them.

Finn's expression darkened further. "No, now. Today," he snapped. The hotel had a ways to go before it was completed. He still felt that Connie's abruptly leaving for a new project didn't make any sense.

Though, he could admit he was more invested than he'd thought.

"Why? Did you two have a fight?"

"No, we didn't 'have a fight,'" Finn retorted angrily. "Her father decided he wanted her working on something else."

"What does Connie say about it?" Brett asked him quietly.

Finn blew out a shaky breath, angrier than he could ever remember being. "She isn't saying anything about it. She's going."

Brett continued to study his brother as he responded. "Did you ask her not to?"

"No," Finn bit off. It wasn't up to him to ask. It was up to her to *want* to stay, he thought, totally frustrated.

Brett gave up standing quietly on the sidelines. "Why the hell not?"

"What am I supposed to say?" Finn demanded.

"How about 'Connie, don't go. I love you.' From where I stand, that sounds pretty simple to me," Brett told him.

Didn't Brett understand what was at stake here? "I'd be asking her to give up everything, that big house, the future she's been working toward all these years. Give it all up and stay here in Forever with me." The inequality of that was staggering, Finn thought.

Brett nodded his head. "Sounds about right."

"Damn it, Brett. I haven't got anything to offer her," Finn cried angrily.

Brett looked at him for a long, long moment. And

then he shook his head sadly. "If you think that, then you're dumber than I thought you were."

Finn gritted his teeth and ground out, "You're not helping."

"You're not listening," Brett countered. "Connie grew up in pretty much the lap of luxury from what she said—and she didn't seem able to crack a smile when she first got here. After working in Forever—and associating with your sorry ass—she's a completely different person. She looks *happy.* That's what you can do for her. You can make her happy," Brett emphasized. "That's not as common a gift as you might think."

Finn waved a hand at his brother. Brett was giving him platitudes. "You don't know what you're talking about."

"Ask her to stay," Brett urged. "Honestly, what have you got to lose?"

"Face," Finn retorted. "If she turns me down, I can lose face."

Brett raised and lowered his shoulders in a careless, dismissive shrug. "It's not such a great face. No big loss. Might even be an improvement," he told Finn, keeping a straight face. And then he turned serious. "And if you don't ask her to stay, you'll never know if she would have."

Finn shook his head, rejecting the suggestion. "If she wanted to stay, she would."

Brett threaded his arm around his brother's shoulders. "Women operate under a whole different set of guidelines than we do, Finn. You should know that by now." Brett suddenly pushed his brother toward the front door. "Now stop being such a stubborn jerk and go tell her you want her to stay. That you *need* her to stay."

"It's not going to work," Finn insisted.

Brett pretended to consider that outcome. "Then you'll have the satisfaction of proving me wrong for the first time in your life."

Finn opened his mouth to argue that rather unenlightened assessment, then decided he didn't want to stay here, going round and round about a subject he felt neither one of them could successfully resolve.

Instead, he shoved the bottle he'd pulled from the shelf earlier back on the bar and stormed out of the saloon.

"Make me proud!" Brett called after him.

HE DIDN'T KNOCK this time. Instead, Finn burst into the trailer, swinging the door open so hard that it hit the opposite side, making a resounding noise.

In the middle of packing, Connie jumped and swung around. "Finn, you scared the hell out of me," she cried, her hand covering her heart, which was pounding hard for more than one reason. Hope began to infuse itself through her—hope that maybe, just maybe "happily ever after" wasn't completely off the table. A hint of a smile broke through even as she held her breath.

And prayed that he would say something she needed to hear.

"Well, then we're even," he replied. "Because the thought of you leaving Forever is scaring the hell out of me."

She let the shirt she'd been folding drop from her hand as she regarded him. Just what was he up to? "You certainly didn't act like it did." It was an accusation more than an observation.

"No, I didn't," he agreed. The temper he'd been grappling with since he'd left her trailer was only beginning to come under control. "And you used the right word—act. I was *acting* like it didn't bother me because I knew that was what you'd wanted since you got here, to show your father that you could handle a project on your own, to show him that you were damn good for the company and deserved to be treated with respect instead of being treated like a lackey.

"And I knew that once you were finished building the hotel, you'd leave. I figured I was okay with that. But just now I had to *act* as if I was—because I wasn't. I wasn't *okay* with that. I wasn't *okay* with you leaving."

"You weren't?"

"No, I wasn't. And I'm not," he told her, changing his tenses to make her understand that his feelings were still ongoing. "Look, I know I don't have the right to ask you to stay, and I don't have anything that's close to measuring up to what you have waiting for you back in Houston. I don't even—"

Connie cut him off. "Ask me to stay," she said softly.

Finn was desperately searching for the right words to convince her to stay. When she interrupted, his train of thought came to a screeching halt. He *couldn't* have heard her right.

"What?"

"Ask me to stay," Connie repeated. "Say the word."

He stared at her in disbelief for a long moment, stunned into silence.

"Stay," he whispered quietly, certain that she was seeing how far she could get him to go. He honestly didn't know his limits right now.

And then he thought he was dreaming when he saw the smile that blossomed on her lips. It almost blinded him with its brilliance.

Connie stood on her tiptoes as she reached up and wrapped her arms around his neck.

"Okay," she replied, the word all but ringing with immeasurable joy.

"You're serious?" he asked.

Her eyes never left his. "I am if you are," she answered.

He hadn't known that a person could be this excited and happy while struggling with shock, all at the very same time.

"I love you," he told her. "You know that, right?"

He could have sworn that her eyes were laughing. "I do now."

"Don't you have anything you want to say to me?" he prodded. He'd laid himself on the line here, opened up his heart to her—and she hadn't told him how she felt about him. He held his breath, hoping that it wasn't all going to blow up on him.

"Kiss me, stupid," Connie responded, doing her best not to laugh.

He tried again. "Don't you have anything to say to me besides that?"

The smile slid over her lips by degrees, widening a little more every second. "Oh, yeah, right." And then she said in the most serious voice she could summon, "I love you, too."

"*Now* I'm going to kiss you stupid," he vowed. "As well as senseless."

She was ready and willing to have him try. All in all, it sounded like a lovely way to go.

"You have your work cut out for you," Connie warned him.

Finn's arms tightened around her a little more, bringing their bodies even closer together. "I sure hope so," he told her.

And he was prepared to love every second of it.

Epilogue

"And you're sure you're up to this?" Brett asked Liam for what seemed like the umpteenth time since yesterday morning when the wedding was given the green light by all concerned.

Standing beside him, Finn and Liam exchanged looks. In their joint recollection, they couldn't remember *ever* seeing their older brother look anywhere so nervous and unsettled. But then, Brett had never been in this sort of a situation before, either.

Brett and Alisha's wedding ceremony was only moments away from unfolding. Because of the extensive guest list—everyone wanted to attend—the couple was getting married in an outdoor ceremony performed at the ranch Brett had inherited.

Everything, including Liam's band, which was providing the music, had been set up outside. A canopy was put up to protect the food just in case the weather decided to reverse itself and go from the predicted sunny to rainy at the last moment.

Right now, the sun was shining, but Brett scarcely noticed. His attention was otherwise occupied by the thousand and one details that apparently went into planning a wedding. Brett was concerning himself needlessly inasmuch as his brothers, especially Finn, had for the most part taken over making all the arrangements.

But, as the oldest, Brett found he had trouble relinquishing control and just sitting back. He had just too much riding on all this.

"It's the 'Wedding March,'" Liam reminded his older brother. "I think I can handle the 'Wedding March,'" he said.

But Brett had to make sure. Liam was impulsive at times. "You're not going to suddenly decide to jazz it up or put in a beat, right?"

"What the 'Wedding March' needs is to have you calm down, big brother," Liam told him. "Just concentrate on remembering your vows and getting through the ceremony. I'll handle the music, okay?" he asked, flashing a sympathetic smile.

Brett blew out a breath, doing his best to get this unexpected case of nerves under control. "Okay."

"All you have to do is keep it together until the minister pronounces you husband and wife. After that, you're home free," Finn counseled.

"No, Finn. You've got that wrong. He's getting married. He's never going to be free again," Liam deadpanned affectionately.

That was enough to make Brett rally. "You two should be so lucky," he told them.

"Not me. I've got a lot of wild oats to sow yet," Liam informed his brother happily. Glancing at his watch, he announced, "Time to begin. Last chance to do something stupid and run," he said to Brett.

"Not a chance," Brett replied. Squaring his shoulders, he went to stand at his designated spot at the front of the newly constructed altar.

As his best man, Finn stood beside him—and thoughtfully watched the proceedings unfold.

"THIS HAS TO be the most beautiful ceremony I've ever attended," Connie told Finn as they were dancing at the reception. "And I've been to more than my share," she confided.

At times it seemed like three quarters of her graduating class had all gotten married in recent years. Because of that, she found that it gave her less and less in common with people who used to be her friends. Their priorities slowly changed while hers had remained the same.

Until now.

"It's incredible," she went on to say, "considering that it seemed as if the whole town pitched in." In her book, that should have yielded a hodge-podge. Except that it didn't.

"They pretty much did—which is maybe *why* it turned out so well," Finn speculated. He knew the world she came from involved wedding planners, something that was completely foreign to his way of thinking. "Wedding planners don't have a personal stake in things turning out well, just a professional one. It keeps them removed."

"Bartender, master builder, wedding organizer. I

guess there's just no end to your talents," Connie teased even though she was only half kidding. "A regular Renaissance man, that's you," she told the man who filled her days and her dreams, as well.

"I don't know about that Renaissance part, but I am a regular man," Finn replied.

Not so regular, Connie thought happily. As far as she was concerned, the word for Finn was extraordinary. Each day she felt as if she loved him a little more. Now that she had made the bold move of detaching herself from her father's company—with the stipulation that she be allowed to finish the hotel she'd started—she had half expected Finn to back away from her. After all, she wasn't that rich woman she'd been just a short while ago, just a woman who was still determined to make her mark on the world—but for a whole different reason.

But instead of backing away, Finn had been incredibly supportive, telling her she was doing the right thing, especially when she told him that she wanted to form her own construction company and take on projects that would help improve the community where she chose to do her work.

The first place she intended to start was on the reservation. The buildings there were in desperate need of repair or rebuilding from scratch. She had enough in her trust fund, left to her by her maternal grandfather, to help her with her goals for a very long time to come.

"How do you feel about marrying a regular guy?" he asked her out of the blue, just after twirling her around as the music went from a slow dance to one with a pulsating beat.

It took her a moment to regain her balance. "Depends on who the regular guy is," she said guardedly. She hung on to her imagination, refusing to allow it to run away with her.

"Me, Connie. Me."

She stopped dancing and stared at Finn, completely stunned. Had she really heard him correctly? "You're asking me to marry you?"

"That's the general gist of this conversation, yes," he acknowledged. "Move your feet, Connie," he coaxed gently. "You're attracting attention."

She did as he asked, hardly aware of moving at all. "Really?"

"Well, you probably always attract attention, looking the way you do, but—"

"No, I'm not asking if I'm attracting attention," she said impatiently. "I'm asking if you're really asking me to marry you. Are you?"

His mouth suddenly felt dry and just like that, he completely understood why Brett had been so nervous earlier. One way or another, this was going to be life-altering for him. If Connie said no, he'd be crushed and if she said yes—well, she *had* to say yes, he told himself. He couldn't live with any other decision.

"With every fiber of my being," he answered her. Then, to further prove he was serious, Finn made it formal. "Constance Carmichael, will you do me the extreme honor of becoming my wife?"

"I don't know about the extreme honor part, but

yes, I'll marry you," she told him as her eyes welled up with tears.

As for Finn, his eyes lit up. The next moment, he sealed their agreement with one of the longest kisses that the good citizens of Forever had ever witnessed.

One of Liam's band members, Sam, nudged him in the ribs and when he looked at Sam, the latter pointed toward the lip-locked couple.

Liam glanced over and then smiled. "Next," he murmured under his breath, because it was clearly indicated that Finn was next when it came to being altarbound.

Liam knew he would be the last Murphy brother left standing alone.

The thought made him smile even more broadly.

* * * * *

4_ST_3

MILLS & BOON®

Want to get more from Mills & Boon?

Here's what's available to you if you join the
exclusive **Mills & Boon eBook Club** today:

✦ *Convenience – choose your books each month*
✦ *Exclusive – receive your books a month before
anywhere else*
✦ *Flexibility – change your subscription at any time*
✦ *Variety – gain access to eBook-only series*
✦ *Value – subscriptions from just £1.99 a month*

So visit **www.millsandboon.co.uk/esubs** today
to be a part of this exclusive eBook Club!

4_ST_4